Bauldr's Tears: Retelling Loki's Fate

Alydia Rackham's Retellings, Volume 2

Alydia Rackham

Published by Alydia Rackham, 2024.

BAULDR'S TEARS: RETELLING LOKI'S FATE

First edition. March 25, 2024.

Copyright © 2024 Alydia Rackham.

ISBN: 979-8215729045

Written by Alydia Rackham.

Also by Alydia Rackham

Alydia Rackham's Retellings
Bauldr's Tears: Retelling Loki's Fate
Ghost: Retelling the Phantom of the Opera
The Tailor of Semenov: Retelling the Legend of Anastasia

Stardust
Stardust

The Curse-Breaker Series
Scales: A Fresh Telling of Beauty and the Beast
Glass: Retelling the Snow Queen
Tide: Retelling the Little Mermaid
Curse-Maker: The Tale of Gwiddon Crow

The Legacy of Constantin
The Last Constantin: A Novel of the Original Vampire

Watch for more at
https://alydiarackham642036291.wordpress.com/.

Chapter One

"LOKI FARBAUTISON," the deep, quiet voice resounded through the white marble courtyard. "You have been accused of murdering an Aesir—a willful and wicked act that cannot, through any cunning, be undone. Do you deny it?"

Slate gray clouds hung low, blocking the sun. Icy wind whipped between the pillars, tugging at the long, black, draping clothes and loosened blonde hair of the crowd of courtiers who hugged the perimeter. All of their pale faces, stark eyes, turned toward the center of the yard, where a young man stood alone.

He also wore black, with tatters hanging down from his shoulders and long sleeves. His long, colorless, shackled hands did not move, nor did his lean form shift. His curly, dark brown hair ruffled in the wind, strands falling down across his white brow.

He slowly raised his head. Beneath ink-dark eyebrows, striking eyes lifted to the far end of the courtyard—eyes like a gray dawn; alive, but distant. The courtiers focused on his angular, handsome face, noble nose, cheekbones and chin, and firm, quiet mouth. They watched him unblinkingly, waiting for his answer.

He took a breath, and slightly lifted his right eyebrow.

"Is there a point in answering?" He spoke lowly, each word elegant and precise. Vapor issued from his lips. The crowd seethed. Their murmurs rumbled like low thunder.

And the first one who had spoken—a tall, white-bearded king garbed in night, seated in a wooden throne on the dais—slammed his hand down on the armrest.

The blow shook the air.

His single sapphire eye blazed, and he gritted his teeth. His wizened brow knotted around his eye patch, and his fists clenched.

"You murdered my son," he snarled. "*You*, who we took in as one of our own. *You*, who have been our...our *friend* for countless centuries. You have betrayed us." The one-eyed king paused. His voice roughened. "You have betrayed *me*."

The court murmured and groaned. Some shielded their eyes, others leaned their heads against their loved ones'. Loki Farbautison twisted his left hand and lifted his shoulder. His chains clinked. As if he could not help it, he glanced to the king's right, where a magnificent, golden-headed prince stood, clad in dulled gold armor, and a heavy thundercloud of a cape that hung from his shoulders to his ankles. For an instant, Loki's gray eyes met the prince's burning blue ones. But the prince's brow twisted, his eyes closed, and he turned his lion-like head away, pressing a hand to his mouth and over his bearded jaw. Loki swallowed, and turned again to the king. He raised his eyebrows.

"What can I say?" he asked.

The king would not look at him. His hand flexed, and he stared fixedly at something to his right.

"You make no defense, you will not answer for your conduct," the king said hoarsely. "Therefore, we must acknowledge that there can be no question of your guilt." He shut his eye, and closed his fist. "You murdered my son, a prince of Asgard. Therefore, there is only one possible consequence."

The court held its breath. The blue-eyed prince turned to hide the tears that spilled down his face. The king lifted his chin.

"Loki Farbautison," he declared into the silence. "You are sentenced to death."

Loki's long-lashed eyes closed. Overhead, a groan of thunder rolled through the clouds.

And it began to snow.

THREE MONTHS EARLIER...

Thunder growled around the thick wooden walls of the house as Marina Faroe crept from the sitting room toward the library, holding only a lit candle in her right hand. As her stocking feet slid across the floorboards, she bit her lip and prayed she wouldn't trip over any of the boxes she had left out. The darkness hung thick and heavy around her, unwilling to flit away as her candlelight intruded. With her free hand, she pulled her long cashmere wrap closer around her very slight form, though the movement made her stiff arm ache from her thumb to her elbow.

She slipped through the pokey corridor, and then her feet brushed across the deep red, tapestry-like carpet of the library. She crossed the room, then reached up and pushed her candle down into a wooden candlestick standing on the carved mantle. Then, she knelt, groped for the matchbox, and leaned into the fireplace to snap flame from a single match, then light the tinder and logs inside.

It was difficult—the last three fingers of her left hand stayed curled close to her palm, and her wrist refused to extend more than halfway, leaving all the work to be done by her right hand, and the forefinger and weak thumb of her left. Besides which, it hurt.

However, after a few minutes of quiet struggle, a small fire danced against the rough-hewn stones, warming her narrow face, and lighting her hazel eyes. She dusted her right hand off on her jeans, then pushed her sleek, unbound black hair out of her face. Taking a breath, she lifted her head, folded her arms, and glanced around the room.

Deep bookshelves covered all the walls, except for the door and the wide fireplace. Empty cardboard boxes sat against the north wall, and their former contents now lined the shelves. Ancient, leather-bound manuscripts, their spines ragged, their pages yellowed, sat in uneven rows, the titles illegible in the flickering half dark. But Marina knew them all—knew them like weathered faces of old friends. They belonged to her dad's collection: volumes of Norse poetry, Viking travel records, maps, folklore, songs and legends. Some had been inscribed by hand, in now-faded ink. Others were first editions of research published a hundred years ago. She had read them all.

Marina sighed, bringing her knees up to her chest and wrapping her right arm around them, leaning back against more unpacked boxes as the scent of burning pine and the crackle of the flames filled the silence.

She glanced up at the softly-ticking, intricately-carved Swiss clock sitting on one side of the mantle. She could barely see its face by the light of the candle—it was past ten. Her delicate mouth hardened. The storm had knocked the electricity out, so she couldn't charge her dead cell phone, and she hadn't set up her landline yet. She couldn't have called her mother in New York at nine-thirty. Even if she had wanted to.

She shifted, pressing her left arm against her stomach, turning her head to consider the empty shelves on the south wall. Tomorrow, she would set her dad's collection of rusty Viking swords on the middle ones, along with his glass cases of beaten coins. She would heft the small, stone idols of Odin, Loki, Thor and Frigga to the very top shelves, so they could be studied, but never touched. And in the far corner, across the room, she would stand the three-hundred-year-old half-tree up, so that all of the wide-eyed, gaping faces and squatty bodies of the dwarves carved into it could be seen in the firelight. And over the mantle...

She got up. Thunder rumbled again, shaking the upper stories. Marina stepped nimbly between the maze of boxes on the floor, and bent over one in the back. She pried the lid open, then reached in with her right hand and pulled on a thick, gold-painted frame.

Carefully, she slid it up and out. Firelight flashed against the glass. She straightened, and held it up. For a long while, she just stood there, gazing at the broad picture within the frame. Then, she turned, moved back to the mantle, and, grunting, managed to lift the picture up and set it there, and let it ease back to rest against the wall. She stepped back, and gazed at it, keeping her left arm pressed to her chest. She took a deep breath, and her lips moved to mouth the words penned beneath the strange drawing. Words she had whispered thousands of times.

"*Stien til Asgard...*"

Silence answered her. Silence that had always been interrupted before by a deep, eager voice forming words of explanation—a bright eye, a roughened hand reaching up to point at the illuminated edges, a smile bordered by a dark, graying beard...

A tear escaped her guard. It spilled down her cheek. She swiped it away, swallowed hard and tightened her jaw—but the flutter of the candle's flame drew her gaze back to the picture. Marina's arms tightened around herself as thunder once again grumbled overhead, and the spring rain broke loose, and lashed the outer walls.

Chapter Two

MARINA TOOK A DEEP breath of cool morning air, thick with the scent of rain, and shut the front door behind her, as the sunlight warmed her whole body. She stepped down the short landing and turned back to glance up at her new house. "New" being a relative word—it was actually only new to *her*.

She could see it better now than she had when she had moved in. Yesterday, it had been cloudy, and she had ducked her head and hauled boxes inside between spats of rain. But today, golden sunshine bathed the whole house, and she stopped on the brick pathway to look for a moment.

Three stories, all dark weathered wood, with a peaked roof and simple, sturdy bric-a-brac around the thick-pillared porch, and upper windows. Marina narrowed her eyes at those dusty, flaking windows. They needed cleaned and sealed and painted. And she was fairly certain that the deep-green, hardy ivy growing up the north side had already slipped its inquisitive fingers in through the windows of the second story.

She took another deep breath, and glanced around at the rest of the yard. The lush, dew-gleaming lawn needed mowed, the rosebushes flanking the path had twisted and sprawled out of their bounds, and the iron-wrought fence surrounding the whole half-acre needed re-painted. And she didn't even want to look at the snarled knot that was the vegetable garden on the north side.

She paused, listening. Birds chirped in the motionless boughs of the towering pines and oaks that surrounded and filled her property, but aside from that quiet, cheerful sound, all remained silent. She nearly smiled. So different from the rushing, wailing, flashing, seething streets of Manhattan.

She turned, adjusted the collar of her draping sweater wrap, and strode down the uneven walkway between the rose bushes, her boots tapping on the bricks. She pushed the squeaking iron gate out of the way, turned and opened the door of her dad's pickup truck—a sturdy, new red Ford that had carried everything of hers up all the winding, sweeping roads from New York to here: an empty house by a tiny town near the Bay of Fundy.

She opened the door and crawled up into the cab—it was like climbing a tree. Her dad had been a lot bigger than her...

She settled, pulled her purse strap over her head and set her purse in the passenger seat, slammed the door, and started the big diesel engine. It grumbled to life as her keys jingled, and she gingerly pulled the truck out into the dirt road, sitting far forward in the seat and steering with just her right hand.

As she drove, the sunlight flashed through the trees and against the left side of her face. Marina rolled the window down, to let the fresh air in. She bit her lip, hoping she could remember the way back into town. She'd driven through it yesterday, late, but it had been in the rain...

She didn't push the truck faster than twenty five, and she didn't listen to any music as she maneuvered the road that wound through a canyon of pines, her left hand resting in her lap. She only came to one fork in the road, hesitated for a moment, wincing, then turned right. After a few minutes, though, she breathed a sigh. Here it was.

Marina doubted this little town appeared on most maps. But it had a medium-sized, stone post office that she could see from here, a wide, sunlit main street lined with a few quaint shops, a two-pump gas station, and a general store at the far end that she hoped would have what she needed.

She pulled up in front of the broad-windowed, brick general store and parked, then opened the door and slid down out of the truck. Her boots crunched on the gravel as she stepped up onto the sidewalk. She glanced to the right and realized that the store snugged up right next to what was probably the only restaurant in town—a white, pleasant little deli with the name *Theresa's* painted in curly writing on the window—and the hanging sign said *Closed*.

Marina pushed the door of the general store open. A bell jangled over her head. She eased inside and let the door click shut behind her.

The shop was small, dimly-lit, and packed with rows of loaded standing shelves. White and maroon checked tiles made up the floor, and jars of old-fashioned candy almost covered the cashier's counter off to her far left.

Before she had taken three steps, a middle-aged man in a plaid shirt and jeans stepped out from behind one of the back shelves.

"'Morning," he greeted her, smiling. "Can I help you find anything?"

"Um," Marina adjusted her purse strap on her shoulder and glanced around. "Paint?"

"Interior or exterior?" he asked, coming closer.

"Exterior," she answered. "I'm painting my window frames."

"It's a nice day for that," he commented. "Yeah, come this way." He beckoned, then started back the way he had come. Marina followed him.

"Is there a specific color you're looking for?"

"They used to be deep green," Marina said. "Almost all the paint is gone now, but I think that's right—some sort of pine green."

The storekeeper paused and glanced back at her, brow furrowed.

"Which house are you painting?" he wondered. "I've sold paint to pretty much everybody in this town, and there's nobody with pine green windows."

Marina almost smiled.

"I'm new in town—just moved in yesterday," she said. "I bought the Stellan house."

The storekeeper, now standing in front of a rainbow of paint swatches on the wall, stopped and looked at her.

"You mean..." He raised his eyebrows. "You mean that old, Danish-looking house on the edge of town?" he pointed. "The one where that author lived for all those years before he went out into the forest and..."

"Yeah," Marina nodded, then shrugged, smiling. "What can I say? It was cheap."

He laughed, then turned to search the swatches.

"Ghosts don't bother you, huh?"

"No such thing," Marina said quietly, the smile fading from her face.

"Tell that to the people around here," the shopkeeper answered, reaching up to pull a couple swatches off the wall. "Especially after most of us have seen or heard more than *one* weird thing in those woods." He turned and gave her a pointed look. "Word to the wise: don't go out there at night. No matter what you think you see."

Marina frowned at him, alarmed, but he was perfectly serious, so she nodded once. He faced the swatches again, and pulled down one more, then handed them to her with another smile.

"Feel free to take these home and see how they look."

"I think I'll actually pick one out now, if you'll give me a minute," Marina said, taking them from him.

"Okay, sure," he nodded. "Take your time. I'll just be up here organizing some stuff by the counter."

"All right," Marina said, and he left her alone in the aisle with three swatches of green. Marina watched him go, her brow slowly furrowing as she rubbed her thumb up and down the pieces of paper.

The overhead radio clicked on, playing oldies. She blinked, and forced herself to look down at the different shades.

After ten minutes of debate, she decided, and took the swatch up to the counter. The shopkeeper eagerly mixed the paint for her, then helped her load up a basket of other supplies she would need, such as paint stirrers, brushes, and scrapers. She bought three gallons of dark green paint, all the other supplies, and a glass bottle of soda, and hauled all of her purchases, in bags, to the front door. Two bags she carried in the crook of her left elbow, and the other two in her right hand. She heaved the door open. The bell jangled.

"Need help?" the shopkeeper called from behind the counter. Marina shook her head.

"No, thanks. I've got it."

"Okay," he answered. "Nice to meet you, Miss...?"

"Feroe," she answered, slipping out. "Marina Feroe."

"Jim Fields," he replied. "Have a good day!"

"Thanks," Marina said, letting the door shut.

A crisp gust of wind blew through her clothes and hair as soon as she stepped down off the sidewalk, and she fumbled in her purse for her keys. She managed to dig them out, bite the side of her cheek and use the keyless entry to unlock the truck. It beeped. Grunting, she heaved the door open and swung her right hand bags up onto the passenger seat.

The bags on her other arm slipped.

She gasped. She scrambled to catch them, scrabbling around her swaying purse— Her left hand wouldn't obey.

One bag slipped and smashed onto the ground.

Her soda bottle shattered.

She wanted to scream something foul. Instead, she gritted her teeth hard, threw the remaining bag up into the truck, and got down to pick up the bag of paint brushes that was now filled with soda.

"Wait, wait—careful!" a voice called out. "Don't cut yourself."

She jerked, startled, and glanced up. At first, all she saw was a pair of work boots and jeans—then she saw the rest of him.

He wore a long-sleeved, blue shirt stained with dirt, as if he'd been working in a garden. He had collar-length blonde hair that lit up like gold in the sunlight. He hurried toward her, his boots thudding on the paving. Her face heated and she looked back down at the mess.

"I won't," she mumbled. "I'm just...stupid..." She twisted her left arm and pulled it toward herself, cursing her useless fingers. She reached out with her good hand and pulled the plastic back, trying to fish the brushes out.

"Wait a second—stop," he urged—his voice sounded like an afternoon wind, warm and deep. It brought her head up again...

And she froze. He knelt right across from her, startlingly near. His face was flawless—pale but ruddy, with soft, strong features and jaw line. His fine hair hung like flax around his brow and ears, and his quiet mouth formed a small smile. But she saw all of this peripherally—for Marina was instantly captured by his eyes.

They were the color of the highest summer sky—pure blue, and brilliant as jewels, and fathomless. His dark right eyebrow quirked, and his smile broadened. He glanced down at the mess. His brown eyelashes were as long as a girl's.

"I can get those," he assured her, reaching down with both dirt-covered hands and swiftly pulling the brushes free of the tinkling glass. Marina's mouth opened to protest, but nothing came out. Her face got even hotter.

"Here," he said, holding the brushes out to her and giving her another bright grin. She managed to take them from him, and then he scooped the bag up and stood. Marina's eyebrows raised. He was *tall*, his shoulders broad. He trotted over to a metal trash can and tossed the mess in. It clanged when it hit the bottom. Marina got to her feet, then realized she was staring at him. She turned quickly, leaned into the truck and stuffed the now-sticky brushes into the cup holder.

"Planning a project?" he asked, and she heard him come back toward her. She turned back around, wishing she wasn't blushing so hard.

"Yeah," she nodded, glancing up at him. He dusted his palms off on his jeans, his friendly look remaining.

"I'm painting some windows," she added, shrugging, still keeping her arm close. He stuck his hands in his pockets and cocked his head.

"That's a big job. Need any help?"

Marina's eyes flashed and she frowned at him. He suddenly laughed.

"I've forgotten my manners," he said. "My name is Bird Oldeson. I'm kind of the town's handyman." He met her eyes again, and inclined his head.

"Oh, I see," Marina nodded. Absently, she noted that he had an accent—it sounded almost English, but with a gentle Nordic lilt that she couldn't identify. She held out her right hand.

"Marina Feroe," she said. "I just moved here."

He gave her a look of startled pleasure, then took up her hand in a gentle hold. His fingers were warm.

"Nice to meet you," he said. Marina allowed herself a little smile.

"Nice to meet you, too," she answered. Then, she turned and climbed up into the truck.

"I meant what I asked you," he said as she shut the door.

"What?" she asked, glancing out the open window as she turned the truck on.

"If you need any help." He wasn't really smiling now—he gazed at her with raised eyebrows. She shook her head.

"No, I think I'm okay," she said. "Thank you, though."

"You're sure?" he pressed, his voice quieter. Marina paused, studying him, then nodded again.

"Yes," she said. "But really—thank you."

He gave her a half smile, then bowed his head again.

"I'm sure I will see you again."

She didn't know what to say to that, so she broadened her smile a little, then put the truck in reverse, pulled out and headed back alone to her old house.

Marina leaned the shaky ladder up against the north wall of the house. It rattled as it hit the sunlit siding. She took the heavy clippers in her hand and gazed straight up. Before she did anything with the paint, she had to get the ivy off the windows of the second storey. Which was going to be tricky.

She clamped the handle of the clippers between her teeth, grabbed one of the rungs of the ladder and set her feet. Then, taking a breath, she started to climb, only occasionally using her left hand for balance. Once she reached the top, she wrapped her left arm around the ladder, took the clippers in her hand and began snapping at the ivy.

The long tendrils fell down in waves, but more and more lay beneath, like a thick carpet. Her arm got sore, and the ladder wobbled, but she worked for several hours without stopping.

Finally, her shoulder couldn't take it anymore, and she sighed, wiped the sweat off her forehead, and started down.

She gathered up the trimmed ivy and hauled it around to the sagging mulch pile near the garden. Then, she came back around, put her hand on her narrow hip and gazed up...

To see that it hardly looked like she'd done anything. She gritted her teeth, frowned fiercely at the remaining ivy, snatched the clippers up from the grass and started up the ladder again.

Marina thrashed. Her sleeping bag tore. She jerked awake, sweating, her heart hammering. She stared at the dark ceiling of the study.

Jerking gasps caught in her chest and she shivered all over. Weakly, she lifted her head and glanced through the door. Gray light of dawn seeped in through the sitting room windows. She swallowed and eased her head back down onto her crooked pillow—and grimaced.

Clenching pain ran up and down her left side and shot through her shoulder, down her arm, twisted through her elbow and clamped down on her wrist. Her arm shuddered, and she pulled it against her chest. Her whole back ached, and she felt like she had a fever.

For an hour, she lay there, breathing deeply, forcing her muscles to loosen, mentally kicking herself. She'd overdone it yesterday. She should have stopped after tearing the whole wall of ivy down, and not tried to tackle the rosebushes by the front walk. She'd known that when she started that last job, but she hadn't listened to herself. Now she was paying for it.

Tears leaked out and ran down her temples. She knew what it was like to wake up fully rested, without any pain. But she couldn't remember the last time she had.

And the last time it hurt *this* much had been about a month after it happened.

She sat up, groaning and gritting her teeth, squeezing her eyes shut. She stayed still a moment, regulating her breathing, trying to stop shivering. Then, she pushed her sleeping bag off herself and crawled to her feet. The ruffle of her long white nightgown tumbled to her ankles. She wrapped her arms around herself, chilled.

"Such an idiot, Marina..." she muttered. She crossed the rug and left the study, turned left down the hall and fumbled with the lock on the front door. If she could just get some fresh air, the ache in her head might go away, at least...

She pulled the thick, heavy black door open. Its hinges squeaked.

Cool air gushed in to meet her, and she closed her eyes and took a deep breath, letting the door go as it swung further open. She stepped up and leaned sideways against the wide doorframe, letting the breeze cool her hot forehead. Sighing, she finally opened her eyes, and gazed out at her gray front yard, hung with early-morning shadow. She lingered on the ragged rose bushes, whose branches still hung wild, disordered and tangled all over the other flower beds and the path.

Then, she caught sight of something on her front step. Frowning, she shuffled out, bent with a wince, and picked it up.

She fingered the flimsy sheets of a small newspaper of ads and coupons. Her mouth quirked as she straightened. The people in her new town didn't waste any time trying to sell things to her...

Her eyes focused on the front page. She frowned.

Right in the middle sat an ad for Svenson's Plumbing, Carpentry and Landscaping—and it listed its employees: Richard Smith, Harry Williams, and Bird Oldeson.

Marina absently pulled her left arm against her stomach, and stared at the name as her unsteady hand held the paper. Then, she clenched her jaw, muttered a Danish curse word under her breath, and turned and went back inside to find a light, hoping the ad listed Svenson's hours.

Chapter Three

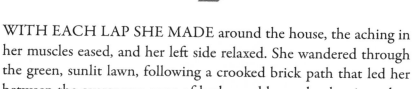

WITH EACH LAP SHE MADE around the house, the aching in her muscles eased, and her left side relaxed. She wandered through the green, sunlit lawn, following a crooked brick path that led her between the overgrown rows of herbs, and beneath a leaning arbor laden with grape vines. Her heels tapped on the dull stone as she passed into the deep shadow behind the house, cast by three towering oaks. She glanced over the half-sunken benches and toppled bird bath, all swallowed by vines and weeds. A little robin alighted on the back of one of the benches and cocked his head at her. She paused, and watched his bright eyes. He chirped once, then fluttered up and away, darting into the forest and out of sight.

A chilly gust of wind issued from the reaches of the woods, and rustled through her hair and clothes and the boughs of the trees. She wrapped her arms around herself and narrowed her eyes at the deep, tangled green shadow beyond the benches, the line of pines and the sagging wrought iron fence. She turned, and resumed her walk.

On the other side of the house, she came again to the rose garden, all in disarray. Many bloomed—red, white, peach and maroon—but they snarled together like an evil fairy's curse. One rosebush in particular made her frown: it bore no buds, and it leaned menacingly up against the house very close to the sitting-room window, just as the ivy had done on the opposite side. She paused and stepped closer to the plant, glancing it up and down. Thick, wicked thorns covered all its branches, and even its leaves. It needed to be cut back, or torn out—but she was afraid it would slice her to shreds if she tried.

Far off, a low rumbling rose through the silence, obscuring the twittering of the birds. Marina's head came up, and she listened. Then, she took a breath and braced herself, and started back around to the front of the house. She picked through the border garden, kicked at a large weed, and halted in front of the steps, her arms still folded, gazing toward the road, toward town, at the approaching pickup truck.

The truck's brown paint gleamed in the brilliant sun, and shovels, ladders and other tools rattled around in the bed. It pulled up in her driveway next to her truck, and the throbbing engine cut out. The next moment, the door creaked open, and the tall, winsome form of Bird Oldeson hopped out onto the gravel.

He wore a tan t-shirt, worn jeans and boots, and gave her a smile that lit the day up even brighter. She reflexively returned it.

"Beautiful morning, isn't it?" he called, striding toward her, his vivid blue eyes glancing all around at the sky, then the gardens and trees, as the light made a halo of his hair.

"Yes," she nodded. "I think the rain did some good."

"Oh, always," he grinned, coming up to stop in front of her. He held out his hand. "Good to see you again, Miss Feroe."

"Thanks," she nodded, and barely took hold of his fingers. She let go right away, blushing, but he didn't act like he noticed. He stuck both hands in his pockets, then looked her house up and down.

"Well, what is it you need done?" he asked, then met her eyes. She smiled crookedly and glanced behind her.

"The question is," she said. "What do I *not* need done."

He laughed. The ringing sound made the birds flutter.

"All right, let me rephrase," he amended. "What do you need done *first?*"

"Well..." she sighed, frowning as she studied her house, then faced him again. "The windows. They leaked during the thunderstorm. The rest of the stuff in the garden can wait a while, but I don't want my furniture ruined if it decides to rain again soon."

"All right," he said, scrubbing a hand through his long gold hair as his brow furrowed. "You have the paint already, I assume—but the windows will probably need sealed, maybe even adjusted, since they've probably gotten crooked as the house shifts."

"Okay, do whatever you need to." Marina folded her arms and cocked her head. "Are you paid by the hour?"

"Yes."

"All right, go ahead," she gestured toward the house. "Bring me any paperwork or questions or whatever—I'll just be down here, trying to get this rose garden under control."

He nodded again, catching her eye and giving her a soft, bright smile that warmed her to her core.

"I'll get started right now," he said, and turned and strode back to his truck, his boots crunching on the sand. Suppressing her own smile, Marina faced the house again and headed back toward the roses.

All day, Marina sat on a short stool with her back to the sun, letting it warm her, as she cut the overgrown roses back away from the path with a set of sturdy clippers. She had managed to find her work gloves, so she was able to thrust her hand into the thorny mess without tearing up her skin—though working with her left hand remained a challenge. Her long braid hung over her shoulder, and her jeans and loose shirt got dirty, but she didn't care. Birds crooned and twittered in the bushes and in the branches of the bordering trees, and a quiet wind rustled the leaves.

Behind and above her, Bird Oldeson perched on a ladder, leaning up against the front of the house. His hammer clacked, the wood of the window frame creaked as he pried and pulled, and the ladder rungs squeaked with each step as he effortlessly ascended or descended to resume or go get a tool. She didn't look at him—she just listened to the patter and tap of his rhythms, and the thud of his footsteps.

When she had gotten halfway down the row of roses, she paused a moment, sat back and winced at her stiff muscles, then wiped the sweat from her forehead with the back of her sleeve. Bird's hammer tapped three times, rapidly. Then, he began to hum.

She froze, then twisted on her stool and glanced up at him.

The sunlight caught half of him as he leaned against the ladder and the wall, deepening the color of his clothes and skin, and blazing against his hair. His hands moved swiftly, deftly, over the loose windowsill as he secured it. He held two nails between his lips, his attention fixed on his work. And he hummed a soft, strange tune that carried through the midmorning air like a breeze.

For a long moment, Marina didn't move or even breathe as she listened, studying the way he moved, trying to remember if she had heard the song before. He used one nail, then the other, and then with his liberated mouth, he began to sing, quietly. She blinked. It was another language—something like Swedish or Danish...But she couldn't tell.

Then he paused, turned his head and looked down at her.

For a moment, her eyes locked with his, and she saw nothing but the shade of the sky. Then he smiled, and Marina's face flooded with heat. She quickly turned back around and began hacking at the bushes with a vengeance. For a few moments, he was silent behind her, and her blush started to hurt.

His hammer *tap-tap-tapped* again. He resumed his lilting hum. And she let herself start breathing—but she did *not* let herself turn around and stare at him any more.

"Ow! *Crap!*" Marina hissed, jerking her hand back and shaking it out, then prying her glove off. She sucked in air through her teeth as she rested her right hand on top of her left, watching a long line of blood bloom from her wrist to her forefinger knuckle.

A thud issued from around the corner of the house. Then, Bird came striding around into the shade, his brow furrowed, his eyes finding her hand.

"What happened?"

"Oh, this stupid rosebush," Marina halfway gestured to the gnarled old plant leaning against the house. She smirked down at her injury. "It bit me."

Bird put his hands on his hips and studied her, then the rosebush.

"What were you trying to do?"

"I want to cut it down and then pull it out," she answered, wincing at the sting that darted up and down her hand now. Bird glanced at her, startled.

"Why?" he asked.

"Look at it. It's not blooming, and it doesn't look like it's planning to," she answered. "Plus, I think it's trying to climb into my window."

He shook his head.

"I think you have the wrong idea."

She frowned at him.

"What do you mean?"

He knelt down in front of it, and reached out toward its thick, wicked branches. Marina flinched back...

But he didn't recoil. Instead, he gingerly moved the branches, feeling them, studying their form. Then, he turned, and picked up her clippers from the grass, and began strategically cutting at the small, withered branches.

"This bush is a different kind from the ones along your walkway," he explained quietly as he clipped. "Those were bought in this part of the country—they were bred for this weather. But this one..." he paused, and pulled a few dead leaves off and flicked them aside. "This is from somewhere else entirely. A different climate, different soil. Picked up on some faraway travels, I suppose. And see, it's a climbing rose, and those are not." He gestured back to the others. The pain of Marina's wound faded as she watched him, measuring what he said.

"It's had to survive far harsher winters than it was meant for, and a lot less sunlight than it needed," he went on. "But it did what it had to in order to survive—it leaned up against the house, near the fireplace here, see? The warmth and shelter of the house has kept it alive. And the one who built the house was wise enough to plant this bush on the south side, away from the brutal north wind—and that same person nursed it and fought off frost and bugs for probably twenty or thirty years before the bush got strong enough to fend for itself. But it wouldn't leave the house then, even though it could." He sat back on his haunches, his arms unbloodied, even though he had been elbow deep in the teeth of that bush. Bird glanced up at Marina, holding her still with his gaze.

"It's a late bloomer," he said, giving her a crooked smile. "But I think, if you'll have a little patience with its difficult attitude, it might turn out to be the prettiest rose you've got."

Marina looked at him for a moment, marveling at the way his speech flowed from practical to decorous, and how he talked about the rosebush as if it were a person.

"Okay," she found herself saying, answering his smile. "I'll see if I can keep from killing it."

He grinned, and stood up, then stepped closer and eyed her cut. "Are you all right?"

"I'm fine," she answered, nodding. "I'll just go clean it up."

"Are you sure? It looks like it hurts," he said, watching her face.

"Ha," she laughed, a bitter gall rising in her throat. "Believe me, I've had a *lot* worse."

His brow tightened and concern lit up his eyes. She forced a smile and stepped around him, heading for the house. And as she pushed open the door, she almost swore she heard him murmur something soothing to that rosebush—but she couldn't understand a word.

Chapter Four

"THERE YOU GO—WHAT DO you think?" Bird asked breathlessly as he hopped down from the third rung of the ladder and trotted across the grass over to her. Marina stood up from her garden stool and dusted her hand off on her jeans, then reached up and adjusted the crooked chain of the necklace that hid under her collar. She shot him a startled look.

"Are you finished already?" she asked. "It's only been two days!"

"Yep," he said triumphantly, folding his strong arms and facing the house. Marina glanced past him and up, and let her eyes wander over all of the now-perfect-and-painted windows.

"Looks great," she nodded. "Very pretty."

"Good," he nodded. He heaved a deep breath. "That means I have time for that herb garden."

Marina blinked.

"The what?"

He strode around the house, past the bushes and toward the side of her vegetable garden.

"Your herb garden," he repeated. "You've got a lot of stuff growing—asparagus, rhubarb, spearmint, dill, garlic...You just can't see them because of all the weeds."

Marina frowned, dropping the clippers from her left hand into the dirt and following him.

"But I..." she tried, blushing in spite of herself. "I...I can't pay you for—I mean, I can't afford—"

"Don't worry about it," he waved her off as he paused in front of a small section of earth that had been plotted out with now half-buried bricks. "My work day just ended a few minutes ago, and the rhubarb has been crying to me all afternoon." He glanced over his shoulder at her and flashed a grin. She paused, and raised a sardonic eyebrow.

"Crying to you?" she said flatly.

"Well, maybe crying is the wrong word," he shrugged one shoulder.

"Probably 'sweetly requesting' would be better. I could say the same thing about the asparagus, just take the 'sweet' part out—asparagus get all stuffy-acting when they're asking favors." He turned back toward the garden. "The spearmint I just had to ignore—they're pushy and overpowering, as you know, unless you keep them at a distance. I can personally only take them in small doses. And the dill is just plain saucy about it, and the garlic is downright loud, making a lot more fuss than is actually necessary, so you see..."

Marina was already laughing too hard to hear the rest, and he trailed off, grinning at her. She calmed down, pressing the back of her wrist to her mouth, hiding her smile.

"So you see," he finished. "They're all whining about the weed situation." He canted his head. "Want to help me get them to shut up?"

"Sure," Marina shrugged helplessly and beamed. "Can't have my herbs complaining, can I?"

"Is this really how you like to spend your Saturdays?"

Bird glanced up at her over the tall stalks and green leaves of the white lilies. He then continued to pull up weeds from between the feet of the elegant flowers and toss them to the side. His arms were dirty up to the elbows, as were the knees of his jeans, and he had a smear of dirt across his forehead.

"Look who's talking," he answered, then sent her a twinkling glance. Marina chuckled, and sat back on her stool. She peeled off her work gloves and tried not to wince as the worn leather came loose of her left hand, then brushed a strand of hair out of her face.

"You've been done with the house for a week now," she pointed out. "But you keep coming back to work in this garden in the afternoons, even though I'm *not* paying you, and now you're here on a Saturday—"

"Would you like me to leave?"

Marina stopped. He met her eyes, perfectly serious, his eyebrows raised.

"No!" she said quickly, sitting up straight. Her face heated up—again, and she stammered. "I mean...No, I'm not telling you to leave. In fact, I like...I mean, I appreciate..." she pulled her arm toward her, then swallowed. "I was just wondering why—"

"You have one of the best gardens I've ever seen," Bird interrupted seamlessly, still weeding. "And one of the oldest. I know you want to fix all this up, make it look nice—but that's a *lot* of work. Lucky for you, I love getting my hands covered with dirt." He tossed a dandelion over his shoulder. "Plus, you just moved here, and you don't know anybody." He sat up, and dusted his hands off. He looked at her squarely, then gave her a quiet smile. "And I won't let anybody sit alone in a great big house if she looks like she needs some company."

For a moment, she just gazed back at him, her cheeks still flushed—but a soft glow guttered to life in her chest.

"Really?" she murmured.

His eyes flickered.

For just an instant, she almost frowned. Then, his expression cleared, and he nodded. She ducked her head, smiling again, and shrugged.

"Well..." she managed. "Thanks."

He was silent for a second. Then, he cleared his throat.

"'course, I may have to say something about the weird color of green that you picked to frame the door..."

She threw a clod of dirt at him. He ducked, laughing.

They continued working in companionable silence, and so the heat in her face faded—but the warmth deep inside her did not.

"How's work today?" Marina asked, taking a long sip of her cherry limeade, then pushing aside the remnants of her sandwich wrappings and leaning back in the red-padded diner chair. She canted her head at Bird, who sat across from her at the tiny two-person table right next to the sunlit ceiling-to-floor front window of *Theresa's*.

"Busy this morning," he admitted, his brow furrowing as he poured more catsup out onto his fries. "Mr. Petrson cut down a line of oaks by his driveway—we had to pull out the stumps."

Marina studied him. He sullenly clenched his jaw.

"You all right?" she asked.

He shook his head, still not looking up.

"It's the oaks."

"What about them?"

"They were healthy," he said, putting the catsup down with more than necessary force. His jaw tightened. "There was nothing wrong with them. And they had to be at least a hundred years old."

Marina frowned.

"Why did he cut them down, then?"

He shrugged.

"Don't know. Didn't like them blocking the view of the bay, I guess," he muttered. He shoved his food basket away and sat back abruptly, crossing his arms and looking out the window. He huffed, and shook his head.

"What right does Petrson have to take them down?" He ground his teeth. "A century they've survived, through ice and snow and drought—and he fells them in one afternoon."

They went silent. Marina bit her lip, and glanced outside at the empty main street. Bird stayed petulantly quiet. Marina hooked her thumb through the necklace at her throat and pulled the chain out of her collar, and fingered the pendant. She glanced at him—he still stared out the window.

"I was thinking of planting an oak off to the side of my house," she said, tilting her head, and glancing back at him.

He looked at her out of the corner of his eye, his mouth still tight. Then, the hardness in his face melted into warmth, and he smiled.

"I can probably get you a good deal on a sapling," he said.

"Good," she smiled at him, the weight of his mood lifting off her like clouds opening up to the sun. She sat forward. "Actually, I—"

"What's that?"

Marina halted. Bird's bright blue eyes had sharpened in a keen stare at her—no, at her necklace.

"Oh, uh—this?" Her brow furrowed and she glanced down at the pendant. Something lodged in her throat. She had to fight for a moment to find her voice again. "My...My dad gave it to me. It's—"

"Mjollnir," he finished, his eyes still fixed on it. Marina's eyebrows shot up.

"You...You know what this is?"

"Sure I do," he nodded. "Could I...?"

Before he could finish his question, or she could answer it, he had reached out and taken hold of her pendant. Their fingers brushed. She gasped, and almost jerked back—then stopped herself to keep from pulling it out of his grasp.

She held very still as he leaned forward, until their heads were not six inches apart. His forehead tightened and his eyes narrowed as he held the pendant with his first two fingers and his thumb. Marina risked a glance down at it—it was a decorative interpretation of Thor's hammer, made of silver, slightly tarnished.

"The designs on it are beautiful—very delicate," he observed quietly. "Is it an antique?"

"I think so," Marina answered, unable to summon much volume with him so close. "But I can't remember. I've worn it for several years."

He didn't answer—just ran his thumb over the "T" portion of the hammer.

"You're..." she ventured. "You're interested in old Norse myths?"

He halfway smiled.

"Ever since I was born." He lifted his bright eyes to hers. "Are you? Or was this just a present?"

"No, I..." she started, her heartbeat starting to pound in her throat. "I mean, my dad and I are Old Norse scholars. Well, I...*I* am. My dad...*was*."

He raised his eyebrows.

"Scholars?" he repeated, mercifully leaving the subject of her father alone. "In what capacity?"

"Archaeology, mostly," she said, absently realizing that he still had hold of her pendant, and had not leaned back. "And...And literature. Dad collected manuscripts and antique books."

"Really?" he sounded pleased, astonished.

"Yeah," Marina answered, surprised.

A slow smile bloomed on his face.

"Would you...I mean, could I see them?"

"Um..." she swallowed hard, but she couldn't think clearly at all with his fingers just inches from her face. "Sure—?"

"I mean, I won't if you don't want me to," he said hastily. "I just think all that stuff is incredible, so—"

"No, it's okay," she cut in. "Sure. Sure, you can see it," she nodded, finally realizing that she meant it. She smiled at him. "Would this evening work?"

He dropped her pendant and leaned back, grinning.

"I'll be there with bells on."

"What a fantastic library," Bird remarked quietly as he stepped through the door, his tea cup in hand, and slowly gazed from one corner of the room to the other.

"Thanks," Marina said, following him in. It was still halfway light outside, but since there were no windows in the library, so it was dark except for the standing lamp, the fire in the fireplace, and the candles she'd lit on the mantelpiece. She put her hands in her pockets and shoved a half-full packing box with her toe.

"Sorry about the mess," she said. "I tried to straighten a little this afternoon, put more stuff up on the shelves, but there's so much. And, you know, I've been outside mostly for the past couple weeks..."

"Sure," Bird said lightly, stepping further in to study the spines of the books on the far wall. Marina paused by the fireplace, watching him in the gold half light. It was chilly this evening—he wore a dark blue sweater and nice jeans and boots, and he had combed his hair. He seemed softer, stronger—and older, somehow. But more vivid, alive—close. He sent a casual glance over at her, and her heart suspended. He smiled.

"You sure you have enough shelf space for all this?" he asked, gesturing to the remaining full boxes and taking a sip of tea.

"Ha, I hope so," Marina smiled crookedly. "I'd hate to leave something homeless."

He came closer, and leaned over one of the boxes. Then, something in his face changed.

"What are these?"

Marina stepped up next to him and looked down.

"Oh—a few of the artifacts my dad came across on our...on our last dig." She paused, forcing that familiar, wicked pain back down her throat. She wrapped her arms around her middle and straightened.

Then, Bird bent down and picked one up. Startled, Marina tried to say something to stop him, but nothing came out. He carefully lifted one of the small, squatty stone figures up out of the box, and held it in front of him.

"Loki," he stated. Marina stared at Bird.

"You recognize him?"

His eyes never left the statue, which he held almost gently.

"Well," he said quietly. "I recognize that it's *supposed* to be him. Being punished by the snake, right?" he glanced at her. For a moment, she thought she saw the skin around his eyes tighten. She nodded.

"I actually think he deserved it, don't you?" she murmured. "For killing Bauldr?"

He was silent for a long time.

"But that brings Ragnarok, doesn't it?" he said. "Makes Loki so angry that he wants to destroy everyone and everything."

"Yes," Marina said carefully, studying Bird's profile. "I suppose so."

For a while, they were quiet. Then, Bird took a low breath.

"*Kjóll ferr austan, koma munu Múspells,*" he murmured.
of lög lýðir, en Loki stýrir;
fara fíflmegir með freka allir,
þeim er bróðir Býleists í för.
Surtr ferr sunnan með sviga lævi,
skínn af sverði sól valtíva;
grjótbjörg gnata, en gífr rata,
troða halir helveg, en himinn klofnar."

Marina couldn't take her eyes from him. The Old Norse words flowed easily from his lips, lilting with his deep voice. When he stopped speaking, she could swear he could hear her heart pounding. But if he did, he didn't show it—he stared at the statue. So she took a breath of her own.

"*O'er the sea from the east there sails a ship*," she translated, hushed.

With the people of Muspell, at the helm stands Loki;
After the wolf do wild men follow,
And with them the brother of Byleist goes."

Bird turned to look at her, fixing his gaze on her. The firelight flickered against his eyes. She swallowed, but he waited, so she went on.

"*Surt fares from the south with the scourge of branches,*
The sun of the battle-gods shone from his sword;
The crags are sundered, the giant-women sink,
The dead throng Hel-way, and heaven is cloven."

She stopped to catch her breath. He watched her.

"You memorized the *Edda*?"

She lifted her eyebrow.

"You memorized it in Old Norse," she countered.

He suddenly chuckled.

"Yeah, well..." he bent, and put the Loki statue back. "I'm a geek like that."

"You're not a geek," Marina said quietly. He straightened, and met her eyes. She cleared her throat and looked the other way, hiding her blush yet again.

She sensed him open his mouth to say something—but then he stopped. She turned, and frowned at him.

He was looking at the framed artifact above the fireplace.

"What's this?" he whispered, his voice entirely different—enough to make a chill run down her spine. He stepped around her to stand right in front of the mantle. He set his tea down next to one of the candlesticks, then didn't move.

"I actually found that in the back of an old library when I was fifteen," Marina explained. "I just thought it was interesting, and so the librarian paid me with it, instead of money, for straightening all his archival shelves." She came up next to Bird and turned her gaze to the subject of her narrative. It was an old piece of parchment, three feet by three feet, its borders illuminated with ships and sea monsters and intricate, twisting knots. In the center had been drawn, in black ink, a broad stone gate, with an arched top—and in the center of the arch stood a carving of Mjollnir, Thor's hammer. Through the center of the gate, a great, gnarled tree stood. And all around the gate stood a thick, thorny forest dotted with disembodied eyes—and a few wiry wolves with lolling tongues lurked between the rocks and shrubs.

"Looks frightening," Bird remarked. "What's the inscription, there at the bottom?"

"*Stien til Asgard,*" Marina said. "It means—"

"Gate to Asgard," Bird finished. She blinked.

"You...You didn't just memorize the *Edda,* did you?" she realized. "You know old Norse!"

"Yes," he nodded absently, then pointed at the drawing. "What did your father have to say about this?"

Marina said nothing for a long moment. It was getting harder and harder to ignore that old pain, that shadow reaching up to smother her.

"He thought it was a real structure," she managed, taking a deep breath. "Another dig site to investigate—maybe a place for ritual sacrifice or something." She glanced down at the floor. "He seemed to think it was around here somewhere, actually."

Bird looked at her sharply.

"He did?"

Marina lifted her head, and nodded.

"Yeah. Which is why I came and bought this house." She paused, and gazed up at the drawing again. "Of course, neither of us believe it's the gate to *Asgard*, but…" she shrugged tightly. "He was interested in it. It was almost enough to…" Her throat closed up, and she couldn't keep going.

Bird stayed quiet for a long time. She didn't look at him. Then, he drew himself up, and turned toward her.

"Hey," he said, his tone easier. "There's still some light out—want to go see if we can find a good spot for your oak?"

"Yeah," Marina sucked in a deep breath, blinking tears back and tightening her arms around herself. She forced a smile and a glance in his direction. "Sounds good."

Chapter Five

AFTERNOON SUNLIGHT flooded the side lawn, and birds fluttered between the branches of the trees beyond the iron fence. Marina sat on a patchwork quilt in the center of the yard, leaning comfortably back against a pillow and a lawn chair, a portable writing table in her lap. She had used masking tape to secure a tall, narrow piece of new parchment. Now her pen, which she had just dipped in red ink, hovered over the top right corner. Carefully, she set the pen tip down, and traced a delicate curl, creating the tongue of a Celtic-style illuminated dragon.

She paused, glanced up, and took a deep breath. The air smelled like pine and roses. She turned to her right, and looked down at Bird.

He lay on his back on the quilt, his head beside her, pillowed in his hands. His long-lashed eyes were closed, the sun beaming across his flawless face. He wore his usual plaid shirt and jeans. A lock of gold hair fell across his forehead. His broad chest rose as he took a breath.

"What are you illuminating?" he asked sleepily.

"Just the first few lines of *Beowulf*," Marina answered, turning back and dipping her pen again. Out of the corner eye, she saw his mouth quirk up in a small smile.

"Just for fun?"

She smiled.

"I'm a geek like that."

His smile broadened, but his eyes stayed shut. She glanced at him again, and her gaze lingered. She traced the perfection of his brow, his nose, his cheekbones, his lips—the shimmer in his hair, and the strong, graceful form of his body. And her heartbeat slowed.

He had been coming to her house almost every afternoon for almost three weeks, bringing with him a ready smile, a cheerful greeting, and the promise of easy, uncomplicated company for an hour or two. Sometimes, the two of them filled those couple hours with long discussions about vegetables, herbs, and breeds of roses as they dug through the garden. Other times, they hardly said five words to each other. But in either case, Marina always felt equally comfortable. Safe, even. Yet, as she stared at him now in the sunshine, suddenly too angelic to be real, pressure built inside her chest, and she swallowed.

As if sensing the change in her mood, he opened his vivid blue eyes—brighter than the sky today—turned and frowned at her.

"What's up?" he asked.

"Bird," she said quietly. He sat up, propping himself up on one elbow and facing her. She gazed back at him for a moment, the ink on her pen drying as she tried to decide what she wanted to say.

"Where..." she began. "Where did you come from?"

He laughed.

"What do you mean?"

"I mean..." she struggled, finally setting her pen down so she could gesture with her right hand. "I feel like I've known you all my life, but..." she looked at him earnestly, unable to articulate that building pressure in her chest. She set the writing desk aside so she could face him. "But I haven't," she finally said. "I've known you for a few weeks, and I don't...I mean, I don't know anything about you. Nothing about your family, or your friends, or...anything."

He waited a moment, watching her.

"Are you afraid of me?" he finally wondered. She frowned for a moment, then shook her head.

"No," she answered honestly. "But...well, sometimes you say strange things, like you know something I don't. Or like you're older than you look."

He gazed back at her for a long moment, almost smiling. He glanced down.

"You want to know about my family?"

She hesitated.

"I'm not trying to pry," she said. "I'm just—"

"Curious?" he finished, meeting her gaze again. "It's okay, Marina—I actually have been kind of rude, haven't I? You've shown me your garden and your father's collection, and I haven't said a word about any of my own stuff."

"You weren't being rude," Marina insisted. "I've appreciated your company."

He smiled again.

"Well, good," he said. Then, he sat up all the way and cleared his throat, glancing out over the flowers. "Who do you want to hear about first?"

Marina shrugged.

"Um...how about your mother?"

"My mother," Bird repeated, interlocking his fingers. "All right. My mother is the best sort of woman there is. Tall, beautiful, and kind of scary when she wants to be. But she takes her role as a mother very seriously—in fact, she sees to it that everyone who comes to visit is always happy and comfortable. If they aren't, well, they'll be sorry."

Marina had to cover her mouth to repress a laugh. His glance sparkled.

"All right, who next?"

"Your father," Marina urged.

"My father lost an eye when he was young," Bird told her. "But that doesn't stop him riding and hunting—he loves that. And he loves having people over for huge meals and telling stories all night."

"Oh, that's awful," Marina murmured. "About his eye, I mean."

"I don't think he misses it anymore. It's been so long," Bird answered. "It happened even before my brother was born, I think."

"You have a brother?" Marina said.

Bird grinned.

"Yes—a *big* brother. He's loud, and he's as blonde as I am, but with a beard—and I've never tried to seriously wrestle him. I think he'd snap me in half."

"He's mean?" Marina winced.

"No!" Bird chuckled. "No, not at all. He's fierce, but I don't think there's one cruel bone in his body. He just...overdoes it sometimes." Bird shifted on the quilt, some of the humor leaving his face. "Then there's my extended family—well, *sort of* extended. They're kind of...adopted relatives. There's one who is good friends with my father—best friends—but he's a lot younger than my father, so he spends quite a bit of time with my brother and me. He's a lot of fun, and brilliant." He paused for a moment. "Likes to cause problems, though."

"What do you mean?" Marina wondered. Bird shrugged.

"Oh, you know—make people angry at each other for stupid reasons, because he likes confrontations and arguments."

Marina frowned.

"He *likes* people yelling at each other?"

"Yeah, I guess so," Bird said. "Thinks it's funny."

Marina scowled.

"What a waste of time," she muttered. "Life's too short."

Bird barked out a laugh—a sudden, uncontrolled sound that he instantly stifled with a snort. She gave him startled look—but he was nodding.

"Yeah, you're right," he said. "You're absolutely right."

As she watched, his abrupt onset of mirth faded—replaced by a look that seemed almost—sad.

"He's...He's always kind of been a fish out of water. Trying to fit in, but...And his brother and sister don't help. His brother's aggressive and has no sense of humor, and his sister—well, she likes to cause problems too. But *she* gets people hurt."

Marina canted her head.

"Gets them hurt how?"

Bird looked the other way.

"All sorts of ways." He went quiet for a long time, and for a second, Marina thought he might be done. Then, he took a breath.

"I think it's probably been very hard on him, all these years," he said thoughtfully. "Caught between two families."

"He likes yours better?" Marina ventured. Bird almost smiled, but the shadow in his face remained.

"I think so. Yes, I think so," he said quietly. "So I'm doing what I can to help him."

For a long while, they remained quiet. Then, he lay back down, and closed his eyes to the sun. Marina couldn't pull her eyes away from him. For what felt like the hundredth time, he held her captive. But the weight in her chest still bore down on her, constricting her ribcage.

"Bird," she whispered, her throat tight as her vision filled with the light of his golden form. She swallowed hard, pulled her crippled hand against her, and made herself speak. "Why did you decide to keep me company?"

He didn't answer. He just smiled faintly. She waited, now unable to draw a single breath. Then, his lips parted, and he sang—softly.

"Bird on a briar, bird, bird on a briar,
Mankind is come of love, so love he craves.
Blissful bird, have pity on me,
Or dig, love, dig for me my grave.

I am so blithe, so bright, bird on briar,

When I see that handmaid in the hall:
She is white of limb, lovely, true,
She is fair and flower of all.

Might I have her at my will,
Steadfast of love, lovely, true,
From my sorrow she may save me
Joy and bliss would me renew."

Marina listened as his deep voice drew out a haunting, sorrowful, *beautiful* melody, which caused her blood to thrill and her heart to hurt. Absently, she realized that all the birds had gone silent, listening. And when he finished, not one of them chirped.

She swallowed hard, speechless, her mind blank. He didn't say anything more. And so, her shaking hand picked up her pen again, and she resumed her illuminating work, as a few subdued birds dared to follow that song with their own.

She knew something was wrong the instant she opened the door. Startled, she stepped back as Bird's tall form came stomping across the threshold, dripping wet.

"What are you doing?" she cried. "Did you walk here?"

"Um..." Bird ran a hand through his soaking hair. "Yes."

"Why?" she demanded. "I wasn't expecting you since the weather is so awful!"

Just then, a growl of thunder rolled overhead, and lightning flashed. Marina quickly stepped around him to shut the door on the dark Sunday afternoon and the pouring rain. The heavy oak thudded as it latched.

"Quick, take your shoes off and put them on the rug here," she instructed, pointing with her good hand. He leaned one hand against the wall and tugged at his boots—one tumbled off, then the other.

"I'm actually on my way to visit my parents—thought I'd stop in and say hi," he mumbled.

"How far away are your parents?" Marina asked.

"Not far," he answered, straightening—and then she saw his face.

"You are *white*," she gasped, stepping closer to him. He had dark circles under his eyes, and the rest of his skin was ashen. "Are you okay?"

He nodded, but frowned and closed his eyes.

"Yeah, I just...I have a really bad headache all of a sudden."

"Come here and sit down." Marina took hold of his wrist and tugged on him. He padded after her in his socks, letting her pull him toward the sitting room fireplace, which she had blazing.

"Wait here a second—I'll get a couple towels," she said, and darted back down another hallway toward the little kitchen. She returned with one large towel and one medium—she draped the big one over the couch and had him sit on it, then handed him the small towel.

"For your hair and face," she said.

"Thank you," he said, leaned his elbows on his knees and began dabbing at his face and scrubbing at his hair.

"I'll, um...go make some tea," she suggested.

"Sounds good," he nodded, closing his eyes and letting out a small sigh. Marina bit her lip, then returned to the kitchen. As she filled the kettle with water and fished out the teacups and saucers from the white cabinet, she listened toward the sitting room—but she only heard the wind whipping around the walls, the clatter of her blue china, and the rumble of thunder.

She set the kettle on the stovetop and turned on the heat, then slipped back out toward the room where he was. She stopped just at the mouth of the dark hallway, watching him.

Bird reached up and unclasped a chain around his neck, then pulled the necklace loose. A silver chain dangled from his hand, a simple pendant shaped like a bird dangling from the middle. He sighed again, winced, turned and lay back on the couch, laying his head on the armrest and closing his eyes. The necklace hung from his fingers, glittering in the firelight. Marina drew in a slow breath. The deep sunset glow from the fire flickered over him, and the curves of the couch, and the faded pattern of the rug. It barely touched the tall curtains and the shadowed paintings on the walls. Bird lay still, his chest rising and falling evenly. Marina wrapped her arms around herself hard.

The kettle whistled. She turned and hurried back to the kitchen.

She laid a tea tray out on the white counter, set the teacups on it, tossed a tea bag into the pot, and snatched the steaming kettle from the stove. Carefully—she'd spilled on herself too many times lately—she poured the hissing water into the teapot.

She had just emptied the last of it when Bird screamed.

She dropped the kettle.

It crashed on the linoleum. Burning drops scalded her ankles.

Marina leaped back, her hand flying to her throat. Then she jumped over the fallen kettle and raced down the hallway—

And skidded to a halt.

Bird thrashed on the couch, eyes screwed shut, hands clamped around the cushions. He sucked in a desperate breath, and let out another wrenching wail. His body twisted, he let go of the cushions, and flung his hands up to protect his face.

"Bird!" Marina cried, darting into the room and throwing herself down on her knees. She grabbed his shoulder and shook him. "Bird, wake up!"

He twitched. His eyes flew open.

He sat up, tearing out of her grasp, and leaped to his feet. She tumbled backward. Her left hand hit the floor. Pain shrieked through her wrist. She yelped.

"What...Where...?" Bird panted. Then, he spun toward her. "Marina?"

She just grimaced, cradling her left hand in her right as she tried to sit up.

"Are you okay?" he asked, his voice clearer now. He bent down, took hold of her elbows and pulled her to her feet—but she could feel him trembling.

"I'm so sorry," he tried. "I didn't mean to—"

"No, it's okay," she managed, trying to fight back her own shaking fit. She lifted her face and looked at him.

If she thought he was white before, that was nothing. And the circles around his gray eyes were practically black. The shadows of his face looked stark in the firelight, his hair disheveled.

"Are you all right?" she whispered, all thought of her hurt arm vanishing. He nodded quickly, swallowing.

"Yeah, I..." he took a deep breath, closed his eyes briefly, and nodded again. "I must have fallen asleep."

"You were *screaming*," Marina said. "What's the matter?"

He looked at her. Absently, she realized he still had hold of her arms. His grip gentled.

"Nightmare," he sighed, glancing past her. "Bad habit of mine." He let go, heaving a shaking sigh, then raked a hand through his damp hair. He turned toward the door. "I've...I think I'd better go."

"Oh, no, don't," Marina urged, her chest tightening. "It's raining so hard now, and you don't feel well—"

"It's okay, I'll be fine," he muttered, suddenly absent and avoiding her eyes. "I'll see you later Marina. Thank you."

"But..." Marina stammered, following him as he strode toward the door. "At least let me...Let me give you an umbrella!"

"It's okay," he said again, ramming his boots on. "Goodnight."

And the next moment, he had pulled the door open, and stepped out into the roaring rain.

The door slammed shut.

Marina stood there in the hall, her left hand still clutched to her chest, feeling the dark house turn hollow all around her.

CHAPTER SIX

IT RAINED ALL THE NEXT day. Never once did it ease, or let the sun peek through for an instant. In the gray dark, as the water lashed the walls, Marina busied herself with unpacking the rest of her cardboard boxes, and carefully hauling some of them up and down the narrow, squeaky, pokey staircase that led to the upper bedrooms. She unloaded her books, clothes, bedding, jewelry, pictures and keepsakes and began arranging them in the tower room, never minding the thunder that cracked and rumbled not far above her head, or the lightning that flashed through the single curved window. She had two lamps—one on the table and one on the dresser—that lit the room well enough. The antique overhead light didn't show any sign of life, though she changed the light bulbs and clicked the switch up and down several times before giving up. She had made up her twin-sized bed, hung her clothes in the tiny corner closet, spread a rug over the creaky wood floor and had stacked half her books in the short bookcase when she heard a trickling sound in the other room.

After pausing just an instant to listen, she got up, hurried out and into the bathroom, her stocking feet padding on the floor...

To discover water leaking through the ceiling and into the claw-foot bathtub. She let out a curse and grabbed a fistful of her hair, staring at the new brown stain on the white paint. She spun around, darted out of the bedroom and back into her room, and snatched up her cell phone from her night stand where it had been charging. She dialed a number, and held it to her ear.

Ring. Ring. Ring.

"Hi, this is Bird. Leave me a message."

Beep.

"Hi, Bird," Marina began. "I...I hate to bother you on a Saturday while you're visiting your family but...I have a little problem. The ceiling in my bathroom is leaking. Thankfully, it's dripping down into my bathtub, so it isn't getting all over my tile, but...I, well—I hope it's just the rain, and not a broken pipe. In the wall." She grimaced at the thought, and curled her left hand up against her chest. "Anyway, if you could just call me back and tell me what I ought to do, that would be great. And then maybe, when the rain stops, you could come over and see...you know, what's the matter. I'd appreciate it. Hope you're feeling better. Thanks. Bye."

She hung up, her stomach tightening. Keeping hold of the phone, she wandered back into the bathroom and gazed at that slow drip, her brow knitting. For several minutes she watched it, but the stain didn't seem to be spreading, and the drips did not get larger or more frequent. She bit her lip, shifted...

Then reluctantly retreated to her room, vowing to listen carefully for any change. She knelt back down on the rug, set the phone on the floor, and put her right hand to work stacking her pocket collection of the complete works of William Shakespeare. Then she moved on to the works of Jane Austen, Charlotte Bronte, Charles Dickens...

But Bird didn't call back.

She finished her room, fixed herself supper, ate it, curled up on the couch and distractedly tried to read a few pages of *Beowulf*—all the while sending glances at her still, silent phone.

When her mantel clock finally struck ten thirty, she gave in, shut her book, put it down and crept upstairs to get ready for bed. She stalwartly ignored the *drip, drip, drip* in the corner as she brushed her teeth, her stomach tightening harder. All at once, that drip didn't matter so much.

Thunder crisscrossed just outside as she got dressed in her pajamas and climbed into bed. She set her phone down on her night table, then snuggled uneasily under the sheets.

Drip.

Drip.

Drip.

The thunder growled again.

But all the dark night long, her phone never rang.

Marina shivered, wrapping her long brown jacket tighter around herself. The day had dawned clear and bright—but suddenly chilly. It almost felt like September back in New York. Her shoes crunched on the sand as she strode down the shoulder of the dirt road. Ancient pines and budding trees hugged the road, and in the brisk gusts of wind that blew her braided hair, she could smell the brine. Brilliant white gulls spun and dove far above in the crystal sky, their cries falling faintly down to earth. Birds twittered in the tangled shrubs on either side, and little white blossoms winked at her from the grass as she passed by.

At last, Marina rounded the corner, and the dirt turned to black paving beneath her feet. The rumble of a few cars greeted her, and as she hopped up onto the sidewalk, the quiet busy-ness of the sleepy main street surrounded her. She strolled under the overhang and past several shops, nodded at a few people who passed her, watched a couple trucks roll by to her left, and admired the colorful banners flapping from the lamp-posts before finally catching sight of the building she was hunting for: a tall, broad, wide-windowed business with a hand-painted red sign reading: *Svenson's Plumbing Carpentry and Landscaping*

Marina hurried across the street between two cars, hopped up, and pushed the jangling front door open. Instantly, the scent of newly-sawed pine flooded her, and she glanced around a cluttered workshop filled with all manner of table-saws, tools, half-done furniture and wood-littered countertops. In some other back room, she heard one of these saws busily whining.

"Good morning!"

She turned to see a man with a white beard and twinkling eyes, wearing cover-alls, carry an unvarnished rocking chair in through a side door.

"Good morning," Marina answered.

"How can I help you?" the man asked, setting the chair down with a *thunk* and dusting off his hands.

"Is Bird Oldeson here?" Marina asked.

The man's cheerful expression vanished, and his eyebrows drew together.

"No, I'm afraid not."

Marina blinked.

"He isn't?"

"Nope," the man sighed, shaking his head as he stepped up to the counter near her. "He quit on me the other day. Said he had some family business he had to take care of in Colorado."

Marina stared at him, not understanding what she was hearing.

"What...? He's gone?"

The man sat down in a chair and nodded, glancing up at her.

"Yeah, moved all of his things out of his trailer yesterday—he stopped by my house to say goodbye last night before heading out."

"But..." Marina stammered, feeling as if the room was tilting sideways. "I thought...I thought all his family lived around here!"

"No," he shook his head. "No family at all here. He's only been here for a few months. He came here for the fishing, initially, then needed some extra pocket money, so I hired him on. It's a shame I had to lose him—he's one of the best workers I've ever had. A real good kid, so friendly, always on time...I'm Jim Larson by the way," And he stuck out a worn, calloused hand. Marina took his fingers, and numbly shook his hand.

"Marina Feroe," she managed.

"Feroe!" he said, his eyebrows going up as he released her. "Bird was doing some work for you, wasn't he? Windows?"

Marina just nodded, trying to keep her eyes focused.

"You're satisfied with what he did, aren't you?" Larson leaned forward, worried. "Like I said, I've never had a better—"

"I've got a leak," Marina cut in. "A leak in my bathroom ceiling. I need...I need someone to fix it."

"Sure!" Larson nodded. "Sure, no problem. I think Richard's got some time tomorrow morning—want me to send him on by?"

"That would be good," Marina nodded. "Thank you."

Mr. Larson may have said something back to her, but Marina didn't hear. She turned and pushed through the door—it seemed strangely silent, now. She trailed back down the sidewalk, looking straight ahead, but the people and cars made no noise, and she didn't see any banners. Her footsteps met the paving, but as if she was walking on feathers. No sand crunched under her heels as she walked down the lane. The flowers were invisible, the trees withdrawn. Gulls flickered overhead, but their voices stayed mute.

She traipsed up the walk to her house, and opened the silent front door. Didn't bother taking off her coat. She found her way to the living room, and stood in the center of the floor for an eternity.

At last, she eased down onto the couch, staring into the empty fireplace, and remained there until the shadows of twilight filtered in through the windows and covered her.

A gust of wind shuddering against the walls made her lift her head.

She blinked slowly. Pulled her arms closer to her chest. Her left hand ached—ached all the way up to her elbow, her shoulder, her whole side. Listlessly, she shivered, and realized it had gotten dark outside. And in this room, a chill had gathered. She glanced at the fireplace. Stayed where she was.

The wind rustled again, with a nasty edge. The branches of that twisted rosebush outside slapped against the window. Marina did not move.

Then...

A howl.

A long, piercing, wailing howl of descending notes that sent a chill crawling down Marina's spine.

Her vision sharpened. She sat up straight.

A wolf.

Close by.

Stiffly, she rose to her feet, and stepped quietly into the dark entryway. She paused by the door, distantly frowning.

There, again. A lonely, rising call leaping up into the night to plunge back down into the silence. As she listened, it came once more...

And another voice joined it. Then another.

She swallowed.

She knew all the old stories liked to exaggerate the wolf's fierceness into a brand of evil. She *knew* they were nothing more than wild dogs, doing what they needed to survive...

A slicing, unearthly song interrupted her thoughts. She wrapped her arms around herself, feeling her body go cold.

They could not be any further away than the edge of her garden. Right there, in those shadowed woods.

She reached out and noisily bolted the front door, then hurried back into the sitting room. Marina knelt on the rug, tossed a few logs into the hearth and lit a fire. Heat bloomed beneath her hand, and yellow light startled her eyes. She tugged her jacket even tighter around herself, pulled her knees up to her chest and sat back against the leg of the couch.

The wolves outside began a chorus of haunting singing, setting her teeth on edge.

A twinkle, out of the corner of her right eye.

She frowned, and glanced over.

Went still.

Then, hesitantly, she reached out, and touched the edge of a delicate silver chain sticking out from beneath the couch. She wrapped her fingers around it, and gently tugged it free.

A small silver pendant, beautifully shaped like a bird in flight, glimmered in the firelight as it hung from the chain by her finger.

Marina gazed at it for a long while.

Then, with clumsy, shaking fingers, she quickly unclasped it—cursing again at her crippled hand—and fastened it around her neck. Finally secured, she reached up and pressed the pendant against her breastbone and burst into tears.

She sank down onto the floor on her left side, heavy tears rolling down her cheeks, curling up tight and sobbing, as the wolves continued their eerie, gleeful choir all around the walls of her house.

CHAPTER SEVEN

MARINA'S EYES FLEW open.

She couldn't see anything.

Wind rushed and battered all around the windows. The fire had burnt itself into low, sinister embers.

Lightning flashed.

For an instant, the whole room blazed in a white flashbulb of light, then plunged back into blackness. Thunder crackled and snarled in answer.

Marina sat up. Her whole back panged, and she couldn't feel her left forearm. She could, however, still feel the tear-tracks on her cheeks. She frowned, shifting uncomfortably. Had the storm awakened her?

Scrape, scrape, scrape...

She tilted her head. The low digging sound cut through even the gale, and seemed to be coming from just outside the window straight in front of her.

Her eyes slowly widened. Her throat locked.

But she climbed to her feet.

Stiffly, she crept toward the window, holding her breath. The rosebush out there scraped against the panes. She held out her right hand and touched the wooden frame.

Another flash of lightning.

She flinched back.

Someone.

Someone was out there. Half-turned away from her, but distinct.

For just an instant, she had seen him—a tall, winsome form. He wore flowing white, and what looked like...

Armor. Shining armor.

An icy-pale, handsome face, and hair like snow.

A *familiar* face.

Crack.

Lightning blazed across the sky. Marina's lips parted.

He was gone.

She turned, dodged around a chair and ran to the door. She unbolted the lock, grabbed the handle and tugged the heavy door open. It gave way, and the wind blasted her. She leaped out onto the porch, her heart pounding.

Once more, a bolt of white electricity sliced through the sky, lighting up her front walk and side lawn like day. The wind whipped her hair. Where was he, *where*...?

There.

There, walking away from her...

Toward that tangle of wicked-looking woods.

She clenched her teeth and sucked in a breath as her heart skipped three beats. She pressed her left arm close to her as her whole body quivered. Her balance teetered on the edge of the step, her whole being suspended...

She reached up, fumbling, and closed her fingers around that bird pendant.

And she jumped off her porch.

She narrowly avoided tripping and crashing into a rosebush, and skidded on a paving stone. But then her shoes caught traction on the grass and she hurried through the darkness, the night clouds roiling overhead. She couldn't see him anymore.

She swished through the herb garden and the shrubbery, the storm gnashing just above her. Gritting her teeth, she squeezed the pendant harder. And she passed the first oak tree.

Silence fell.

The wind died.

Marina jerked to a stop, panting. She shifted, looking all around—leaves crunched under her feet. Her breath suddenly rang too loudly through the forest. Not even the slightest breeze disturbed the uppermost branches of the ancient trees.

"Ohhhh..." she rasped, leaning back and going cold down to her bones. "I should..."

Something.

A movement...

A light.

Far, far ahead of her. Low to the ground. Quiet blue...

And growing.

Filling the woods—but the deep black shadows remained. As if the light and the dark had grudgingly agreed to share this corner wilderness.

Marina stood motionless, barely breathing.

Then, she slid her right foot forward. Then her left.

Very, very carefully, she picked her way between the tangled tresses of the wild vines and the sprawling ferns, rustling through the dead underbrush as she moved.

Less than a hundred yards, and the light grew brighter with every step. She fixed her attention on it, trying to distinguish what was making it, and see if it was standing still...

She drew close. Rested her right palm against the rough bark of an oak, and leaned into its shadow. Her eyes narrowed...

The light moved.

She jerked.

It hoisted up in one, swift movement—

And she saw him.

A man.

A *different* man.

He towered, perhaps six-and-a-half feet tall. He had wild, windblown blonde hair, half tied back; and a short beard. His face—handsome, striking and carven, his eyes blazing, his strong, heavy brow frowning fiercely. He wore a dark blue cloak that draped over his chest and flowed over his arms and down his back—and the cloak rustled without a breeze, and transformed into clouds of rolling vapor around his ankles. His metal bracers glittered, as did the silver embroidery on his trousers, and the high buckles on his tall boots. At his wide belt hung a great hammer, its rune-covered head glimmering. And in his left hand he held up a small lantern, from which the blue light shone.

Marina wrapped her fingers around her throat.

And the next instant, someone else strode into the halo from the lantern.

Him!

It was him—the one she had seen outside her window. His long white clothes flowed and whispered like summer clouds, catching and reflecting every bit of light. His spare armor, shining on his shoulders, upper chest and forearms, glittered with tiny jewels. He lifted his flaxen head, and spoke.

And when he did, she knew his voice.

Bird.

"What are you doing here?" he asked the bearded man with the lantern.

"I came to find you," the bearded man answered in a deep, rumbling voice, turning toward him. "Mother wanted you this morning, but you were *nowhere*." The taller man searched Bird's face with his vivid eyes, and his brow knitted differently. "What were you doing?"

"Running an errand," Bird replied, sighing and glancing around. "We should go, before your storm lifts."

Marina's eyes flashed.

The bearded man looked straight up, then back at Bird.

"All right, come." He kicked his head back, and turned...

Halted.

Bird's form stiffened. Both men stared at the ground.

Marina's breath slowed.

A mist came crawling through the dead leaves from somewhere off to Bird's far left. An unnatural, gray, snake-like mist, with creeping fingers and slithering tendrils. Slowly, the two men lifted their heads and gazed into the woods, toward the source.

Marina's heart skipped a beat, and she could no longer hold her breath. It started coming short and sharp. But she couldn't even move, let alone turn and run.

A new figure slipped into view. Silent on the underbrush—graceful, smooth and deadly.

A woman.

She wore draping black—it drifted all around her in shadow, and dripped from her limbs like ink into water. She had ash-white skin, and raven hair that fell all the way down to her knees. Marina could only see her in profile, but she glimpsed her right eye—and it had no white. All black, like obsidian. When she saw the two men, her comely mouth smiled, and she languidly canted her head, showing off her slender, icy neck.

Marina's soul trembled.

"Hello, Bauldr," the woman purred, glancing at Bird and flashing her eyebrows. "The new armor suits you."

"Hel," the bearded man frowned at her. "What are you doing on Midgard? I thought you had party business with Sif at Bilskirnir."

Marina's knees went weak. Still, she couldn't shift an inch.

The woman—*Hel*—shrugged her pale, bare shoulders.

"I was curious," she said lightly. "I saw the little one dash off across the Asbru and thought to myself 'Hm.'" She crossed her arms. "'*What* is the prince doing at this late hour visiting the mortals?'"

She arched one of her inky eyebrows at him. "Does Nanna know where you are?"

Bird shifted, swallowed. Hel blinked.

"Oooh. I see." She smirked, then gave a coldly-amused glance at the bearded man. "Well. We're all entitled to a little fun, aren't we?"

"No," Bird suddenly snarled at her. "Not at all."

She just gazed at him saucily, her arms still crossed.

"So I'm to assume Thor only came to retrieve you because he was *lonely?* Is that it? Lonely for the baby brother?"

"Hel," the bearded man heaved a sigh and rolled his eyes. "If you weren't Loki's sister, I would kill you. Right here, on this spot. I've told you that, haven't I?"

She laughed out loud, then winked at him .

"Oh, yes—but you're quite fond of me. You'd never do that."

"Sure," Bird muttered. Then he faced her squarely. "So why are you *really* here? Get lonely too?"

She bared her teeth in a grin.

And Marina realized with horror that her teeth were *sharp*.

"I am here with Fenris," she answered. "He's taking my pack for a run."

And suddenly, wolves yipped and howled around them all, their disembodied voices shrieking through the forest. Hel turned her face toward Marina, glancing about casually...

And Marina's stomach turned over.

Hel's face...

The right side of it was beautiful—smooth and perfectly formed, if pale as death. The left side...

Was a skull.

Though long, straight bangs tried to hide it, there could be no mistaking. No skin, no muscle—only bare, whitened bone, and a gaping hole where her eye should be.

Marina began to shiver violently. Her vision blinked in and out.

"You shouldn't do that," Bird warned Hel. "Let them all loose to run. Not so close to a town."

"Why?" Hel turned back to him, frowning. "They don't go past the borders of the woods, and if any mortal is stupid enough to come in here at night with wolves howling—well, that's his own fault."

Marina gulped.

"We're going home," the bearded man cut in. "Are you coming?"

"On such a lovely night?" Hel spread out her hands. "Of course not! Go on. Don't worry about me."

"We've never wasted any time *worrying* about you," Bird rolled his eyes.

"Good night, Your Highnesses," Hel grinned. "I'm going to have some more fun playing."

"Don't break anything," Thor warned. She made a terrifying face at him. He just looked at her flatly, and together he and Bird strode off into the woods, away from Marina.

Hel watched them go, then casually turned around and swept off the way she had come...

And disappeared into the dark.

Marina's fingers closed tighter around her throat. The bearded man and Bird still strode straight away from her, the lantern flickering, and growing dimmer.

Wolves cackled behind her.

She spun around.

She couldn't see anything. But she could hear them moving around through the underbrush, darting back and forth, panting, sniffing...

She stood away from the tree, stared after Bird, her breath catching...

And hurried after him.

She fought to keep her feet quiet on the rustling leaves as she caught up—but as soon as she got close enough to their backs, she hesitated. Fell back. Clapped a hand over her mouth.

She could not show them that she'd seen them. She could *not*.

But maybe...Maybe they could lead her out of the forest, closer to some civilized spot, *away* from the wolves and that *woman,* and she could find her way back to her house...

The two men kept walking, never looking back. They strode noisily, the bearded man's boots making a racket. Bird tread more lightly, but not carefully.

They wound between the trees, gradually heading downhill until Marina lost her bearings. She wrapped her left arm around her middle, praying that she wouldn't trip and fall down the slippery, shadowed incline.

Up ahead, the scenery changed. The trees stood back, and the path opened up into a small clearing. The two men kept walking. Marina slowed to a stop.

There, right in the center of the hollow, stood a tall stone doorway.

Thick, broad, set stones, with vines clinging to them—vines that almost hid the deep, carved runes in the granite. And up on the lintel, right in the center...

Unmistakably.

Mjollnir.

A seal of Thor's hammer.

Just like in the picture above her mantel.

"*Stien til Asgard...*" she whispered.

This was it! This was the very place that had sparked her father's imagination and teeth-gritting determination—the *reason* she had moved here to that isolated house next to these frightening woods...

But why were Bird and the stranger coming here? Were they...

Were they disciples of the Norse myths? Men who actually still worshipped the old gods? Had they come here for some kind of ceremony, or...

But what about the bearded man's cloak? The cloak that looked like it was made of storm clouds...?

And what about *that woman's face*...?

She stopped, and grabbed a branch. She stared at the two men, her thoughts battering around in her head.

But the bearded man with the lantern did not hesitate. He did not pause to say a prayer, he didn't lay down any flowers or wreaths or treasures as an offering. Neither did Bird.

Instead, as one, they stepped through the door, into the darkness...

And the lamp went out.

Marina quit breathing.

Then, she gasped. It echoed in the stillness. She strained her eyes, *sure* that they still had to be there, just hidden in the dark—

A deep, rugged, chesty snarl.

She whirled.

There, just behind her, bathed in a rare shaft of moonlight...

A wolf.

A giant, black wolf, with eyes like burning coals.

It gnashed its gleaming teeth, curling its lips and laying its ears flat against its head. Its horrid eyes fixed on her. It lowered its great head.

Her heart gave one awful *bang* against her chest.

She ran.

Marina pelted down the hill, straight toward that door, her pulse skyrocketing, her hair flying out behind her. The wolf—on her heels—she could feel it—

She threw herself through the doorway.

Tripped and slammed into the ground. Buried her head in her arms and curled into a ball...

Silence.

She pulled in a breath. Lifted her head. She opened her mouth, but nothing came out.

She lay on a bed of wet stones. Cobbles. And, as she dared to sit halfway up and look around, she realized she was lying on a bridge.

A long, road-wide stone bridge running straight off into the distance—and disappearing into thick fog. Fog also stood like walls on either side of the bridge, concealing everything from her but the flickering iron lamps that perched upon the bridge's sides.

"*What*...?" she whispered, suddenly dizzy...

But there.

There.

Almost invisible in the fog: a light. A blue light.

The lamp.

"Wait!" she cried. She clambered to her feet, gritting her teeth as pain danced around all the bones in her left arm. She limped forward, steadied herself and picked up her pace. Her shoes clacked on the stones as she broke into a run. "Wait, wait!"

"What was that?" a muffled voice up ahead demanded—it sounded like the bearded man.

"I heard it, too," Bird replied, hushed.

"Wait, there's...There's wolves in the...*wait!*" Marina called, picking up her pace.

And all of a sudden, she *ran* right into him.

Slammed into a shoulder, a chest—tried to catch herself—

Hands grabbed her shoulders. Her head jerked up...

She found sky-blue eyes, and a familiar, pale, handsome face framed by blonde hair.

"Marina?" he exclaimed.

"Who is this?" the bearded man demanded—and stepped closer. Marina gaped at him. He loomed over her, his wide shoulders casting a shadow even in the fog, his brow scowling, his gaze like lightning.

"Calm down," Bird let go of Marina to put a hand on the bearded man's chest. The bearded man's eyes narrowed to slits, and cut straight through her.

"Am I..." Marina gasped, reaching out to grip the front of Bird's tunic. "Am I dead?"

The bearded man bent closer and tilted his head, studying her.

"You don't appear to be," he remarked. "Who are you? Where did you come from?"

"I came from...from back there," she pointed. "I saw Bird go into the woods, so I followed him, and then the wolves chased me through the door..."

The bearded man looked sharply at Bird.

"She calls you Bird."

Bird sighed, and glanced down at the ground.

"Who is this, Bauldr?" the bearded man asked.

"Bauldr..." Marina mouthed, unable to make any sound.

"Marina, this is Prince Thor, son of Odin. My brother," Bird wearily gestured to him. "Thor, this is Marina Feroe. A mortal."

"A *mortal?*" Thor roared, shaking Marina down to the soles of her feet. "What—*How* did she follow us? How can she *see* us?"

Bird sighed again, turned to her, and reached up. He touched Marina's collar with his fingertips, and moved it aside...

Thor's eyes fell on the chain around her neck. Marina blushed.

"You gave that to her?" Thor growled, glaring at Bird.

"No," Bird shook his head. "I left it at her house."

"What were you doing in her *house?*" Thor pressed, baring his teeth.

"I told you," Bird replied calmly. "I had errands to run."

"Wait, wait..." Marina interrupted, feeling unsteady. "Thor. Thor?"

"That is my name," Thor bit back, then focused on Bird again. "Take her back where she came from. Get the necklace and *come home*. Enough of this nonsense."

"I'm not taking her back," Bird replied, meeting his eyes squarely. "You—"

"No, you heard what Hel said," Bird countered. "She and Fenris are in those woods, and I know they're looking for trouble. I'm not going to take Marina back there to leave her in her house all alone. And it's our fault she left her house and came this way in the first place. We were careless. Besides, she knows all our proper names now, and she's found the gate to the Asbru. It's too late."

Thor ground his teeth. Glowered at Marina. She trembled.

"She cannot stay."

"I know that," Bird agreed. "Just for tonight."

Thor huffed like a bull.

"Fine," he decided. "Come on. We are late as it is."

"Where...What's happening? Where are we going?" Marina flinched as Bird pulled away from her to follow. Bird paused, and met her gaze. He gave her a half smile—but his bright eyes remained earnest.

"Somewhere safe." He held out his hand. "Come on."

She swallowed, stared at his hand...

Reached out and took it. He wrapped his fingers around hers and gently pulled, and she found herself walking with him, trailing after the thunderous stranger into the mist.

CHAPTER EIGHT

FOR SEVERAL LONG MINUTES, Marina couldn't say anything. The only noises she could hear were three sets of footsteps against stone. Bird's fingers, the single warmth on this chilly, fog-bound bridge, kept secure hold on her hand. She tried with all her might to keep her heart-rate down, to slow her breathing...

"Where are we going?" she finally whispered again. "Really." She turned and glanced up at Bird. He took a long breath, and let it out slowly. Tiredly.

"We are going to Asgard."

All kinds of responses leaped onto Marina's tongue. But none of them even made it to her lips.

"It's not far," Bird continued. "Just at the other end of this bridge."

"But..." she finally stammered. "This bridge...Has it always been here?"

He quietly smiled.

"Sure."

"Then why can't everyone see it?" she asked.

"Because they don't have the key." He glanced down at her neck where the bird pendant rested. A strange thrill ran through her body—the necklace tingled on her skin.

For a long while, she attempted to gather her spinning thoughts, listening to the tap of their footsteps. At last, she risked another question.

"That was...That was Hel," she breathed. "Back there. It was really her."

Bird briefly met her eyes.

"You saw her?"

Marina said nothing. He nodded.

"Yes, it was her."

Marina felt even colder than before.

"And that...That is Thor."

He nodded again.

"Yes."

"How?"

He reflexively smiled.

"What do you mean, how?"

"How?" She wrapped her left arm tighter around her middle. She turned again, and urgently searched his face.

"Marina," Bird began, adjusting his hold on her hand. "I know you know all the stories. All of the myths and legends about us, inside and out—everything." He smiled at her. "I saw how brilliant you are."

She blushed again, but listened with all her might. He went on.

"But I'm fairly certain you do *not* know what actually happened, in most cases. Who we really are, where we really live, what we've really done."

"Who are you?" Marina whispered.

"We *are* Aesir," Bird replied. "But we are not gods, as so many people thought for so long. We're sort of..." He frowned, pondering. "We are elf-like. Or...We live a lot longer than the people of Midgard. But we can be killed, or die of old age. Very old age. And some of us have special abilities, like being able to change our shapes, or talk to animals, or bring down lightning—"

"And I should do just that to you for starting this *again*," Thor barked, turning to glare at Bird over his shoulder. Bird chuckled softly.

"He will?" Marina breathed.

"No," Bird breathed back. "But we should hurry a little faster."

And so they picked up their pace, and caught up with Thor.

Marina asked no more questions. She was tempted to try to convince herself that she was dreaming—but she could tell the difference between reality and a dream, and she could *smell* this fog, hear the footsteps, feel the paving beneath her feet and her hand in Bird's. And she *certainly* could feel the electricity buzzing all around Thor's cloudy, rolling cloak.

They trekked for perhaps an hour, the handle of the lamp Thor held squeaking, and the clothing of both men rustling.

Then, very gradually, the fog began to lighten.

Far ahead, the clouds took on a pinkish tinge, and a breeze wafted through the still air. It touched Marina's hair and face—and it wasn't cold. She took a deep breath, and smelled...

Grass. And something blooming. Clover?

Minutes later, the fog brightened, a gust of wind billowed through their clothes...

And the mists cleared.

Marina's eyes went wide.

The three of them stepped through a stone arch and onto an earthen road, in the broad center of the late-afternoon sun.

To their left, looming, white-barked beeches stretched their leafy branches to the dome of the airy, cloud-dotted sky, lining the road like soldiers at march. Off to the right rolled green fields touched at the edges with the gold of the sunset, and interrupted by wandering stone walls. In the distance stood a carved wooden barn with a prowling dragon decorating its peak. The wind whipped playfully through the grain, making its heads snicker to each other, and filling Marina's lungs with a fresh, sun-baked scent. She twisted around...

To see the stoic arch, marked with Mjollnir as well...

But through it spread a plain grassy field, dotted with purple clover, and buzzing with bees and white butterflies.

The wind called again, blustering her hair into her face. She turned toward the front again.

"Are you okay?" Bird asked. "You've gone white."

"Wouldn't you?" she muttered. He laughed. The sunlight through the branches of the beeches played across his features, and danced across his eyes. She almost managed to smile back.

"Come on," he said, squeezing her hand. "No wolves to worry about here."

A ragged clatter sounded from behind them. Marina and Bird turned to look...

A huge, burly man with red hair and beard, wearing a work shirt and trousers, drove a thick wooden cart up the road toward them, grasping the reins of two massive, muscular black horses in his weather-worn hands.

"Your Highnesses!" he called. Thor halted his headlong march and turned. The man on the cart drew up beside them, and pulled back on the reins. The horses stopped, snorting. The great man on the cart stood up. He loomed taller than a tree.

"Aelfdane!" Thor's knitted brow instantly cleared, his eyes brightened and he actually smiled. "Shouldn't you be at home putting the boar on the spit?"

"I had to deliver one more load—and as I plan to drink a great deal tonight, I knew would not be able to accomplish anything tomorrow!" Aelfdane answered merrily. Thor laughed—the sound shook Marina's bones.

"If I may be so bold," Aelfdane went on. "It's no chariot, but my cart is at Your Highness' disposal if you would rather skip the long walk to Bilskirnir."

"Do you want to ride, Bauldr?" Thor asked Bird.

"Why not?" Bird answered, grinning up at Aelfdane. "Thank you!"

"My honor, sirs," Aelfdane gestured to the back of his cart—then frowned at Marina. "What do we have here?"

"A guest," Bird answered, pulling Marina around to the back. He opened the tail gate of the cart and, without a moment's strain, lifted Marina up into the back. She quickly grabbed hold of the edge. Bird then hopped up and landed on his *feet* like a cat. Before Marina could object, he had picked her up under her arms and set her on a bench bolted to the inside wall of the cart.

The next moment, Thor had also leaped up, his boots thudding, his weight jostling the whole rig. He flopped down onto the floor, sat back and folded his arms.

"All set?" Aelfdane called, sitting down himself.

"Yes!" Bird told him, easing down next to Marina.

"Then we are off!" Aelfdane announced, and slapped the reins against his horses' backs. The cart jolted, Marina caught her balance, and they rolled on ahead.

The wheels jiggered and rattled as the horses trotted along, their hooves clacking against the hardened dirt. The harnesses jingled and the boards creaked, and Bird tilted his face to the sun and closed his eyes.

Marina gazed at him for a moment, speechless. Then she caught movement out of the corner of her eye. She turned to the road behind them.

Men and women came trailing out of the waving fields on either side—all handsome, tall and beautifully-built, their faces ruddy, their blonde hair mussed, their clothes dirty from a hard day of work. They slung shovels, hoes, hammers, axes, rakes and scythes over their shoulders and fell in behind the cart. The small group soon grew to a crowd of dozens, and they all spoke easily to each other, laughing and talking about how much each one was going to eat and dance and drink that evening. Some of them shouted greetings up to Thor and Bird, who called back and waved at them. Sparrows burst out of the bordering shrubbery as the commotion passed, taking to the sky in startled, twittering clouds.

Then, toward the back of the crowd, a young man piped up in a strong, clear tone, singing a cheerful song in a language Marina didn't recognize. It almost sounded like Norwegian—but not quite. In less than a moment, almost every one of those tramping behind the cart hand started singing too, loudly, so that the their mixed and rowdy voices resounded across the fields. Marina glanced over at Bird. He caught her eye—and winked. She pressed a hand to her head and laughed, baffled.

Together, this troupe wound up the road, ascending a gradual hill. Marina began to taste new scents upon the air: baking bread, roasting meat, some sort of spice...

"If your guest cares to see it," Aelfdane prompted. "It is Yggdrasil."

"What?" Marina straightened, then turned and stared at Bird. He said nothing, just inclined his head toward the fore. Carefully, Marina stood up, just a little, so she could see past Aelfdane's broad shoulders and fiery head...

And all the breath left her.

Upon the horizon stood a stocky, black, craggy hill, from which countless glittering fountains spilled and tumbled like silver ribbons. And upon the crown of this hill grew a tree.

A tree the size of a mountain.

Ancient, weather-bitten, gnarled and twisted, its trunk the width of a canyon, its branches stretching so high and wide that its leaves eclipsed the sun, and clouds gathered around its elbows. The sky all around it had turned to paintbrushed orange, setting off the green of the tree's billion gold-dusted leaves. And within the trunk, Marina caught sight of a thousand twinkling lights.

"Are those..." she realized. "Are those windows? In the tree?"

"Of course!" Thor answered. "It's the seat of our father, Odin the king."

The cart jiggled. Marina sat down hard, her knees going weak. Even so, she could still see those heaven-reaching branches—and they stayed just where they were, no matter how many times she blinked.

"Are we going there?" she managed.

"No," Bird replied, sighing. "Unfortunately."

"Unfortunately?" Thor sat up, frowning at him. "What's so unfortunate? You are coming to *my* house—is it not good enough for you?"

Bird chuckled, leaned back and kicked Thor's boot.

"I just meant that Mother and Father won't be there with us."

"Everyone *else* will be," Thor huffed, re-settling himself. "Tyr, Freya, Nanna, Eir, Bragi, Gmot, Ran, Loki—"

Marina swayed as each name hit her, going lightheaded. Neither man noticed.

"Have Hel and Fenris been uninvited?" Bird folded his own arms. "They didn't act like they wanted to come after all."

"Pffft," Thor waved it off. "Fenris always gets drunk and starts fights and Hel causes problems without drinking anything. I am happy if they don't come. I only invited them because of Loki."

"Loki doesn't care for their company much, either," Bird pointed out.

"You cannot tell *them* that," Thor countered. "Besides, one cannot invite just one of the Farbautisons and leave the other two out. That would start a war by itself."

Bird chuckled and sat back again. Marina swallowed, glanced at them both, then ventured another question.

"What is everyone celebrating?"

"Some battle a long time ago," Bird told her. "None of us remember."

"Except it is an excuse to eat, drink, dance and stay up all night," Thor added, closing his eyes. Bird nodded at him.

"Exactly."

Marina watched Thor for another moment, but much of the tension had melted from his face. She bit her lip, staring at that mighty frame, then regarded Bird.

"What?" he asked.

She shook her head.

"I'm not..." she murmured. "I'm not here. I can't be."

"And why not?" he asked, watching her.

"Because," Marina answered. He laughed. Marina's brow knitted.

"Look, don't worry," he assured her. "It'll all make sense eventually. You'll see."

She didn't answer—but then he reached out and took her right hand in his, and squeezed it. Warmth shot through her, and she answered the pressure.

"And here we are!"Aelfdane announced, pulling back on the reins. The cart rolled to a stop. "Bilskirnir! Welcome home."

"Thank you, Aelfdane," Thor grunted as he sat up, then slid off the back and landed heavily. He turned, and held out his arms to Marina.

"Come, little thing," he urged. Marina's eyebrows shot up, and her gut tensed. But she stood, shuffled toward the edge—

Thor grabbed her waist, and all at once she stood on the grass. She tipped, grabbing hold of the cart wheel. Bird hopped down next to her, grinning.

"Happy feasting!" Thor shouted, and Aelfdane waved at him, and drove off.

"Come on, come on," Thor said, charging off the road and up between two unbelievable oak trees. A wave of sparks raced down his cloak, snapping like fireworks. "My wife will have my head."

Together, Marina and Bird followed Thor between those same trees...

Onto a broad lane, bordered on each side by ranks of oaks—and ending in a giant mead hall.

Marina's steps faltered.

A huge wooden hall, all carved with snarling, wide-eyed faces, knots, runes and curling dragons, loomed higher than the trees. Its guest wings, spreading from either side of the hall, stood three stories high each, lamps and candles flickering in their windows. Soldiers strolled along the rooftops, their armor and spearheads gleaming in the evening sun. The mighty front gates, painted with shimmering gold, bore the image of Yggdrasil; and a great wooden Mjollnir—a trinity knot in its center—rested above the lintel.

Three lonesome notes from a horn burst out through the quiet evening, sending the birds in the trees fluttering. Shouts rose up from the guards. The front gates swung open.

Voices spilled out. Voices, and bustling, and hurrying feet, and the clanking of metal dishes. And the scent of honey bread. The two brothers strode right in.

Marina hesitated, reflexively pulling her left arm against herself.

"Come on," Bird beckoned. "I need to show you to Sif."

"Sif?" Marina croaked. Bird beckoned again, so she tried not to wince, and followed him.

Her feet met a smooth wooden floor—and, as her eyes adjusted to the slightly-dimmer light, she attempted to figure out where she stood.

A balcony with a railing—almost a catwalk—lining the perimeter of the massive hall. Directly in front of her, wide stairs led down from this balcony to the main level of the hall. Long tables and benches covered the stone floor, all set with platters and twinkling jeweled goblets, and decorated with bursting bouquets of purple and white flowers. In the very center, a roaring fire blazed in a rectangular pit. All of the pillars in the place had been wrapped in living vine that bloomed with delicate pink blossoms. Marina could smell them from here. Lilac. And far above, the roof somehow let in the light from the sky—indeed, panels had been lifted that they could easily lower if it began to rain. Brightly-clad servants darted back and forth down on that lower level, carrying trays, brooms, rags, vases, bottles and knives. They called to each other, barking orders, and their voices battered around and magnified in the wide, wooden space.

"Your Highness!" a masculine voice called, and Bird's brother stopped halfway down the stairs. A young man wearing cream and brown darted out of one of the side doorways and onto the balcony, then leaned on the railing.

"What?" Thor demanded.

"There are not enough rooms for all the men coming," the young man reported.

"*What?*" Thor said again. "Sif forced me to check the list four times before I was able to invite anyone—how did that happen?" He turned around and stomped back up the stairs, nearly shaking them loose.

"My lord, with Fenris *and* Loki *and*—"

"Forget Fenris, he's not coming," Thor replied, swinging around the corner and striding up to the servant. The servant blinked.

"He isn't?"

"No, he is on Midgard."

"*Midgard?* But—"

"Show me which rooms you mean," Thor instructed. "We'll get this sorted."

"All right, this way..." the servant said, and the two of them vanished back through the door.

"Come on," Bird said yet again, and Marina trailed after him down the stairs, marveling at the way his clothing still swept around him like a mist. He strode across the floor. The servants dipped into quick bows as he passed—and then those same servants followed Marina with curious glances. She ducked her head and fixed on Bird's back.

That is, until she saw *her*.

A lady, standing up on the dais, arranging the flowers on the head table before the two wooden thrones.

She had to be almost as tall as Thor—curvy, muscular and elegant, with a spill of golden hair that reached all the way down to the floor. She wore a velvet scarlet gown embroidered with gold, its sleeves flaring around her wrists. She turned and looked at Bird with long-lashed, moon-blue eyes, and her sharp, stunning features brightened. Her red mouth smiled, and she held out her pale hand to him. Marina was suddenly struck by the certainty that she had seen a Renaissance painting of this woman somewhere in Sweden.

"Bird!" the lady cried. "You're early!"

"Really?" Bird caught up her hand and kissed it, then laughed. "All Thor would talk about was that we were late!"

The woman laughed—a lively ringing—but then her smile faded as her moon-blue gaze landed on Marina.

All at once, Marina felt like a withered weed. She gulped, and tried to look away. The lady turned back to Bird.

"Is this from Midgard?"

"Yes," Bird answered.

"Oh, poor thing," the lady mused. "What is this one dying from?"

Marina frowned and looked up at her, but the lady returned to arranging the flowers.

"She's not dying," Bird corrected. "She followed us home."

"Aha," the lady chuckled. "Well, I am certain your mother will not let you keep her."

"I'm not keeping her," Bird replied. "She's just staying the night."

The lady paused, then whirled and pinned him with a deadly look.

Bird rolled his eyes.

"*No*," he insisted.

Marina's mouth fell open—and then her face burned.

The lady's eyes narrowed.

"Sif, I give you my word," Bird said. "I only need you to find her a room with the other maidens. Just for tonight."

Sif studied him for another moment, and then she sighed.

"Very well." She motioned to Marina. "Come with me, little one."

"I'll see you soon," Bird assured Marina, then strode off toward one of the side doors. Marina watched him go, a chill passing through her.

"Come," Sif said, her voice harder. And Marina forced herself to follow the great lady, realizing she didn't have much of a choice.

CHAPTER NINE

"IT IS VERY SMALL, BUT this is the only room I can spare," Sif said, pushing the door open. It squeaked. Marina had traipsed after her down a very long, wooden corridor to the very last room on the right. Now, she peered inside, trying not to stand too close to Sif's imposing figure.

The first thing she glimpsed was a four-poster bed with beautifully-carved wood and dark green drapes. Furs covered the stone floors, a trunk sat at the foot of the bed, and off to the right, a fireplace crouched, a low fire flickering and bobbing in its throat. A wardrobe waited in the far corner.

Marina smiled.

"Good enough," Sif decided. "You may want to change into a dress before you come to the feast. There are several in the wardrobe." Sif lifted her chin, and looked Marina up and down. Marina shrank back an inch.

"You *are* coming to the feast, yes?" Sif asked, arcing a lovely eyebrow at her.

"Am I invited?" Marina wondered.

"That is probably the reason Bauldr brought you," Sif decided flatly. "To force you to eat something. You desperately need it." And with that, she turned and swept back down the hall.

Pausing for just a moment on the threshold, Marina shook herself, turned and entered the bedroom, shutting the door behind her.

Marina bit the inside of her cheek as she finally opened her door and stepped out into the corridor. She wore a loose, light-weight, sleeveless blue dress that trailed on the floor behind her. She had found a silver linked belt to wrap around her waist, and a simple clip to tie part of her hair back, but she felt strange, and *knew* she was under-dressed.

But now, as she hesitated in the hall, she could smell it—the food. Roasted apples and baked pears, pies, boar and toast. Her mouth watered. Swallowing, she started forward.

I'll find him in the hall, she told herself. *He won't be hard to see...*

She wore her own shoes, still. The shoes in the trunk had been two sizes too big. She hoped no one noticed. Hoped no one else ran their eyes up and down her body, the way Sif had. She achieved the door, paused one more time, then stepped out onto the balcony.

The mead hall below had already filled with people. Men and women, all lavishly and comfortably dressed in loose summer garments, their fingers and wrists and ears and necks glittering with gold, silver and jewels. The women—handsome and strong—all had long, lovely blonde hair pinned up on their heads like crowns. The men—broad-shouldered and bearded—wore mixes of leather and linen. They all laughed, embraced each other, kissed cheeks and shook hands as they sipped from the sparkling goblets. The dull roar of their conversation rose to the rafters. In the far corner, a group of musicians beat on drums, tapped their feet, and played upon flutes and fiddles. The lively tune skipped over all their heads.

Mesmerized, Marina crept toward the edge, and rested her good arm on the railing, gazing down across them all. She didn't even notice him walk up.

"What do you think?"

She jumped, and turned to her left to see Bird right next to her, his elbows braced on the railing, too. She halfway smiled, the tension in her chest easing, then considered the crowd.

"I think it's wonderful," she answered. "Everything."

"Do you?"

His voice sounded odd—different.

She faced him, meeting his eyes.

And his vivid, sky-bright gaze captured hers. She forgot what she was going to say.

He tilted toward her, then reached up with his left hand and brushed a strand of hair away from her face. But he did not draw back.

He cradled her neck with his fingers, then stepped into her, looking intently down into her eyes. Marina's breathing picked up, her heart started to hammer.

He bent his head, tipped to the left. His nose brushed hers. He paused for just a moment, drew a deep breath...

And gently closed his lips over hers.

Marina's eyes fluttered shut. She gasped through her nose—and instantly the smell and taste of peppermint raced through her senses.

His right hand slid slowly down, around her waist, and his arm softly wrapped all the way around her, pulling her against his chest. She gave in, melting against him. He pressed deeper, his mouth moving carefully, subtly against hers. Her head spun—she lost her balance. His thumb traced her cheekbone, sending a shiver all through her.

"All right, enough of that."

Her mind staggered.

That voice! That voice belonged to...

His lips—his lips changed form. Softened further—warmer, more delicate. They moved against her lips again, insistently. The arm holding her strengthened. The scent of peppermint drowned her. His hand on her neck wandered down—his thumb pressed against her throat.

She forced her eyelids to open...

And she looked, stunned, into a pair of half-open, glittering *emerald* eyes.

His mouth lingered deliberately on her lower lip, then finally broke from it. But he stayed just an inch away, just a *breath* away...and grinned.

Marina stared, paralyzed.

He was tall—taller than Bird. Lean as a blade, with good-looking, pale, angular features—eloquent dark eyebrows, a perfect nose and an expressive mouth. A mouth that now bore a satisfied smirk. Curly, blazing-red hair crowned his head, and he wore forest green, lavishly embroidered with blue.

Out of the corner of her vision, Marina glimpsed Bird standing behind him. But somehow, she couldn't tear her attention from the brilliant eyes of the man who still held tight to her.

"She's a thin, young little thing, isn't she? Rather like a baby bird," the stranger remarked, his voice lilting, deliberate and musical—with an undertone that set Marina's heart thudding. The stranger reached down and lifted Marina's right arm, running his hand underneath the bare length of it until it lifted and stretched out to the side. He watched his own progress, his brow furrowing slightly, as his fingers met hers. He found her hand, guiding it with his fingertips, and almost interlaced their fingers—then turned her wrist so her palm rested down upon his.

"Fragile," he mused. "Breakable. And...crooked."

His gaze trailed back up, and he considered her face.

Then, he glanced down. And caught sight of her left hand curled uselessly against her chest.

His attention sharpened. His eyebrows drew together. And his eyes themselves flooded with a penetrating aqua. At the same instant, a deep brown started at the roots of his hair and rippled through the rest of his locks.

"Hm," he said—and touched the back of her hand with his fingers.

Marina leaped backward, wrenching herself out of his arms, tears scalding her eyes. He let her go. Her cheeks flared with heat, and she turned her right shoulder toward him, shielding her entire left side.

For just an instant, his gaze flashed, that aqua brightening to a blue...

And then he kicked his head back.

The emerald in his eyes washed back through. His hair seemed to catch fire, so quickly did it return to red. He glanced to his right, where Bird had stepped up. Bird folded his arms and sighed. The stranger mimicked him.

"That wasn't very nice," Bird said.

"I was *very* nice," the stranger sneered, flashed his eyebrows at Marina, then attended to Bird. "What is she doing here, anyway?"

"Do you even know who *she* is?" Bird wanted to know.

"Come to think of it, we haven't been introduced," the stranger said lightly, and faced her. "Formally."

Marina almost bared her teeth at him.

"Marina Feroe, may I present Loki, son of Farbauti," Bird gestured. "Loki, this is Marina—my friend from Midgard."

"Ah, your friend from *Midgard*," Loki repeated, grinning again. "Well, isn't this interesting. Where is Nanna, by the way?"

Bird's cheeks colored.

Marina's glance flitted back and forth between the two men. The floor felt like it was tipping again...

Nanna.

She knew that name.

"Come on, Marina," Bird threw a glare at Loki as he walked past him and up to her. Bird touched her shoulder and turned her, urging her to walk with him.

"What, you're going to eat without me?" Loki called.

"Well, come on, then!" Bird shouted back as he and Marina started down the stairs. She risked a glance over her shoulder at Loki—

He caught her eye and gave her a wicked grin. Quickly, she faced front again, and vowed to ignore him for the rest of the night.

"So tell me, little one," Thor slammed his stein down, wiped his hand across his mouth, and propped his forearms on the edge of the table. "What are you?"

Marina hesitated. Thor sat at the head of the very long table. To his left on a bench sat Bird—and Marina sat to *his* left. And right across from Bird, in a tall chair...

Sat Loki. Awash in colorful candlelight.

She would not look at him.

In front of all of them sprawled plates and trays of delicious food and drink—berries, apples, potatoes, turkey, pheasant, rabbit, chicken, venison, goat, grapes, breads, nuts, wine and mead—a lot of which had now been devoured. Marina had eaten all of the turkey, potatoes, apples and toast on her plate, but it had not been a challenge, because she had forgotten to eat the whole day before. Now her stomach was full, she felt stronger, and a little steadier. With Bird right next to her, she dared to lift her face to Thor—but his aspect had softened even further since the last time she had studied him, and the flamelight from the candles warmed his eyes and his encouraging smile. She reached out and dipped her right hand into a fingerbowl, attempting to keep her fingers from shaking.

"Can I ask...what you mean?"

"What are you?" Thor said again, and cleared his throat. "A seamstress, a cook, a field worker, a gardener—a wife?"

Loki sat back in his chair and snorted. Marina tried not to notice, and wiped her hand on a napkin.

"I'm an archaeologist."

Thor considered.

"I'm afraid I'm not familiar with that word. It has been a very long time since I walked any streets in Midgard."

"She studies ancient cities, ancient people," Bird said. "She finds what they left behind—their houses, their art, their writings, their bones. And from that she tries to piece together what their lives would have been like."

"Are there enough places like that to keep you occupied?" Thor frowned, taking another swig of mead.

"Midgard is littered with fallen kingdoms, remember?" Loki reminded him, lifting a careless eyebrow and crossing his arms. "I'm surprised everyone doesn't trip over all the graves and cracked monuments of dead kings."

"And what is so interesting about these...dead kingdoms?" Thor wondered, eating a grape.

Bird didn't answer for her, so Marina shrugged one shoulder.

"They...tell us about our past. About discoveries those people made, and how we became what we are now."

"They have such tiny memories, you see," Loki said as an aside to Thor.

"Not everyone has the privilege of living forever," she murmured, looking straight at him.

Loki blinked. For an instant, she thought the green in his eyes faded toward blue, and his hair darkened.

"She doesn't study all of them, though," Bird told them. "She's an expert on our old friends in the north."

"You are?" Thor sat up.

"Marina's brilliant," Bird spoke up. "Knows everything about us. Or—what the Midgardians *think* they know about us, after all this time."

"Really?" Loki sparked and sat toward Marina, his chair creaking. "What they *think* they know, eh? What do they think they know?"

Her face got hot.

"For one," she shot back. "They know you're a usurping trouble-maker that causes more damage than he's worth."

Loki laughed out loud and slapped the tabletop with a *bang*. Every single flame in the room leaped at the sound, as if suddenly delighted. Thor broke out into chuckles that rolled like a great stone through the hall.

"And *how* did they find that out?" Loki crowed. "I was trying so very hard to keep it a secret!"

"No idea," Thor shook his maned head. "Nosing about in your business."

"So rude," Loki decided.

"Indeed," Thor agreed. "So, what else, little one? What else do people *think* they know?"

"I'm..." Marina stopped.

"Go ahead," Bird urged. "You know the stories better than I do."

"I...It's mostly family things," Marina admitted. "Like...Stories about Odin and his...He has several sons, doesn't he? Bauldr by Frigga, Thor by Fjorgyn—"

"Hold—*Fjorgyn?*" Thor raised a hand.

"I...She is in charge of the earth..." Marina frowned. "Isn't she your mother?"

Loki choked, turned away and put a hand across his smirking mouth.

"She...is the groundskeeper..." Thor said slowly, baffled. Loki gagged on his laughter now, and almost turned all the way around in his chair.

"She is shaped a little bit like a potato," Bird whispered in her ear. Marina balked.

"Ugh, look at that!" Thor exclaimed, holding up his stein, shutting one eye and staring down into it. "Empty!" He slammed it down. "Traust! Traust, have you fallen asleep?"

"Who is Traust?" Marina whispered to Bird.

"He's sort of...the housekeeper?" Bird replied. "I can't think of a better word for him."

"Traust!" Thor bellowed.

Marina cast around the room, but no one came running.

"Where is he?" she wondered.

But next moment, Marina watched, stunned, as Thor's stein filled itself up from bottom to top, and the froth overflowed and spilled down the sides.

"Haha, thank you, my friend!" Thor lifted the stein and hefted it toward the ceiling, then took a large gulp. "Tell me, girl," Thor said, after setting down his drink. He scooted forward. "Who else do you think is...Well, all right, who have they told you is *married* to whom? Of us at the table, here?"

"You..." Marina started, trying to pull her attention away from his foaming drink. "You are married to Sif."

"Yes," Thor nodded.

"And you..." Marina lowered her voice. "You have a mistress, a giantess named Jarnaxa—"

"*No*," Thor cut in, wide-eyed.

"No?" Marina murmured.

Bird covered his mouth. Loki writhed with the effort of keeping silent.

"Can you imagine?" Thor looked sideways at Bird.

"No," Bird said solemnly. "Sif would cut your head off. *Off.*"

Thor nodded slowly. Loki's laughter finally got the best of him, and he gasped and chortled, wiping at his eyes.

"What about Loki?" Thor wanted to know, jerking a thumb at him.

"In our books, Loki is married to an Aesir named Sigyn," she told him, unable to keep from glancing sideways at Loki.

"Wait—Sigyn?" Loki gasped, trying to sit up straight, but failing. "*Sigyn?* That...That old hag in charge of...What is she in charge of?" he turned his watery eyes to Thor. Thor grinned.

"The royal chickens."

"*The chickens!*" Loki repeated, nearly asphyxiating.

"Haha, perhaps you went to a matchmaker," Thor suggested, shoving Loki'sv shoulder.

"No, impossible. I wouldn't pay her!"

Thor truly laughed now—it rattled the platters.

"Loki also gave birth to a horse," Marina stated pointedly.

"A...A what?" Loki's smile faltered as he blinked away tears.

"What?" Thor repeated. Marina looked to Bird, but he just waited, quietly amused. So she nodded.

"A horse. With eight legs."

"I...ahem..." Loki cleared his throat, his amusement vanishing. "Who...How would *I* give *birth* to a..." Loki trailed off, and he stared uncomfortably at her. Bird snorted loudly.

"Bahaha!" Thor slapped Loki's shoulder so hard he almost knocked him over. "You win!"

"Win what?" Loki scowled, his eyes flaring purple.

"Most humiliating Midgardian story," Thor told him.

Marina glanced down at her lap—but then Bird bumped her shoulder with his and smiled crookedly.

"What?" Thor cried again.

"There might just be one about *you*," Bird admitted.

"*Bahaha* yourself," Loki shoved Thor back.

"What—no, no, you must tell me," Thor insisted, picking up his plate and setting it aside. "It cannot be as bad as a horse."

"It might be," Loki said loftily. "You don't know what it is yet."

"Tell me, this instant," Thor commanded.

"Don't keep them in suspense, Marina," Bird warned. "They're likely to kill each other over who has the worst story."

"I already won," Loki countered, the full blaze of his green and red returning.

Marina glanced at Bird again. He nodded to her.

"Go ahead."

She gathered herself, gripping her hands together under the table.

"Well—"

"Wait!" Thor held up both hands. "If she's to tell a story..." He lifted his voice and bellowed to the other end of the hall. "Bring me a stool! Set it beside me! The little thing is going to tell me a story!"

Marina's face burned and her heart thudded against her breastbone. All of the Aesir started muttering, and Marina felt them turn and look at her. A servant immediately hurried down the aisle toward them, his feet pattering, hauling a wooden stool.

"As you please, Your Highness," the young man panted, setting it down to Thor's left with a clack.

"Come here," Thor beckoned to Marina. "Come sit here, so we can see you."

Marina froze, but then Bird got up and offered her his hand. She winced, took it, and stood. She climbed over the bench, and then he easily picked her up and set her on the stool. Now her head was higher than Thor's, and everyone at the whole table could easily see her if they wanted to. She felt the heat drain out of her face.

"Speak," Thor bade her, taking another swig of mead. "Tell us this horrible tale of yours."

"Yes, please do," Loki said snidely.

Marina tucked her left hand against herself, a quiver running down through her whole body as Loki's eyes narrowed. She cleared her throat—but when she opened her mouth, nothing came out.

She looked down at Bird, panicked.

"You know which one I mean, Marina," he said easily. "Go on. It's one of my favorites."

She swallowed, cleared her throat again, took a breath...

"There are several versions of this story," she managed. "But I think...I like the version my dad told me best." She swallowed. "Once upon a time..." she said, unable to think of anything else. "You wake up...Your Highness...and discover that Mjollnir isn't anywhere in your room." She paused, grasping her left hand with her right. "It's been stolen."

"How?" Thor demanded. "No one can pick it up but me!"

Loki snapped his fingers and grinned. Thor frowned at him.

"What?"

"Well, it's obviously *magic*," Loki said, as if Thor was stupid.

"You did it, then!" Thor pointed at him. Loki's mouth fell open.

"I did not!"

"How do *you* know?" Thor cried. "You don't even know the story!" He whirled on Marina. "Did Loki do it?"

"No," Marina admitted.

"See?" Loki gestured sharply at her.

"But he goes to find out who *did*," she went on. "So...he borrows Freya's winged cloak and flies all the way to Jotunheim—"

"That would be a nice thing to have," Loki remarked. "A winged cloak."

"Be quiet," Bird told him.

"...And he sees Thrym, the king of the Frost Giants, standing on a cliff," Marina said. "Loki lands beside him, and asks him about their problem. Thrym admits he took the hammer. He's very proud of himself for stealing something right out from underneath Thor's nose. Loki tells him that Thor wants it back. Thrym says no."

"You ought to kill him," Thor muttered.

"I ought to try, yes," Loki nodded. "If I wanted to wind up pasted to the side of the mountain."

"Shut up and let the little thing talk," Thor ordered. Loki searched the ceiling in exasperation, scooted noisily back and propped his feet up on the table.

"Talk," Thor said again to Marina. She risked a glance around—

To see that many of the other Aesir had started listening to her. They had quieted their conversations, and their blue eyes found her.

"Well," Marina shifted tightly, her voice low. "Thrym tells him that the only way he'll give Mjollnir back is if they bring Freya to be his wife."

"Hm," Loki said, putting his elbow on his armrest and propping the side of his head on his fist. "That'll go well."

"Mm," Thor grunted. "So what do we do?"

"Um...Heimdall has an idea—"

"Who is Heimdall?" Loki made a face.

"I don't know anyone named Heimdall," Thor told her.

"Um..." Marina faltered. "Well, *someone* has an idea—"

"Who?" Loki pressed.

"Loki does," Bird filled in.

"All right," Marina said quietly. "Loki does."

Thor openly groaned and rubbed his eyes.

"Ah, so it's *my* idea." Loki grinned.

"He says Thor should put on a dress and veil and pretend to be Freya, and when the giants let him in, he can steal Mjollnir back."

A rippling chuckle ran through the ranks of Aesir. Thor peeked over his hand.

"A *dress?*"

Loki waggled his eyebrows at Thor and kept grinning.

"And Loki volunteers to go along as Thor's bridesmaid," Marina added.

"Wha—?" Loki sat up straight.

The laughter got louder, vibrating the tables.

"Serves you right, Horse Face," Thor muttered.

"You know, he's going to *keep* calling you that," Bird warned Loki.

"Not if he wants to go on living," Loki said pleasantly.

"What next?" Thor pressed. Bird put his elbow on the table and his chin in his hand, and gave Marina a twinkling glance. So she bravely went on.

"The two dress as women—but Loki doesn't have to wear a veil, since he can't grow a beard."

Several Aesir shouted and clapped. Thor sat up and puffed out his chest. Loki rolled his eyes.

"Oh, as if I *care*."

"I can't grow a beard either," Bird pointed out.

"That's because you're a baby," Loki answered.

"So what does that make you?" Bird countered.

Snickers darted through the crowd. Loki stuck his tongue out at Bird. This caused a racket of amusement among the others—Loki glanced over and winked at them.

"Silence!" Thor roared. "I want to hear the story." He pointedly turned to face Marina, and raised his eyebrows.

"The two of them ride in Thor's chariot over the bridge and all the way to Jotunheim," she went on. "And when they get to the giant's door, Thrym looks at Thor strangely. Because he...doesn't exactly have a girlish figure."

Loki hid his face in his hand.

"Of course," Thor said, gesturing carelessly. "I hope I weigh more than a *woman*."

"Trust me, you do," Bird muttered. Thor flicked a crumb at him.

"Thrym says something about it," Marina told them. "But Loki says that it's because Aesir women are very strong and hardy—for doing housework."

Somebody threw a biscuit at Loki's head. He ducked and batted it away.

"Wait, *I* didn't say that!" he cried.

"And when they sit down to the feast," Marina said. "Thor eats almost everything on the table. And when Thrym says something about *that*, Loki says that his bride hasn't eaten for several days, because she's been so anxious to get married to him."

"You stupid oaf, you can't even control yourself for one night," Loki chided. "We're supposed to be in *disguise*. As *women*."

"How am I supposed to fight if I'm hungry?" Thor wanted to know.

"You're always hungry," Bird remarked.

"Very true," Thor confessed, pointing at him.

"Shut up and let her get on with it," Loki kicked at the legs of Thor's chair.

"Yes, get on with it," Thor said.

"Another...problem," Marina went on. "Thor's eyes burn red when he is ready for battle."

"They do?" Thor frowned. Then, he sat up. "I mean, yes they do!"

Bird laughed.

"And...even though Loki told Thor to keep his eyes down, he does look up once at Thrym."

"Of course you never listen to me," Loki muttered.

"And so what does Loki say about that?" Thor wondered.

"He says your eyes are red from crying, because you've been wanting to get married so badly. Either that, or you have a cold."

"That sounds fairly stupid," Thor lifted an eyebrow at Loki. Loki shrugged.

"I'm doing my best with what I'm given."

"What next?" Bird asked.

"They are about to start the wedding ceremony when Loki reminds Thrym of their bargain, about Mjollnir."

"Thor's forgotten because he's drunk," Loki added.

"And so Thrym brings out the hammer and shows it to them..."

"And I take it up, and with Mjollnir in my hand at last I call lightning down upon them all!" Thor shouted, shaking his fist in the air. "The giants fall before my might, and burn upon the instant—" He slammed his hand on the table. "And with a *crack* of my thunder everyone in the room is *dead!*"

All the Aesir burst into cheering.

"Everyone except *me*, I hope," Loki looked at him.

"Of course not *you*," Thor scoffed. "What would I do without my bridesmaid?"

Everyone laughed heartily, stood up and applauded. Marina ducked her head, guarding her small smile. The next moment, many courtiers got up from their seats and eagerly approached Thor to congratulate him on his imaginary victory, swallowing Marina in a swirl of activity—but not one of the towering, impressive men or women addressed her, or even acknowledged her. They stepped around her to shake hands with Thor and make their remarks, never looking at her once...

Except Loki.

He watched her. He did not sneer or speak. His eyebrows drew together, and firelight illuminated his sapphire eyes. Quickly, she looked away, slid down off her chair, and retreated to Bird's side. But through the rest of the evening, Bird grew strangely distant, and so the two of them fell into uneasy silence until the master of ceremonies called everyone to the dance.

CHAPTER TEN

DUSK HAD THROWN ITS cloak over Asgard, filling the glen behind Bilskirnir with purplish shadow. Marina stepped out onto a broad back balcony overlooking the grassy clearing ringed with unlit torches. All of the Aesir, including Bird, had now trailed out of the mead hall, through a lower door and out onto the lawn. Though Bird had asked, Marina had politely refused to come with him. So he had directed her up a set of stairs to the balcony, so she could at least watch. She rested her shoulder against a wooden pillar as a cool, careless breeze touched the edges of her hair.

The Aesir hurried out, led by Thor, Bird, and Loki. Thor grasped his shimmering cloak, pulled it off and tossed to a startled servant. Loki stripped off his long-sleeved coat, revealing a sleeveless tunic beneath, complete with dozens of long, colorful ribbons that streamed from the collar. He threw his coat off to the side—it landed under a tree. He made a gleeful remark to Thor, who laughed in response and loudly clapped his back. Bird chuckled and shook his head at them. The other Aesir gathered around and began shouting to Loki, urging him on. Marina's brow furrowed as she observed.

Loki held up his hands, walking backward, as if to placate them. They all fell silent, folding their arms, waiting. He stopped, took a breath...

Lowered his hands and rubbed them together. He then brought them up to his mouth, cupped them open, and *blew*...

Brilliant white, living sparks gusted from his palms and leaped into the air. He fiercely flicked his fingers, and more shot out. Everyone cheered. The sparks grew and pulsed, dipping and bobbing through the glen, lighting it up like near-day—but bathing everyone in a soft, wondrous pearly light.

He whirled around, hopped, and *clapped* his hands.

Every one of the waiting torches burst to life, throwing a merry red glow against the pearl, and filling the glen with heat.

Marina pressed her fingers to her lips, then stayed still.

Four men suddenly darted out of the house, holding their gleaming instruments aloft. A roar of delight launched up from the Aesir. The musicians drew to a breathless stop in the center of the glen, readied their instruments and began to play.

The pipes and fiddles cut through the night. The drums pulsed through Marina's chest. Wild music—beautiful, and slightly savage. A flurry of movement consumed the Aesir as they reached out and grabbed each other by the hands or arms, throwing their heads back and crowing happily as they did; and then, all bare-footed, they plunged into a twirling, dizzying dance, circling and circling around the musicians.

Thor took hold of his wife around the waist and lifted her high in the air—she giggled like a girl. Together they led the troupe, Sif a lithe and fascinating figure—elf-like and flawless; Thor moved like a bear, chuckling all the while. Bird hopped up and perched on top of a pile of barrels, swinging his legs in rhythm, just observing and smiling, until someone tossed him a wooden flute, pointed at him—and he shrugged and started to play along.

Loki snagged a gorgeous, slender, freckled, fire-headed woman dressed in yellow and kissed her flat on the lips straightaway. She shoved him back and laughed. He tickled her ribs. She shrieked. He then snatched up her hands and tugged on her, and soon the two of them caught up to Thor and Sif. But *these* two...

Marina tilted her head, and laid the side of it against the pillar.

These two both danced with grace and strength, never missing a step. Loki pulled the woman close to him, and their feet flew.

Her dress flared out like the petals of a flower, and her burning hair came loose, flying out behind her like a flag. Loki's ribbons flashed a rainbow all around him, his hair like a lit candle, his face shining, and together they grinned dazzlingly, winked and flirted, weaving in and out of the other couples.

An hour had passed before Marina realized she hadn't been watching anyone else.

Finally, the musicians halted, gasping for breath and sagging against each other for support. All the Aesir sprang to a halt, then clapped their hands. The musicians bowed.

A bustling sound disturbed the area beneath Marina—and the next moment, several large barrels of mead appeared, hefted by large manservants. Every one of the Aesir's faces lit up. All at once, everyone snatched up their mugs and shoved between each other to fill them with the frothing liquid. They drank and drank, and offered toasts, and spilled it on each other—which caused even more merriment. Loki took three full steins in his fists and hurried over to Thor and Bird. Together, the three of them drank, and chuckled about some joke Loki told. Then, Bird made a remark to Loki and raised his eyebrows pointedly—Loki gazed at him a moment, his levity vanishing...

And all at once he reached around Bird with his left arm and pulled him in to an almost tender embrace. He closed his eyes, and his brow furrowed as he rested his head against the side of Bird's. Bird encircled his waist with his arms. For a moment, though the dancing leaped to life all around them again, the two stayed as they were. Loki then murmured something. Thor reached over and patted Bird on the back, and Bird backed up. He offered a wan smile to Loki, then to Thor. Thor, beaming like sunshine, reached up with both hands, and rested one against the side of Bird's head, and the other against the side of Loki's. Loki laughed, and gripped Thor's wrist. Thor took hold of their hair and gently shook them, then grabbed the stein out of Loki's hand. Loki barked at him, and Thor pushed him toward the dance again. Loki made a face at him, spun around, and instantly snatched another young, beautiful woman—this time, one with blonde hair and a red dress. Together, these two turned the dance into a stunning, frenzied storm that Marina could barely track—but neither could she pull her attention away.

Finally, the high moon smiling down on them all, the musicians screeched to another halt and fell down on their backs, panting. The Aesir hopped up and down, demanding more. Loki bent in, leaned his partner backward and kissed her obnoxiously. She batted him off. Laughing, he straightened up.

And then, Loki looked up at Marina.

He didn't search for an instant. He just turned, lifted his face, and met her eyes. His smile faded, and his gaze penetrated completely down through her.

She swallowed, and stepped back from the railing. He did not break contact.

So she did.

Her vision blurring, she faced the other way, found the door, and re-entered the mead hall, stumbling her way down the corridor until she found her room.

Marina rolled over in bed for the thousandth time. Stared up at the gray ceiling. Let out a long sigh. She reached up and pressed her hand to her face, her stomach tightening.

And her lips burned.

She pressed her hand over her mouth and ground her teeth. Green eyes flashed in front of her memory, too close for any comfort. She pulled in a breath, and suddenly tasted peppermint—

A hot glow started in her chest and she screwed her eyes shut.

She sounded insane, even to herself.

Bauldr?

Nanna?

Thor?

Loki...?

She sat up, and tossed her covers off herself. For a long moment, she just sat on the edge of her bed, tamping down the rate of her heartbeat.

"You seek the prince?"

Marina shot to her feet and threw herself back against the wall.

"Who's there?" she gasped.

"It is I, only," came a grating, deep voice. "Here—above the fire."

Marina's whole left side shivered.

"What...*What?*"

"Come near, young one," the voice urged. "I cannot hurt you."

Marina stood locked in place.

"Come," the voice said again—and that time, she caught sight of movement.

And then...

The fire in the hearth blazed to life. Light flooded the room...

And a wooden, bearded face materialized onto the mantel, turned its wooden eyes, and looked at her.

It smiled. Its lips creaked.

"Come," it said for the third time. "I mean you no harm."

"Who are you?"

"My name is Traust." It blinked. Its eyelids clicked.

"You...*You* are Traust!" she cried.

"Yes," he said. "And you are Marina, daughter of Aaron and Irene."

"How did you know that?" she asked, risking a step closer.

"You stepped across my threshold," it answered. "I am the heart of Bilskirnir —and I reach into the depths of each heart that enters. But worry not. I am also a secret-keeper."

"You...What did you ask me?" Marina wondered, shaking her head to clear it.

"Do you seek the prince?" Traust repeated.

"I...don't know," Marina confessed, taking another step closer. "I just can't sleep."

"Mhum," it said, as if it understood. "You still do not believe in where it is you stand."

"No," Marina whispered. "How can I?"

Traust considered her.

"Ask me a question, then," he said. "Something you have been wondering about, but dared not ask anyone...Not even the Beautiful Prince."

Marina crept closer, canting her head.

"Why?" she asked.

"Because you wish to know," he countered.

"All right," she drew herself up. "Where is Valhalla from here?"

"No one can reach Valhalla from here," Traust replied.

"They can't?" Something inside Marina's heart wilted.

"No," Traust said. "Because, despite the great legends you learned on Midgard, Valhalla is unreachable even by the All-Father, and cannot be entered by way of Asgard," he said. He fell quiet, and Marina thought he might not say any more.

Then he took a breath. And when he spoke, his tone was low and deliberate, each word formed to perfection, each phrase flowing and pausing and lifting like a quiet melody.

"But the Aesir often believe they can see Valhalla, when the sun strides through the high gates and stands watch over the great seals, giving light to the grand throne room gilded in gold," he said. "And there at the head of it waits the throne of the kings of Asgard—long-bearded fathers of mighty helms and heavy hammers, who ruled in days long sped with a quiet hand and a steady eye. The throne was hewn of a block of living gold by careful-fingered smiths, and has not stirred from its place since the age when the giants shivered the roots of the realms." He lifted his chin, just an inch. "Beneath it lies the chamber of illustrious arms, where lives the All-Father's staff when he is weary of battle, along with captured treasures from hundreds of wars that even he has forgotten. And in the far reaches of the chamber, in a coffin of stone, sleeps a broken sword whose name no one remembers.

"Above the great hall, stretching higher than any mountain, reach the mighty limbs of Yggdrasil, catching daylight and starlight in their leaves as they watch the gate to the Asbru bridge as it holds its hand out to Midgard.

"Below, near the heels of the roots, spill ten-thousand fountains of healing water, clearer than the sky and purer than snow, and they feed the gardens where bend the trees that are older than the realm. They glimpse the first of the sunrise, and witness the coming of the day as it flashes like lightning through the waiting sky." Traust's eyes moved, as if he were watching something very far away.

"And when the sun falls and twilight pulls its cloak over the sky, night never truly descends," he murmured, in a soft, rasping tone. "For a quiet light remains in the west, touching the edge of the silver water on the far side of the great tree. Sometimes, if one stands alone and listens, he can hear the sea birds sing his name, feel the surf call on the wind, and many a man will begin to wish to make sail, and meet that light where it stands." He paused, his gaze flickered, and his wooden brow tightened. "But then a lamp will come to life in a chamber above him," he whispered. "The scent of roasting meat and stewing lintel will reach his breath, and the strum of a lute will touch his ears. Then, someone will call his name, call him inside, to the light and the warmth." His words quieted so Marina almost could not hear him. "And he will forget the shine on the water, and remember the people he loves—and that he is home."

Marina felt her knees weaken, and her hand fluttered toward her heart. Traust considered her—and quietly smiled.

"I know all of this, Marina daughter of Aaron," he said. "And yet, I have never seen it. I have only read the hearts of those who have. How much more can *you* believe, who have seen?"

"Why did he bring me here?" Marina whispered, staggered.

"Ah," Traust smiled. "And this is the *true* question you wished to ask."

Marina said nothing.

"I cannot tell you," Traust confessed. "You must ask *him*."

"I can't wait till morning," Marina gritted, shifting restlessly.

"Then luck is with you," Traust said. "For just moments ago, he left my walls, and I believe he stands upon the road out in front of my gates. Perhaps you should go to him now."

Marina stared at the wooden countenance.

"A dressing gown hangs in the wardrobe," Traust said. "Be certain to take it. It would not do to catch a sneeze."

Marina hesitated for just an instant, then felt her way to the wardrobe and opened it. Groped inside...

Found a housecoat, tugged it out and put it on. Tied the sash tight, then stood in indecision in the middle of her floor.

"Go," Traust urged. "The night is waning fast."

Marina started toward her door, then pulled it open. Moonlight spilled in through the windows of the corridor outside. Giving one last look back at the carven face, she stepped out and wandered down the length of it, listening to the quiet.

Something caught her eye. She stopped.

Outside—there, through the trees. A figure in white, standing in the road.

Just as Traust had said.

A chill passed through her.

She strode forward, out onto the balcony of the mead hall, turned right and found a smaller front door next to the great double doors. She opened it, and the night scents washed over her. She ventured out onto the shadowed lawn, the moon lighting her way. She clutched the collar of her robe close to her throat, her bare feet swishing through the cool, dewy grass. Bugs chirped in the trees. No wind disturbed the leaves.

She made it to the border of oaks, and peered out at the person standing.

Bird. His arms folded, gazing off into the distance.

"Hello?" she called.

He came out of his reverie, and turned his head toward her. He smiled.

She waited.

"Hello, Marina," he murmured. "How do you suppose that rosebush is doing without you?"

Marina sighed, her chest loosening, and she stepped out onto the road toward him.

"I wondered if it was actually you," she confessed.

"Hm," Bird chuckled, glancing down. "Yes, Loki is something else."

"I don't like him," Marina decided, lighting by his shoulder. "He's arrogant and awful."

Bird considered her, his brow furrowing.

"I wish you wouldn't say that."

Caught by his tone, she lifted her eyes to his.

Lit by the moon—they were fathomless, ethereal. And earnestly sad.

"Why not?" she wondered.

He said nothing for a moment, then glanced out ahead of him.

"I'll just say this," he told her. "One of the greatest storytellers, magicians, poets, musicians, healers and warriors alive sat at the table with you this evening. And it was not me. And it was not my brother."

Marina's mouth tightened, but all at once she couldn't bring herself to argue with him. Instead, she memorized the way his beautiful profile looked in this light.

"What are you watching?" she wondered.

"Home," he murmured. Marina turned...

Yggdrasil's majestic shape spread across the horizon, black against the night sky, its branches and trunk twinkling with a thousand lights that reminded her so much of fireflies.

"I still can't believe it," Marina muttered. She felt his smile.

"Sometimes I can't either."

For a long while, they stood silent.

Marina couldn't take her eyes from him. And a deep pain started in her ribs.

"Bird," she finally whispered, very softly. "Is your name really Bauldr?"

He did not stir for a long moment. At last, though, he slowly faced her, and drew himself up. And as the silver moonlight cascaded over him, something in his bearing changed—softened, aged. He looked deep down into her eyes, his own bright as crystal. He nodded, once.

"Yes."

Marina's brow tightened as she searched his features.

"Why did you start coming to my house?"

A soft breeze touched his feathery hair. And as it did, sorrow drifted across him—and pierced Marina in the heart.

"Marina," he whispered. "I'm going to die."

Her throat closed. She didn't move.

Bauldr glanced out toward Yggdrasil again, his movement heavy.

"For several years now, I've been having dreams that I would be killed," he went on. "I know all the old stories that you learned on Midgard—stories that I've taken to be prophecies. Yet, in my visions, I can never see whose hand actually shoots the arrow. I can never be sure. But it doesn't matter. I've told no one but my mother about it. I've learned enough to know that trying to stop a prophecy from coming true might actually make it happen."

Marina tried not to tremble. It didn't work.

"Marina," Bauldr said again, earnestly coming back to her. "If I told you that you could help me, if only you'd be brave and willing...Would you?"

"Of course," she gasped. She nodded hard. "Of course, what do you want me to do?"

He took up her right hand and held it in both of his. And the next moment, she felt three small, smooth, cold objects in her palm, where there had been nothing before. She turned her hand over...

Three round, glassy stones sat quietly in the cup of it. One dark blue, one blood red, and the other deep green. They felt warm against her skin. Bauldr cradled her hand.

"These are Wishstones," Bauldr told her. "The blue one is *hide,* the red is *unbind.* The green one is *flee.* You only need to hold one tight in your hand and think of what you need it to do for you, and it will be done."

Marina watched the way the moonshine whispered across each icy surface.

"I know that I am utterly selfish to ask this of you," Bauldr said, bending close to her. "And I never would, if I feared only for myself. But I don't. Whatever evil thing is to happen to me, it will also twist around my brother, my mother, my father, all my friends—and my realm. I can feel it. And you are our only hope."

"What do you want me to do?" Marina asked him, lifting her face again. He halfway smiled.

"You'll know when it's time."

And he slipped his hand around to the back of her neck, stepped in and pressed a kiss to her forehead.

Warm, golden light swelled through her mind, and chills shot through her arms and fingers.

He drew back, lowered his head and gazed at her.

"Thank you, Marina," he whispered. "Now you should go back to bed."

"I don't want to leave you." It just fell out before she'd calculated. But he just smiled gently.

"The best way you can help me now is to rest," he said, stroking her cheek. "It will be all right. I promise."

"But..." Words failed her. All of a sudden, she could think of nothing she'd rather do but lean up and kiss his fair lips...

Bauldr stepped back from her, and dropped his hand.

"Goodnight, Marina," he said, inclining his head. "I'll see you soon."

She closed her fingers around the Wishstones and pressed her fist to her heart. She nodded.

"Okay," she breathed. "Goodnight."

And she turned, and walked back up between the towering shadows of the oaks, toward the great mead house. She pulled the door open, stepped in, turned left into the corridor that led to her room—

Jerked to a stop. Her heart jumped into her throat.

Loki stood there, arms folded, leaning sideways against the first window frame, gazing out across the front lawn. He wore black nightclothes, and in this light, his russet hair caught edges of gold. His pale brow knitted in thought, his eyes silvery. He turned and looked at her. The edge of his mouth quirked.

"So you've gone and done it too, hm?" he asked, lifting his chin.

"Done what?" Marina demanded, closing her fingers tighter.

"Fallen in love with the little prince," Loki nodded out the window, then regarded her. "There's nothing unique in that, you know. Practically every woman in Asgard has done, at one point or another."

Marina clenched her jaw and started to walk past him.

"Do you know what Lady Sif said about you?" Loki called. Marina halted, but didn't turn around.

"She said she thought you were another one of Bird's pets," Loki remarked. "You see, sometimes, when he's on Midgard, he'll find mortals that are ill, and he'll feel sorry for them and bring them here to spend the rest of their days. It's a bit pathetic, but we've all gotten used to it. And judging by the state you're in, I can see why my lady made that assumption."

Marina twisted and faced him, clenching her jaw. He beamed, and chuckled.

"You're so easy to upset—look at you," he shook his head. "Like I said before: fragile. And crooked."

Marina's blood raced, but she couldn't think of an answer. So she gave him one last hard stare, faced front again and hurried back to her room, feeling his attention follow her.

She hurried in and shut the door, then leaned back against it, frowning at the inexplicable tightening in her ribcage. She turned around, found the lock and *clacked* it into place, then turned toward the fireplace...

Traust's face had disappeared. Only the plain, rough-hewn mantel remained.

Biting her lip, she climbed into the bed, lay down and buried herself in the covers, clamping the Wishstones against her.

Sunlight touched her eyelids. She drew in a deep breath, and sighed. She shifted her legs beneath warm blankets, turned over onto her back.

Birds twittered somewhere outside. Her face tightened, and she stretched.

Box-springs squeaked.

She frowned.

Drip. Drip. Drip.

She shot into a sitting position, her eyes opening so fast she had to fight to focus.

A small, circular room. A closet in front of her, a bookshelf to her right, a rug on the wooden floor, a window off to her left looking out over a morning garden...

Home. She was in her bedroom at home.

Home?

Her hand jerked up to take hold of her hair—

Three tiny somethings flew out of her grasp and clattered across the floor.

She twitched. Then she flung off her covers, clambered out of bed, and scrabbled for them. Her hand landed on the first, then the second, and finally the third, near one of her slippers. Panting, she settled onto her knees, holding the little pebbles in her hand.

One blue. One red. One green.

Hide.

Unbind.

Flee.

CHAPTER ELEVEN

MARINA STOOD NEXT TO a dead pine, making no sound.

Listening to the wind as it whispered through the highest needles of the trees.

Gazing down into the hollow at the carved stone archway.

Tracing the details of the Mjollnir crest at the top. The runes that marked its edges.

Never stepping any closer.

It would be two months tomorrow since she'd awakened in her room and spilled Bird's Wishstones all over her floor.

Two months.

Every day, she left her house early in the morning and hiked around the side of the house and past the border of that forest, all the way down the hill to stand in front of the vine-covered arch and listen to the quiet.

Every time she crossed into the shadow of the reaching trees, she had to bite back a chill, and ignore the remembered voice of Jim Fields from the hardware store...

"Word to the wise: don't go out there at night. No matter what you think you see."

"Yeah, well..." she often muttered. "Too late for that."

But she never passed through the arch.

She almost had, once. She'd stepped right up to the stones to try to make out the runes, to perhaps translate them...

But she had stopped, breathing very carefully, gripping the little bird pendant between her fingers and staring through to the forest on the other side.

That's all it looked like. More forest. No foggy stone bridge, no flickering lamps.

But she could feel it.

Like static electricity a hand's breadth away. She could almost touch the surface of it when she got this close.

It's how she knew she hadn't dreamed it all.

That was why she came back every day, without fail. To remind herself, when her memories started to get hazy and doubt crept through her veins.

She drew in a long breath, then slowly let it out. She turned, and trudged back through the needles up the hill. She lowered her head and pulled her left arm close, her right hand fingers working thoughtfully against each other. And halfway up the hill, just to make sure, she absently touched her hip pocket where the three Wishstones waited.

A breeze brushed over her tabletop and rustled the papers. She quickly picked her pen up and pressed the side of her hand down on the top paper to keep it from blowing off the slanted desk. She glanced to her left, out through the half-open window, and leaned her shoulder against the frame.

The late afternoon slant of the July sun filled the side garden, lighting up all the buds and blooms, tingeing the tips of the rose petals with gold, and catching the wings of the white and purple butterflies flittering through the clover.

The breeze whispered again, carrying that scent in with it—clover. She propped her elbow on the sill and touched her lips to the back of her hand, drawing in a careful breath. Absently, she glanced sideways back down at the paper underneath her right palm.

These past few weeks, she had carefully pencil-sketched out the front of a great mead hall in great detail, making certain to include all of the knots and growling faces peering out from the corners of the wood, and decorating the borders of the page in the manner of an illuminated manuscript. Today, she had just started inking the fine lines.

Slowly, she slid the top page out of the way, tilting her head as she studied the papers beneath it. She ran her eyes across the title page, done in monk-like calligraphy:

THE AMENDED EDDA by Marina Feroe

She pushed that page aside, and re-read the first few lines for the thousandth time, written out in her usual hand:

BITS and NOTES
The Two Sons of Odin
Only two.
Born to Odin All-Father, and his wife Frigga, the queen of Asgard.
Thor: eldest and wielder of Mjollnir, the thunder-hammer. He dwells in a vast mead hall called Bilskirnir, encircled by ancient oak

trees and anext the country highway, with his wife, the Amazonian, beautiful and golden-haired Sif.

Bauldr: youngest, bringer of light and warmth, friend to all things that grow. His kin have also given him the pet name of "Bird."

Marina swallowed the pain in her throat and pushed that paper out of the way too, skipping over the rest of the writing. She narrowed her eyes at the next title.

THE THREE CHILDREN OF FARBAUTI

LOKI

The youngest, most forward, obnoxious and unconventional of the three children of the Jotun giant, his appearance seems to change with his mood—alternating from bright and flashing when he is mocking or clever; to dark and penetrating when he is calculating or cold. He is very unlike both Thor and Bauldr in manner and character, yet for some reason the sons of Odin and Frigga seem to endure him, and even enjoy his company. He is rude, conceited, flirtatious, rakish, shallow, invasive and callous, though he seems to be talented in the area of magic and illusion, which is perhaps why the other Aesir put up with him—

Marina blew air out through her lips and shook her head. That would never work with her publisher—she knew that. She wasn't sure *any* of it would, even posing as a fictional addition to the Edda, but *that* particular commentary had just started to sound...

She pushed it out of the way, frowning at the next page.

FENRIS

The middle son of Farbauti.

Commands a pack of wolves.

Would rather run around in the forest with them at night than go to parties.

Marina bit her lip. She might have to leave him out altogether. She'd never actually *seen* him, after all. She pushed to the next page.

HEL

The eldest child of Farbauti—

Cold wind blew through the window.

Marina sat up straight, pushing down hard on the pages even as they flapped and rustled like autumn leaves. She looked outside.

Dark clouds rolled over the sun. The garden fell into shadow.

And in the far distance, thunder rumbled.

She narrowed her eyes, then pressed her left forearm to the windowpane and pushed down. It creaked, but the window slid shut.

Outside, the tops of the trees began to lash. She watched the toiling sky for a moment, then pushed her stool back and got up. She needed to shut the other windows in the house before it started raining.

Marina opened her eyes.

Frowned.

She stared at the dark wall and black bookshelf in front of her. Then, she grimaced...

Realizing that she was wrapped with death-like urgency in her sheet and light blanket. And her whole body ached with the effort of curling herself in a tight ball on her bed. She groaned, shifting under her covers, her left arm twanging and tingling. Finally, she sat halfway up, her hair hanging in her face.

The wind gusted around her tower, howling and wuthering. But...

It didn't sound right. It didn't sound like the full-throated roar of a summer thunderstorm. It sounded like...

She stiffly pushed off her covers, her brow furrowing sleepily, and put her feet onto her wood floor.

"Oh, oh, *oh!*" she cried, pulling them back up onto the bed.

Her floor felt like ice.

She blinked several times, trying to wake up, feeling goose bumps rise on her bare arms and legs. She forced herself to get up out of bed and hurry across her frozen floor to the closet. She threw the door open and dug around toward the back, finally wrenching her winter bathrobe out from where it hung on the back hook. She threw it on and wrapped it around herself, her teeth chattering, then stuffed a pair of socks on her poor feet. Then, she shuffled to the window, pushed the curtain out of the way and looked out.

And her blood ran still.

In the dull moonlight light filtering through the clouds, a pure white blanket shrouded the garden, and flakes pouring from the heavens drenched the full branches of the trees.

Snow.

Marina tossed another log onto the blazing fire and glanced over at the little flickering television in the corner. She grabbed the fire iron and re-arranged the wood. Sparks shot into the air.

Unable to stand it, she had finally dug out her winter chest and put on her jeans, long-sleeved-shirt, a sweater, socks and boots. Then, she'd puffed down into the icy basement to try to light the furnace, but it wasn't working. So she'd hurried up into the sitting room to start a fire and turn on the news. It was two in the morning, but all the newscasters had already worked themselves into a frenzy.

"...all over the state, and spreading southwest at a blinding rate. The same thing is happening in Europe. Sudden frosts have swept across Sweden and Norway, and snowstorms are moving over Scotland, England, Ireland, Germany and France."

Marina sat back on the rug and watched as the harried weatherman, his red tie askew and his hair messy, waved his hand frantically over a world-wide map, where white clouds rapidly built and began to obscure Europe, the northern United States and Canada. Marina bent her knees up to her chest and wrapped her right arm around her legs, the sound of the weatherman's hurried voice fading to the back of her attention.

The wind whistled outside her walls, buffeting the flames of her fire. That sharp, rasping hiss of a January gale.

And it was July. July fifteenth.

She turned, and stared at the black window, where fingers of Jack Frost had begun to creep over the panes. All of her muscles slowly tightened, her heartbeat thudded against her bones, and she closed her fingers into a fist.

What had *happened?*

Scrape...

Marina glanced over the back of the couch toward the door.

An odd, distant shuffling. Crunching.

Outside.

She swallowed.

The shuffling came closer, drawing around the corner of the house, nearing her front door.

Then, it stopped.

Her throat closed.

A *gust*—

Wind sucked down the floo and flared the fire in the hearth. Marina gripped the bird pendant around her neck.

Silence. She waited.

Tap, tap, tap.

Marina blinked, mentally stumbling. She stayed completely still.

Then, slowly, she climbed to her feet, and edged around the couch. Her boot soles sounded loud on the wood. She stepped down into the entryway.

The dark front door rose up in front of her. She tried to keep her breathing low, even as her heart danced around against her breastbone. A tremble shot through her. She hesitated.

Tap, tap, tap.

She jumped, gritting her teeth.

Then, finally, she reached out and gripped the cold handle. She worked the latch. It clacked open. She tugged on the door. The hinges squeaked, and it swung open.

A blast of wind stinging with snow hit her—nearly blinded her.

Then, she opened her eyes...

And threw herself backward.

A tall, white-skinned woman dominated the doorway. Her head nearly touched the top frame. Midnight spilled from her shoulders and down into her skirt, flooding into the floor of the entryway like inky poison. Thick black fur lined her collar and the cuffs of her velvety coat. Luxurious black hair tumbled from her head down around her shoulders, but it did not conceal her porcelain neck and luminous, refined features...

Or the left side of her face.

Which had no skin.

Only a bare skeleton.

Her flashing black gaze captured Marina and pinned her to the floor. The half of her mouth with lips curved upward, and she inclined her head elegantly.

"Hello, Marina," she said, her voice pleasant and cool. "May I come in?"

"Who are you?" Marina gasped.

"Don't be silly," the woman chided. "You know who I am."

Marina squeezed the bird pendant so hard it cut into her hand. She nodded once.

Hel.

The other woman's lightless gaze wandered casually through the entryway.

"Enjoying this weather?" she asked. "I am. Ever so much. It's been so long since I got to wear my black coat." She smiled and reached up with both hands and adjusted her furry collar. "Summer is so tiresome and hot, don't you think?"

Marina gulped. Said nothing.

Hel sighed.

"Well, if you're not in the mood for small-talk, I'll get to the point." She canted her head, and looked frankly down at Marina. "Little Bird left something here and I've come to get it. If you'll just step out of the way and let me look, I'll find it myself and be on my way."

"He didn't leave anything here," Marina rasped.

"I know for a fact he did," Hel shot back. Suddenly, she narrowed her one eye. "And you know something about it, don't you?"

Marina's heart stopped.

"Whatever evil thing is to happen to me," Bird's soft words lit her memory. *"It will also twist around my brother, my mother, my father, all my friends—and my realm. And you are our only hope."*

"I don't know what you're talking about," she stammered.

"Oh, yes, you do!" Hel took a step inside. She towered over Marina. "He told you, didn't he? He told you about his tears?"

Marina stared at her.

"I don't—"

"Don't *play* with *me*, mortal," Hel bared her pointed teeth. "He told you where they were and he told you how to bring him back, didn't he? *You're* the one he trusted!"

"What?" Marina cried. "I don't know what you're...I mean, no, I don't have—"

"You're *lying!*" Hel snarled, her left eye blazing red. She advanced further in, the blackness swirling around her swelling through the hall. Her hands balled into fists.

"Give it to me now, and I might let you live. Test my patience and I will *kill you.*"

Marina turned and ran.

She bolted down through the dark hall, frantically praying she wouldn't trip.

Hel howled, and tore into the house after her.

Marina leaped down a short set of stairs, dodged to the left, skidded down another darkened hall and raced toward the back door.

She slammed into it.

Snow caught the outside edge.

She shoved and *shoved*—

Icy air rolled in.

A lamp on a hall table just behind her shattered violently.

Panting, Marina forced her way through the small opening and darted out into the snow.

The cutting blizzard whirled all around her. She staggered, knee deep, toward the shadow of the woods, then picked up her pace, running as fast as she could. Her breath shredded in her ears. She dove past the first row of pines and kept going—the snow was not as deep here. The ground sloped down and away from her. She slapped through the tangled, crunching underbrush, sliding through the ice, her breath a cloud around her head.

Her back door bashed open. An inhuman roar sliced through the storm.

And a chorus of piercing wolvish howls replied.

Marina's heart clenched with terror and she sprinted down the hill, holding her left arm tight against her, batting branches out of her face with her right. It was *so dark*—at any second she could tumble into a hole or fall into water or slam into a tree...

Wait.

She jerked to a stop.

A pack of feet pattered through the snow behind her. Huffs of lathered panting surrounded her.

She rammed a shaking hand into her hip pocket and pulled out a stone. She had no idea which one it was—it was almost pitch black.

"Get me out. Get me out of here," she hissed. Nothing happened. She stuffed it back in and pulled out another one. "Get me out of here!"

A sharp growl.

She spun around.

A massive black wolf, the size of a bear, galloped down the hill straight for her.

She put the stone back and yanked out the last one.

"Get me out of here!" she cried.

Snap!

A quick gunshot of bright light.

A wrenching sensation in her chest—

She fell forward.

Crashed down onto stone, and ice...

And her hearing flooded with the chilled, indifferent song of rushing water.

She held very still for a long moment—but her breathing still rattled. She shivered hard. Gradually, she realized that she sprawled face down on black rock.

She lifted her head, and glanced around.

A stream. A thin, ice-choked stream. It ran by her feet. She lay on the slick, jagged bank. Leafless trees crowded in around, and darkness hid everything beyond them. But the moon peeked down through thready clouds, flooding the space with white, stark light—and causing the rippling water to glimmer like liquid obsidian.

She shivered and crawled to her feet, letting her breath out in a puff of vapor. She stuck the Wishstone back in her pocket and wrapped her arms around herself.

She had no idea where she was. But, if the silence was any clue, she was at least far away from Hel.

She shivered again.

And caught sight of something. She frowned upstream, listening.

The little trickle of water spilled out of the mouth of a very tall, broad, toothy hole in the side of a cliff. The abyss echoed softly with dripping...

And something else.

Breathing...?

And...

There.

A low, grating moan.

Marina's eyes went wide.

Someone was inside that cave.

She quickly pushed her numb fingers into her pocket again, and fished out that same Wishstone. She opened her mouth...

The moan lashed out in a cry of pain. Then, a shuddering, keening groan.

She paused.

That someone was also hurt.

Setting her jaw, she slipped the stone back into her pocket and picked her way forward across the black, slippery rocks.

When she reached the mouth, she hesitated, then hopped over the bit of water and edged inside the cave. She slowed, trying to make her eyes adjust...

Strange.

Just a few paces in, there was apparently a hole in the ceiling—moonlight filtered down into a small portion of an inner chamber. She started toward it.

Her footsteps scraped and rang as the water jingled coldly. She pressed her hand against the frozen wall, biting the inside of her cheek. Then, at the edge of the pool of light, she dared to open her mouth.

"Hello?"

Her voice echoed. The rippling water replied.

And then...

A chain—heavy, rugged and wet—slithered across the surface of an uneven floor.

A terrible shiver raced through her blood.

And suddenly, as if a curtain had drawn back, she could see him.

He sprawled in crucifix, feet toward her, on a broad slab of stone. His feet were bare, but he had torn black trousers and a ripped, ragged, long-sleeved black shirt that lay open, exposing the whole of his muscled, pale chest—the skin of which had blistered and broken. Shackles gripped his ankles, and their short chains bit into the cave floor. His arms, pulled out to either side of him by suspended chains, hung just inches above the floor. His fists glistened with blood.

And his head, half in shadow, rested back against a pillow of rock.

His face was white, his lips gray. Straight ebony hair stuck in strands to his head and neck with sweat.

And his eyes burnt like red coals—no pupil.

Burnt a hole straight through Marina.

"Well," he said hoarsely—and the small comment resounded like clanking metal. "If it isn't Bird's little pet." And a smile flickered across his marble features like a dying candle. Blood showed on his lips and teeth. He had bitten himself.

Marina instantly recognized his voice.

"*Loki*," she breathed.

He cleared his throat, shifted his left shoulder uncomfortably, then sighed.

"I know. It's a bit hard to recognize me at the moment. Don't look quite as dashing, I'm afraid. Forgive me. Didn't know you were coming."

Images darted through Marina's head—illustrations from old manuscripts, library books and documentaries; carved idols...and descriptions from the Edda...

Her eyes darted up above him, searching for a writhing body, the gleam of scales...

She saw nothing.

"So," Loki said, lifting his left hand. All the muscles in his torso strained, lifting the heavy manacle. He winced, and forced his fingers to open and close twice. "Why do I deserve the honor of *your* visit upon my dying day?"

Marina blinked. He looked at her, and barely lifted an eyebrow.

"Or have you come to spit on me?"

"Spit on you?" Marina repeated, hardly able to make a sound.

"Thor's cousins have had a go already," Loki added. "Very well-aimed, too."

The edge of Marina's heart panged.

"Why would they spit on you?" she asked, drawing her arm close.

"Oh, haven't you heard?" he asked, looking at her evenly. "They tell me I've killed a prince."

Marina stared at him.

She curled her fingers around the pendant, her gut turning to lead.

"No."

Loki said nothing. Just held her gaze with his glowing scarlet one.

A low gurgle issued from above him.

Loki's head jerked and his attention twitched upward. His body twitched also, and he bared his teeth. He tugged against the chains—they chewed into his wrists. He pulled hurriedly back, *pulled...*

Water trickled out from a hole in the rock near the ceiling. It dripped down, sparkling in the moonlight—

Splattered across his chest.

The drops *hissed* like scalding tar—steam shot up. It ate into his flesh—turned it red, split it open.

Loki screamed.

He arched his back and thrashed. His shrieking howl ricocheted through the cave, shocking Marina back against the wall. The scream broke into choked, panicked cries. He spasmed, his muscles shivering. He tugged uselessly on the chains, contorting half into a sitting position...

The steam calmed.

His frame released.

His heels thudded against the stone. He fell back against his rocky pillow, gasping. He blinked his eyes open.

Tears trailed down his face. With an effort, he focused on Marina again.

"Forgive me," he swallowed. "I'm in no fit state to entertain."

Marina's insides churned—blazes of furious heat tore at her while the echoes of Loki's shriek turned her blood cold.

"You...You killed Bird?" she gritted. Loki swallowed again. More tears tumbled, ran down and dripped from his chin. His expression didn't change.

Marina felt a tear of her own escape. It wandered listlessly down her cheek.

"Why?" she mouthed.

"Hm," he chuckled blackly. "You wouldn't believe me if I told you." Suddenly, he smirked as his eyes sparked. "And you never did like me, did you little twig?"

Marina couldn't answer. Her head reeled—she felt as if her legs might give out...she wasn't getting enough air...

"Not that it's...any of my business..." Loki sighed again, leaning his head back and gazing up at the ceiling. He blinked slowly. "But...if you *didn't* come to throw rocks at me...What are you doing here?"

"I...I didn't come here on purpose," Marina answered sharply, through trembling lips. "I had a Wishstone—"

He frowned, wearily tilted his head. Considered her.

"A Wishstone?"

Marina shut her mouth. Loki shifted his right shoulder this time.

"Where did you get one of those?"

Marina's fingers curled tighter around her pendant. Loki watched her movement...and his look intensified. He met her gaze.

"Running from something?"

Marina didn't answer. More sparks crossed Loki's eyes.

"From some*one?*"

Marina's mouth worked, but she still said nothing. He gave her a narrow look.

"You're being chased."

"I'm leaving," Marina snapped, feeling sick. Unsteadily, she started for the mouth of the cave. "I didn't *want* to come here, and I'm not wasting time talking... talking to *you*, you...You deserve to...You... Go ahead and die."

"Anyone I know?"

Marina jerked to a stop. Clenched her quavering right hand. Slowly, she turned her head, and looked back at him.

Loki watched her gravely, eyes like flame.

"It's my sister."

Marina shivered.

"It is," Loki realized. "Fenris, too? Both of them?"

"I..." Marina tried, shaking.

"Why? What do they want?" Loki demanded.

"I...I don't—"

"They must want something, or you'd already be dead," Loki went on, lifting his head off the stone. "And you probably have it. Don't you?"

"No. Not that I..." Marina shook her head. Couldn't finish. Loki arched an eyebrow.

"They *will* kill you if you don't give it to them. You know that."

Marina locked in place.

The chains clanked. Loki moved his feet—halfway sat up.

"Look..."

Marina jerked her attention back to him. His blazing eyes cooled to deep maroon. His eyebrows drew together.

"Let me go."

"What?" Marina whispered, baffled.

"Get me out of these." He tried lifting his hands again. The metal clinked. His imploring look sharpened as sweat trickled down his forehead. "Bird is dead, Thor is in Asgard and the Aesir will *not* help you. Hel and Fenris and their pack are coming after you and they *will* find you. Get me out." His voice lowered. "I know you can."

"And *why*..." Marina bit out. "Would I do *that?*"

"Because," he replied. "I'm the *only* one who can keep you alive."

Marina said nothing for a long moment. Loki held her gaze...

Then winced and glanced anxiously upward. Turned back to her.

"Why would *you* care about keeping me alive?" Marina demanded.

"Look, it's an exchange," he said, looking up again.

Marina stared at him. He started to breathe faster, and sat further forward, even though it strained his arms. His shredded shirt began to come loose.

"You see what they're doing? They're poisoning me. They've *executed* me. My *brother* and *sister* and my *friends.* I tried to tell them. None of what happened—none of it—is as it appeared."

"What do you mean?" Marina wanted to know.

His gaze cut into her.

"Let me go and I'll tell you."

She said nothing. Loki twisted his left wrist.

"A life for a life, Marina. I'll owe you my life—you'll have me in slavery. Please."

The gurgling sputtered through the upper cave. Loki jerked on the chains.

"Marina, I beg you, please," he gasped, his wide eyes searching her face. "Please, please, let me help you. You don't know them—they fly over the ground at night, like they have wings. They'll catch you and kill you and *eat* you and they won't...Marina," He made fists. "They think you have something they want and they *will not* give up until they have it or you are dead. Trust me."

Marina stared at him.

Loki held her gaze in a vise.

"Please, Marina," he whispered again.

The water dripped.

It flashed in the light.

It scalded the back of his neck.

He roared, fell back and hit the ends of his chains. The terrible *clash* bashed through the cave, deafening Marina—warmth drained out of her face.

Gasps tore through him—his eyes widened sightlessly. He writhed again...

His brow twisted and tears streamed down his temples. He released a strangled, helpless sob that tore Marina lengthwise.

Shakily, Marina reached into her pocket and withdrew the Wishstones. With quivering fingers, she picked out the red one, and put the others back. She crept forward, across the slippy rocks, toward Loki's left side. Sweat and blood gleamed on his skin and his lips. Blearily, he blinked his eyes open, and halfway looked up at her.

"I want you to know, before I do this," Marina said slowly, evenly. "That I hate

you."

His lower lip twitched.

"Fair enough," he muttered, his voice watery.

"You swear you'll help me," Marina said, squeezing the Wishstone. He nodded, sighing.

"You have my word."

Marina hesitated. Clenched her teeth. Held the Wishstone out over him, half wondering if it would work...

"Let him go," she ordered.

Snap!

White light flashed.

The manacles cracked loose of Loki's ankles and broke off of his wrists.

"*Gaahhhh...*" Loki choked, his arms going limp. Blood dripped from his fingers. Marina pulled her hand back. For a moment, Loki just lay there, eyes closed, catching his breath. Then, slowly, he rolled over onto his side and forced himself into a sitting position. He scooted away from where the water would fall, then tried to get to his feet. He started up, then lost his balance and had to reach out and catch himself on a low rock. Marina watched him. He closed his eyes again, sweat dripping from his black hair. He grimaced, pushed himself off, and finally stood on his own. He cleared his throat.

"All right, then." He lifted his left hand and tried to snap his fingers. They slipped across each other—and shook. He huffed tiredly. "Oh, fine." He muttered. Glanced up at Marina. "Thank you." And he clapped his hands.

He was gone.

No flash, no sound.

He was just *gone.*

Marina's mouth fell open.

She spun around, searching the reaches of the cave.

Nothing. No one. It was completely empty, except for the whispering waters.

Her gut twisted.

And then...

A faraway, lonesome, trailing *howl.*

CHAPTER TWELVE

"STUPID. STUPID, *stupid,* " Marina hissed, stumbling through the darkness, further into the cave, hugging herself tightly. "Sure. You have a master's degree in Norse myth. Sure, you've memorized the Edda. Couldn't remember Loki plays *tricks* on people? You're a genius."

She'd fled from the mouth of the cave and left it far behind. Now, she followed its winding path by feel, occasionally reaching out to touch the cold, moist wall, her feet splishing through the thin stream. Every few paces, she would pause, and listen for the wolves.

She hadn't heard anything for several minutes.

Didn't mean anything.

She swallowed, her brow tensing. Her legs ached, and her entire left side panged with deep, painful spasms. She had to rest soon.

She pressed on for fifty more feet, and then the cave walls started to feel drier to the touch. She stepped to the right, out of the stream...

And blundered into a small, raised alcove. She sighed, shivering, sank down and sat on the floor, her back to the wall. She wrapped her right arm around her knees and bent her head, curling up into a ball. For a long while, she just concentrated on breathing in...out...in...out...

Bird.

Bird...

She gasped, and lifted her head. Stared straight out, into the pitch blackness. She couldn't see anything at all. Her heart pounded.

"What..." Her voice caught in her throat. "What am I going to do?"

Silence answered.

An ache tingled across her head and centered in the middle of her forehead. She winced, the back of her throat stinging.

She could freeze to death. And she had no idea where she was. She could be in Norway. Or Siberia. Or Romania. Or about a mile from her backyard—she had no clue. No way to know, and no way to find out. She hadn't been thinking of a particular place when she'd used the Wishstone—but did that matter? Did it *decide* where to take her, or was its job merely to get her *away?*

But why had it brought her to Loki? Of all places? Was it drawn to other uses of magic? Or other pieces of Asgard, wherever they might be?

And Bird...

Bird...

Her heart hurt. So did her head. It felt like her very bone was cracking. She reached up, swallowing tightly, and rubbed her forehead.

A powerful light suddenly swelled across her vision.

She sat up straight.

Froze.

Blinded. Blinded by sheer, radiant sun-like light. She blinked, trying to focus...

A mountain.

A distant, black, steep, double-peaked, snow-covered mountain rose up in front of her, surrounded by pines—and a deep cave penetrated the rock between the two peaks. Her vision swooped forward, straight into the throat of that cave...

And in its depths, there suddenly flashed a golden, multi-faceted stone.

It blazed across her mind.

And then—

She saw Bird. Lying on a slab of stone, robed in white, his hands folded on his chest. He looked peaceful.

No.

He looked dead.

But—

In the back of Marina's mind, that gold stone abruptly flashed...

And Bird's blue eyes flew open.

Marina jerked.

She stared ahead, at blackness.

The cave.

The stream softly gurgled just inches from her boots.

She shot to her feet.

Frantically, she caught herself against the wall. Started breathing so hard and so fast that her vision blinked in and out.

"I..." she tried, rasping. "I have to...I..." She started forward, splashing into the stream. Halted. Shook herself hard, to clear her head. Then, she shuffled toward the cave entrance again as quickly as she could, impatiently trailing her right hand against the wall.

Minutes later, she passed the moonlit room where Loki had lain. She paused.

No chains hung from the ceiling. No shackles lay on the floor. An eerie chill swept over her skin. She kept going.

Finally, she broke out of the cave and stepped out into the stark, snowy, forested night. The stream widened and rushed. She couldn't feel her feet.

Marina folded her arms, hopping across the stream again and searching between the branches, trying to find the stars. If she could just discern a few constellations, she might be able to figure out where exactly she was...

A shiver shook her. Her teeth rattled. Thin, gray clouds had begun to wash across the moon, and the frozen leaves obstructed so much of the sky. She had to find a more open space, so she could see.

She turned around, peering through the darkness. The land upstream slanted fairly steeply, like a foothill. Maybe, if she followed the stream up, she might run across a better vantage point. And from there, she might also be able to see the lights of a town, or even just a house.

Which she would *have* to find. Soon.

She closed her numb fingers and started up.

C

MARINA TRUDGED THROUGH knee-deep snow, the lunar light filtering down between the thin, leaning pines, creating dark and light crisscross patterns all around her. She trembled constantly, sucking in her breath in short, painful gasps. She couldn't feel her feet or legs up to her thighs, and she had no sense in her arms up to her elbows—except for the jagged pain that constantly needled up and down her left side. She knew it had to be about four in the morning...

Which meant that dawn was still too far away.

Up, up a steep, uneven hill, stumbling through snow-bound underbrush, trying desperately not to fall down. If she ever *did* fall...

She squeezed her eyes shut for a second, knocking that thought aside. She just had to get to that ridge up there. She could see the moon shining onto the snow...

Finally, she dragged herself to the border of the light, and crossed into it. She turned, her jaw chattering so hard she feared she might bite herself...

And gazed out, from the side of a low mountain, on a silent, rolling black forest. It stretched on as far as she could see in every direction. Not a single light blinked—no light at all, except for the cold moon, and the icy stars. Nothing moved. Not even the wind.

Marina let out a gasp through chapped lips, tears springing to her eyes. She fumbled in her pocket and pulled out the stones, then put two of them back, keeping the green one. She squeezed it against her heart and closed her eyes.

"Get..." she stammered. "Get me out of here. Get me out of here..."

Nothing happened.

She blinked her frozen eyelashes and opened her eyes. Pried open her palm and stared down at the emerald stone.

"Come on," she rasped. "Come on, get me out of here!"

Still nothing.

"Handy little things, those Wishstones."

The voice rang out through the winter.

Marina whirled around, her heart slamming into her ribs.

High above her, perched at the edge of a cliff...

Hel.

Moonlight gleamed against her hair. Night slid from her robes and oozed down the mountain. Her eye flamed red, and she grinned at Marina.

"Too bad they each only work once."

Marina spun and leaped down the hill, throwing herself back into the darkness. But the next instant, she heard Hel cackle—

And dozens of wolves, in chorus, howled in fiendish delight. She heard them spill down the incline, billow through the snow, and give chase at full throttle.

She couldn't make her legs move! She lurched forward, tugging in sharp breaths that cut through her lungs, plowing through the snow, pumping her arms—

Her foot caught.

She yelped—slammed into the snow.

She plunged into the icy, stinging fluff, face-first, then rolled. Then—

Her hip crashed into a tree. She let out a strangled cry, trying to claw her way to her feet, shaking the snow out of her face. She slipped into a standing position—

Jaws snapped behind her. She leaped back—her shoulder hit the tree—

She looked straight into the teeth of that huge, black wolf.

It heaved a thunderous snarl that vibrated its whole, muscular body. Its frosted hackles stood on end, its ears flattened to its skull—spit dripped from its fangs. And its eyes lit like the fires of hell.

Marina screamed, and threw her arms up over her face.

FLASH!

Lightning exploded in front of her.

The wolf keened sharply and leaped backward, stumbling. Marina's eyes dazzled—for an instant, she couldn't see anything—

And then...

A tall, lean, black-clad figure materialized *right* there. He faced the wolf, his hands up, palms out.

He clapped his hands.

Light *burst* from them like a concussion, striking the wolf and knocking it back. It fell into the snow, wildly shaking its head.

The stranger spun on his heel, and found Marina.

High-collared, woolen, winter garb, short cape and silver belt; white, handsome, angular face; dark, curly hair, hawk-like eyebrows and piercing gray eyes. He reached out toward her.

"Your hand please, Twig."

"Wha—" Marina tried. "*Loki?*"

"Your *hand*, woman!" he barked.

A legion of wolves suddenly burst through a snowdrift, clashing their teeth together, lunging toward them—

Marina grabbed his hand.

A hot, flaring thrill shot down her arm and down into her chest. All at once, she felt like she weighed nothing.

Loki whirled her around, pulled her to him and leaped down the hill. Marina followed him—their feet flew over the snow, hardly leaving a trace. The wolves screamed after them, barreling between the trees with the swiftness of phantasms.

A wolf darted in, snapping at Loki's right leg. Loki slapped the air with his right hand—blue sparks sprang from his fingertips and bit into the wolf's face. The wolf veered and struck a tree. The others barked and shrieked. Loki squeezed down on Marina's hand.

They wove through the forest, kicking up clouds of snow in their wake, skidding down the steep hill. Loki shoved her toward the left, they took a sharp turn...

"Oh, *no!*" Marina cried.

"Hold tight!" Loki said.

And they raced full-tilt toward a cliff.

Before Marina could even form a thought, Loki had thrown her over the edge.

For one horrifying, heart-stopping instant, she hung in the icy, thin air over a thousand foot drop.

Then—

He caught her.

Wrapped his arms all around her—and his cape enveloped them. Chills submerged her.

She grabbed his collar, gritted her teeth and ducked her head.

They fell.

Her heart leaped into her throat and her stomach flipped. Wind howled past them. They plummeted toward the ground like a stone. Marina couldn't breathe. She braced herself to impact and die—

They slowed.

Tilted. Turned upright.

Marina opened her eyes.

They drew to a quiet halt.

Her feet sank down into the snow. So did his.

She sucked in a hard breath and pulled sharply back, out of his grasp. His cape fluttered loose of her. Panicked, she glanced all around...

They stood at the bottom of a narrow, sheer-sided ravine. The moon gazed indifferently down on them from far overhead, creating a slice of pale light that cut jaggedly across this small, thin space.

Loki stood in front of her, half in black shadow, hard and striking. He glanced around them, too, as if gauging the cliff wall.

"What...What..." Marina tried, her lips trembling again.

"Sh," Loki muttered, his breath a vapor. "They are still up there."

Marina looked up, straining her hearing...

The low whuffling of a dozen noses sniffing disturbed the snow far overhead. She wrapped her arms around herself and turned back to Loki. He crept away from her, toward the southern cliff wall, eyeing it. He assessed a slight recess no wider than ten feet, then nodded once.

He brought his left hand up to his lips, rubbed his fingers together, then blew on them.

Gold and red sparks bloomed on his fingertips. He flicked them toward the ground.

They leaped off, and struck the snow. Marina watched, entranced.

The sparks took root, and from them blossomed wooden sticks—they grew straight up with astonishing speed, creaking and whispering and broadening as they did. Soon, they reached out to each other, tangled and entwined, to form four knotted, branchy walls. Up and up they climbed, perhaps ten feet, but only five feet wide. The walls thickened, the gaps closed.

Then...

A window pushed through, and opened—

Only for shutters to materialize, and slap across it. Another window did the same, then two more above them. A door opening yawned into existence in the middle, and then the door itself clapped it shut. The walls leaned, and wound together at the top in a sharp peak. A chimney sprouted like a mushroom, and wooden shingles spilled down the slant of the roof.

Dozens of grotesque and ugly wooden faces then poked out of every angle and post, blinking their eyes open and sticking out their tongues. Smoke sputtered and then sighed from the chimney—but it didn't trail upward very far before disappearing. An iron goblin's face shoved out through the center of the door and spat out a circular knocker, then gripped it in its teeth, glaring out at the two of them.

Marina gaped at it all.

A perfect Norse playhouse, from nothing.

"Come inside," Loki sighed, glancing back at Marina. "You look half dead."

He strode forward, rubbed the goblin's nose...

And the door eased open. Light spilled out. Loki pushed the door aside and stepped in.

"We..." Marina started. "Will we both fit?"

He didn't answer.

Clouds rolled across the moon. Marina bit her lip. She couldn't feel it. Wincing, she stepped forward, slogging through the snow again...

Then slipped through the gap between the post and the door.

"Shut that, will you," Loki ordered. "It's far too cold."

Marina couldn't say anything. She could only faintly push on the door to close it. It latched easily.

She stood on a fur rug, in an entryway that was only four feet deep. Straight ahead of her, hugging a wall, climbed an extremely narrow   set   of   worn   wooden   stairs—almost   straight up—accompanied by a gnarled banister. To her left, only a foot away, waited a closed, five-foot-high door, carved with the image of a spindly kitchen witch sweeping up a pile of spiders. To her right, through a four-foot-by-six-foot opening, she glimpsed a dark, pocket-sized library, every wall packed to the throat with dusty, beaten leather books. The far wall held a low, stumpy stone fireplace where more ugly faces protruded, and a lively fire burned in the hearth. A short-legged, high-backed chair sat on either side of the fireplace. The stuffing was falling out of both of them. A woven rug covered the floor, and red, tapestry-like curtains obscured the front window. Loki stood in front of the fireplace, which only came up to his waist. He rested his graceful hand on the mantel and leaned his weight against it, lowering his head.

Marina couldn't conjure a single question. Everything in here seemed impossibly close and jammed together—but it was all still *infinitely* bigger than it should have been. The outside of the house was *tiny*, appearing barely big enough for the two of them to stand inside together, and yet...

Loki cleared his throat.

She made herself look at him, stunned.

"Are you a bit warmer?" he asked, regarding the flames.

She opened her mouth. Nothing.

"Come closer to the fire," he beckoned offhandedly. Marina couldn't move for a long time, but when he didn't say anything else, she ventured through the door and into the little library. Carefully, she drew up next to him, feeling the heat of the *very real* fire swell across her legs and start to thaw them out.

She peered up at Loki's flamelit face as he frowned down at the mantel. The light glanced across his gray eyes and touched the edges of his chestnut hair. He had dark circles under his eyes, and his lips were colorless.

"You came back," she said.

He blinked, and looked sideways at her.

"I said I would."

She couldn't answer. His frown deepened.

"I said I *would*," he repeated.

"You *disappeared*," Marina countered. He lifted an eyebrow, incredulous.

"Did you expect me to be of any help to you like that?" he asked, straightening and folding his arms. "You did *see* me, didn't you?"

"Yes, I saw you—"

"I had nothing—no provisions, no shoes, no clothes," he interrupted. "No way to keep either of us warm, to feed us or to set us in the right direction. So I left for half of a healing spell and to fetch Festning, here. I was gone for ten minutes. But in that time *you* decided to go trekking off to who-knows-where and get yourself pulled into toothpicks for wolves. Brilliant plan."

"It was not a *plan*," Marina shot back. "You *left*."

"I promised I would help you," Loki retorted.

"That doesn't mean very much," Marina said, wrapping her own arms around herself. "I'm aware of your reputation."

He considered her a moment, then laughed quietly and shook his head.

"My *reputation*." He turned back and glanced across the bookshelves above the fireplace, and shook his head again, his mouth tightening. He fell silent. Marina took a low, careful breath.

"Tell me what happened."

"What happened when?" Loki asked.

She hesitated.

"To Bird."

He faced her.

"No."

Marina's eyebrows went up.

"You said you would."

"Well, now I'd rather not," he answered flippantly.

"You gave me your word," Marina reminded him.

"Ah, so *now* you expect me to keep my word?" he remarked. "You know, it's always been painfully obvious what you think of me, Twig. If I cared about it enough, I might be offended." He shrugged. "But, though I don't wish to mince words here, I've now saved *your* life. Our contract has been fulfilled. I could honestly throw you out into the snow right this moment and go do whatever I wanted."

Marina's gut tightened.

"Will you?"

He thought for a second.

"Not yet."

"Why not?"

He smirked coldly. His eyes darkened.

"Because I'm curious."

She gave him a narrow look.

"About what?"

"About what you're going to tell me in the morning," he strode past her, ducked through the door into the entryway, then faced the stairs. "Go on, then," he pointed upward.

She stayed where she was.

"Go on where?"

"Oh, and you were so anxious to explore earlier," he jabbed. He reached up and rubbed his eyes. "It's just a bedroom. And I swear, there's not a troll up there anymore."

Marina had no idea if he was serious. He dropped his hand and gave her a pointed look, then gestured impatiently toward the front door.

"Or, by all means, sleep outside if you'd find that more comfortable."

Marina swallowed, and stepped out of the library onto the fur rug. She cast an uneasy glance up the skinny stairs.

"Where will you be?" she asked.

"Why? Are you afraid you might need me if you have nightmares?" he sneered. She glared up at him. He snorted.

"A witch used to live here, so you should find enough womanish clothes and brushes and everything you think you need up there. There's only a few good sleeping hours left," he warned her. "Go."

She turned away from him, grabbed the banister and started up. Her feet creaked loudly on each step—a different note each time. She reached the landing, and looked back down to Loki...

He watched her for a moment, his face solemn and pale. Then, he turned and re-entered the library. Marina gripped the railing. Then, she lifted her head and assessed the cherry door in front of her.

A garden scene had been carved into this one—a little bridge over a stream, stone walls, and a cottage hung with ivy and roses. She reached out and touched the brass handle, then worked the latch and pulled the door open.

It gave way without a sound. She stepped inside.

Stopped.

"Oh..."

It was huge. Well—at least as big as her room back home!

Dark wood walls and ceiling, wood floors padded by thick furs, a curtained four poster bed just to her right, with its head back against the right-hand wall; a hearth with a bright, live fire in the far corner; a wardrobe just across from her, a vanity and washbasin next to that, and a large trunk at the foot of the bed. A lamp in a hurricane burned on a nightstand next to the bed. The whole room smelled like fresh pine and cinnamon. She finally ventured further in, and shut the door. She moved through the room, studying it all, catching sight of more of those faces peering out from the walls—but these had their eyes closed, and looked much more smooth and elvish. She knelt in front of the ornate chest at the foot of the bed and lifted the squeaky lid.

Inside, folded neatly, lay a soft, white fleece nightgown and knee-high soft-wool socks. That was all. Marina gazed at them for a while...

Then stripped off her soggy clothes, laid them out on the rug in front of the fire, and quickly donned the nightgown and socks. Warmth and softness enveloped her.

The next second, exhaustion hit her in a wave. She swayed—had to reach out and grip the cool post of the bed. She took hold of the thick down comforter, pulled it back, and pulled the sheet back as well. Sighing heavily, she dragged herself into bed, underneath those heavy covers, and barely summoned the strength to blow out the lamp before she sank down into the warm and fell asleep.

CHAPTER THIRTEEN

"WELL...WHO IS THIS?"

The creaky female voice made Marina frown, and slowly open her eyes. Thick blankets buried her, and delicious warmth nearly smothered her. She sighed deeply, then shifted and peeked up over the edge of her covers.

"Good morning!" came the scratchy voice again—

And Marina caught sight of a wooden face sticking out of the center of the mantle off to her right. An old woman's face, with big eyes, spiky hair, pointed chin, a hooked nose and only a few teeth—which Marina could see because she was grinning widely. In afterthought, Marina noticed that the window directly across from the foot of her bed had been blanketed with Jack Frost, but bright morning light filled the room.

"Good morning," Marina managed hoarsely, swiping her hair out of her face.

"Ah! A young lady!" the wooden face gasped, her grin broadening even further. "The young lady I thought I heard come over the threshold last night! Marina is your name, isn't it?"

"Yes," Marina nodded, sitting up further and rubbing her eyes, trying to wake up.

"It has been so very long since anyone has slept in this room!" the wooden lady went on. "Is everything in order? Did you find what you needed?"

"I..." Marina dropped her hands and looked around. "I found a nightgown and socks in the chest, but I haven't had time to..."

"Oh, yes, certainly, certainly, and—But where are my manners?" the wooden lady interrupted herself. "You may call me Bestemor, if you wish to call me anything at all! I am the heart and secret-keeper of Festning."

"Festning?" Marina repeated.

"That is the name of this little house!" Bestemor replied, chuckling like sticks rubbing together. "Did Loki not tell you?"

"He...may have," Marina confessed. "I can't remember."

"He's a dear boy," Bestemor said. "Even if he doesn't scrub out the floo like he ought, or dust in the corners. But what can one expect from a Jotun, anyhow?"

Marina kept her opinions to herself, only half-smirking.

"If you're ready to get up, you'll find underclothes, trousers, a dress and boots in the chest," Bestemor told her cheerfully. "And through the wardrobe will be your washing-up, as well as brushes and everything else!"

"Wait—through the wardrobe?" Marina sat up. Bestemor's wooden eyes widened.

"Oh, dear, he's in the kitchen. I must go see to it that he doesn't burn anything." And at once, her face dissolved, leaving a plain wooden mantle in her place. Marina stared for a moment, then finally threw off her covers and got out of bed. She hesitatingly stepped up to the chest, wondering what Bestemor had meant. There hadn't been anything but the nightgown and socks in there last night...

She bent, and opened the lid...

And lo and behold—there lay undergarments, a fitted pair of black trousers, a long-sleeved, velvety green dress and stockings.

"Ha," she remarked. Carefully, she reached down and touched the soft sleeve of the dress.

Yes, it was real.

"Ha," she said again, smiling. She pulled the clothes out and laid them out on the bed, then took off her pajamas and socks and got dressed. The new clothes felt wonderful—snug, comfortable and fitted as if they had been made for her. Even the knee-high black boots. After rustling the skirt of her dress and smoothing it, she faced the wardrobe. Smiled wryly.

"I shouldn't be surprised at anything now, should I?" she murmured. She stepped up toward it, and worked the little brass handle. She slowly pulled the heavy door open...

She laughed out loud now, and then covered her mouth as delighted chills raced all over her skin.

Inside the wardrobe waited a cream-colored bathroom. A clawfoot tub with faucet stood off to the left, a beautiful side table covered in brushes, combs and teeth-cleaning supplies stood to the right, and a mirror and sink hung on the wall straight in front of her. Wood paneled the walls, and a fleece rug covered the floor. She stepped inside, careful to leave the door wide open, and gazed, awestruck at her own clear reflection for a long time. Finally, she addressed herself frankly.

"This is impossible, you know."

"Oh, not at all," came a smooth, refined feminine voice. Marina jumped.

Another face appeared, blooming out of the wall just above the mirror. It was a beautiful face, with billowing hair, large eyes, a perfect nose and full mouth. She looked like she was made of delicately-carved maple.

"Hello," Marina said cautiously.

"Good morning," the face answered. "I am Skjønnhet, and this wardrobe is my domain. How are you this morning, Lady Marina?"

"I'm...doing well," Marina managed. Skjønnhet smiled.

"Very good. Shall I draw you a bath, or are you wishing to prepare for the day quickly?"

"I think I'd better get ready," Marina decided. "Though a bath does sound really wonderful."

"I shall draw you one later this evening, then," Skjønnhet said kindly. "Please use whatever you like here. And if you need anything, you need only call my name."

"Thank you," Marina said, meeting Skjønnhet's eyes—and suddenly finding that she did mean it.

"Have a delightful day, Lady Marina," Skjønnhet bid her, and melted away.

Marina, her long hair brushed and braided, her teeth cleaned and her face washed, finally emerged from her bedroom and paused on the landing. She listened, trying to figure out where Loki could be in this little house. Bestemor had said he was in the kitchen—could that be the door with the witch on it?

Gingerly, with her right hand on the wall the whole time, Marina picked her way down the steep, narrow staircase, and stopped in front of that door. Setting herself, she grabbed the doorknob and twisted it. Opened the door.

Stared into a large, fully-stocked larder. Large blocks of cheese, bags of potatoes, garlic, onions, carrots, flour, and sugar packed the wooden shelves, and salted meat hung from the ceiling. Barrels of mead and wine lined the floor. Marina eased inside, but it was dark in here, and abandoned. Frowning, she drew back and shut the door. She stood there for a while, hand on the doorknob, then stepped across to the library. She didn't have to go in to see that, though a fire burnt in the fireplace, nobody was in there. She took a breath, but stopped herself from calling out loud. Had he gone outside? She started toward the front door.

"Oh, haloo."

Marina spun around as the witch door abruptly opened and Loki stuck his head out.

"What—were you in there?" Marina demanded, putting a hand to her heart. He raised his eyebrows.

"I've been in here," he said. He wore a loose black shirt with its collar flung open, black trousers and boots. Strands of his curly dark hair hung across his white forehead. His eyes still looked bright and gray, with shadows under them. He looked tired. He glanced Marina up and down, then shoved the door carelessly aside. "Come in and have something to eat." He turned, and re-entered the room...

The room that was *not* the larder.

It was a kitchen.

A very small one. Straight across stood a wooden counter and washing station. Cupboards hung above it, all carved with forests and vines. An iron wood stove sputtered in the far corner, and in front of it were a little square table with two benches. It all smelled like burning pine, and bacon grease.

Marina couldn't move.

"Ah, there she is!" a familiar voice cried. Marina twitched and glanced past Loki to see Bestemor's face grin out from one of the cupboard doors.

"Come in, dearest!" Bestemor called. "Come in and eat!"

Numbly, Marina obeyed. She ventured into the little space, edging around Loki toward the table where a plate of bread, cheese and bacon had been laid out, along with a cup of milk.

"Yes, yes, sit down," Bestemor urged, swimming across the wall to rest by the stovepipe. "You look starved! Eat something!"

"Thank you," Marina murmured, and eased down onto the bench. She watched Loki, who stood at the counter. A front window, to his left, let in bright morning sunlight, only slightly filtered by white cotton curtains. Loki quickly put a loaf of bread back into the breadbox, then set to washing and drying another dish, cup and knife. He didn't look at her. So, Marina picked up the cheese and ate it, and then the bread and bacon, swallowing each bite with gulps of milk. It all tasted very good—made from scratch, she could tell—and rich. She had just finished the last sip of milk when Loki turned and crossed his arms. His gaze cut down through her, and she stilled as she sat, her hand on her cup.

"So," he began. "Would it be possible for you to tell me why it is Hel and Fenris are chasing you?"

Marina held his gaze and pulled her hand back down into her lap.

"Not until you tell me what happened to Bird."

The edge of his mouth curled up. Marina's gut tightened.

"Ah, you see..." He flashed his eyebrows. "Now that I've saved your life, given you a place to sleep and food to eat—sanctuary, if you will, I no longer owe you anything. And..." he stood away from the counter and took a step toward her. His lean form loomed over her in this tiny place. His eyes flashed. "If I lose my patience, I'll just get the information from my brother and sister in exchange for *you*."

Marina swallowed.

"Loki, you oughtn't treat our guest that way," Bestemor chided. Loki glanced at her.

"Give us a moment, please, Bestemor," he said—but his polite words carried an edge. The spindly face blinked, and her mouth downturned, but she reluctantly faded away. Loki leaned back against the counter and folded his arms, then regarded Marina.

"So," he said again. "What's your pleasure?"

"Why should I trust you?" Marina wanted to know.

"I never said anything about *trusting* me," Loki replied. "Just use your brains. Tell me what I want to know, or I'll toss you over to the wolves. Simple as that."

Marina studied him. He watched her with a look of ice.

"I..." Marina finally started, glancing down at her empty plate and trying to scramble her thoughts together. "When I was in Asgard, Bird told me that he'd been having dreams that he'd be killed—but he didn't know how or when it would happen. So he asked me for my help, and he said I would know what to do when the time came." She risked a look up at Loki.

He gazed back at her, his eyebrows drawn together, his eyes deep blue. He said nothing. Marina went on.

"And so I...I didn't have any idea what he was talking about, until *she* came to my door, and said something about his *tears,* and bringing him *back...*"

"What?" Loki cut in. "*Back?*"

"That's what she said," Marina insisted. "And I still didn't understand until..." She trailed off, suddenly feeling foolish.

"Until what?" Loki pressed, leaning toward her, his eyes lightening back to gray. "What?"

"After you left, I went further up into the cave," Marina said, squeezing her left hand with her right. "And when I sat down to rest, I saw..."

"What did you see?" Loki asked softly, intently. She looked up at him.

"A mountain," she said. "A mountain with two peaks. And there was a cave in between the peaks. Inside the cave was a gold-colored stone. And then I saw Bird lying there. It looked like he was dead. But when I came closer...his eyes opened. And I got this feeling, all of a sudden..." She swallowed. "That I *had* to go out and..." She couldn't bring herself to finish.

Loki's eyes narrowed.

"When you were in Asgard...did Bauldr kiss your forehead?"

Marina's cheeks flamed. But she nodded once.

Loki didn't speak for a long time. He didn't even breathe.

Then, he suddenly straightened and turned around, stepping away from her. He stopped, putting his left hand over his mouth.

"What does it mean?" Marina asked, pushing the bench back and standing up. "Is he...Is he not really dead?"

Loki didn't answer. Marina closed her hand to a fist.

"Is he dead or not?" she demanded.

"He is dead," Loki muttered.

"Then what?" Marina kept on, her heart starting to pick up. "What does it mean?"

Loki stayed silent for several minutes. Marina waited, holding her breath.

"It means," he finally said, lowering his hand. "That I have to get that stone out of the mountain before Hel and Fenris kill us."

"Why would they want to kill us?" Marina gasped.

"Because," Loki looked at her over his shoulder, his eyes ocean-blue again. "Bauldr told you how to bring him back from Helheim."

Marina stood stunned.

"Is that possible?"

Loki tilted his head.

"Some say so."

"With a *stone?*"

Loki ignored her, his attention drifting off. Marina shifted gears.

"Why would they want to *kill* us for trying to bring him back?"

Loki's aspect darkened.

"Ask them," he muttered. He stepped back toward her and picked up her plate and cup with one hand. He carried them to the sink.

"I'd rather not," Marina answered. He said nothing. Marina frowned at him as he vigorously scrubbed soap suds all over the plate and cup, then rinsed them in the clean water. And she noticed, for the first time, heavy bandages bound around his wrists underneath his loose sleeves. A cold feeling settled down through her.

"And...why do *you* want to get the stone?" she asked slowly, wrapping her arms around her middle. "To finish the job and make sure Bird stays dead?"

Loki took the cup and hurled it at the wall in front of him.

It *smashed*—pieces exploded and shattered all over the counter.

Marina jumped back and knocked her bench over with a bang.

Loki set his hands on the edge of the counter, bowed his head and closed his eyes, his jaw clenching. His hair blackened. Marina didn't move.

"I wish," he rasped. "That you would stop calling him Bird."

"That's..." Marina started trembling. "That's his name."

"Only to his family and most intimate friends," Loki answered back. Marina swallowed.

"I'm his friend."

Loki sneered down at the suds, then shook his head and chuckled poisonously to himself.

"Listen, you little broken, crooked thing..." He raised up, opened his eyes and looked at her. Fire overtook the blue in his gaze until his eyes smoldered. "You've memorized scraps of nonsense stories passed down by word of mouth from your half-deaf ancestors. So you *condescend* to understand us and how we think and what our lives are like. And that can be amusing at dinner parties." He leveled a paralyzing look at her. "But the truth is, you don't know anything about anything—and *somehow* your visit to Bilskirnir and the hospitality shown to you by every single Aesir, despite your offensive presumptions, failed to teach you that." He threw the plate down into the water. It splashed all over. "You are stupid and ignorant and you judge your hosts and saviors by thousand-year-old hearsay." He advanced two steps closer, raising his eyebrows and pointing at himself. "You want to know what happened to Bird but you're surprised when I'm disinclined to tell you? Well, here's the reason, then." He leaned down toward her, bracing his fingertips on the table, liquid savagery in his voice. "It is *none* of your blasted business. You are a stranger to the house of Odin and you are a stranger to me. Conceited, snobbish *mortal*—you are *nothing* to any of us. You are here and you'll be gone—" he snapped his fingers in her face. "—before anybody notices." He glared straight into her eyes. "Just stay out of my way and be thankful I'm honoring my word—no matter how worthless you think it is."

He shoved on the table. It rattled.

Marina jumped back again. He stood up straight, narrowing his eyes. At last, he lifted his chin and turned away.

"Now get out of here and find clothes fit for snow," he bit out. "I am packing up the house and leaving in half an hour. If you don't want to be killed when the walls fold up, I suggest you hurry."

Marina stared at him, ice in her veins. He stayed where he was. So she crept around the table, avoided looking at him at all costs, then shoved through the door and bolted up the stairs.

E

Marina stood outside, hands in her pockets, ankle-deep in snow. After she had staggered up the stairs and flung open the door, she had then frozen in the center of her bedroom for fifteen minutes, fighting back a horrifying fit of shuddering.

Finally, she'd been able to gather herself enough to go open the trunk, and there found find knee-high fur-lined snow-boots, a knee-length leather-and-fur gray coat with a deep hood, and gloves. She had hurried into them, feeling weak, sick and jumpy all at once, tightly tied the sash on the coat and climbed down the stairs just as Loki's dark form had strode out of the house ahead of her.

Now, she watched him from a safe distance as he faced the little pale-wood house, its thin chimney quietly puffing like an old man's pipe. Loki wore a knee-length coat as well—black—its sleeves, edges and hood lined with gray fur. His ruffled, curly hair now matched the deep tint of his coat, and his skin looked as white as the snow. His narrowed eyes studied the house for a long time.

He lifted his bare hands, cupped them and blew into them, then rubbed them swiftly together. Then, he cleared his throat, and casually crooked his fingers toward the house.

The chimney sucked noisily down into the roof.

Marina straightened.

The shingles curled up and clattered up to the peak, then vanished—

The peak split open and retreated in both downward directions, rustling and clattering as the walls began to melt. The shutters slapped open and disappeared. The door swung open and was gone. The window and door holes winked shut; the walls disintegrated and everything trailed down into the snow, until all that remained were tiny red sparks.

Loki beckoned with his fingers again.

The sparks leaped up, whizzing through the air, and landed in his palm. He closed his hand. For just a moment, his fist glowed. Then, the light faded.

He huffed, and drew himself up. His breath clouded around his face as he turned and looked at her. He still had circles around his vivid eyes—eyes that now mirrored the color of the hard winter sky above them.

"We walk during the day," he said shortly, putting on a pair of gloves. "Neither Hel nor Fenris are too fond of traveling while the sun is up. And any use of magic to transport us would be like shooting up a beacon right in their faces." He glanced at her sideways. "Good news is, the same goes for them." He waved his left hand out to the side, and a pearly-handled, waist-high crook blinked into existence. He grasped it, and planted it firmly into the snow, then kicked his head to the side. "Come on." And he started off, heading up the ravine through the deep, flawless snow, Marina trailing after, keeping her mouth firmly shut.

CHAPTER FOURTEEN

THEY HIKED FOR SEVERAL hours in silence, traipsing up the floor of the ravine, snow crunching beneath their boots. The narrow canyon wound and bent, thin trees tangling around each other and hugging the stone walls. Marina tried to follow in Loki's footsteps, but often his strides were so long she couldn't manage it. She stumbled more than once, but he ignored her, and pressed onward even if she started falling behind.

All day long, as she strained to keep up, silence pressed in around her—muffled, weighty silence, only broken by the persistent *stump-stump* of their boots.

Finally, the ravine opened up to a wide, steep valley. Forested foothills and then mountains loomed to either side. Pines hung thick with snow, and here and there, Marina caught sight of bushes and vines whose bright, eager blooms had frozen mid-life. Loki, several paces in front of her, wove easily between the trees, pausing only occasionally to glance around and listen.

But then the snow got *deep*.

All of a sudden, Marina found herself stumbling into thigh-deep white fluff. Loki did the same—only he sank almost up to his waist.

"Oh, for the sake of..." he muttered, following that with several low Norse curses as he jerked his crook out of the snow. He switched his walking stick to his other hand, bit the fingers of his glove and pulled it off, then snapped his fingers several times, impatiently. Then, he rammed his glove back on, bent his knees and jumped nimbly into the air.

Ice flew. He kicked his feet out and landed—

On the snow. His boots only sank perhaps a centimeter. Heaving a quick sigh, he bent and slapped the snow off of his trousers, tossed his crook easily into his left hand and strode onward, as easily as if he were strolling on cement.

Marina stayed where she was. Staring at him in disbelief.

But also stuck.

After a moment, she shook herself, set her teeth and battled her way forward, swinging her arms with the effort of lifting her legs. But when she got to the place where Loki had sunk, she tripped and fell face-first.

She threw out her right hand to catch herself, but it went straight through and the snow swallowed her.

"Gah," she sputtered, rolling onto her side as downy ice buried her. She tried to sit up, to stand up, but her feet slipped and snow collapsed in around her shoulders.

A hand gripped her right upper arm.

The next second, she lifted straight up into the air, pulling free of the snow.

Loki held her with one hand, as if she weighed no more than a loaf of bread. She stiffened, her breath catching.

He bit off his glove again, snapped his fingers, then flicked the shoulder of her coat. He set her down.

Her feet rested on the powdery snow. They sank about as far as a leaf would.

"There," Loki said around his glove, then stuffed it back on his hand. "What would you have done without me?" He re-conjured his walking stick with a flourish, then started forward.

"Thank you," Marina said, half stunned.

He stopped. Frowned. Glanced over at her.

Started onward again.

Marina stared down at her feet, oblivious to the ice and snow covering her.

"Magic," she realized.

"Very astute," Loki remarked. She looked up at his retreating back.

"But...I thought you said magic would be too obvious," she said. "That Hel and Fenris would find us."

Loki spun on his heel and faced her.

"Well, this right here is what you would call *Practical* Magic," he pointed at Marina's feet with his stick. "And it's not uncommon on Midgard at all. If you looked closely enough you'd find it working in most of your communication devices, computers, and," he almost smiled. "A few German and Italian-made sports cars."

Marina looked at him in surprise. He assessed the trees around them.

"What we have to avoid is Flash Magic. Instant transport of ourselves, or the house—anything that creates too much light or heat or noise." He lifted an eyebrow at her. "Any of that, and they'd come running."

"Right," she murmured.

"Which means we have to walk faster," he said, catching up his stick and continuing on. "I trust you'll be able to keep from blundering into any trees without my assistance."

Marina just grinned to herself as she watched herself take one step forward, then another, then another. She didn't sink at all, even though the snow wouldn't have held up a small bird that landed on it.

"This is incredible," she whispered.

"Sorry?" Loki looked back. She found his eyes, and halfway smiled.

"This is incredible," she repeated, a little louder. He watched her a moment.

"All right, no more dallying. Come on," he ordered again—and this time, Marina easily kept up with him.

Marina sighed. It came out as a cold shudder, and she wrapped her arms around herself. The sun had gone down half an hour ago, and the temperature had plunged. Her trousers were wet; she'd lost feeling in her toes, her ears, her nose and her fingers. Her left side ached and twinged. Clouds still covered the sky, so darkness dominated the valley. She could barely see Loki's black form in front of her, facing the cliff. He disappeared his cane, pried off his ice-coated gloves and breathed into his bare hands.

Red sparks blazed from his fingers like fireworks, and hit the snow. With renewed fascination, Marina watched the little house, Festning, grow up out of the sparks—twining and twisting—until light glowed through the gaps in the shutters, and she could glimpse a faint puff of smoke emitting from the chimney.

"Let's get inside," Loki huffed, striding forward. "I'm about to expire."

Marina hurried after him. He tapped the metal goblin's nose and the door swung open. Loki swept in, Marina on his heels.

As soon as her feet touched the fur rug, she felt her weight settle again. The spell had broken. She shut the door behind her and pulled off her gloves, her nose and cheeks stinging.

Loki, just a foot away from her, coughed and stomped his boots on the rug. He then dashed the snow off his coat, unbuttoned it and pulled it off, and hung it on a peg near the kitchen door—a peg Marina *knew* had not been there last time. He wore the same black, high-collared winter clothes as before—though Marina thought she detected a faint pattern of silver embroidery in the sleeves.

Loki scrubbed his fingers through his hair, turned and ducked into the library, heading for the fire. Marina pulled off her own coat, very careful of her stiff, aching left arm, and hung it up on *another* peg that had certainly not been there before. Carefully, watching his back, she ventured into the library after him. She edged closer to the fire, wanting to stretch her hand out toward it...

Loki caught sight of her. Frowned.

"What are you doing?"

She jumped.

"I..."

"You have your own fireplace, don't you?" he asked. "I mean, Bestemor lit it for you last time."

Marina nodded.

"And you'll want to change into something that isn't wet," he added, turning back to the fire and folding his arms. "I know you're probably accustomed to eating more than once a day, so we'll dig out something hot once you're ready." He fell silent, staring intently down into the flames. Marina hesitated, then withdrew, turned around and made for the staircase, forcing herself not to look back at him.

Marina trailed carefully down the creaky steps, her right hand pressed to the wooden wall as she watched her feet, trying not to trip on her skirt. Now, she wore a warm, long-sleeved red fleece dress, dry trousers, stockings and leather shoes, and the ache in her side had faded.

She reached the bottom and approached the kitchen door, which stood a little open. Clattering noises issued from inside. She pushed it aside, and eased over the threshold.

Fire burnt in the stove, and the door of it hung open. Two candles on wooden spools flickered on the little table, and a glowing lamp with glass chimney sat on the counter, back near the wall. Otherwise, the kitchen felt dark—but the flamelight richened the darkness, and brought out the colors of the wood. In here, it smelled like roasted meat and boiling potatoes, and perhaps spiced cider...

Loki stood off to the left in front of the counter—a knife clacked against a cutting board. Marina stepped slowly up to his right side. Pulled her left arm up against her.

"Anything I can do?" she asked quietly.

"Yes," Loki answered, focused entirely on the salted meat he was busily slicing into pieces. "There are more potatoes in the sink, there. Cut them up, and put them into the bigger pot that's on the stove."

Marina found the bowl of potatoes and hefted them out onto the right side of the counter.

"I need a knife," she said. Loki pulled open a drawer near him and whipped out a flashing silver knife, and presented it to her handle-first.

"Thank you," she said, and took it. He said nothing, just returned to work. Marina, in a slightly-awkward-but-practiced manner, held the potato down with the side of her crippled hand and cut with her strong right one. In very little time, she had finished the potato, set down the knife and carried the pieces over to the large, simmering pot. She dropped the potatoes in, careful not to splash, then returned to cut up the others. She had hardly put the last one in the pot before Loki dug five long carrots out of a burlap sack and set them down at her station. Without a word, she started in on those, too. Loki finished his meat, carried it in both hands over to the pot and tossed it in, then returned. Marina traded places with him, dumping the carrots in this time.

"Come, put these bones in there," Loki said, holding out two meaty bones to her. "Oh, and start stirring it." He picked up a long wooden spoon and held it out, too. "After it boils a while, cool it down and taste it. We may need to add pepper."

Marina nodded, took everything in her right hand, stepped to the stove and eased the bones down into the hot water, reveling in the feeling of the steam washing over her hands. She also eased over and took a breath of the other simmering pot. *That* was where the lovely scent of spiced cider came from. Then she took up the spoon and started stirring the stew, taking deep breaths of the delicious, rolling smells.

Clink. Clink. Clink.

She frowned, and peered down into the pot. She could hardly see anything, because of the dim light, but she could almost be sure...

"There's a nail in the bottom," she realized.

"Mhm," Loki replied, tapping on the curved, old-fashioned faucet. Water gushed out. He began scrubbing his cutting board.

"Why is there a nail in the pot?" Marina asked.

For a long while, Loki didn't answer—and she started to wonder if he had heard her.

Then, he drew a breath—and when he spoke, his voice was so low Marina didn't dare move, for fear of missing a word.

"Once upon a time," he said. "In a land faraway, a starving tinker traveled the narrow, rocky road between one village and another. He had found no work in the last village, nor the one before, because a great famine clutched the kingdom, and no one could pay a tinker—though there were plenty of broken hinges and windows and chairs and buggy wheels. And so he walked, carrying nothing but his tools, his large cooking pot—long bereft—and the clothes on his back. He knew that if he did not find food soon, he would die."

Marina watched him, listening, her stirring hand falling still. Loki tapped the faucet again and the water stopped hissing. He pulled the cutting board out of the water, took up a towel and began drying it.

"As the tinker approached a village, a small stream joined the road on which he walked. As he listened to the flow of it, to him it sounded as if it were simmering. And he got an idea. So, he went down to the stream and filled his cooking pot with water, and dropped a nail into the bottom of it. Then, he carried it into the center of town." Loki finished drying the cutting board, opened a lower cupboard and slid it inside. He shut the cupboard door, stood up and opened another, glancing through its contents. "There, he built a fire, and stood up his small spit and hung the pot from it. He started stirring the water, humming happily to himself. Soon, villagers passing through the square became curious, and asked him what it was he was doing. 'I am making nail soup,' he answered. 'Which is the finest meal one could ever wish for! Miraculous and filling! Though, it will not be quite as delicious as it *could* be, as I am still missing a few things.' 'Such as?' Asked the butcher.' 'Oh, a bone of any kind, to add just a little more heartiness.' 'I can spare a bone,' answered the butcher. 'If I can have a taste of the soup when it is finished!' 'Certainly!' said the tinker. And so the butcher hurried off, then brought back a ham bone and dropped it in the pot. More people walked by, and inquired as to what was going on. Both the tinker and the butcher told them about the fantastic soup—but the tinker said it still would not be quite as good as it could be without a vegetable or two. 'I have one last carrot,' said an old lady. 'I have two potatoes,' said a young wife. 'I have some dried basil and parsley,' said a gardener." Loki fished out two small jars, opened their lids and set the lids on the counter, then brought the jars over to Marina. He set one jar down, then took a pinch out of the other. The scent of parsley sparked up. He tossed three pinches into the pot. Then, he picked up the other jar and threw several pinches of basil into it. Marina watched him as he stood just close to her. She stayed very still. He set the basil jar down, then held out his hand to her, studying the boiling water. Marina carefully handed the spoon over to him. He began to stir.

"Word soon spread throughout the village," he went on. "That if you brought an ingredient for this miraculous nail soup, no matter how small, then you would get to taste it. Soon, the pot was full to the brim with good things, and all the people gathered around with their empty bowls, their mouths watering at the smell. At last, the concoction was finished, a ladle provided, and everyone, including the starving tinker—was helped to a steaming bowlful of this miraculous nail soup."

Marina studied Loki's angular face, half hid in shadow, half touched by the flamelight from the candles.

"It was a trick," Marina mused.

His bright gray eyes flicked up to hers—and remained, gazing at her. He barely lifted his right eyebrow, quietly earnest.

"Not all tricks are evil, Twig," he murmured.

Marina's throat closed. She didn't answer. She only gazed back up at him, captured.

He shifted, taking a quick breath.

"Why don't you set the table," he suggested. "Bowls and cups are in the cupboard, spoons in the drawer."

Marina nodded, stepped back from him and walked around the other side of the table, then opened the cupboards.

"I'm surprised we're using spoons," she remarked quietly.

"This isn't Bilskirnir," Loki replied. "We're civilized, here."

Marina suppressed a smile, and pulled out the utensils. She held her left arm snugly against her chest as she set the table. Then Loki brought the pot over and set it down on the table, and ladled the stew out into both bowls. He took the cups back to the stove and ladled cider into each of them. Then, he sat down. Marina sat down across from him.

Together, they ate in silence, their wooden spoons clacking against the wooden bowls. The stew was rich and divine, and the spiced hot cider filled all of her senses, trailing down her throat like liquid Christmas. She ate everything, only now realizing how famished she was—and by the time she was finished, her whole body felt warm and drowsy.

"Best get to bed," Loki advised, picking up his dishes. "We're to start out early tomorrow. I don't like the idea of staying in one place any longer than we have to."

Marina frowned sleepily, knowing there was something she ought to say...

"I'll help wash."

"No, go to bed," he ordered. So she nodded, slowly got up, and headed to the door.

"Goodnight," she said absently. He didn't answer—but she felt his attention follow her. She left the kitchen, climbed the stairs, and, full and tired, entered her room.

CHAPTER FIFTEEN

"WHAT'S THIS, THEN?"

Marina wore her nightgown and socks now, and had just climbed into the sinking warmth of her bed when Bestemor's face appeared in the mantel.

"What's what?" Marina yawned, pulling the covers up over herself.

"What is troubling you?" Bestemor asked. "With your left arm?"

"Oh," Marina reflexively smiled—it became a wince. "I...hurt it. Several years ago. Now I can't move my fingers or my wrist very well. My elbow sometimes doesn't...either..."

Bestemor frowned.

"And it cannot be fixed?"

"No," Marina shook her head. "It's actually *been* fixed as much as it can be."

"Oh, tosh," Bestemor countered. "You ought to have Loki see it."

Marina gritted her teeth and stared at Bestemor.

"No," she said flatly.

"Why not?" Bestemor wondered. "He knows all sorts of things. He can—"

"He's killed someone," Marina bit out, vivid pain suddenly swelling through her and clawing the inside of her throat.

How? *How* had she let that fade to the back of her mind?

Bestemor watched her softly. And smiled.

"He is a good boy, Lady Marina," she said quietly. "You'll see."

"What in the *world* would make you believe that?" Marina shot back. "Didn't you hear what I said?"

"I know what you said," Bestemor replied calmly. "But I also know a great deal more about it than you do."

"Then tell me," Marina urged.

"I cannot," Bestemor said.

"Why not?"

She smiled quietly again.

"Because it is not my secret to tell."

Marina looked away from her.

"Get sleep, Lady Marina," Bestemor advised. "You have a long journey tomorrow."

Marina ignored her. The fire flickered. And when she glanced back, Bestemor's face had disappeared.

"Where are we? Exactly?" Marina asked, hushed. Loki stood very still several paces ahead of her. He studied the sky through the thin, crowded trees, his breath escaping his lips in vapor.

"The Caribou Mountains," Loki answered, keeping his voice low. Marina's eyes widened.

"We're in *Canada?*"

He nodded, still looking around.

"We're heading north, toward that double-peaked mountain. If we keep up this pace," his eyes narrowed. "We should be there by tomorrow afternoon."

He fell silent. But he didn't start walking again. Marina took a breath and held it. She listened.

"What?" she finally murmured. "What is it?"

"Not sure," he whispered. "A feeling."

He pulled off his gloves and put them in his pockets, and, still studying the woods, he rubbed his palms together.

Light shimmered between his hands, like the reflection of moonlight on water.

Then...

An elegant mahogany longbow bloomed in his grasp, alongside a leather quiver of silver arrows. He quickly looped the quiver's strap over his shoulders, and held the strung bow in his right hand.

Marina shivered.

He glanced back at her.

"Come on."

Marina's whole body ached, and her right arm spasmed with fatigue. She eased through the door of Festning, leaving the freezing darkness outside, and sighed, leaning back against the doorframe.

It had to be past midnight. The moon had come out, lighting a silvery path in front of them, so Loki had insisted that they press on even at night. At the beginning of the day, he'd cast the spell again that made them both light enough to walk on the snow—but Marina estimated that they'd walked close to twenty or twenty-five miles.

Loki took off his quiver, rested his bow against the wall and pulled off his coat. He winced as the sleeves passed his wrists, then hung the coat up.

"I'll put the rest of the nail soup on the fire," he muttered, shoving against the witch door.

It opened to the larder.

Loki heaved a sigh and let it fall shut.

"Kjøkken," he snapped.

Marina watched him. That word meant "kitchen."

He pushed on the door again...

And there it was. Candles and lamps flared to life, to reveal the kitchen instead. Loki strode in, leaving the door open. Marina wearily pulled off her coat and hung it up, then trailed into the kitchen after him, so sore and beaten she couldn't even summon any more surprise.

Marina's eyes jerked open. She stared at the dark ceiling.

Her heart hammered so hard she could feel every single rib.

Icy sweat coated her body. She clenched her right hand around her covers and gritted her teeth as terrible pain raced all up and down her left side.

Light blazed—fire roared in the hearth.

She gasped and pushed the covers out of the way. Bestemor's face emerged on the mantel.

"Lady Marina!" Bestemor called sharply. "You must go down and help him!"

"What?" Marina rasped, forcing back another wave of pain.

"Hurry, hurry!" Bestemor cried. "He needs you!"

Marina pushed her covers off herself and slid out onto the floor, fighting back the stiff cramping that threatened to lock her up.

"Put on the shoes in the trunk!" Bestemor ordered. "And wrap up in the long coat!"

Marina pried open the lid and found the shoes Bestemor meant—she was able, with a little struggle, to tug them on. Then, she wrapped herself in the ankle-length brown housecoat lying there and tied the sash.

"Hurry! Oh, hurry!" Bestemor pleaded. Marina stumbled toward the door and pulled it open, stepped out onto the landing...

Froze.

Festning was dark. And silent.

And the front door hung open.

Snow spilled over the threshold. Snow and moonlight.

And voices.

"Don't, little brother. It doesn't have to come to this at all," a man's voice—deep, rich, sophisticated yet quietly pleading, crawled through the night up toward her. "You know what we want and you know you can't just keep running and expect to lose us."

"We aren't having this conversation, Fen," another voice—*Loki's*—replied evenly. "Not after what the two of you did to him."

"We didn't do anything," the first voice—"Fen"...*Fenris!*—countered. "We were nowhere near when it happened. That was you."

Marina crept forward, setting her arm against the right wall and stepping down onto the furthest right-hand side of the first stair, praying, praying...

It didn't squeak. She stepped down onto the next stair. And the next, and the next...

"Do *not* play with me, Fen," Loki spat—but his voice shook. "I'm not some Aesir courtier whose brains you can twist in whatever direction you feel like. I know *precisely* what happened. Do you think I'm stupid?"

"Of course not," Fenris replied gently. "Don't be ridiculous. But..." he paused. "I also know you have no proof either way."

Marina sneaked into the library, edged up to the window and pushed the thick curtain just an inch aside.

Out there, in the pool of moonlight that filled the little clearing in the woods, stood two tall, lean men. One was clearly Loki, wearing his same black winter garb, his back to the house, his arms folded.

Facing him—an even taller man in a high-collared, rugged, patched, knee-length, fur-lined coat. He had windblown, curly chestnut hair; high, prominent cheekbones and strong, stern features; a set mouth, frowning brow and bright, piercing eyes.

"I mean to *find* proof," Loki shot back at him.

"I know," Fenris answered, gazing at him in an open, almost sad way. "But what do you think that will solve?"

"I will show it to them," Loki said deliberately, leaning toward him. "I'll show them the *truth* about what happened, not the lies they've been led to believe."

Fenris raised his eyebrows.

"And who led them to these lies?" he wondered. "You know Hel and I did not. We fled Asgard as soon as it happened. The Aesir brought you to trial and convicted you all on their own. These precious friends of yours. The ones you chose over your own family."

Loki stared at him. Said nothing.

Fenris took a step toward him. Then another.

Marina tensed, watching...

Fenris stopped in front of Loki. Reached out with his right hand and lightly gripped Loki's elbow...

And lifted his left hand, and laid it affectionately against the side of Loki's head. He dipped his own head, to meet Loki's eyes, and softly smiled.

"You are my brother," he said quietly. "You live next to my heart. Look at what has happened, here. The Aesir have abandoned you—but *I* have come to bring you home."

Loki took a shivering breath. Fenris lowered his hand to rest on Loki's shoulder.

"I never wished this upon you. But now that it has happened, I hope you can finally see the truth."

"No," Loki shook his head. "I don't."

Fenris took fistfuls of Loki's coat.

"They are not like us, Loki!" he cried, shaking him once. "The three of us are savage elves, born to roam the wilds and live as we please—not in fashioned palaces and fortresses playing with manners and niceties. They cannot understand us, they cannot know us. And look! They've *more* than proven that to you! Forget Asgard and their feeble affections." Fenris searched Loki's face earnestly. "Come with me. And give the girl to Hel."

Marina's whole body went cold. She backed away from the window.

"And how would that solve anything?" Loki demanded. "How would that clear my name?"

"Clear your name? Whatever for? You're free!" Fenris laughed. "We three could live in this realm, or any realm at all besides Asgard. Odin hardly holds sway over the entire universe. We're tricky and clever. It's more than possible."

Marina's right hand closed around a cold fire iron. She gritted her teeth.

"And what would Hel do to her?" Loki asked slowly. Marina watched Fenris through the little gap in the curtains.

He shook his head, releasing his hold on Loki.

"That can't matter to you. Bring her out, be done with it, and Hel and I will stop pestering you. We can move on, you, Hel and I, as a pack again." He held out his hand, palm up. His eyebrows drew together. "We need you, Loki. Please tell me that you'll come."

Marina picked up the heavy iron. Spread out her stance and waited, her heart thundering.

Waited.

"No."

She blinked.

Had he said—

Fenris looked at Loki, startled. He slowly lowered his hand.

"I told you, Fen," a female voice sliced through the darkness. "There wasn't a point to this errand. You've been wasting your time."

Fenris glanced to his left.

And Hel, in all her nightmarish majesty, caught in the silver light, swept out of the forest and straight toward her brothers. She fixed Loki with a severe, terrible look.

"Listen," she snapped. "I'm tired of all this dancing around. Are you just doing this to be irritating?"

"I'm doing it to clear my name of murder," Loki snapped back.

"Well, you can't," Hel retorted. "You know why? Because you're guilty. You did it. Everyone knows that. *You* know that. The Aesir don't believe your fairy story, but the good news for *you* is that Fen and I don't *care* either way. So bring out the little stick and I'll break her neck and all this stupidity can finally be over with. I'll buy you a round of drinks in Fort McMurray. Come on."

"A prince died," Loki murmured.

"I never cared if that stuck up, too-pretty Aesir was alive or dead," Hel waved it off. "Why should I? I was never good enough for anyone in Asgard—so I don't keep myself awake worrying about their opinions."

"Bring her out, Loki," Fenris advised.

"I will not," Loki snarled—and tears suddenly choked his voice. "You know what she has, and that it could ruin you. I'll not give that up, not now. Especially if all you're going to do is kill her."

"All right, fine," Hel said. "I'm done here."

She slapped Loki.

He staggered back, his hand flying to his face.

Marina saw drops of blood hit the snow.

Hel shook herself, fast, like a dog shaking off water...

And white hair swept across her whole body. She swelled with muscle, her arms and legs lengthened, her hands and feet became clawed paws. Her head become that of a great, savage wolf—missing one eye—and in an instant her other red eye blazed in the darkness. In an instant, she stood upon all fours and lunged at Loki.

Loki caught his balance and backhanded the air.

A light *cracked* right in front of Hel's face.

Fenris withdrew.

Hel ducked Loki's blast, skidded to the side and charged toward the front door of Festning.

Loki leaped on top of her.

He tangled the huge wolf's legs. The two tumbled into the snow.

Hel roared, fangs bared, and battered Loki with her paws, knocking him off and pinning him to the ground. Loki kicked her, grabbing fistfuls of her mane—

Hel twisted her head and snapped her jaw shut on Loki's right arm—biting down hard.

Loki screamed.

Marina moved.

She hefted the fire iron and raced toward the door, then out into the night.

Cold air hit her, and a chaos of thrashing, howling and snarling.

She brought the iron up, pelted toward them, reared back and swung it with all her strength.

She hit Hel across the face.

The *clang* echoed through the woods.

Hel spat out Loki's arm.

Loki sprang up, snatched the iron out of Marina's grasp and hit Hel again.

The iron flashed in the moonlight.

Hel yelped and dodged back, startled.

Loki swung around, hooked his arm around Marina's waist and hurled her back into the house, leaping with her.

The two crashed onto the floor. Loki flipped over and kicked the door shut. It slammed.

"Festning!" Loki shouted.

And then—

The floor lurched. The walls tipped.

Marina's stomach plunged.

Darkness swallowed them.

Roaring wind howled against the shutters.

Marina took fistfuls of the fur rug and buried her face in it, holding on as tight as she could. She felt Loki press up against her back—and he threw an arm across her, bracing her in place.

The whole house tilted one way, then another, and Marina suddenly felt as if it were...spinning.

Then, her gut suspended, and for an instant she and Loki lifted an inch off the floor. She scrabbled for the rug. Festning plummeted toward the ground.

"Easy, easy!" Loki cried.

The walls creaked. Branches slapped the outer walls and scraped the windows.

They slowed down. Marina and Loki fell back onto the floor.

The foundations thudded to the earth.

Silence fell.

And then filled with Marina's panting, and Loki's gasping.

Loki collapsed onto his back, pulling his arm off her, breathing hard. For several seconds, Marina couldn't do anything but try to calm her spinning head. Finally, though, she caught her breath enough to speak.

"What...Was that your brother?" she tried, weakly pushing off the ground to try and sit up. Loki chuckled.

"Ah, yes," he muttered. "My family: the circus."

Marina caught her balance, pulling her left arm to herself, and planting her right hand on the rug...

Her palm met warm liquid.

"What—?" she yelped, jerking her hand up. She quickly rubbed her fingers together, trying to feel...

Her stomach turned over.

"Bestemor, we need some light!" she called, scrambling to sit up all the way. The next moment, every lamp and candle in the house blazed to life. The entryway lit up, and suddenly Marina could see...

Blood. All over her hand and all over her arm. All over the side of her dressing gown.

And Loki. Lying on his back, staring up at the ceiling, his face white, his breathing labored. Three bright red lines stood out on his right cheek.

His right sleeve had been shredded.

And deep, torn, bloody puncture marks marred his skin.

"Oh, she bit you...She bit you," Marina realized, edging toward his left side.

"Yes, I believe so," he sighed, swallowing.

"We've got to...We've got to stop this bleeding," Marina decided. "What..."

"Dearest!" Bestemor called, emerging above the doorway. "Get him up! Bring him into the kitchen! I will show you what to do!"

"Can you stand?" Marina asked him. He closed his eyes. Nodded.

With a deep, swift breath, he sat up, pulling his arm in close to him and then cradling it with his other hand. Hissing through his teeth, he climbed to his feet. Marina followed him, hanging back.

"Support him!" Bestemor barked. "You cannot have him falling and hitting his head!"

Marina jumped up to Loki's left side and grabbed his arm. Together, they shuffled toward the kitchen door. Marina put her shoulder against it and pushed it open, hoping that it didn't lead to the larder...

It didn't.

The kitchen, fully alight, waited for them.

"Here, sit down," Marina pulled out a bench for him. He thudded down onto it, groaning.

Bestemor's face bloomed over the sink.

"Top left hand cupboard, bottom shelf. Little wooden box," she said. Marina tugged the door of it open and found the box. Pulled it down. Flipped the lid.

The bottom of the box was lined with several layers of what looked like very thin, blunt silver needles.

"What are these?" Marina looked to Bestemor.

"They are Seamstresses," Bestemor replied. "Take one out and lay it across the wound. It will slip through and create a single stitch that goes deep down as far as it needs to, to sew all they layers together."

"I see, I see," Marina said quickly, grabbed the box and hurried over to the table. She sat down to the bench next to Loki's right, scooted closer, and dragged a flickering candle over so she could see what she was doing.

"All right, let me look," she urged, holding out her hand. He didn't move.

She looked up at him. He was already gazing back at her, his white brow twisted.

"I'm sure it hurts," she said. "But you have to let me see it."

He swallowed, then slowly lowered both his arms, laying his right one down on the table. Marina winced a little, studying his torn skin. She set her teeth.

"Be right back," she said. She got up, hurried to the cupboard and got a towel, brought it back and eased it underneath his arm. She returned to the sink, rolled up her sleeves and lathered up her hands. She rinsed, then, and dried off, then filled up a bowl of water and tossed some clean rags into it, then came back and set it down. Quickly and carefully, she pulled the strips of soaked, torn sleeve away from the bleeding wounds and pushed them up toward his elbow. He helped tug a little, with the trembling fingers of his other hand. Then, she found the deepest, longest wound, which started up near the inside of his elbow and trailed down to mid forearm. She picked out one of the silver Seamstresses, scooted forward, bent closer and set the tiny thing against the very top edge of the bite.

She let go. The little piece laid there for a moment...

Then bit down into his skin and synched down.

Loki squeezed his eyes shut. Marina glanced up at him. Didn't say anything. Picked up another one. Set it just next to the first one. It bit and synched as well. Loki's breathing unsteadied. And his right thumb twitched. Twitched again. Marina looked down at it. Her brow knitted...

But there was nothing else for it. She only had two hands.

She forced her left elbow to unbend, and she set the side of her hand against his.

His slick, bloody fingers caught hers, and weakly curled around them. Squeezed. Marina bit back a pang—it *hurt*—but she had no right to complain. She gathered herself, and picked up another Seamstress, and set it next to the second. It stitched neatly. Loki's throat made a soft choking noise. She studied his face again—but his eyes stayed shut. Marina picked up another.

"When I was little," she began quietly, in a low, soothing voice. "I used to like climbing trees. My parents and I lived in New York City, but every summer we would take a trip upstate to my grandparents' house, out in the country. I used to climb this huge oak tree in their backyard." She set another Seamstress down, and another. Loki's fingers tightened on hers. She took a tight breath, and kept talking. "One day, when I was up there—I think I was maybe ten years old—I tried to pull myself up on a branch, not knowing it was dead. Two branches broke and I fell, but luckily I landed in a big mulch pile. It was only a few seconds later, after I figured out that I wasn't dead, that I realized my whole face was bleeding." She steadily kept putting Seamstresses down as she talked, until she reached the end of that wound. Carefully, she tilted his arm to the side, to expose a shorter, but much deeper one. She reached for another Seamstress, and kept with her story. "My parents came running out. They'd seen me from the back window of the house. My mom scolded me for climbing the tree, told me I was never allowed to climb another tree again. My dad got down and helped me up, and made sure I could still see out of both eyes. Then he decided that a smaller branch had lashed me across the face and cut me open. So they called the ambulance and I got in. The doctors put butterfly bandages on it and ice, and my dad rode along with me." Marina finished with that bite, and started on the third and last one—a hunk of his flesh that had been torn back. She ignored the fact that the towel beneath their forearms was now drenched in blood. She picked up another Seamstress and set it down on his skin. "When we got to the hospital, they numbed my face, and the doctor started stitching up the cut. He said he had to make very small stitches with a very small needle, so he wouldn't leave much of a scar. It didn't hurt anymore, but it still felt very strange, and I was very scared. My dad sat beside me the entire time and held my hand. And he said, 'Just look at me, Marina. Just look at me. I'm right here. Just concentrate on me, okay? Just concentrate on my voice. Everything's okay. Everything's okay now. You're being so good. So brave. The doctor will fix you up and you'll be good as new. In a few weeks you'll never even see that anything happened.'" Marina set the last Seamstress down, and it sank its teeth in. Marina reached over and pulled the wooden water bowl closer, found one of the rags in it, squeezed it out, and started wiping the delicate skin all around the stitches. "'Look over here at me,' he said. 'Stay still for the doctor. It's okay to cry if you want to, sweetheart. You're being so good. It's almost done. Almost done.'"

Loki's breathing had evened out. Marina concentrated on cleaning, dipping the rag into the water, squeezing it out, and wiping again.

"'No shame in tears,' he said. 'You've been to battle—nothing to be embarrassed about. You can tell everybody that the *tree* came away with two broken arms.'"

Loki made a soft, choking snorting sound in response. She glanced up at him.

In the candlelight, his gray eyes were brilliant with tears. Twin drops of crystal water had already trailed down his cheeks. And he gazed at her steadily. As if he had been, constantly, for quite a while.

She met his eyes for a moment. Loki swallowed. But he didn't look away. And a very, very small smile rested on his lips. Marina returned to her work.

She worked her way down his arm, then gingerly pulled her left hand out of his grasp. His fingers eased open, and she bathed his long, graceful hand.

"Bestemor," Marina spoke up. "Bandages?"

"Same cupboard, dear," came the answer. Marina carefully got up, hurried to that cupboard, dug through it, and found a spool of wide, white bandage. She brought it back and sat down.

"Lift up your arm a little, please," she said. Loki did. She managed to pinch the end of the bandage with her bad hand—enough to start the wrap going up near his elbow. Then, slowly, she wrapped and wrapped his arm.

"Is it too tight?" she asked.

"No," he answered, his voice watery. "It's fine. Thank you."

She looked up again. He still watched her. She turned back to the wrapping.

"So..." she murmured. "Your magic can't do anything about this? Make it heal faster?"

"Nothing...can heal family wounds," he replied. "Nothing but time. I'm told."

She stopped. Lifted her eyes to his. He gulped, and another tear tumbled down. He took a breath.

"I'm sorry I shouted at you," he murmured.

Marina said nothing—but she nodded slowly.

They gazed a moment longer, but neither said anything. And the soft crackle of the stove fire filled the quiet as Marina finished, and tied off his bandage.

CHAPTER SIXTEEN

MARINA GAZED INTO THE whispering flames, blinking slowly as its warmth washed over her, soaked into her. She sat in front of the hearth on the rug, cross-legged, wrapped in a fleece blanket. To her left, his head toward the mantel, Loki had stretched his lean length across the floor, facing the ceiling. Black furs draped over him up to his shoulders, and his head rested on a pillow from one of the chairs. He stared at the ceiling of the library, but his grey eyes had unfocused. A line tensed the skin between his eyebrows. He hadn't stirred since she had covered him up.

Marina watched him. She couldn't imagine what time it was—the chaos of the night had disoriented her—but even if dawn was nearing, she had a feeling they wouldn't be traveling anywhere. Loki's face hadn't regained any color, and his hair had darkened even further, if that were possible. Absently, Marina glanced around the little room.

One of the armchair's legs had broken off when the house had hurtled through the forest—the chair had fallen on its side, off to her right. A good number of the books had also burst from their places on the shelves, and now lay like strewn leaves, their pages sprawled open. She drew in a deep breath, but her ribs tightened, and she winced. Looked back at Loki.

The fire spat out a shower of sparks—the crack shocked through the room. Loki didn't blink. Marina shifted, wrapped her blanket tighter around herself, and tilted her head to the side, studying the way the red embers deep inside the fire pulsed like a heartbeat. Her lips parted. And, very quietly, she spoke the words that surfaced in her mind.

"*Silent is my garment when I tread the earth,*" she murmured.
Or dwell in the towns or stir the waters.
Sometimes my trappings lift me up over
The habitations of heroes, and this high air,
And the might of the welkin bears me afar
Above mankind. Then my adornments
Resound in song and sing aloud
With clear melody—when I do not rest
On land or water, a moving spirit."

She felt him turn his head and look at her. Cautiously, she met his bright eyes. His brow furrowed further, and he swallowed.

"I've heard this one," he said softly, his voice hoarse. "Erm...It's some sort of waterfowl."

The edge of Marina's mouth quirked up, but she didn't answer. Loki closed his eyes, heaved a quick sigh, then nodded once.

"I remember. It's a swan."

Marina allowed her smile to show, just a little. She tucked her blankets closer to her neck and turned back to the fire, her thoughts drifting off.

"*I speak through my mouth with many voices,*" Loki said into the silence, his voice low and deliberate. Marina straightened, then frowned at him. He attended to the ceiling again, and went on.

"*Skillfully I sing with many beautiful notes*
Loud and strong, with all kinds of tunes
I sing as I must, unhampered, unhindered,
I am the nighttime, songster of old
I bring joy to the folk who dwell in the towns
When I sing out with my sweet tones
They sit at home, silent. Tell me my name
Who brightly imitates the bards of the kings

And loudly foretells many welcome tidings."

"Wait, what was that first part?" Marina asked, scooting a little closer to him. "I am...the nighttime. Songster of old..."

Loki gave her a look out of the corner of his eye, almost smiling as well.

"And it's a pleasant sound," she mused. "With *different* tunes—so it's not an owl." She studied his profile in the flamelight, and took a guess. "A nightingale."

He took a deeper breath, shut his eyes, and smirked.

"Your turn."

Marina's mouth opened—and she paused. Snorted lightly, suppressing a grin until it disappeared, adjusted her blankets, and strained her memory.

"All right, um...I...*I saw a tree with bright branches
Stand high in a grove. The tree was happy,
The growing wood. Water and earth
Fed it well, till wise with time,
It met with a change: it was deeply hurt
Dumb with bonds, covered with wounds,
But adorned in front with dark ornaments
Now it clears the way for a treacherous foe
Through the might of its head. By storm they plunder
The hoard together."*

"That's a battering ram," Loki said, almost before she had finished. Marina bit her lip, an odd warmth traveling through her.

"Very good," she muttered.

"My turn," Loki decided, eyes still closed. And even as she watched, a tinge of auburn flushed through his black curls. Marina marveled as quiet surprise swelled in her chest, but she didn't say anything, and hardly breathed as she waited, catching every move on his face.

"All right. Ahem..." he lightly cleared his throat.

"*Me the wet ground, exceeding cold,*

First brought forth from within itself.
Neither am I wrought of woolen fleece
Nor of hairs, with skill; I know it in my mind.
I have no winding wefts nor any warp in me;
Nor with strong rods does the thread resound for me,
Nor the whirring shuttle move across me,
Nor the weaver's rods anywhere smite me.
Worms do not weave me with fatal wiles
Which fairly adorn the fine yellow web
Yet nevertheless, the wide world o'er
One will call me a joyful garment for heroes." He opened his eyes partway, tilted his head just a little, and gave her a weary, but halfway-sly, glance.

"*Say now truly, you cunning sage*
Learned in language, what this garment may be."

"Ha," Marina ducked her head away again. "Um...All right, so it's a piece of clothing, but not made of anything that clothes are made of."

"I don't know what trick you're trying—I'm not giving you any hints," Loki sighed.

"I don't need hints," Marina lifted her chin.

"Mhm. Of course," Loki grunted.

"I don't," Marina answered. She reached up and pushed her hair out of her face. "It's a piece of clothing that only heroes wear. And you become a hero by fighting and winning. So...men who fight wear armor. But armor is in pieces. It's not one thing, like..." Her mind lit up. "Like chain mail."

"Brilliant," Loki said flatly. "Though I don't know why you're allowed to do so much talking."

"I'm allowed," she countered. "I started the game."

"So you devise the rules?"

"Yes."

"Fine."

"Fine," she moved even closer to him, leaning in. "My turn."

"Oh, you have another one?" he raised his eyebrows.

"I do."

"Let's have it, then."

Marina let the blanket fall off her shoulders as she straightened up again.

"My head is forged with the hammer
Hurt with sharp tools, smoothed by files
I take in my mouth what is set before me
When girded with rings I am forced to strike,
Hard against hard, pierced from behind.
Must draw forth what protects at midnight
The heart's delight of my own lord.
Sometimes I turn backwards my beak
When, protector of treasure, my lord wishes
To hold the leavings of those had driven
From life by battle-craft, for his own desire."

"The rings give it away," Loki whispered. "And treasure. It's a key."

"These are too easy for you," Marina sighed, shaking her head.

"All right, I'll give *you* an easy one," Loki grimaced, shifting under his covers until he lay partway on his left side, facing her. His eyes opened, completely colorless and silvery now, the auburn vanishing from his hair as it blackened to raven.

"I was alive but said nothing, even so I die," he said, his brow knotted.

Back I came before I was. Everyone plunders me,
Keeps me confined, and shears my head
Bites my bare body, breaks my arms
No man I bite, unless he bites me;
Many there are who do bite me."

Marina went cold down to her bones and stared back at him. She swallowed hard, her eyebrows drawing together.

Then, his lips weakly curved, and his aspect softened.

"Come now, Twig," he murmured. "It's an onion. Nothing to be frightened about."

She gulped again, and his ghostly mirth faded.

"Lady Marina."

Marina twitched, and blinked the water from her eyes. She turned around, and saw Bestemor bloom into being next to the kitchen door.

"Yes?" Marina managed through her tense throat.

"There is a potion in the kitchen cupboard, in a brown bottle," Bestemor creaked, smiling. "It will ease his pain, and help him to sleep."

"Oh. Oh, all right," Marina nodded, gingerly extracting herself from the blanket and getting to her feet. She padded across the thick rugs, pushed through the witchy door, and peered through the dim kitchen toward the cabinets. She rifled through a few of them before she found a tall brown bottle in a far corner. She pulled it out and bit the cork, then pulled it out with a *pop*. She set the cork down on the mantel.

"How much do I give him?" she called into the air. Bestemor obligingly appeared in a cabinet door.

"After what has happened to him, he may drink all of it if he wishes," Bestemor chuckled. "It cannot do him any harm."

Marina nodded, and Bestemor melted away. Making sure she held the bottle securely, Marina turned and left the kitchen, and went back into the library.

"This is for you," she said. Loki glanced at the bottle, then partially sat up, pulling his good arm from beneath the blankets and holding out his hand. Marina knelt back down on her blanket and gave it to him.

"Thank you," he muttered, and took three generous gulps. He lowered the bottle, swallowed thickly and licked his lips, making a slight wince.

"Always has a sour aftertaste," he remarked, setting it on the floor. "I suppose it should, considering it's made of batwing and fish scales."

Marina frowned sharply. Loki caught her eye, then snorted and smirked a little.

"Do you always believe everything people tell you?" He shifted, and lay gingerly back down on his pillow.

"Yes," Marina answered, lifting her chin. "Until someone gives me reason not to."

"You know, Twig..." Loki sighed, gazing at her softly. "I haven't told you a lie yet."

Marina lifted an eyebrow.

"Not even about batwing and fish scales?"

He smirked.

"I wish."

Marina's mouth tightened, and she glanced down at her hands in her lap.

"Would you like me to stay here with you?"

"And what, if I may be so bold, do you plan to do if the hounds of Hel come barging through the door?" Loki asked flatly. Marina bit the inside of her lip, nodded once, and stood up.

"All right," she said. "Goodnight, then." She turned and started toward the stairs.

"Marina."

She stopped, and glanced over her shoulder to see Loki had almost sat up again, his eyes bright. His brow tightened.

"That isn't...quite what I meant."

She said nothing. Just watched him. He swallowed, and turned his head.

"But...I'm sure you'd be much more comfortable in a bed." He looked briefly at her. "Goodnight."

She studied him for another moment, then found herself smiling just a little.

"Goodnight, Loki." And she climbed the stairs up toward her bedroom.

The soft hum of a crackling fire lulled Marina awake. She took a deep breath and slowly blinked her eyes open to find her chamber filled with morning light. She groaned and stretched, shifting under her covers and realizing she had not moved since she had put on a new nightgown, crawled beneath the burying comforter and lost consciousness deep last night.

Slowly she sat up, pulling her left arm in, and running her other hand through her hair. Carefully, she slipped out of bed and walked across the rug toward the frosted window. She pushed the curtain further aside and squeakily rubbed her hand against the frost that coated the pane. The chill bit her fingertips. In a moment, she could see out into a pine forest, draped in snow, and sparkling with edges of gold. It had to be close to midmorning.

"Bestemor?" she called, still peering out into the still, wintry wood.

A *creak* sounded from the hearth.

"Yes, Lady Marina?"

"What is Loki doing this morning?"

"He is sleeping," Bestemor replied. "He fell asleep soon after he drank the draught you gave him, and hasn't wakened since."

"Mm," Marina said quietly. "I'd imagine we're not traveling today."

"I should hope not!" Bestemor cried. "Not after what happened to all of us!"

Marina turned around, and regarded Bestemor with furrowed brow.

"I'm sorry—I didn't ask about *you* last night," she said. "Are you all right?"

Bestemor scrunched her mouth, then twisted it sideways.

"A bit splintered, I think, but still sound," she finally decided. "Nothing that hasn't happened before!"

Marina only nodded, then started toward the wardrobe.

"I think I'll take a bath, then," she said.

"All right, very good, dear," Bestemor said. "I'll see if there some cold things in the larder you can have to break your fast." And with that, she melted away and was gone.

CHAPTER Seventeen

MARINA, MUCH REFRESHED, wearing a deep red, fleecy gown, trousers and boots, her hair braided back, crept down the stairs, listening. However, no sound issued from the sitting room except the drowsy sputter of the fire. She reached the bottom of the steps and eased around to look...

The blankets lay folded on the seat of one of the armchairs. She stood up straight, listening...

A slight clatter beyond the witchy door. She turned and pushed slowly through...

Loki stood by the stove, stirring a steaming pot. He held his right arm bent close to him, and worked with his left, frowning into the cloud that rose up from the boiling. Marina hesitated there, her hand on the door. He looked pale, his hair still very dark, with dark circles under his eyes.

"You're standing up," she remarked. He glanced over at her. For a moment, his eyes flashed a deep green, before returning to gray.

"Only just." The edge of his mouth quirked up as he returned to stirring. The spoon clacked against the metal edges of the pot. Marina took a deep breath, and frowned.

"What is that?" she wondered, stepping in and letting the door shut behind her. "It smells like...gunpowder." She ventured closer, trying to see in. "It isn't...breakfast?"

He snorted tiredly, that crooked smile returning for just a moment.

"Only if you'd like to be poisoned. Or turned invisible—I'm not sure which it would do to you at the moment."

Just then, Marina noticed a different sound accompanying the clank of the spoon and the pan: a tiny jingling, down at the bottom. She lifted her attention, and studied Loki's pale features, an idea sparking in the back of her mind.

"What is it?" she whispered.

"Be a love and get in the left hand cupboard for me," he asked instead, nodding toward it. "Get the two blue bottles and the one yellow one, and bring them here."

Marina frowned again, but maneuvered around the table and went to the cupboard. She opened it, and found several colorful bottles up high, filled with various cloudy mixtures.

"Two blue and one yellow?" she asked.

"Mhm," he said absently. Biting her lip, she reached up with her right hand and plucked each one down, then tucked two of them against her chest with her bad arm, and picked up the last one and carried them over.

"You can set the two blue ones on the table," Loki instructed. "Let me have that yellow one." He held out his right hand. Marina awkwardly bent and set the blue ones down with a clatter, then set the yellow one in his palm.

"Are you sure...?" she winced. He gripped the cork with his left-hand fingers.

"Yes, I—*ah!*" he tugged, and suddenly hissed through his teeth—and almost dropped the bottle. Marina lunged and snatched it, catching his fingers in hers as well.

"Aha...Well...Hm," Loki said shakily, letting her have the bottle. He pulled his hurt arm against his chest, he clenched his jaw and he squeezed his eyes shut. The remaining color washed out of his face.

"Do you need to sit down?" Marina asked, stepping closer to him.

"That...might be a good idea," he murmured. Marina quickly set the bottle down on the table, then shoved the bench over behind him. It scraped loudly against the floor. Carefully, Loki sat down, letting out a tight sigh. Marina waited, watching him. For several moments, he did nothing but breathe—she counted as his shoulders tensely rose and fell.

"Should I go that draught for you?" Marina asked quietly. "Is it by the fireplace?"

"No, I drank it all last night," Loki muttered.

"Oh." Marina shifted, her brow knotting. "What can I do?"

His head came up, and he looked at her. His eyebrows drew together, and a brilliant blue colored his eyes—and remained. He swallowed.

"Can you help me finish this?" he asked quietly.

"Is it more draught?"

"No," he shook his head. "It's…I'm fixing your Wishstones."

Marina blinked.

"What do you mean?"

"You've spent them and they've stopped working, yes?"

"Yes," Marina nodded. "Hel said they each only work once."

He smiled—a little tiredly, but that soft blue shone in his eyes.

"Well, luckily for you, I'm something of a magician." He shifted in his seat, tensed, then released a low breath. "Open the yellow bottle."

Marina picked it up, then lifted it to her mouth to bite off the cork—

"No-no-no!" Loki's left hand darted out and grabbed her wrist. She jerked, narrowly catching the bottle—her eyes flew to his.

"*What?*"

"On no account should you put that near your mouth," he gasped. "You'd be dead before you could swallow."

Marina's face flushed and her heart started to hammer—but she ironed out her expression and lifted her chin.

"Well then, how..." She cleared her throat and regathered herself. "How am I supposed to open it?"

"Here," he let go of her and held out his hand. "I'll hold the bottle and you pull out the cork."

She handed it to him. He gripped it, and she dug her fingernails into the cork. With a swift *pop*, the cork came loose. An acrid scent, like burnt hair, rose into the air.

"Now," Loki sighed. "Pour all of it into the pot—keep it low so it doesn't splash. It will eat your skin."

Marina held the bottle carefully, the hot steam flowing up around her hand, and lowered it as far as the heat would allow. She tipped the bottle, and let the strange, greenish liquid pour out into the mixture, hissing and gargling when it hit, turning the potion an angry red color

"What is it?" Marina glanced at him.

"Dragon spit," he answered.

"Hm," Marina wrinkled her nose. "Remind me never to get bitten."

"That would be ideal," Loki remarked. "Now, pour half of this blue bottle in." He lifted it to her. She put the empty yellow bottle on the table and took the blue bottle from him. She gave him a sideways look.

"Open it however you like," Loki shrugged one shoulder. "It's extract of dandelion."

Hiding her own smile, Marina bit off the cork, and poured half of the clear liquid in, just as he had instructed. It instantly calmed the red color, turning it to a placid gold.

"All right," she sighed, setting that bottle down too and looking to him.

"Stir it, and wait a few minutes," Loki said. She picked up the handle of the wooden spoon and did so, watching the liquid inside froth and foam, listening to the jingle of the stones on the bottom...

"Now pour just a fourth of this last one in," Loki said. Marina put down her spoon, took up the bottle and waited. Loki looked at the bottle, frowned, and canted his head.

"It's aconite, but it should be fine." He gravely met her eyes. "Unless...you're a werewolf."

"Ha. You've found out my secret," Marina tossed her head and looked away. Loki almost chuckled.

"Well—that changes things, madam."

She bit back a laugh, turned so he wouldn't see, then bit off the cork and poured exactly a fourth of that mixture in. The potion transformed to a pleasing, creamy yellow. Silence fell—and all at once it felt strange. She lifted her head to find him studying her.

"What?" she asked.

"Why do you do that?" he asked, that earnest blue back again.

"Do what?" She uneasily reached for the spoon again.

"Hide your face," he said, his voice quiet. "When what you really want to do is laugh."

Pain slid down Marina's throat, and she turned back to the potion. She lifted her left shoulder, and it remained there, tense.

"It's better not to," she whispered. "Allowing yourself to be...silly and happy...is a risk. Too much of a risk." She fell quiet, waiting for him to comment...

But he didn't. She could just feel him listening. She pulled her left arm tight to herself, and released the words into the quiet.

"The only one who's made me feel close to that is Bird."

She heard Loki take a breath, and slowly let it out.

"Well..." he ventured. "He made everyone love him." Loki slowly rose to his feet, neared the pot across from her and leaned down into the steam. He closed his eyes.

"*Lysta,*" he hissed.

The pot shook.

The water suddenly shrank and dissolved and disappeared...

Leaving two brilliantly-colored stones shining on the clean bottom of the pot.

Loki opened his eyes and looked at Marina.

"My gift is certainly not to make everyone love me," he said. "But it *is* my gift to make everyone laugh." He lifted an eyebrow. "Whether she wants to or not."

Marina stared back at him, mouth tight.

"Now!" Loki briskly straightened up. "I feel like getting drunk. Want to join me?"

Marina snorted, and clapped a hand over her mouth.

His eyes sparked with vibrant green, and he leaned toward her, grinning.

"I *will* win, Twig," he challenged. "Count upon it."

She instantly sobered her face, lowered her hand and lifted her chin.

"No, you won't," she retorted. "And you're not getting drunk, either."

"Tosh," he waved her off. "You're no fun."

"You already knew that."

"We...have to do something about that," he grunted, sitting back down.

"You're not fit to do anything," she reminded him. "Except to go back out there and lie down."

"I have to make more draught..."

"I can do that. Bestemor can help me. Now go."

Loki gave her a wry, indignant look, rose to his feet, and headed toward the door.

But halfway there, he slowed, reached out and put his hand to the table, and his shoulders sagged.

Marina immediately went to him, her knee knocking against the bench, and took hold of his arm.

"Are you all right?"

"I'm fine," he assured her faintly, looking paler than ever. "Just give me a moment."

Marina waited, her hand gripping his upper arm, until he took a bracing breath, straightened, and nodded slightly.

"I can make it across the hallway, I think," he said. "I'll be fine until there's more of that draught."

"Are you sure?" Marina pressed.

Loki glanced down at her, smiling crookedly.

"Admit it, Twig," he said quietly. "You're just a little fond of me."

Marina lifted her head.

"No," she said. "I don't like you at all."

Loki winked at her, touched the back of her hand lightly with the fingertips of his wounded hand, then moved carefully through the door and out of the kitchen. Marina stayed just where she was, listening. But no violent sounds of falling or tripping greeted her, and so she finally relaxed her shoulders, and turned to face the cabinet.

"Bestemor? I need your help, please."

They stayed put for three more days. On the night of the first day, it began to snow, and poured so steadily that soon it had covered the lower windows of the house. Loki spent most of his time lying before the fire, sleeping or drowsily reading books. Marina straightened the clutter that had been caused by their sudden flight, replacing all the fallen books onto their shelves, putting the furniture in order, although some had been badly broken, and wiping the dried blood off the doorframes and the floor. The two of them ate cold things from the larder, or Marina occasionally made a nail soup of her own. Loki always ate everything she brought him, without a single complaint.

In the evenings, they challenged each other with riddles, and told stories. Marina recited several of Grimm's fairytales to him, and other folk tales that she knew. Loki enjoyed Rapunzel and Beauty and the Beast, but decided his favorite was The Peasant's Clever Daughter. In turn, Loki entertained her with fantastic tales of elves, dwarves, sprites and spells unlike any she had ever heard. As he spoke, gesturing precisely and delicately with his good hand, the firelight caught in his hair like embers, turning his locks chestnut and amber, and his eyes gleamed with a bright green—like a spring morning. The flow and ebb of his words transported Marina to deep and ancient lands—she could smell the must of the bogland, feel the cold wind gust across the moors; hear the haunting, wild songs of the elves as they perched around the flickering fires in the woods, plucking lute strings and eating grapes, nuts and flower petals...

Finally, on the third day, Marina got dressed and came downstairs to find Loki wearing his travel clothes, standing near the door.

"Are we leaving?" she asked, hesitating. He nodded, then gestured toward the door.

"The snow's stopped. You go and eat breakfast—I'm going to dig us out." He grasped the latch, tugged the door open, to reveal a solid wall of snow.

He sighed briefly, then brought his hands up, rubbed them together and breathed into them. He then flicked his fingers, and blue sparks darted out, and bit into the snow. As Marina watched, the balls of lights pushed into the ice, creating holes that widened every second. Loki glanced back at her.

"This will take a moment," he reminded her. "But once I'm finished, we'll need to be off."

She nodded, went into the larder, and found some bread and cheese for herself.

After she had eaten, she dressed for the cold, and found the doorway clear—the snow formed a kind of steep ramp up and out of the house. She started to step through—

"Wait, wait," Loki called from above, then skidded down the short hill and onto to the threshold. He brushed snow out of his hair, then pulled off his glove. "Here. We'll lose you otherwise." He snapped his fingers, and tapped her forehead.

Instantly, she felt herself lighten, her feet barely dusting the rug.

"Come on," Loki urged, turned and hopped up the ramp. Marina followed, skating on the top of the snow and grinning stupidly—until she saw Loki watching her, and she buried her smile.

She lifted her face and took deep breaths of the bright, frosty air, enjoying the feel of the sun flashing through the white treetops—she felt like she hadn't seen it in ages. Absently, she noticed the sounds of Loki's hands striking together as he folded up the house, and the next moment, when she turned, she found the house vanished, as if it had never been there. Loki flicked his wrist and his walking stick leaped into being, slapping into his palm. He pulled his gloves back on, then nodded to her.

"Shall we?"

Two more days, they hiked up the ever-steepening, snow-locked hill, weaving between massive, shrouded boulders, picking across ice-choked streams, avoiding the piles of huge branches that had broken beneath the massive weight of the sudden winter. They kept quiet as they traveled, the deathly stillness waiting like a listening ear all around them, threatening to carry their voices far through the valleys, and either return with an avalanche, or an enemy.

In the evenings, they maintained their ritual of riddling and tale-telling, eating their meals by the fireside. Bestemor often lingered in the wall as well, smiling to herself, quietly humming, and sometimes inserting a comment that would startle both Marina and Loki, especially if they had been deeply listening to each other.

The first day of hiking, Loki strode more slowly than he had before, and Marina kept a wary eye upon him, walking close behind him in case she needed to catch his arm. The next two days, however, he improved, and much of his color returned. Marina became quite glad of it, for she soon had no energy to expend on looking after him—the air was getting very thin.

And then, suddenly, they reached it.

"Wait..." Marina gasped, stopping next to a large outcropping of snow-piled rocks, which Loki had passed.

"What?" he asked softly, coming back to her, his feet almost soundless. Marina narrowed her eyes against the glare of the sun on the snow, and bit her lip. She tilted her head, trying to remember...

And a deep *jerk* tugged on the center of her forehead.

"Oh!" she slapped a hand to her head as she took three involuntary steps forward. Loki grabbed her right arm.

"What was that?" he demanded.

"I..." She swallowed, staring straight at the rocks. "I think it's here."

"What? It's...It's solid rock," Loki said, assessing it.

That *jerk* came again, making Marina lunge clumsily forward. Loki almost slipped in an effort to keep hold of her.

"I...I don't know why I keep..." Marina tried, her pulse skyrocketing.

"It's a spell..." Loki breathed—

And the next second, Marina was yanked by a completely invisible force out of Loki's grasp and *straight* at the rock—

And through it.

A painful throb of terror banged through her heart—

And she stumbled two steps onto a smooth, stone floor.

She clenched her fingers around her coat collar, fighting to regain her sense of balance, making her eyes focus...

The darkness shrank back. Ahead of her, in what looked to be a small, rough-hewn round room, a small wooden chest lay on the floor. Open.

And light poured from it.

Memories flashed back to her. Memories of that vision that had swelled through her mind. The golden gem deep in the mountain...

She started forward, her footsteps ringing in the small stone enclosure. Battling to catch her breath, keep her head from spinning, she carefully knelt down on the cold floor in front of it...

And gazed down at a quarter-sized jewel that shone with all the facets of the summer sun. Heat radiated from its surface, touching her cheeks and nose. The swimming, glittering surface dazzled her eyes—and from deep within it, a soft noise seemed to breathe out...

Almost like voices...

Marina vacillated for a very long time, studying every feature and edge of that gem. She could feel power pulsing out from it, in an ancient language she couldn't understand.

What would happen if she touched it?

She glanced behind her at the black wall through which she'd passed. Loki clearly couldn't follow her. She gritted her teeth.

She had no choice.

She stretched out her hand, breathed a quick prayer, and picked it up.

Chapter Eighteen

WARM.

The stone felt warm in her fingers, even through her glove, and a strange sound seemed to ring through her head when she carefully turned it this way and that. A soft jingling.

Golden light flashed from inside it, reflecting into her eyes. Other than that, it kept its secrets.

Marina slowly stood up, cupping it in her palm. Then, she took a careful breath, and turned and faced the way she had come.

She couldn't see the wall she had obviously come through—darkness hid it. Her stomach sank, and a chill passed over her. What if she couldn't get out?

She started toward it, biting her lip...

The light from the stone glanced up and out, suddenly showing her a solid rock wall.

Her mouth tightened. She put the stone in her bad hand, stretched out her good one, squeezed her eyes shut and *pushed*...

Fingers caught hers.

Jerked her hard.

She tumbled forward—

Blazing sunlight hit her face—she opened her eyes.

"Marina!"

She blinked, trying to refocus—

Loki bent close to her, his hair blazing with locks of gold, his earnest eyes a brilliant green. He let go of her hand and grabbed her hard by the shoulders, rapidly searching her face.

"Are you all right?" he demanded.

"Ha!" she exclaimed, looking around her to find herself on that same snowy path. "Yes. I'm fine."

"I couldn't get through!" Loki panted, his grip on her loosening but his gaze intensifying. "I tried everything I could think of, short of bringing the mountain down—" He stopped himself, brow furrowing. "What did you see?"

"I...I found it," Marina breathed, and made herself uncurl the fingers of her bad hand as far as they would go, to let the sunlight fill the gem. It glittered and winked at him against the dark fabric of her glove.

Loki's attention fixed on it—auburn rippled through his hair, deepening its tone. A penetrating, stricken, solemn blue overtook his eyes, catching the full brightness of the snow.

"What is that?" he whispered. Marina stood up straight.

"You don't know?"

Loki, unblinking, leaned just an inch closer.

"I might have an idea," he murmured. "But I'm not willing to try anything out here." He glanced up and around, his eyes darkening to ocean blue, his hair to dark chestnut. "Come on. We'll find a better place to put Festning."

The rest of the day, they toiled part of the way back down the mountain, toward a thick forest that waited like a black curtain below them. As the light faded, they finally reached a set of towering boulders that loomed like goblins standing in a circle, all surrounded by very old pines. Wasting no time, Loki strode into the center of them, flicked the red sparks onto the snow, and Festning bloomed, leaning its back against one of the snow-draped gray stones. As soon as the knocker spat out, Loki pushed inside, and held the door open for Marina to follow.

She sighed as warmth washed over her, her fingers aching from holding the stone so tightly all day. She'd been so afraid of dropping it into the plunging snow...

The door shut noisily behind her, and Loki whipped off his coat and gloves, raked a hand through his hair, and then held out his hand.

"May I see?"

Marina looked up at him—all grave and pale again—and set the stone in his palm.

He jumped slightly at its touch, all sorts of colors sweeping through his hair before settling again on a deep brown. He then closed his fingers around the gem, turned and swept into the sitting room.

Marina quickly hung up her own winter things and followed him, wrapping her arms around herself and watching him closely. He neared the fireplace, his back to her. She approached his right side, peering at him, to see that he stood with his eyes closed, the gem pressed between both his palms. He pulled his hands up close to his face, his brow knotting. Then, slowly, he knelt on the rug in front of the blazing fire. Without quite knowing why, Marina knelt next to him.

Then, Loki opened his hand, and breathed three times onto the stone. Then, he whispered a single word.

"*Syna.*"

And he tossed the stone into the fire.

Marina gasped—

The fire *cracked,* spitting wildly and leaping up the chimney. It changed hue, deepening to an almost living, liquid, burning gold.

And then, Marina began to see shapes inside the flame.

They rose up, ghost-like at first, but gradually clarifying, taking on color and edges, until at last they stood within the hearth, fire sputtering around their feet, as real as life—only small.

A long, grand hallway, lined with pillars and decorated with hanging banners. A tall, broad-shouldered man with a white beard and long white hair, wearing majestic dress armor, a patch covering one eye, strode down the center of the corridor toward them.

Marina, hardly able to breathe, heard the thud of his footsteps against marble, the jingle of his armor...

It was Odin. It had to be Odin!

A young man—a teenager—darted out from a side corridor and drew up beside Odin's right. It only took an instant for Marina to recognize him.

He wore a flawless, sleeveless white tunic and trousers, tied with a rope belt, his golden hair flowing around his shoulders, his handsome face tilted toward the king. Very young. But still very familiar.

Bird. Bauldr.

She gasped, a painful stabbing sensation traveling all through her chest.

"Father," Bauldr said, trotting to keep up with his long strides. "Why have you put Fljotur in the stable with the old horses going out to pasture?"

"Fljotur is not to be ridden," Odin answered.

"But I need him!" Bauldr protested. "Thor, Loki and I are to go hunting this afternoon, and I wouldn't consider taking another mount."

"Fljotur is not to be ridden," Odin answered, stopping and turning frankly toward his son. "Not until I give the word. Is that understood?"

Bauldr's jaw clenched, but he nodded. And he did not follow his father as the king strode on.

The image blurred, and the next moment, the fire showed them Bauldr once more, pushing into the stable, glancing gingerly around, and then hurrying inside up to a magnificent cream-colored stallion.

"Father wants you for his *own* hunt tomorrow," Bauldr muttered, pulling open the stall and slipping inside. The horse nickered at him, and rubbed his shoulder with his soft nose.

"He doesn't want you to be tired because of me—but you're *my* horse, not his." Bauldr began taking blanket and saddle off the wall and draping them over Fljotur's back. "You're coming with me today, just like I promised, and you and I will give Loki and Thor a run for all their gold."

The images swam together once more, and then solidified...

To reveal Bauldr standing beside an imposing fireplace, his face bruised, his right arm in a sling. And tears in his eyes.

Odin paced back and forth in front of him, his hands clenched behind his back.

"What did I tell you?" Odin bit out. "What were you not to do?"

Bauldr swallowed and did not speak. Odin stopped pacing and faced him.

"Answer me!"

"Ride Fljotur," Bauldr choked.

"I said you shall *not* ride Fljotur!" Odin thundered. "Did you think that I was giving that command for my own amusement?"

Bauldr bit his lip and shook his head, tears brimming.

"I...I didn't know he was injured..."

"Did you not trust me?" Odin shot back. "And do you know so little about your own animal that you cannot tell that he was already lame before you took him out of the stable at break-neck speed? Did you care so little for him?"

Bauldr's tears spilled down his cheeks.

"He was one of the finest stallions ever bred in Asgard, and now we have had to kill him," Odin snapped. "You injured him so badly he would never have been able to stand again. And in the process, you nearly got yourself killed as well." He gestured to Bauldr's cast, while Bauldr hung his head.

"You shall not receive another horse," Odin told him. "And you shall not go riding again. Not until you can learn to care for others more than yourself, and to listen to your father."

Bauldr said nothing, just let his tears drip from his chin.

"Go on, go to bed," Odin sighed. Bauldr stood for just a moment, then turned and left the room.

Marina's throat felt thick. She couldn't speak as the images dissolved...

Replaced by Bauldr once more—but he looked different. He looked almost exactly the way she remembered him the night of the feast. He stood by a window in a large, dark room, gazing out, his arms folded over his chest, his gaze absent and sad.

Odin stepped slowly behind him, approached a small table and poured himself a goblet of mead.

"You caused a stir by bringing that Midgardian woman to the feast," Odin remarked. "You really ought to break that habit, Bird—I know that Lady Nanna is deeply hurt by it."

Bauldr's expression darkened.

"I have never aimed to harm her."

"Yes, but you are doing so, nonetheless. And you are being inconsiderate to the Midgardian," Odin countered. "Bringing their kind into Asgard, especially those who are not dying of a terrible disease, is cruel. Allowing them to stay is forbidden, and teasing this little girl with our realm, our feasts, the goodness of our life, and then sending her back there to that land of death and darkness is unkind. You must see that."

"At this point in my life, I do nothing without reason, Father," Bauldr murmured.

Odin paused, gazing at him, the moonlight from outside the window illuminating the myriad scars and wrinkles on his wizened face. He stepped up to his son's side, his eye bright, his brow furrowing.

"Bauldr," he said quietly. "I know that you and your mother have been in secret council with each other for many months now. And though I have pressed her, she has sworn she cannot tell me the subject of your deliberations. I can see that something is troubling you a great deal, weighing heavy on your spirit." Odin stepped even nearer. "Could you not trust me enough to tell me what it is?"

Bauldr's gaze sharpened, and filled with sorrow. He sighed shallowly.

"Do you know," he whispered. "I have never ridden a horse again."

Odin blinked. Bauldr slowly lowered his head, and sighed again.

"Goodnight, Father," he said, turned, and left the king standing there, staring into his goblet, his expression broken.

The image faded. The flames retreated and dimmed. The timbers sparked—snapped—

And the golden stone spat out onto the hearth rug, and lay there silent, and glimmering.

Marina pressed her quivering fingers to her mouth, trying to make herself breathe again...

She glanced over at Loki.

His hair had turned black as the feathers of a raven. His eyes bright as starlight; grey as a winter morning.

And as he stared into the fire, where the image of Bauldr and Odin had just stood...

Twin tears rolled down his cheeks.

Marina's lip parted, but she couldn't summon any words. She could only shift slightly toward him, wanting to reach out, to touch him...

His brow twisted, his nose snarled, and he swallowed, bowing his head. Abruptly, he climbed to his feet, and stood still for a moment.

Then, without saying anything, he turned and went into the kitchen, shutting the door behind him.

Marina lay on her back, tucked deep in her blankets and comforter, staring at the ceiling. The muttering fire in her hearth burnt low, casting strange shadows across the walls and curtains and carvings.

Her heart churned and her thoughts spun around and around, but she couldn't make sense of most of it. That stone had clearly been showing them some of Bauldr's memories—but why? Why those? They didn't seem to have anything to do with bringing him back to life. The only aspect they had in common was Odin, and a deep familial disappointment she could still feel in her bones. The sight of Bauldr, right there in front of her—but completely untouchable—burned her almost as badly as putting her hand into the flames would have.

But...

Loki.

Even right now, recalling the image of his tears filled her with a cold, painful ache—and a strange, pulling desire to smash something, or *fix* something, or just...

She thrashed, and rolled over onto her right side, biting the side of her cheek.

None of this made sense. She had been awake for hours fighting with it, and it only became more muddled each time she turned it over. Her head pounded with the effort—worse than when she had stayed up all night studying for her final exams...

She winced, the pain thudding through her skull, and she reached up and rubbed the middle of her forehead—

FLASH.

Bright, crystal-clear images covered her vision.

She suddenly seemed to swoop on the wings of a crow down a narrow mountain path—one that looked familiar...

Down, down, reeling and zagging, to the bank of a wide, frothy river. She then turned and raced downstream, skimming the icy surface, following its bends and twists and traveling miles in an instant, until a violent stretch of rapids—

And her vision swerved to the left, and dove down a narrow path through thick woods, to a little glen where a pile of giant stones stood...

A small opening waited, and she plunged inside, was hit by a striking, silvery glow...

Marina jerked, threw her covers off and leaped to her feet before she knew what she was doing.

She stood there on the rug, cold sweat breaking out all over her, her left arm pulled tight to her chest, her eyes wide as she stared at the placid flames sputtering in the fireplace in her room.

But the memory of what she had just seen remained impossibly vivid. She knew she would be able to walk out the door this minute, and find that very spot, without any doubt.

Panting, she pressed her right hand to her forehead. No wonder she hadn't been able to make sense of what she and Loki had seen—there wasn't any use trying.

The golden stone was only the first piece of the puzzle.

Chapter Nineteen

"LOKI?" MARINA, DRESSED, with her hair braided, hesitated on the threshold of the sitting room. Loki, who sat in the unbroken armchair to the left, a cup of tea in his hands, looked up at her through the steam. Hair dark, eyes slate-grey. He frowned as he caught her expression.

"What?"

"What is it that we found?" she asked carefully. "What did we see?"

Loki sighed, lowering the cup and saucer into his lap. He reached up and rubbed his eyes.

"I've been thinking about it all night," he admitted, lowering his hand. "From what I can tell, it's some kind of Soul-Spark or Soul-Splinter...or even a Soul-Anchor. Maybe a combination of all three of them."

"What are those?" Marina wondered, coming closer to him.

"A Soul-Spark is what's needed to wake a person up out of a sleeping spell—one that's deep as death," he explained. "A Soul-Splinter is an actual piece of your spirit that you copy and put into an object you create, to preserve its memories. Like a library, or a memorial. A Soul-Anchor latches your spirit to this world, and acts as a long rope, a lifeline if you will, to keep the entire soul from traveling all the way into Hel or Valhalla."

"Why did it only show us those two memories?" Marina asked. Loki's mouth tightened and he shook his head, his gaze wandering into the distance. Then, he dipped his head, and fingered the handle of his teacup.

Marina steeled herself, took a deep breath and another step forward.

"I know where another one is."

Loki's head came up. Blue rippled through his hair.

"Another one what?"

"Another one of the stones," she said. "I had a kind of...dream...last night. Just like the first time. And this one took me down the mountain, down a river, into a forest and then to a clearing with a stand of rocks—and there's a silver stone inside."

Loki stared at her—and in that moment, a kaleidoscope of brown, gold, green and sapphire swirled through his eyes. Then, in an instant, they settled upon a steely blue, and he got to his feet.

"We've no time to waste," he announced. "Get your snow clothes—we've got to go."

With Festning folded up and dissolved, leaving not even a footprint upon the snow where it had stood all night, Marina and Loki—lifted by the snowshoe spell—left the encircling rocks and started further down the mountain. Marina led the way, images from her vision rising up constantly in her mind.

Soon, she came across a narrow descending track, something like a deer trail, and together they followed it, the bright, sharp sunlight filling the spaces between the trees.

"It's a relief to be going down," Loki commented from behind her, swinging his walking stick. "Maybe I'll be able to breathe again soon."

"You're having trouble, too?" Marina glanced back at him.

"What, couldn't you tell from my blue nose?" he asked indignantly.

"Ha. Couldn't see past my own blue nose," Marina muttered, then tossed her head a little and offered a crooked smile. "I thought you'd be made of tougher stuff."

"Oh, never underestimate us Jotuns," Loki advised. "We're perfectly prepared to be weak at the most inopportune moments."

Marina glanced back at him again, catching the unmistakable thread of pain woven through his casual tone. He didn't look at her, just carefully maneuvered around a thick, snow-laden shrubbery. Marina slowed her pace, and lingered back to walk beside him, hesitating as she formed her question.

"Do you remember it?" she finally asked. "What happened to Bird's horse?"

"I do," Loki nodded. "He rode out to meet us on the green—Thor and me. And then Fljotur's leg just..." Loki's expression shrugged, and he shook his head. "It folded like paper. Bird flew through the air and landed so hard we all thought he'd broken his neck. And Fljotur just flailed and screamed to wake the dead."

"That's terrible," Marina whispered.

"It was," Loki said quietly. "None of us had ever been so angry. Or so..." He trailed off, and swallowed.

Marina watched him as they walked, studying his profile.

"What did you do?"

"I...Well, I threw myself off my horse," Loki said, ducking beneath a low branch. "And I ran to where he'd fallen. I could hear Thor right behind me. The palace guard had already come out, but they hadn't reached him yet. I got down beside him, and he looked..." Loki suddenly stopped.

Marina waited. But Loki didn't go on. She frowned.

"What did he look like?"

Loki glanced over and met her eyes—and his clouded to gray.

"Never mind," he murmured, turning to face the path ahead. "Suffice to say...one of my least favorite moments of my life. Up...until then."

Marina fell silent, turning that over and over, listening to the silence that fell in the wake of his words.

As midday approached, Marina began to sense a low sound rising through the trees—a deep rush, one that she could feel in the center of her chest.

Water.

They were coming upon the river. She and Loki followed the deer track down through the trees, the terrain becoming ever rockier.

"Isn't it odd," Marina noted. "That we hardly ever see any animals?"

"They were probably killed by the frost," Loki answered—and pain needled straight through Marina's heart. She didn't say anything for the next two hours.

Finally, they emerged from the line of tall pines, and found themselves upon the banks of a wide, mighty, gushing river—white foam frothing at its edges, shards of ice breaking loose and tumbling downstream, along with branches and dead leaves. It roared like a faraway battle. Loki turned to her.

"You said we have to head downriver?"

Marina regarded him—his tall, lean black form cut out against the sky, his skin still white as the snow, his eyes a pale blue, his black hair caught by the open breezes. She nodded.

"All right, then," he said, and pulled off his gloves. He waved a hand, and his walking stick disappeared. He then clapped his hands three times, then squeezed them to fists. For a moment, he just stood, his eyes closed. Then, he cupped his palms together, as if keeping a moth captive. He opened a slight gap between them, and breathed inside. Then, he turned and faced Marina.

Startled, she saw his hair flush to auburn, his eyes glitter with emerald.

"What?" she asked.

"Hold out your hand," he instructed. Marina, transfixed by the sudden change in his looks, did as he asked.

The next moment, a soft weight rested in her palm.

She blinked, stared...

A little Norse longboat, the length of her hand, sat there. It had no mast or sail, but its prow curved like a dragon's head and spat out a long tongue. The back of it also curled with a wicked tail, and circular shields had been hung upon its sides. Perfect, miniscule detail—a museum replica. Better than that. The *real thing*, at a thousandth of the size.

"Oh...!" Marina gasped, captivated.

"Now, bring it up to your mouth," Loki instructed, stepping close to her. "And say *staekka*."

She lifted her attention, meeting his gaze—to find it filled with lively green.

A green she almost remembered seeing before.

Keeping her eyes upon his, she lifted the little boat toward her lips.

"*Staekka*."

The tiny boat creaked.

Marina jumped.

"Now, come here. Quickly," Loki advised, touching her shoulder. He led her over to the edge of the river, and bent down. "Set it in the water."

Even as Marina squatted down beside him, the boat began to swell in her grasp, lengthening and becoming heavier and heavier...

Quickly as she could, trying not to capsize it, she set it down in the shallows.

And the boat continued to grow.

It stretched, its neck straining, its tail curling, until it was about five feet long.

"Give it a push," Loki said, and Marina shoved on its stern, urging it out of the mud and into the deeper water, just to the edge of the current. And as she rose to her feet, watching, the boat billowed out into a magnificent full-sized longboat, perhaps twenty-feet long from stem to stern. And it turned its fierce prow downstream, and began to leave without them.

"Come," Loki urged, holding his arms out to her.

"What?" she arched an eyebrow.

"Have you learned how to fly when I wasn't looking?"

"No...?"

"Then come here. Unless you'd like to wade."

Marina stood still, feeling her face heat up. He gave her a crooked smile.

"Don't you trust me yet, Twig?" He held out his hands even more insistently, and raised his eyebrows. "I promise not to kiss you."

Her cheeks instantly burned.

Blue glittered through Loki's eyes, and his smile almost faded.

He glanced over his shoulder.

"All right, the boat's leaving," he said, stepping up to her. "Beg your pardon."

And he scooped her up and cradled her.

The next moment, they lifted off the ground. Marina threw her right arm around his neck and pulled her left in close.

They skated just over the surface of the river and easily caught up to the boat. Loki eased them down onto the wooden floor of it, and set Marina down on a bench. She thudded to her seat with a grunt, and grabbed the wooden edge. Loki then hopped over her bench, and several of the others, and made his way to the fore. He patted the dragon's head, then peered past it.

"Dreki will keep us on course," Loki said, looking back over his shoulder at her. "All we have to do is hang on through the rapids."

Marina gasped and swiped at her eyes after an ice-cold wave leaped the side of the boat and lashed across her face. She shivered hard, then gritted her teeth, holding onto the bench as best she could. Loki still stood at the fore, seemingly untroubled, his cape gusting behind him as the boat careened wildly through the foaming currents.

Marina had felt the snowshoe spell break as soon as Loki had picked her up—she sat as heavily as normal inside this boat as it rocked and tipped, the water roaring all around them, spray striking her face and soaking her coat.

Her muscles shook, her left side ached, but she didn't say anything. She knew Loki couldn't do much better than this boat—any sort of flashy magic to protect or hurry them along could still attract Hel and Fenris. And she'd rather contend with a little damp and cold than *them*, any day.

It happened before she could think.

The boat swerved around a bend, the tail struck a rock—

And Marina launched out of her seat.

For half a suspended heartbeat, she hung in the air—

Then slammed down into the water.

Breath drove from her lungs.

Cold slapped her chest and gut.

Light, dark, light, dark all spun around her head, her hair wrapping around her face like a wet rag. She bowled end over end and then spun like a rolling pin, her hands and legs striking slick, round rocks...

Rippling tingles of pain raced all across her skin. And agony grabbed her whole left side in its teeth and wouldn't let go.

And in that swirling tangle, she could almost hear the deafening, rhythmic CRASH-CRASH-CRASH of a truck tumbling down a rocky hill—the windshield shattering and spraying glass at her face—striking her head on the steering wheel—the seatbelt snapping against her neck...

Light faded—the bubbling roar of the water gave way to a sharp buzzing all through her skull. She choked, reflexively sucked in—

Water filled her lungs. Her eyes went wide, but saw nothing.

Terror darted through her chest—

BOOM.

She *felt* it in her bones—a deep, powerful THUD right next to her—

Water gushed out and away from her—sprayed up into the air—

A hand grabbed her left arm—bound like a vise around it—wrenched it—

Her head broke the surface. Blurry light blinded her.

For an instant, she lifted up and out, then slammed onto her back onto something hard and unmoving.

Her body jolted—a gagging spasm took her throat and gut—her muscles clamped.

She thrashed onto her side and *coughed*...

Ice water spewed from her mouth and nose—she pulled in a breath that tore her lungs, then coughed and coughed again, her vision spinning, her head throbbing, her hearing dull. She curled into a ball, only vaguely aware of a heavy form lying mostly on top of her, arms braced to either side...

Her mind spun again, clouding, as screaming pain gnawed dagger-like fangs all up and down her left side. She broke into violent shivering, almost sensing shards of glass dripping from the floor onto her head and shoulders...the seatbelt twisted around her...her left arm crushed to splinters...

"Dad," she rasped, her lips trembling. "Dad. My dad. I have...I have to get to my dad. Get me...Get me out of here. I need...I need to see my dad..."

"Marina?"

She frowned hard, unable to focus, the masculine voice muddy in her head...

"Dad?"

"Marina." Hands took hold of her face and turned her. Warm hands. Thumbs wiped gently at her eyes, clearing the water. She blinked rapidly, still shaking so hard and feeling like she might throw up.

"Marina? *Alskling,* can you...can you hear me?"

No. That didn't sound right. She blinked again...

And managed to focus on a young man's face just a few inches from hers. Ice-pale, piercing blue eyes; wet black hair plastered to his head and collar. He breathed raggedly, his gaze searching her. He cradled her neck as he lay on top of her—warmth radiated from his body, and it stung her skin.

She worked her mouth, couldn't make any sound. She squeezed her eyes shut, quivering, and only managed to make her lips move, though no sound came out.

"Loki."

He let out a breath in a gust, leaned down and pressed his lips to her forehead. In the same movement, he pushed his forefinger into her breastbone.

"*Leita...leita...leita...*" he breathed, his warm mouth moving against her skin, his finger shoving painfully against her bone. "*Finna...finna...finna...*"

She felt something go coursing from his mouth and his hand and into her bloodstream—a restless, searching power, flickering and winding through her limbs, centering around her bones, tracing her spine...

Then, it sucked back out of her, retreated into his mouth—and he exhaled. More heat washed over her. His mouth softened against her, and she heard him swallow.

"All right," he whispered—and it sounded shaky. "Come on." And he crawled off of her. For a moment, the daylight sky above dazzled her vision. Then, he bent over her and picked her up. He pulled her against his soggy chest and walked away with her. Wet rocks scraped and slithered beneath his boots.

Marina's vision still blinked in and out, and every muscle shook. She pulled her arms tight in to her chest, her stomach muscles twitching, her jaw clamped.

Loki's footsteps quieted as he strode into the snow, and shadows crossed them. The temperature plunged. Marina tried not to let her chattering teeth bite her tongue or cheek...

He let go of her with one arm, lowering her feet to the ground. With his free hand he snapped his fingers and then blew on them. In seconds, Festning had sparked loose, bloomed on the ground and risen to its full height. Wasting no time, Loki picked Marina back up and pushed through the door.

The waves of heat inside the entryway sent awful prickles all over her. Loki charged up the stairs, turned and shoved into her bedroom, then awkwardly worked the latch on the wardrobe and pulled that door open. Marina's vision finally sharpened enough that she could see the creamy-colored wood of the bathing room, the mirror, the bathtub, the dressing table, the stacks of fuzzy towels, the soaps and thick rugs...

"Skjønnhet," Loki panted. "Run a bath. Not too hot."

Skjønnhet's face emerged from space above the mirror, her brow knotted with concern.

"Yes, sir," she answered, and immediately the tub faucet spat out steaming water. Loki immediately carried Marina over to it and set her down on a stool. He then unfastened her coat, pulled off her gloves, and tossed those heavy winter garments onto the floor. He picked her up again, and set her down in the tub, wet dress and all.

Warm water flooded over Marina's legs, shocking her—and instantly clearing her head. She grabbed onto the edge of the tub with her right hand, but her left she pulled in tight. In no time, the water filled the tub, soaked her clothes, and Marina's spasms calmed. She took deep breaths as the heat melted into her muscles, and the pain subsided.

Loki heaved a great sigh and sat down beside the tub, bracing his elbows on the edge and covering his face with his hands. Marina, her hair stuck to half of her face, heavily turned her head and looked at him.

"Are you all right?" she whispered.

He sighed again, and lowered his hands, folding his arms one on top of the other. And he looked back at her. Eyes still as blue as the winter sky, dark circles around them. He'd gone so white again, his lips were grey. Grave as death, intense as lightning.

"You made me lose my boat," he murmured. "Do you realize how many utterly humiliating things I had to do to obtain that thing?"

She stared at him. He raised his eyebrows.

"I hope you appreciate my sacrifice, Twig," he said.

She blinked, uncertain...

And he smiled at her.

And all at once, his eyes flushed golden, and deepened to a rich, shimmering green—while his hair took on edges of flame, deep russet at the roots. He reached out and gently pushed her hair out of her face and behind her ear, his fingertips lingering for just a moment on her cheekbone. Then, he set his hands on the edge of the tub.

"Skjønnhet will look after you," he said, dragging himself to his feet. "I'll be downstairs by the fire."

And she watched him go, listening as the wardrobe door latched behind him.

Marina lay in the tub for a long time, staring at the ceiling, the dull gush of the water spilling from the faucet filling her head. Finally, after all the clenching tension had eased, the pain had passed, and a heavy weariness pulled through her whole frame, she decided to get out.

She sat up, but her water-logged clothes now fell like lead. So she carefully undressed there in the tub, leaving the clothes behind, and stepped out and grabbed a towel. The bathroom itself felt warm as a fireside, so she didn't resume shivering. After she had dried, she reached for a dressing gown, wrapped it around herself, and went out into the bedroom. In the trunk she found more dry underclothes, socks, soft trousers and a new green dress with long, form-fitting sleeves. She dressed in front of the burning hearth, her eyes drooping shut as she waves of heat washed over her. Finally, she stood clothed in the center of the room, her hair hanging wildly and half-toweled around her shoulders. She didn't care.

Sighing and pulling her arms in again, she glanced at the door. Loki had made a joke, but Marina wasn't blind. He had looked terribly pale.

She crossed the room in her stocking feet, opened the door and went down the pokey stairs. She stopped in the doorway of the sitting room to find Loki, wearing dry clothes, lying on his side on the rug, a handful of tools spread out beside him. The broken chair was propped up on a stack of books, and he held the detached leg in his right hand. With his other hand, he was feeling the wood of the shattered joint—exploring, almost caressing, his brow furrowed, his eyes closed.

"What are you doing?" she asked.

"Fixing the chair," he answered absently. She took a few steps closer.

"I've never seen anybody fix a chair with their eyes closed," she remarked.

"I don't fix things the way people usually do," he answered in a murmur, his brow tightening. "In order to know what is broken, you have to touch it. You have to feel it. You have to *know* it. The depths, the heart of it. You have to know *why* it was broken, and how. What made it this way, and what its original shape was." He opened his eyes. His hand went still. He looked at her.

"How do you feel?"

She shrugged.

"I've felt worse."

He studied her a moment, then picked the tools up off the rug, and put them and the broken leg off to the side.

"Look what I found," he said, sitting up and then climbing to his feet. He turned to the mantel, and picked up a smooth red wooden box. He held it out to her. She took it, frowning with interest down at the design on the top.

"This looks like...Stormont Castle," she realized. "In Belfast."

"It is," Loki nodded. "I stayed there once. I had to get a souvenir."

"Is it a..." Marina began, awkwardly trying to use her stiff left hand to lift the lid...

Loki reached out and did it for her.

The next moment, a lively music machine began playing a lusty waltz that Marina didn't recognize.

"What song is that?" she asked. Loki looked at her in surprise.

"You don't know it?"

She shook her head.

"Ah, I have to show you!" Loki said, taking it from her but leaving it open, so the music still played. And then, in a frank, storytelling voice, he began to sing.

"In a neat little town they call Belfast,
Apprenticed to trade I was bound
Many an hour's sweet happiness
Have I known in that neat little town!"

Loki put on an earnest, sad face, and leaned closer to her.

"A sad misfortune came over me
Which caused me to stray from the land
Far away from my friends and companions
Betrayed by the Black Velvet Band."

He held out his hand to her. Marina stared at it—but he just waited.

And so she took his fingers.

He pulled her toward him, and kept singing, as casual as anything.

"Her eyes they shone like diamonds
I thought her the queen of the land!
And her hair it hung over her shoulder
Tied up with a Black Velvet Band."

And the next moment, he had wrapped his hand around her waist, took up her right hand in his left, and spun her gently in a circle, right in the center of the room.

Marina's breath caught, and she looked up at him, inexplicably speechless.

"I took a stroll down Broadway
Meaning not long for to stay," he went on.
"When who should I meet but this pretty fair maid
Come traipsing along the highway."

In an instant, Loki twirled her again, faster—her head spun. And his eyes sparked as he gave her a pointed, stunning look.

"She was both fair and handsome
Her neck it was just like a swan's
And her hair it hung over her shoulder
Tied up with a black velvet band!"

He urged her into a swift waltz step—and *somehow*, the room opened up for them. They did not trip, they didn't hit the chairs or the mantel or the wall. The sound from the music box swelled high all around them, and Loki sang—his voice filled the world.

"Her eyes they shone like diamonds
I thought her the queen of the land.
And her hair it hung over her shoulders
Tied up with a black velvet band!"

The music sped up—or seemed to—and flooded the sitting room. Loki kept hold of her hand and twirled her out. Her skirt bloomed out around her knees, and then he drew her back in, caught her against his chest, spun with her twice, until warm dizziness whirled all around her.

He bent close and made a face at her—crossed his eyes and stuck out his tongue—then beamed brilliantly.

Marina, startled, let out a giggle. She reflexively tried to put her hand over her mouth, but Loki didn't release her fingers—and instead spun her around again, and again. The room stretched bigger and bigger—her body thrummed with warmth, her hair flew wildly around her face.

And Loki, delighted, laughed.

Like wildfire, the ringing, unrestrained sound caught in Marina's heart. It tickled through her chest, filled her head, and all at once she burst out laughing too.

It cracked through her ribcage, loosening like rust upon a pipe, thrilling through her blood. It mingled with Loki's laugh—like melody and harmony—the song from the box danced like birds all around them.

That laugh burst something inside her. Delicious feelings flushed through her body—but all at once, her muscles went weak...

And she suddenly realized that tears had spilled down her cheeks.

She choked, her smile vanishing, and she tipped toward Loki's chest, her heartbeat skyrocketing.

Loki stopped instantly, catching her shoulders. Reflexively, she curled her right hand fingers through the front of his shirt.

And a cry escaped her. She slapped a hand over her mouth, her face twisting, her knees going limp.

Loki lifted her, and eased her down on the edge of the unbroken chair. Scalding tears raced down her face, dripping across her hand, and sobbing took her in seizure.

Loki knelt down on the floor in front of her, his face lifted, his eyes fixed on her face. He leaned his chest against her knees, his careful hands resting against her sides.

"I'm...I'm sorry. I'm sorry," Marina gasped, shaking her head. He mirrored that action, watching her, his hair going dark, his eyes sky blue. Then, he lifted his hand, and took hold of the forefinger of her useless left hand.

And he said nothing. Just slowly pulled it toward him.

"I...I was living in Norway with my dad." The words spilled out of Marina's trembling mouth, tears running down. "Excavating a Viking burial site...One day he fainted. I took him to the doctor...X-rays...said he had a brain tumor..." She swallowed convulsively.

Loki drew her hand closer and closer to him, never taking his eyes from her. Then, he pressed a kiss to the back of her knuckles.

A strange, hot sensation shot through her bones and entered her veins, reaching up through her whole arm. She caught the collar of her dress in her right hand, her hair falling into her face.

"He started treatment and it was terrible. I thought he was going to die every time," she rasped. "He couldn't come out with me to the site anymore...but he kept making me go...he wanted to know what I was finding..."

Three sharp twitches shook her frame. She choked, and more tears dripped. Loki, his gaze never wavering from hers, pushed her sleeve up to her elbow. His fingertips pressed deep into her skin, slowly running across the surface, deeply feeling her bones, caressing...exploring...

"One day he was feeling much better, he even got up and made breakfast, and he said if I went on ahead, he'd meet me there after lunch," Marina said, her words coming in an uncontrolled rush. "So I went, and it started to rain. Our cell phones never got any service up there...Svenka came running through the storm to tell me that the ambulance had come to my house and taken my dad to the hospital..."

She twitched again as Loki squeezed her elbow with both hands, pushing both his thumbs hard into her joint.

Pain lanced through her arm and entire left side—sharp and raw and vivid.

"I ran out through the rain—I had to get to my truck!" she sobbed. "I got in and started down the mountain to go find my dad, but it was raining so hard I couldn't see, and I didn't know that the road was washed out, and so I drove right into the middle of it, and it turned my truck over and broke my windshield and my windows and my arm went out the window and the door rolled over it, and then I landed in the middle of a stream, upside down..." She swallowed, choked again, her stomach rocked.

Loki pulled on her arm, dragging his fingers hard into her muscles, pushing his thumbs into the tendons on the underside. Her skin flared red. Tears poured down Marina's face, running down her neck. She clamped down on the collar of her dress.

"I almost bled to death and drowned—my head was underwater almost up to my nose. Somebody found me...I don't know how long...and turned the truck back over and got me out. He put me in his truck and drove me to the hospital...*gah*..." Marina hissed through her teeth—then let out a bound-up howl as she squeezed her eyes shut.

"My dad was dead! I woke up in the hospital and he was dead—they told me he was dead, he'd died before I ever heard about—he died in the next room and I wasn't there, I was upside down in a river because of some stupid Viking burial and the rain and my stupid, *stupid* truck—" She covered her face again, letting out a wrenching wail.

Loki twisted her wrist. He pried open her fingers, interlaced them with his—and dragged them open.

Marina arched her back away from him, gasping, her throat latching shut, hot tears filling her eyes.

He pressed his lips to her open palm—with a heat and fervor that almost burned her skin.

And warmth—warmth like a May morning, like intoxicating sunlight, living and rich—spread up from her fingertips, across the back of her hand and her palm, into the bones of her wrist, through her forearm and elbow, to her shoulder and then down her side, tracing her ribs, penetrating her muscles.

And all at once...

Everything resettled.

She blinked, her passion calming, her breath slowing.

Her eyebrows drew together. She blinked again, and the tears cleared from her eyes.

And she stared down at her hand.

It lay loosely in Loki's palm. Her arm stretched out, her fingers open and relaxed.

No surgery scars at her wrist. No crooked joints.

Perfect.

As if nothing had ever happened.

She gasped violently. Looked up at Loki.

His breathing unsteadied. His gaze locked on hers. And sparkling tears ran down his face, too.

Chills racing all through her, she dared to command her arm to move.

It obeyed. She lifted her hand, turned it over.

No hitch in the tendons of her wrist or elbow. No pain. No stiffness.

She closed her fingers to a fist. Opened them again.

Smooth. Easy. Strong.

Her attention jerked up to Loki. Her mouth opened.

She couldn't speak.

And he gave her a broken smile that glittered with tears.

She threw her arms around his neck, clawing at him and burying her face in his collar, sucking in a gasp that shocked her to the core.

Instantly, he wrapped his arms around her too, and pulled her against him.

Marina marveled at the feeling of her left hand threading through his hair, shudders running through her as she squeezed her eyes shut and broke into weeping again. The scent of peppermint drowned her, his warmth enveloped her. She felt him lay his hand against the back of her head, and rock her very gently side to side.

Endlessly, they sat there, the only sound the fire crackling in the background. Finally, her heart warm and thundering, Marina drew back, her cheek brushing his, and gazed at him—just inches away.

He stared straight back at her—breathless, his lips slightly parted. His hair had blushed almost to the tone of red wheat, his eyes emerald. Marina's gaze flickered across his features, her arms still wrapped around his neck...

He almost whispered something—some kind of pain touched his brow...

His lips ghosted across hers.

"He is here!"

Loki twitched. He pulled back, his head coming around—

Marina opened her eyes, her pulse thudding...

Bestemor, alarmed, pressed her face through the wall, and yelped before she was fully visible.

"He is here!" she hissed. "Out before my door."

"Who?" Loki gasped, letting Marina go and standing up.

"Your brother."

Chapter Twenty

LOKI SAT FOR JUST A moment, then shot to his feet and strode toward the door. Marina, swiping at her face, got up and followed as best she could, all her muscles trembling.

"I knew they'd come, just not so quickly," Loki muttered. "It wasn't like I had a choice..."

Marina frowned, wondering what he meant...

Loki pulled the door open.

Cold tumbled over the threshold. Moonlight spilled down across the snow, making marble giants out of the trees outside.

And just five feet before the door stood Fenris.

Tall, lean; with pale, carven features. Long black coat, fur around the collar, his hands in the pockets. Tousled chestnut hair, high cheekbones, and eyes like a winter morning. His gaze fixed on Loki, then drifted down to meet Marina's.

"My lady," he said, his voice deep, deliberate and smooth. "I don't know that we've been introduced."

"Where is Hel?" Loki demanded, pressing close to Marina's side.

Fenris' attention flicked to him, but returned almost immediately to Marina. She couldn't move, couldn't breathe, under the penetration of his cold, brilliant look.

"She isn't here," Fenris answered absently. "She's gone home."

"Why?" Loki asked.

"She believes there is no point in reasoning with you anymore," Fenris replied, reluctantly pulling his regard from Marina up to his brother. "I am disinclined to agree with her. Or rather..." he raised his eyebrows, and again turned to Marina. "I believe there is someone else with whom I may reason quite successfully."

"*No*—" Loki yelped—

Fenris pulled his hand from his pocket and snapped his fingers.

An invisible hook lodged in Marina's chest, jerked her forward—

SNAP.

Blackness.

A sharp gust of wind.

SNAP.

Her feet landed in the snow. It crunched beneath her shoes, and she sank up to her knees. She jerked her eyes open and gasped.

She stood in a snow-steeped clearing, encircled by towering, icy trees. In the center loomed several large boulders, leaning against each other. The stars and moon pricked the vast sky above.

And Fenris stood right in front of her.

She gasped again and leaped away from him, pulling both arms close to her chest.

"Please," Fenris said, drawing both hands out of his pockets and holding them up. "I'm not going to harm you. I only mean to tell you who I am."

"I know who you are," Marina spat. "You're Fenris Farbautison, Loki's brother."

Fenris' eyes glittered unreadably in the moonlight.

"I am indeed," he replied. "And you are Marina Feroe."

Marina said nothing—just clamped her jaw. Fenris took a step closer to her, then another...

And then fell to one knee in the snow, and caught hold of her skirt.

"Then, my lady, since you know who I am," he said, his voice burning. "I beg you to have mercy on my brother."

Marina's eyes flashed as her heart broke into a feverish pounding.

"What do you mean?"

"Please," he said again, softly. "Release him to come back with me."

"He doesn't want to go with you," Marina shot back.

"I know," Fenris nodded, his brow knotting. "Because he hopes for an outcome that cannot be."

Marina closed her fingers around her collar.

"What do you mean?"

"You have come to the conclusion that if you gather all of these stones that Bauldr left behind, that he can be brought back from the dead," Fenris said, gazing at her openly and gripping her skirt. "Is that true?"

Marina stayed silent.

"You are clever, and I know that you love Bauldr," he whispered. "As deeply as a mortal can. But you cannot understand what has happened." He watched her earnestly. "For long ages, Loki, Hel and myself wandered the realms together, as close as any brothers and sister can be. But when Loki met Odin and his sons, our lives changed. Loki began to wish to be an Aesir, to make a home for himself in Asgard. And while he is brilliant and talented, he could never be as strong and powerful as the eldest son, nor wise or as beloved as the youngest son. Not in their eyes, anyhow. Loki could never belong with them—it is so utterly wrong, so against his true nature. That is why he and Bauldr have resented each other for centuries, Lady Marina," he said, a hint of pained helplessness crossing his brow. "I do not know why it happened on that particular night, I don't know what caused the argument, what happened in their minds, what made Loki take up his arrows against his friend." His breath caught in his throat, and his eyebrows drew together as he gazed up at her. "But he did. I watched it with my own eyes."

Marina went cold down to her bones.

"Do you not understand?" Fenris squeezed her skirt. "If you bring Bauldr back to life he will call down a vengeance upon Loki unlike any the world has ever seen. Look at what has happened!" He gestured to the wintry forest. "His beloved springtime cut at the throat. Birds, flowers, fauns—frozen to death. Nothing would wrench his heart more than this." Fenris' eyes began to shine with tears. "The second possibility—and what I fear most—is that this may not, in fact, be a way to bring him back to *life*. The stones may instead simply be Soul-Splinters, meant to bear witness to the truth of his death. If Loki gathers them, and returns with them to Asgard..." Fenris' tears spilled over, and trickled down his cheeks. "They will show the king and Thor and all the Aesir what they already know, and prove without a doubt that Loki shot Bauldr through the back with a mistletoe arrow, and killed him."

Marina swallowed hard—it sent a powerful ache through her whole body.

"Then they would have him in their grasp again, utterly condemned," Fenris whispered, his lip trembling. "They won't listen to any kind of reasoning—they didn't the first go round. And this time, there would be nothing I or anyone else could do about it. For having escaped once, he has proven himself too dangerous for their liking—and they would simply behead him where he stood."

Marina pressed her hand to her throat.

"You have traveled with my brother," Fenris persisted, taking her skirt in fistfuls. "You have seen that he does not have a wicked heart. He has spared your life time after time. Risked his *own* life by using magic to save you from the river this very day—that is how I found you! Yet he thought of you and your safety above his own. Do you not owe him his freedom, at the very least?"

Marina gulped again, and Fenris leaned closer.

"Please," Fenris said for the third time. "If you must gather the stones, keep them past these next three days, so that Bauldr's body is no longer captive in Helheim—let his body turn to dust, so that he won't return in some twisted, vicious form and kill my brother." His voice broke, and more tears fell. "And do not let Loki take the stones back to Asgard, for they will not set him free as he hopes. There, they will only be used as swords to pierce him."

Fenris reached up and caught Marina's hands—and she was stunned to feel that his quivered.

"If you have any honor in your heart," he breathed. "Gather them, look at them, and you will see the truth of what I've told you. Keep them safe. And then crush them. Do not speak of them to anyone for all the rest of your life on Midgard. And tell Loki to come home to his brother and sister." He entwined his fingers with hers, his tears brilliant in the moonlight. "Do not take them to Helheim. Let the dead remain so. And save the lives of those who live."

Marina, shaken to her core, couldn't speak. Couldn't tear her eyes from him.

He leaned forward and fervently kissed her fingers, then dropped his head, sniffed loudly, and let go of her. He got up, snow all over his knees, and turned away.

"Something powerful lies within those rocks there," he pointed toward the icy boulders. "I can feel it, but I cannot go in. I wonder if it might be another one of the stones you seek." He looked at her, his gaze tired and empty. "If you are able to enter, the magic should be loud enough to call Loki to you." For a long moment, he just gazed at her. "Remember what I've said," he finally murmured. "I shan't be able to return to say it again."

And with a black gust, he dissolved into a cloud of sparkling smoke, and disappeared.

Marina stared down at his empty footprints, wrapping her arms tightly around herself, shivering.

For several minutes, she stood alone in the snow, his words—and his tears—sinking through her.

Then, the icy cold creeping up her legs, she looked up...

And abruptly recognized this place.

This clearing was the very place she had seen in her vision.

Bracing herself, she crept toward the large rocks.

With every step she took, an invisible tendril seemed to wrap around her, tugging on her...

And suddenly pulled her straight at the face of one of the rocks.

She snapped her teeth shut, flinched back—

But the next second, she stood inside a very tiny stone room. And before her on the floor, lying on a purple velvet pillow, lay a stone.

Fenris had been right.

Square and silvery—like a cut of moonlight and starlight. It almost seemed to laugh quietly, with the voices of fairies. She stepped toward it, bent down, and picked it up. It sat lightly in her palm, warm as the other one had been, and even more brightly twinkling. She closed her fingers over it, and pulled it toward her breastbone, her heart twisting.

A tingle, at the back of her head. Almost like a distant bell. She frowned, turned around...

Stepped back toward the blank wall...

And slipped through the stone, and stood outside in the snow once again.

"Are you..." A choked voice cut the silence. "Is it you?"

Marina, startled, found the source—

Loki perched, off-balance, at the edge of the clearing, wearing just his black shirt, trousers and boots—no coat—his face white as death, hair inky-black, wide eyes that caught the moonlight. He let out a strangled breath which clouded around his head.

"It's me," Marina managed, though she couldn't summon much volume.

Loki staggered, then hurried toward her, kicking through the snow. He lunged at her and grabbed her by the upper arms.

"What did he do to you?"

"Nothing," she shook her head and looked down. "Nothing."

"What did he say?" Loki demanded. "Marina, look at me."

Her mouth tightened, but she finally lifted her face and met his eyes. He waited, his breath held, his eyebrows drawn together. She folded her arms tightly over her chest, clenching the stone in her fist.

"He said that he saw you kill Bird," she whispered. "And that if we try to bring him back to life, Bird will kill you. Or...if these stones are just Soul-Splinters, and you take them back to Asgard, the Aesir will condemn you again and cut off your head. Because they'll know the truth. He...He says that if I have any honor, I'll gather them all up, and just keep them until Bird's body turns to dust in three days. And tell you to go back to him and Hel."

Loki said nothing. Just stared at her.

Then, slowly, he let her go.

He turned his head to the side, away from her, his jaw clenching. And even in this light, she could see blue ripple through his hair—and blazing red cross the irises of his eyes.

He stepped back, and wouldn't look at her. Then, he faced away from her completely, flicked the red sparks from his fingers, and planted Festning on the ground. It grew up to its full height, he stepped toward it, and wordlessly pushed open the door and went inside, letting it slam behind him.

Marina sat on the edge of her bed, legs crossed, wearing her nightgown, letting the firelight play across her renewed hand. She turned it over, palm up, then palm down; opened and closed her fingers, practiced sliding the corner of the sheet through her fingertips, feeling the lace edges of her gown...

When she'd entered the house, she'd seen Loki standing with his back to her, facing the mantel. She had felt like she should say something—but she couldn't think of a single word. Not with Fenris' tears lingering on her skin, the echoes of his grip still wrinkling the skirt of her dress...

So she had kept silent, gone up the stairs and into her room, changed into her nightclothes, brushed and braided her hair, and sat there on the bed, turning her memories over the same way she turned her now-perfect hand.

"Ah!" the crackly voice issued from above the mantel, and Bestmor's cheerful, wrinkled wooden face emerged. "You finally let him look at your arm, did you?"

Marina almost smiled.

"I'm not sure I did," she murmured. "I don't know how he got me to...Or, why I let him..." She trailed off.

"It is part of being a healer, I daresay," Bestemor supposed. "Not just knowing *how* to mend something, but *wanting* to mend it. And finding a way to do it."

Marina's throat felt thick, and she stared down at her hands.

"What is wrong, child?" Bestemor asked quietly.

"I'm afraid," Marina whispered.

"Why?"

She took a slow breath, and looked up at the friendly wooden face. Bestemor waited, quiet and open.

"I spoke to Loki's brother Fenris."

"Yes?" Bestemor's eyebrows went up. Marina nodded.

"He said that Bauldr would kill Loki if he came back from the dead."

"Nonsense," Bestemor spat. "Why would he do that, if he knew Loki had helped bring him back?"

"I don't know how it works," Marina confessed, lifting a shoulder. "I don't know what's involved in putting a soul back in a body. He might not be...himself."

"Do you not think that such a thing has occurred to Loki?" Bestemor said pointedly. Marina hesitated.

"Maybe."

"And I would suppose that Loki has thought about that risk, and decided it is worth taking."

Marina lowered her head, and nodded.

"What else troubles you?"

Marina looked up again.

"Fenris said that if these stones are only Soul-Splinters, and we take them to Asgard, they'll prove once and for all that Loki is a murderer. And they will kill him."

Bestemor studied her for a long moment.

"And...you do not wish for them to kill him."

Hot tears suddenly spilled down Marina's cheeks.

"No," she gasped, wiping her face with both hands—but tears kept coming as a strange fire coursed through her blood. "No, I don't. But I'm...I have no idea what really happened. I can't believe that he would *murder* Bird like that, but Loki has never denied it, and Fenris says he saw him do it—and said that if I watch more of the stones, I would see that he's telling the truth..."

"You have asked Loki to tell you," Bestemor surmised.

"Yes," Marina sniffed. "He won't."

"Have you considered that perhaps something else happened?" Bestemor ventured.

"What could that be?" Marina asked, blinking to clear her eyes. "If it isn't what it looks like, why wouldn't he just *tell* me?"

Bestemor didn't answer, and the whole of Marina's chest ached. Bestemor clicked her few teeth together.

"It is a pity Loki does not just ask Prince Thor for help."

Marina sat up straight, wiping the last of her tears away.

"What? Thor?" she repeated. "I thought...I thought he chained Loki underneath that...that..."

"Oh, no, dear," Bestemor shook her own head. "The Prince could hardly bear to stand beside his father at the trial, and afterward he secluded himself inside his home, and would not come out. I do not think he has been out since."

"How do you know?" Marina asked.

"Traust, the heart of Bilskirnir, told me so himself. I think you met him once," Bestemor replied.

"You can talk to other houses?" Marina's eyes went wide. Bestemor nodded.

"Yes, sometimes, when the starlight is right!"

"Why...Why do you think Loki should ask Thor for help?" Marina asked, leaning closer to the hearth.

"Because Bauldr's body must be retrieved from Helheim, must it not?" Bestemor asked. "Very soon?"

"Fenris said that in three days his body would turn to dust," Marina breathed.

"All manner of terrible creatures live in Helheim," Bestemor frowned. "Wraiths, goblins, trolls, ghosts, dragons. Not to mention Hel herself! Even Loki will be afraid to enter it without another warrior or magician by his side. Not to mention, he has no one to discuss all these ancient magicks with, since you do not know them. Perhaps that is what is keeping him awake now..."

"But why Thor?" Marina pressed.

"Oh, dear Marina," Bestemor's forehead knotted. "Thor loves Loki with all his heart—as much as he ever loved Bird. I do not think he believes in his spirit that Loki could do such a dreadful thing, but since no one brought evidence to dissuade him or the king, what can he do?"

"You think he would come help us," Marina gasped. "You think he would, if Loki asked him."

"Loki will not ask him. He is too afraid to look into the prince's eyes." Bestemor pursed her lips. "But I think the prince would certainly come if *you* asked him."

"Me?"

"Mhm," Bestemor nodded. "He liked the story you told!"

"Ha! That doesn't mean he would *listen* to me," Marina said.

"He would," Bestemor answered back. "He wants his brother back. And he wishes for someone to prove Loki's innocence. Just as you do."

Marina stared at the kindly, wrinkled wooden face, and closed her hands into fists.

"How to I ask him?"

"Command me to go to Traust," Bestemor replied simply. "I will tell him to tell his master where to come."

Marina stopped breathing, feeling the world tipping sideways.

"Bestemor," she whispered, feeling the full weight of each word. "Go to Traust in Asgard, and tell him that Marina Feroe—the little thing who came to the banquet this summer—begs Prince Thor Odinson to come to her aid."

"I shall," Bestemor answered, smiling, and disappeared.

Chapter Twenty-One

FLASH.

Swooping through the pines, break-neck speed, following a winding deer trail.

The forest folded back, and a great clearing opened up, split by a meandering, ice-choked stream. Near the center of the clearing stood a towering oak, all alone—and blackened with death. It had been struck by lightning long ago, engulfed in flame...

Yet it stood, stone-hard, cold and dead, the heart of it throbbing with a hidden power; a secret deep within its bark...

FLASH.

Marina opened her eyes and shot into a sitting position.

And the next moment...

Thunder.

It shivered through the bedposts, trembled through Festning's eaves.

She gasped, staring at the ceiling and gripping her covers. Her heart hammered as she searched through the darkness...

A soft, icy *creak* reached her hearing...

And the window to her left slowly swung open.

She sat frozen for a long moment. Then, she slowly crawled out of bed and crept toward the window, the terrible cold wafting in, nipping her feet and legs.

Outside, the moonlight coated everything in silver...

But dark, thick, snarling clouds moved to overtake that moon. And in the depths of the storm, lightning darted and danced.

Marina put her hands on the window frame, her breath catching as her mind raced. Quickly, she glanced down at the snow below...

Spun around, stripped off her nightgown, flung open the trunk and threw on a thick underdress, a woolen over-dress, boots, a scarf, and—

To her surprise, her hand met another long coat at the bottom of her trunk that hadn't been there before. She snatched it up and pulled it on as well, reached into the pockets and found gloves, then charged toward the window.

She hesitated just a moment, then braced herself and jumped out.

Cold air hit her face.

She fell for a split second—

Then hit the snow. Sank up to mid-calf. She spun around, glanced back up at the playhouse-sized Festning...

Smiled briefly at it, turned and hurried off into the night, toward the rumble of that ethereal growling.

Her breath puffed in vapor around her head as she jogged onward, between the trees, toward the persistent sound of deep, electric crackling. Snow kicked out in front of her, sparkling in the moonlight. She had put her hood up, and now clutched the front of it with her right hand to keep it from flying back. The shadows of the trees flashed all around her, even as the clouds loomed closer and closer to the moon...

All at once, she burst out of the trees and onto the bank of a river. Panting, she stared up at the billowing black clouds that stretched like the wings of a dragon...

Movement caught her eye. She yanked her attention down...

And it caught on a lone figure standing just there, on her side of the river.

Six and a half feet tall, at least. Long, wild, sand-colored hair and beard, laced with the pearl of moonshine. Armor glittering with captured starlight, a heavy hammer hanging from his belt; dark trousers, rough boots sunk deep in snow. A stormy cloak spilling from his broad shoulders, clouding around his ankles, casting fog all around him in a smoky halo. Handsome and terrible, with a darkened brow, hard mouth, and luminous blue eyes that flashed a gaze across the distance between them.

Marina's heart banged, and she instantly pushed her hood back and fell to one knee.

"Your Highness," she managed—and her shaking voice carried through the silent night. "Mighty Thor. I beg you to have mercy and hear me."

"I intend to hear you," Thor rumbled—she felt in her bones. "When Traust told me that *Bestemor* of Festning had sent word at *your* command, I wondered who else might be your choice of companion here on Midgard." Thor strode toward her, the storm seethed around his feet, and the air sparked. His dreadful eyes burned. "Who else but Loki, who *murdered* my brother."

"I...I have another story to tell you," Marina tried, staying on her knees in the snow, but daring to sit up and hold his gaze. Thor slowed to a stop, his brow frowning.

"A true story this time," Marina added. "One that could save your brother's life."

Thor's eyes flashed, a potent mix of anguish and rage searing across his face.

"What do you mean?" he growled. "I watched him *die*."

Marina shifted, earnestly holding his gaze.

"When I came to visit you in Asgard," she began. "Bird told me about the dreams he was having—dreams about being killed."

Thor's head twitched away, and his jaw tightened. Marina made herself go on.

"He asked me if I'd be willing to help him. I said yes. And then, when the snowstorm came, Hel came to my house."

Thor's attention returned to her instantly. Thunder snarled overhead.

"What did she want from you?" he demanded.

"She said Bird had left something at my house," Marina answered. "I had no idea what she meant—and she tried to kill me. I ran from my house, out into the forest. Bird had given me Wishstones, and I used one of them to escape. And it took me to where Loki had been chained."

Thor's cloak stilled, his whole frame quieting as he listened with the intensity of white flame. Marina risked a breath.

"Loki told me that Hel and Fenris were after me, and if they caught me they'd kill me. He offered to help me stay safe from them—and he did. He has. And together, we are trying to find the stones that Bird left for me."

"What stones?" Thor stepped even closer to her.

"We've found two so far," Marina told him. "A golden one in a mountain, and a silver one in a pile of stones. When Loki looked at the golden one in the fire, it brought up memories of Bird and Odin together. Loki isn't sure what they are—they might be Soul Splinters." Her voice quieted. "Or he hopes...We both hope...that they are Soul-Anchors."

Thor looked down at her, his countenance stormy and unreadable.

"And...why do you hope?"

"Because," Marina said breathlessly. "If we can gather them all and then get his body from Helheim we can bring him back to life."

Lightning *cracked* through the sky. Thunder muttered in answer.

"And why," Thor gritted. "Would Loki want to do that?"

Marina gazed up at him, her heart sinking.

"I don't know," she confessed. "But Hel and Fenris found us once, and tried to convince him to abandon any idea of going back to Asgard and forget about finding the stones, so he could be with them again. He refused. Hel almost killed him."

Thor drew in a deep breath and let out a long sigh, lowering his head, even as his jaw clenched again. Stillness fell for a long moment.

Then, Thor suddenly opened his eyes and looked up, past Marina.

She frowned, confused, and twisted to see...

Loki stood in the edge of the moonlight. He wore his coat, and held his long black bow in his hand.

He stared back at Thor. Eyes vivid as the sky. Eyebrows drawn together, lips parted. As if stricken in the middle of a breath, a word. Fixed on Thor.

No one moved or spoke.

The river rustled in the background, icy and absent.

Then, Loki sucked in a tense breath that echoed through the clearing.

"Thor," he acknowledged, his lower lip trembling.

Thor inclined his head.

"Loki."

"Fancy seeing you here," Loki tried, bright pain crossing his features as he nervously shifted his grip on his bow. He breathed unsteadily, swallowed, and took half a step forward. "What...What brought you to this...cheerful corner of Midgard?"

"The Little Thing," Thor gestured minutely to Marina. "She asked Bestemor to speak to Traust, and to bring me here."

Loki's eyes darted to Marina before returning to Thor.

"Why?"

"She asked for aid," Thor replied. "So I came, because Bestemor had sent the message. And Bestemor is never far from *you*."

Loki swallowed again. Thor stayed just where he was, but lifted his chin.

"The Little Thing says you have found Bird's Soul Anchors. And that you want to bring him home."

Loki's mouth worked for a moment before he managed to speak.

"I...Well, I believe...I *think* that's what they are, yes," he said. He gazed at Thor openly. "And I...Yes," he whispered. "Yes."

For a breathless moment, Thor remained still. Then, he strode forward, past Marina—and dew bloomed all over her sleeve as his cloak brushed her. His feet vibrated the frosty ground, his cape swelled and bannered like a thunderhead behind him—

And all at once he grabbed Loki by the front of his coat and shook him.

Thunder sliced the sky and shook the trees.

Marina leaped to her feet.

Loki dropped his bow, his hands flying up.

"You *swear* to me that this is the truth. That this is what you wish," Thor snarled in Loki's face. "To bring him home for his own sake—no one else's, not even your own." He shook Loki again, hard. "For his *own sake*."

Loki, pale as death, his hands limply holding Thor's wrists, stared straight back into that vicious face. A tear spilled down his cheek, fractured the starlight, and fell from his chin.

"For his own sake," Loki whispered.

Silence fell. Thor's red-hot gaze bore through Loki's, and his knuckles whitened. Loki did nothing—only stood, fingers resting on Thor's bracers, motionless as stone.

Slowly, Thor's iron grasp relaxed, and he let go.

Marina started breathing again.

"Show them to me," Thor commanded, taking a step back. Marina carefully climbed to her feet, watching the two of them.

"The stones," Thor clarified. "Let me see them."

Loki swallowed, then nodded. He took off his gloves and put them in his pockets, then rubbed his hands together as if to warm them. Then, he lifted his right palm off his left...

And there in his left palm lay one gold stone and one silver. Their inner light beamed out against his skin, and danced across both Loki and Thor's faces.

Marina started, and then hurried toward them.

"How...How did you...?" she asked Loki. "I never showed the silver one to you—you left before I could—"

"You put it on the mantel in your room," Loki answered her, without looking at her. "When Festning folds, it enters my blood. I know everything inside it, and I can bring any of it outside if I want to."

"It's a clever trick," Thor admitted in an absent mutter, intently studying the incandescent stones. Then, he held out his hand.

Loki's fingers almost twitched shut, and fear filled his eyes, but Thor said nothing, just waited. So, gingerly, Loki tipped the stones into Thor's hand. Thor roughly picked each of them up in his free hand, studying them, pressing them. Then, he held them back out to Loki.

"I believe you are right," he said—his tone so different that it stunned Marina. Thor gently set the stones back in Loki's hand. "I have seen a Soul Anchor before."

"You have?" Loki said sharply. "When?"

"I was very young, out hunting alone," Thor answered. "I met an Olympian musician on the road who wished to bring his wife back from the dead. He needed me to guide him through the mountains toward Helheim. He showed me her anchor. It was the color of obsidian, and felt much like this, only heavier."

"Did it work?" Loki asked, his eyes suddenly sparking with emerald.

"No," Thor shook his head.

Marina's heart skipped a beat.

"Why not?" she gasped. Finally, Thor turned to regard her—and the storm had gone out from his countenance.

"Afterward, he told me that his adventure failed for two reasons," he answered. "The first was that there was only one stone—and there cannot be. There must be many; one for each person she regarded most dear to her. And each stone must hold the memories of a deep regret. A time that she did harm to each person, and never repaired it. Those regrets had to be seen, and forgiven, before she could return."

"And what was the second?" Loki asked, his voice low, his glance careful.

"He had no time to mend the mistake," Thor replied heavily, turning back to Loki. "A body can only lie in Helheim for a very short time before it turns to dust."

"Three days!" Marina cried faintly, looking at Loki. "That's what Fenris said—that's all we have left..."

Thunder growled again. Thor turned to face her, frowning.

"Do you know where another stone is?"

"I...yes," she managed. Loki's eyebrows went up, but Thor spoke first.

"Then let us go find it," he said, pulling his hammer from his belt and hefting it. "Before my brother slips further from us."

"Wait—you're..." Loki stepped forward and held up a hand. "You're coming with us?"

"That is not the question," Thor answered back. "The question is...are *you* coming with *us?*"

Marina jumped. Loki's mouth fell open.

"Are you..." Loki blinked, baffled. "Do you even know where you're going?"

"No, but Little Thing does," Thor pointed his hammer at her. Marina shifted uneasily.

"Yes, but—" Loki stammered.

"The quest is simple enough, is it not?" Thor asked. "Find the remaining stones and see into them to find the memories they hold, then forge on to Helheim to take Bird's body."

"*Yes*, but Hel, Fenris and *all* of their wolves are on our trail!" Loki cried. "Fenris *found* us just hours ago—before that, Hel nearly tore off my arm!" Loki strode toward him, gripping his injured arm. "We've been trying to hide from them *and* the sight of anyone in Asgard, I've not been using any loud magic for fear of attracting attention, and we've *just* managed to stay alive this long. Not to mention that you are talking about going into *Helheim*." Loki pressed even closer to him, biting out his words. "You know as well as I do what lives in those passages. And according to the law laid down by *your father*, Hel *owns* Bird. She owns him. To get him back, we will have to break through several multi-tiered spells and *steal* him."

"Aha. Then it seems you need to come along after all," Thor said pointedly, giving him a look that *almost* resembled a smile. Loki stood up straight, gestured helplessly and tried to say something, but nothing came out.

"What about the wolves, and Fenris?" Marina asked.

Thor spun his hammer in his grip, then grasped it tight. Lightning snapped behind him, and his scorching gaze landed on her.

"I am not the kind to hide from anyone, or anything," he growled. "If man, beast, Jotun or goblin crosses me I shall crush his bones. And if the underworld devises to keep me from laying hold of my brother again, I will bring Hel's own mountain down upon her head."

Alarmed, Marina looked over at Loki...

To find him gazing at Thor's profile, his features softened, his hair and his eyes tinged with gold. And, just for a moment, the edge of his mouth curved up.

Thor turned his head, and gazed directly back at Loki.

Something passed between the two men in that moment. Something Marina could not decipher—but the air grew heavy with ghosts and memories, and light from another realm seemed to touch the edges of their hair and clothes.

"Why did you not to call to me?" Thor asked quietly. Loki's eyebrows drew together.

"I...was afraid," he murmured. And said no more.

> Thor studied him a moment, then drew himself up and beckoned to Marina. "Come. Tell me where you believe this one is. Loki, get your bow."

Her legs going weak, Marina hurried up to him, scrambling words together.

"Erm...That way," she pointed. "In a big clearing, by a river—there's an oak tree that's been burned, and it stands by itself—"

"Yes," Thor cut her off. "I saw it as I passed over." He then reached down, and without any hesitation, slid his arm around Marina's waist and snatched her up, yanking her against his huge, armored chest.

"Come, Loki," Thor urged, holding Mjollnir straight out in front of him. Loki picked up his bow, slung it across his shoulders and strode back to them, reached out and grabbed Thor's bracer, curling his fingers through the laces.

Static shot down Marina's spine.

"Wait! What about flashy magic?" she yelped.

"You won't find a lot of subtle tactics where Thor is involved," Loki muttered.

"I prefer to accomplish something rather than dither with potions," Thor answered, shifting his stance and looking into the sky.

"It isn't *dithering*," Loki shot back. "And at least it doesn't get anyone's nose broken."

"No one who has given birth to a horse may have any say about what is and is not subtle," Thor retorted.

Loki stared at him. Marina's mouth opened in surprise—

BOOM.

A deafening *bang* slammed into the ground. Blinding light blazed down from the clouds and enveloped them. Marina screamed and screwed her eyes shut—the white burned through her eyelids.

A blast of awful, chilling wind—

A lifting, a weightlessness...

And suddenly, they thudded onto their feet, on snowy ground.

Thor released her and she stumbled away, frantically rubbing at her eyes to try and clear them...

It took several moments for the dazzle to vanish, but when it did...

The stream beside her swirled and chattered its icy teeth. The moon shone down upon the great, wide clearing.

The skeletal oak, all blackened and dead, stood alone in its very center.

And once again, that hook lodged in Marina's chest, and pulled her straight toward it.

Chapter Twenty Two

MARINA STOOD UPON THE threshold of Festning's hearth room, leaning her shoulder against the doorframe, three stones pressing their heat in to the palm of her left hand.

Just minutes ago, she had stopped a mere foot from that scorched oak tree, and before she thought about it, she had put out her hand and it had passed *through* the blackened bark. She had almost jerked back—but then her fingers landed upon the hard edges of a warm stone. When she had grabbed it and pulled it out, the gem's swirling sapphire depths had captivated her. It looked like someone had arrested every wrathful storm and rolling sea and hidden it inside.

Now, she, Thor and Loki had retreated inside Festning, which Loki had planted beside the oak. Thor had shoved his way through the witchy kitchen door to find something to eat. Loki had immediately entered the hearth room, braced his right hand against the mantel and stared down into the flames. His appearance had cooled again—black hair with edges of silver, his eyes violet.

Marina closed her fingers around the stones, a terribly unsteady sensation in her bones as she stared at his back.

For a long moment, she just stood there, tension building in her chest and throat. Finally, she made herself step inside, and creep up to see him in profile—though she kept her distance. She gazed at his stony face, lit by the flicker of the flames, and risked a deep breath.

"What's wrong?"

He looked at her sideways.

And she didn't recognize him. Hard, stark and foreign—it pierced through her heart. Loki's mouth tightened.

"You can't guess?" he asked pointedly, with soft deadliness.

Marina blinked.

"I..."

He quickly returned his attention to the fire.

"You actually *listened* to Fenris," he said. "And you..." He stopped, and gestured behind him toward the kitchen door without moving his head. His tone lowered to a whisper. "I trusted you."

Marina's heart banged. She took half a step toward him.

"I told you everything Fenris said," she insisted. "But I...I worried about it—"

"Why?" Loki snapped, his eyes returning to her and burning red. "What would make you believe *any* word that came out of his mouth?"

"Because you haven't told me *anything* about what really happened!" Marina countered, starting to shake. "You promised to tell me, but then you decided not to, so I'm left to my own imagination. I don't know what to think!"

"So you thought you'd call Thor?" Loki demanded, straightening up, one eye going grey while the other flared with scarlet, that same stark and foreign expression dominating his face. "Do you *realize* what could have happened?"

"I called him because Bestemor said he would help," Marina tried. "That he wants to believe you're innocent, and he wants to get his brother back."

Loki turned toward the fire again, grinding his teeth. He fell silent. Icy goosebumps raced across Marina's skin as she almost felt something slipping through her grasp...

"Do *you* think I'm innocent?" Loki murmured.

Marina's mouth opened—but no words came out.

He looked at her. Saw her face.

And again, it was like she'd never met him.

FLASH.

She sat down in a chair, hard.

Images and sensations barreled through her head, swallowing her vision, spinning her balance. She grasped the stones in a death grip as pictures coalesced and swam...

Her eyes snapped open.

Loki and Thor stood in front of her—Thor held a goblet in his hand. Both towering men watched her with furrowed brows and intense eyes.

"What is it?" Thor rumbled. "What did you see?"

"I..." Marina gasped. "I know where the next stone is."

"Where?" Thor asked.

Marina glanced over at Loki, whose gaze had chilled to grey.

"It's at my house."

BOOM.

Marina blinked over and over, again trying to clear her vision of the blinding, flickering dazzle. Thunder rolled up and back through the sky. Her feet sank down into the snow. Stillness fell.

Finally her vision clarified, even as the footsteps of her companions crunched through the snow away from her.

They stood beside a house. A three story wooden house with a thick-pillared porch, bric-a-brac decorating the porch and upper windows; surrounded by snow-shrouded gardens. The building itself looked like a gingerbread house, since at least a foot of white icing stood upon its roof, window-sills and porch. The dawn touched it all with pale pinkish light—and of a sudden, it snapped from foreign to extremely familiar.

Her hand flew to her heart.

Loki and Thor had already started striding toward it, leaving deep swaths behind them. Marina hurried after them, the freezing air hurting her face and lips...

And all at once, her knees went weak and she had to stop, as a deep, powerful hurt traveled all through her.

Her roses. The ones she'd spent all that time pruning and fertilizing whilst Bird stood up on the ladder, humming that mysterious tune that had somehow thrummed through the chords of her memory...

Tears sprang to her eyes as her glance fell upon the herb garden beside the house—or rather, where it should be. Now, a three-foot drift buried it.

"Well, maybe crying is the wrong word. Probably 'sweetly requesting' would be better. I could say the same thing about the asparagus, just take the 'sweet' part out—asparagus get all stuffy-acting when they're asking favors. The spearmint I just had to ignore—they're pushy and overpowering, as you know, unless you keep them at a distance. I can personally only take them in small doses. And the dill is

just plain saucy about it, and the garlic is downright loud, making a lot more fuss than is actually necessary, so you see..."

A flash of sky-blue eyes—a halo of golden hair. A smile that stole her breath away.

Marina squeezed her eyes shut, the frost nipping at her ears and nose.

Absently, she heard deep footfalls thud against the wood of the front steps.

"The door stands open," Thor rumbled.

Two tears rolled down Marina's cheeks. Quickly, she opened her eyes and wiped them away with her glove.

Both Thor and Loki stood on the porch, their stances light and taught. Slowly, Loki took his bow off his shoulder and notched an arrow to the string. Thor pulled Mjollnir from his belt, spun it once, then lowered his head.

He and Loki exchanged a glance, then Thor turned and regarded Marina.

"Keep right behind us, Little Thing," he commanded. Marina nodded, pushed through the drifting snow, then climbed up the stairs behind them. Loki didn't look at her.

Instead, he took a low breath, set his teeth, and stepped through the snow that had drifted in the open doorway. Thor followed on his heels, and Marina trailed after, her feet lost in the rolling fog of his cape.

The towering Aesir and Jotun moved into the entryway, silent as death. They flowed into the sitting room, casting furtive, hawk-like glances into every corner. Marina watched them, hardly breathing, as they crept through that dark, icy room into the library, where frost covered all of the books and artifacts. From there, into the kitchen, where Jack Frost coated the windows with lacy patterns, and the linoleum proved treacherously slick beneath Marina's boots. Loki's hands remained steady on his bow and long, wicked arrow; Mjollnir rested easily in Thor's hand.

Loki first, then Thor, then Marina, trailed up the stairs. The two vast men filled the small passage—more so than they had in Festning, somehow, and they investigated the empty guest bedroom, the bathroom, and Marina's room. Marina lingered at the top of the staircase, awkwardly feeling that there simply was no room for her between the other two.

Finally, Loki let out a low sigh, straightened up and slid his arrow back in his quiver, and put his bow on his back. Then, he pulled off his gloves, reached out with both hands and pressed them against the wall of the landing.

"Hm," he muttered, running his palms over the wallpaper.

"What?" Thor wondered.

"Did you get a sense, when we walked in here?" Loki asked him.

"A stale one, yes," Thor answered. "Hel has been here."

"Yes, but besides that," Loki said, his brow furrowing. He met Thor's eyes. "Doesn't it seem a little familiar to you?"

Thor's eyebrows raised, and then he looked around. Something settled in his expression.

"Yes."

Loki nodded, then glanced darkly down at Marina.

"Things are starting to make sense, now," he said—in a strange, cold tone. "Let's see if we can wake him up, shall we?" And he started toward her, to go down the stairs. Alarmed, Marina hurriedly turned around, trotted down the steps and got out of his way. He swept past her, followed by Thor, and the two of them strode straight into the sitting room. Marina followed, burning with questions, yet suddenly afraid to ask any of them.

Loki stopped in front of the fireplace, rubbed his hands together, breathed into them, and then *clapped*.

Fire exploded in the fireplace.

The front door slammed shut.

All the lamps blinked on and burned bright.

Marina *felt* heat and light race up the flue—and then flood through the whole room, along the walls, up the stairs, into the kitchen—down into the cellar, through the pipes, through the heater...

The floor vibrated. Something like spices and licorice and gunpowder filled the air so she could taste it...

And then...

The very nature of the light within the room seemed to change. It deepened, richened, like ancient sunlight. And there stood Thor, with his stormy cloak, the firelight gleaming against his armor, across the intricate surface of Mjollnir, making his handsome, rugged features glow, and his eyes sparkle like sapphires. Beside him, Loki—black of midnight and white of snow, in striking contrast—hair blushing to the color of chestnut, eyes like the sea, his sharp profile seen through the feather of arrows and the string of a bow. Both men looming like mighty and terrible spirits that suddenly seemed unreal as a painting.

Marina couldn't speak.

Then, Loki took a step back, and rapped his knuckles on the broad wooden mantel three times.

"Hello," he called. "You have visitors."

Marina suddenly frowned, took three steps forward—stopped—

For a few moments, nothing happened.

Then...

The wood in the center of the mantel rippled. Loki took another step back, folding his arms across his chest and watching carefully.

The wood kept swimming, pushing outward, cracking and squeaking...

Until it formed a face.

The face of a wizened man with a hooked nose; merry, wrinkled eyes; pointed chin, and no teeth—all the shade of deep cherry. He blinked slowly, as if trying to focus, his jaw working as he gummed thoughtfully. Finally, a line formed between his eyebrows, and he focused on the two men in front of him.

"Loki, son of Farbauti," he creaked—sounding unmistakably like the spit and crackle of a fire. "And Thor, son of Odin."

Loki leaned toward him, startled, and peered into his face.

Then, he flashed an unguarded smile.

"Farfar."

"What?" Thor cried, coming closer as well.

"Thor, this house is Hjärta," Loki declared.

Thor straightened, looking around with widened eyes.

"By Jove, it is!"

Marina's mouth fell open.

The wooden man, apparently called Farfar, grinned—and indeed, he didn't have a single tooth.

"We wondered where you'd gone!" Loki said, straightening up. "How long ago were you planted here?"

Farfar gummed again, squinching his eyes as he thought.

"I should say, perhaps two hundred years, I should say," he whistled. "Never moved since, I should say."

"Who brought you?" Thor asked.

"I knew him, *liten* prince Bauldr," Farfar answered, his face drooping. "I knew him."

Marina swallowed hard. Loki and Thor looked at each other.

"For what purpose did he bring you?" Loki asked.

"For certain, to guard his tears. For certain to find a guardian for them," came the creaky reply.

"A guardian," Thor repeated, frowning.

"Indeed, yes," Farfar grinned. "There she is. Indeed, yes." And he looked at Marina. Loki and Thor turned to face her. Her face turned hot.

Loki's eyes just narrowed for a moment, and then he faced Farfar again.

"Yes, I suspected as much," he stated. "You said 'tears.' Do you mean there is more than one of them here?"

"Aye, *pojke*, aye," Farfar replied.

"Can you give them to us?" Thor asked, taking a step toward him.

"No, *pojke*, no."

Loki and Thor glanced at each other again.

"Why?" Loki wondered.

"I can only give it to her," Farfar replied. "If she be willing, that is. That is."

"Come here, Little Thing," Thor beckoned—though he smiled a little when he said it. Marina, swallowing again, ventured around the couch and up beside Loki—which made her shiver—and stood in front of the wooden man. Farfar beamed at her.

"A pretty *kvinna,* for sure, for sure," he said. "Brave *krigare,* too. Of course, of course."

"May I have the tears?" Marina asked quietly.

Farfar grinned again...

Then opened his mouth wide and stuck out his tongue.

And upon that wooden tongue sat a brilliant ruby, flashing and stunning as a drop of fire. Marina reached out and picked it up—it pulsed in her grasp.

Farfar pulled his tongue back in and smacked his lips.

Marina felt both Loki and Thor press closer.

"Where's the other one?" Loki wanted to know.

Farfar's eyebrows went up.

"I cannot know, *pojke*, I cannot know," he answered, his eyes going wide. "He kept it a secret from me. I cannot know."

"But is it here?" Thor pointed at the floor.

"Yes, *pojke,* yes," Farfar nodded. "Yes, somewhere. Yes."

Loki looked flatly at Marina.

"Any ideas?"

Marina's head jerked up and she looked at him, then at Thor.

"I...no," she managed. "I didn't even know *he* was here..." She gestured helplessly to Farfar.

Silence fell. The fire sputtered. Loki sighed heavily.

"I'm tired," he muttered. "And I'm hungry. I'm going to make food, and then I say we should have a look at the ones we've got."

"Agreed," Thor nodded, and followed him to the kitchen, leaving Marina behind. She watched them go...

And when she faced the mantel again, Farfar was gone.

Chapter Twenty Three

MARINA SAT ON THE FLOOR, wrapped in a blanket, leaning her shoulder sideways on the couch and facing the fire. She had taken her coat and gloves off and laid them on the armchair across the way.

The dawn bloomed against the frost-covered windows, making them glow, and filling the room with soft light. She smelled hot food cooking in the kitchen, but somehow she couldn't make herself get her legs under her, and go into a room where he was. Not again.

Heavy footfalls. Coming toward her. She glanced up to the right to see Thor towering over her—and smiling at her.

"Here, Little Thing," he said, holding a steaming bowl down to her. She blinked, then reached up and took it from him.

"Thank you."

"Loki was only able to salvage some things from your larder," he said, sitting down heavily next to her and crossing his legs. "So he's made due with a nail soup."

Marina's throat thickened and her eyes stung. All she could do was nod. Shakily, she picked up the spoon and dipped it into the rich reddish liquid, finding potatoes, canned chopped tomatoes, mushrooms, hamburger, canned corn and peas. She brought it to her mouth and tasted it. Hot, flavorful—a little salty, and delicious. It slid down her throat and warmed her whole body. She almost started crying.

"Forgive my rough manners," Thor spoke up, taking a sip of his own soup right out of the bowl. "But all this while I have been calling you Little Thing, which is rude."

Marina halfway smiled.

"I don't mind."

"But your name is Lady Marina, is it not?"

"Just Marina," she answered, glancing over and meeting his brilliant eyes. "I don't have a title."

"Yes, you do," he countered frankly, looking into the fire. "I've just given it to you."

Marina blushed, ducked her head, and smiled again.

Just then, a slight breath of air against the back of her neck...

And Loki swept silently into the room cradling his own bowl of soup, and sat down a little in front of Thor. He didn't look at her.

But somehow, Marina couldn't tear her eyes from him.

He set the soup down on the rug, rubbed his hands together, breathed into them...

And produced the silver stone. It caught the firelight and the dawn, and snapped sparkles out toward them.

Three times he breathed onto it, then whispered,

"*Syna.*"

And he gently tossed it into the hearth.

The flames flashed, and took on a marvelous silver hue. And, just as before, they coalesced into figures. Figures of people.

Marina heard Thor stop breathing. And, out of the corner of her eye, she saw him lean forward, unblinking, and fixate on those figures.

A tall, beautiful, middle-aged woman with long, curly hair, half of it done up and wound around an elegant circlet. She wore a sweeping gown with fitted sleeves and an ornate belt. Her lovely face was filled with distress, her eyes wide, her fingers squeezed together. She paced with short steps beside a chair—a chair where a young man sat, his expression closed and dark, his fingers draped over his mouth.

Bauldr.

He had matured—he looked exactly the way he did when last Marina saw him. Handsome, with shining hair. Yet, she could still not be sure *when* exactly this had happened, since Aesir seemed to change so little, no matter how much time passed...

"*Alskling*, I beg of you not to worry any more," the woman urged, her voice slightly unsteady as she faced him. "I have done everything that can possibly be done. The spell I have laid on you is unbreakable. Nothing in Asgard or anywhere else can possibly harm you."

"Then why don't my nightmares stop?" he asked, his voice hard and weary, staring straight out in front of him.

The woman stopped her pacing, then knelt down beside the chair, reached out and stroked his hair away from his ear.

"Sometimes we have nightmares," she murmured. "We all do. But we mustn't let fear dominate our lives."

Bauldr shot out of his chair and turned his back on her—she stared up at him in alarm.

"You know nothing of it, Mother," he snapped at her. "Being plagued *every* fortnight for more than two-hundred years by visions of your own red blood spilling out all over your hands?" He turned to her and held out his hands, palm up, his face pale and his eyes stark. His mother stared up at him, stricken.

"They are not just *nightmares*," he bit out. "They are real. And no matter what you, or father, or Loki can conjure, they *will* find a way of coming true." And with that, he fled the room.

His mother sat there, gazing at the place where he had gone.

Then, she sank further to the floor, covered her mouth with her hand, and broke into weeping that shook her whole body.

Marina heard Thor swallow hard. She glanced over at Loki...

His eyes shone, his brow knotted, and he did not look away from that woman.

Slowly, the picture faded, the flames regained their natural color.

And the stone rolled out of the cinders and onto the rug. Loki gazed at it for a moment, then picked it up and vanished it again.

"Strange," Thor whispered. "To see him..."

"I know," Loki breathed.

Marina gripped her blanket around herself, again unable to look away from him.

"What..." Thor cleared his throat, and began again. "What does the golden one show?"

"It shows Odin," Loki answered quietly, head bowed. "And Bird, when he lamed Fljotur."

"Ah," Thor said roughly, and dipped his own head, and swallowed again.

"And..." Loki took a breath. "Odin telling him he shouldn't have brought Marina to Asgard."

Thor looked at him.

"Did Bird tell Father that she was to be the guardian of these stones?"

Loki shook his head, and Thor frowned in answer.

"What others do we have?" Thor asked, setting his stew bowl down.

"Marina has the others," Loki muttered, pulling at a loose bit of the rug tassel.

"My lady?" Thor held out his hand out to her.

"They're in my coat pocket," Marina said, far quieter than she had meant to. "On the chair, behind Loki."

Loki sat up and turned, pulled down her coat and stuck his hand in her pocket. The pulled out the gleaming stones, then laid the coat back where it had been, still avoiding her eyes. He picked up the stormy blue one, breathed on it and said the magic word, and threw it in the fire.

The fire snarled and blazed, turning turquoise, then sapphire, and clouding all around with smoke. And in the swirl and pulse, a figure coalesced which was unmistakably Thor himself. And he chased after Bird down a long hallway. A hallway Marina recognized.

It looked like Bilskirnir, Thor's mead-hall. And Thor and Bird were wearing the clothes they had worn the night of that midsummer feast and dance—when Marina had come.

"Brother," Thor called. "Brother, wait."

Bird slowed, breathing tightly, and stopped to face a railing. He braced his hands on it and lowered his head. Thor caught up to him, his brow furrowed, his gaze intent.

"Bird, what is going on?" Thor demanded. "You bring a Midgardian woman here, one who bears no ailment except a crippled hand—and you walk with her in the moonlight, *kissing* her, all just a fortnight from your own *wedding*."

Marina's heart jolted. Her gaze flashed over to Thor, then Loki...

But both men fixed on the flames before them.

"Nanna is a mere league from here, staying with Mother and preparing the hall for *your* feast," Thor reminded Bird, pressing closer. "And what are you doing?"

"You have no idea what I'm doing," Bird answered in a low, guarded tone. Thor stopped, frowning harder, and leaned around so he could see Bird's face. He paused, studying him, then spoke again, carefully.

"Have your dreams come again?"

Bird cast his gaze down, and his mouth hardened.

Thor reached out and put a broad hand on his shoulder.

"You fear the spell is not sufficient to protect you?" Thor asked. Bird did not answer. Thor leaned even closer, his eyes bright and earnest.

"Tell me, Brother," Thor pleaded. "Tell me so that I might seek out this evil and destroy it—no matter where it lies. Please."

Bird let out a shaking sigh.

"I dare not tell you," he whispered, then turned his head and looked directly at Thor. "I dare not trust anyone."

Thor stared at him. His lips parted, but he clearly couldn't speak. Pain crossed Bird's face—but he pulled out of Thor's grip, turned and walked away, leaving Thor gazing into the empty air, his hand grasping nothing. The image faded away. The fire turned golden again. The stone rolled out onto the rug.

Thor covered his face with his hand. Loki turned to see him—eyebrows pulled together, eyes a deep and brilliant green.

Thor grunted, loudly cleared his throat again, then rubbed his face with both hands and dropped them. His eyes gleamed, and his eyelashes shone wet. He gazed blankly at the rug.

Loki bit the side of his cheek and lowered his attention. For a long while, they all sat silent.

At last, Loki lifted the red stone, whispered the word and threw it in.

A shimmering rainbow burst out, then decided upon yellows, oranges and deep reds. And clarified into a picture of Marina—herself—hurrying down a street in town, in the full springtime.

She gasped, sat up straight, and battled to remember when this had happened...

Ahead of her stood a building: a tall, broad, wide-windowed business with a hand-painted red sign reading: *Svenson's Plumbing Carpentry and Landscaping*

Marina hurried across the street and pushed the jangling front door open, and glanced around a cluttered workshop filled with all manner of table-saws, tools, half-done furniture and wood-littered countertops.

"Good morning!"

She turned when a man with a white beard and twinkling eyes, wearing cover-alls, carried an unvarnished rocking chair in through a side door.

"Good morning," Marina answered.

"How can I help you?" the man asked, setting the chair down.

"Is Bird Oldeson here?" Marina asked.

The man's cheerful expression disappeared.

"No, I'm afraid not."

Marina paused.

"He isn't?"

"Nope," the man sighed, shaking his head as he stepped up to the counter near her. "He quit on me the other day. Said he had some family business he had to take care of in Colorado."

Marina stared at him.

"What...? He's gone?"

The man sat down in a chair and nodded.

"Yeah, moved all of his things out of his trailer yesterday—he stopped by my house to say goodbye last night before heading out."

"But..." Marina stammered. "I thought...I thought all his family lived around here!"

"No," he shook his head. "No family at all here. He's only been here for a few months. He came here for the fishing, initially, then needed some extra pocket money, so I hired him on. It's a shame I had to lose him—he's one of the best workers I've ever had. A real good kid, so friendly, always on time...I'm Jim Larson by the way," And he stuck out a hand. Marina took his fingers.

"Marina Feroe," she managed.

"Feroe!" he said as he released her. "Bird was doing some work for you, wasn't he? Windows?"

Marina nodded.

"You're satisfied with what he did, aren't you?" Larson leaned forward. "Like I said, I've never had a better—"

"I've got a leak," Marina cut in. "A leak in my bathroom ceiling. I need...I need someone to fix it."

"Sure!" Larson nodded. "Sure, no problem. I think Richard's got some time tomorrow morning—want me to send him on by?"

"That would be good," Marina agreed. "Thank you."

Marina turned and pushed through the door. She trailed back down the sidewalk, looking straight ahead, her face blank—and a depth of sorrow in her eyes that shone so clearly, almost written across her whole frame.

The image faded and disappeared. Marina, as she sat wrapped up in the blanket, felt her face burn, and her heart pang like something had stabbed it.

Images rose again, and this time she recognized them instantly.

It was her, and Bird, standing on the road outside Bilskirnir in the moonlight. Facing each other.

"I know that I am utterly selfish to ask this of you," Bird said, bending close to her face. "And I never would, if I feared only for myself. But I don't. Whatever evil thing is to happen to me, it will also twist around my brother, my mother, my father, all my friends—and my realm. I can feel it. And you are our only hope."

"What do you want me to do?" Marina asked him, lifting her face. He halfway smiled at her.

"You'll know when it's time."

And he slipped his hand around to the back of her neck, stepped in and pressed a kiss to her forehead.

Marina watched herself as she closed her eyes, her whole body leaning into him...

He drew back, lowered his head and gazed at her.

"Thank you, Marina," he whispered. "Now you should go back to bed."

Her eyes went wide.

"I don't want to leave you."

Bird smiled gently.

"The best way you can help me now is to rest," he said, stroking her cheek. "It will be all right. I promise."

"But..." Marina stopped. Her gaze flickered down to his mouth. She leaned up toward him, closing the distance...

He dipped down toward her, just for an instant...

Then slowly stepped back from her, and dropped his hand.

"Goodnight, Marina," he said, inclining his head. "I'll see you soon."

She closed her fingers and pressed her fist to her heart. She nodded.

"Okay," she breathed. "Goodnight."

And she turned, and walked back up between the towering shadows of the oaks, toward the great mead house. Bird stood alone in the road, watching her, then turned and gazed out ahead of him at the towering shadow of Yggdrasil.

The images faded, the fire returned to normal. The ruby hopped out of the hearth, and lay by the sapphire on the rug.

Marina felt like something was sticking into her side. She winced, that uncomfortable, stinging feeling twisting around in her chest. She pulled her knees up against her, trying to form words...

"Bird is engaged?"

The words fell out. Hung in the air.

"Yes," Thor replied. "He was."

Marina swallowed, then swallowed again.

And for some reason, she looked up at Loki.

Who gazed right back at her. Eyes green as a rainy spring. Forehead knotted. Mouth soft, lips parted.

She got up, gripping the blanket, and turned away from them.

"I'm going upstairs to bed," she stated. Then, without looking back, she strode toward the stairs and climbed up to her room.

Chapter Twenty Four

MARINA WOKE UP.

She stared at the ceiling above her and frowned, trying to remember where she was...

Oh. Right.

Her house. Her own house. Her own little bedroom, with the bed in the center of the room, the wardrobe that was not magic, the frosted window that faced the garden...

Not Festning.

Blankets and comforters piled on top of her. The room lay quiet. How strange it sounded, not to have a low fire crackling in a hearth nearby...

She adjusted the way she lay, automatically favoring her left side...

And a wave of ease and reflexive relief washed through her as she realized she didn't have to—that actually it felt *wonderful* to lie on that side.

She sat up. Tears sprang to her eyes again. She pressed her eyelids with her fingers, fighting them back, and sniffed.

And then, slowly, as she gazed ahead of her into the softly-lit room—for it had to be afternoon now—memories began rising, unbidden. Like water bubbling up into a dry cavern.

She sat up, her breath stilling in her chest as she frowned, carefully clicking the mental pieces together. Wondering at them...turning them over...

She slid out from beneath the heavy covers, pulled her boots on, and, shivering, found her long coat and gloves, put them on and left her room.

She crept out onto the landing and went down the stairs, avoiding the ones she knew squeaked. Marina passed the living room and glimpsed Thor lying on the rug in front of the fire, covered in several blankets, sound asleep. Sunlight glowed through the ice-covered windows. She smiled faintly, glanced around...

She didn't see Loki anywhere. Setting her jaw, she made her way to the front door, grasped the handle and opened it.

The cold daylight spilled inside as the hinges creaked. She quickly stepped out and shut the door behind her, struck by a bracing breath of winter air. Her own breath fogged around her face as she looked around her yard. Sunlight shone blindingly upon the virgin snow all around her, making it look like mounds of sparkling sugar. Her boots crunched on the ice and snow piled on her porch as she started forward, down the steps, and out into the sunlight herself.

Carefully, she waded between the drifts toward the side of the house, following what she remembered of the path, studying...frowning...

There.

Completely shrouded by snow so that it looked like a hunched tree. That wild, ungainly rosebush that she had almost torn out so long ago. Leaning against the fireplace for warmth.

She paused, and then stood very still. Gazing at its burdened form beneath all of that crushing, paralyzing ice...

She closed her eyes, trying to remember what warmth felt like, and the sound of the wind through the leaves, and birdsong...

"Planning a little landscaping?"

She opened her eyes and turned toward the voice.

Loki stood there at the corner of the porch in his black trousers and boots, and a form-fitting black jacket with a thick velvet collar, his hands in his pockets. His curly hair had gone to ebony, and gleamed in the sunlight; and his eyes had turned to a slate gray that nevertheless appeared so striking that for a moment, Marina couldn't look away.

"Hello," she said.

Loki blinked, and swallowed.

"Hello."

For another long moment, she held his gaze, and neither of them moved. Then, Marina turned back to the rosebush.

"I *was* thinking of landscaping, actually," Marina confessed quietly, wrapping her arms around herself.

Loki's footsteps swished through the snow toward her, but he stopped a short distance away.

"Well, you might have to re-think your garden's theme," he suggested—and she could feel his dark smirk. "Something more along the lines of ice-sculptures or gingerbread, perhaps?"

The corner of Marina's mouth quirked up, even as memories kept tugging on her...

"I was going to tear out this rose bush this past summer," she murmured. "Because I thought it was obnoxious and mean. Look at the thorns." She pointed. "They're so long they're sticking through the snow."

She heard and felt Loki take three steps closer, cautiously.

"Mhm," he grunted. "So...why didn't you?"

Again, that sensation rose up inside her, swelling, *almost* coalescing into clarity...

"Because of something Bird said," she said, her brow furrowing as she called up his words from the golden haze of a faraway afternoon. "He said...'This bush is a different kind from the ones along your walkway. Those were bought in this part of the country, bred for this weather. But this one...'" Marina reached out and touched one snow-covered leaf. "'This...is from somewhere else entirely. A different climate, different soil. Picked up on some faraway travels. It's had to survive far harsher winters than it was meant for, and a lot less sun than it needed.'" Marina's voice lowered as light began to dawn in her mind...

She kept going, careful with every word, every thought...

"'But it did what it had to in order to survive. It leaned up against the house, near the fireplace. The warmth and shelter of the house has kept it alive. And the one who built the house...was wise enough to plant this bush on the south side, away from the brutal north wind. And that same person nursed it and fought off frost and bugs for twenty or thirty years...before the bush got strong enough to fend for itself. But it wouldn't leave the house then, even though it could.'"

Marina *felt* Loki's breathless silence—the tension against her shoulders, the *almost*-realization, the *almost*-words...

"He said, 'It's a late bloomer,'" Marina whispered. "'But I think, if you'll have a little patience with its difficult attitude, it might...turn out to be...'" Suddenly, she turned, and looked straight up into Loki's eyes. "'...the prettiest rose you've got.'"

He gazed right back at her, caught full in a sunbeam—and for the first time, though his eyes shone emerald, she could see dozens of other colors sparkling there, like the facets of a jewel. And though the depths of his curls remained black as pitch, the tips, highlights and edges shimmered with auburn, red, silver and gold. His angular face, pale as snow—yet he blushed. And his breath caught in his chest.

The two of them stood, frozen, not daring to breathe—and Marina's heart hammered so hard she was sure he could hear it.

Finally, she forced a breath in through her tight throat, a warm shiver running all through her.

"Loki."

"What?" he whispered, his gaze flitting all over her face.

"I think..." She stopped, swallowed hard, then tore her attention away from him to stare at that gnarled bush once more. "I think it's in there."

Loki instantly stepped closer to her, frowning intently down into the snow-covered leaves.

"What is?" he murmured.

Marina gingerly reached up and pulled the glove off her left hand. She didn't know why—it just seemed *correct* to use that one, instead of her right hand...

Then, trying not to wince, she knelt down, stretched out her fingers and pushed them past the first layer of dusty ice.

Cold kissed her skin. Brittle leaves brushed the back of her hand and her palm. Thorns prodded her, running along her fingers as if tasting her—but they didn't stab into her. Slowly, slowly, she kept going, pushing deeper and deeper, waiting for that bush to slash her open like it had before...

Then, she felt that pull again.

Deep inside her chest.

She had to scoot closer, so that her front touched the outer branches, and her arm delved in past her elbow. She sensed Loki standing uncomfortably beside her, still holding his breath, as if on the edge of flinching back...

Miraculously, the thorns didn't bite her. Her fingers met the cold main stem of the vine, all knotted and bristled. She slid down, closing her eyes, searching...

There. A hollow spot in the heart of the rose. She pressed her fingers inside...

And met warmth.

Her eyes flew open.

She picked the unseen object up, and felt it. A small, sharply-diamond shaped piece as hard as steel, and warm as a summer day.

She closed her fist around it, keeping it tight in the hollow of her hand, and gradually drew her arm back out, snow knocking loose and sparkling in the sunlight.

Then, she climbed to her feet, faced Loki...

And slowly opened her fingers.

There in the center of her palm lay a gorgeous emerald, more beautiful by far than any of the other stones. Deep within its facets gleamed blues, purples and turquoises that Marina had never imagined. It dazzled in the sunlight, sending splintered rainbows across her dark coat and Loki's. She glanced up at him.

He stared down at that stone, a strange, quiet, almost frightened look on his face. His hair had caught silver, his eyes deep blue.

"I think it's yours," Marina murmured, and held it out to him.

Loki met her gaze. Stood motionless for a long while.

Then, hesitating, he held out his bare hand, palm up. Marina set the stone in it. Their fingers brushed.

Another deep, warm shiver raced through her.

"Well," Loki said quietly, then cleared his throat. "Let's have a look then, shall we?"

Together, but wordless, they ventured back inside the house. After knocking the snow off their boots and removing their coats, they entered the sitting room to find it empty, the blankets folded on the couch.

"He might be in the kitchen," Marina ventured softly. "Should I call him?"

"Not yet," Loki answered without looking at her—but moving to stand in front of the fire, his brow dark and pensive. He breathed onto the stone, then whispered,

"*Syna*," and tossed it into the flames.

They blazed a terrible green, outlined with yellow, and leaped high up the chimney. In an eyeblink, figures appeared—two men on horseback, trotting through a wide open field.

Marina, helplessly drawn forward, knelt in front of the fireplace. She felt Loki do the same, not far from her.

The men—Thor, wearing loose-fitting clothes, a dagger at his belt and a bow and arrow slung over his back. Loki, clad similarly, with a sleeveless tunic; his hair wildly curly and red, his face beaming with smiles. He and Thor laughed together as their steeds kicked through the tall grass.

A whistle cut the day. The men pulled back and turned to look.

"Ah, there he is," Thor chuckled. "Took him long enough."

Marina frowned, but the scene didn't shift. She just watched, spellbound, as Loki and Thor observed someone else far away, with placid amusement on their faces—

That suddenly flared into terror.

"My God," Loki cried, his voice breaking in two as his hair blanched to white and his eyes to grey.

"Bird!" Thor roared—

And together, Thor and Loki kicked their horses, who broke into a blinding gallop. The men bent over the necks of their steeds and raced back whence they had come, Loki pulling ahead almost instantly.

Then, in the background, the horrid, wrenching screams of an injured horse. Loki left Thor far behind, his steed sucking air like a jet engine—

And then Loki flung himself out of the saddle.

He twisted midair, landed on both feet and charged forward, then skidded and threw himself down beside...

A young man who lay face down in the grass. A young man in tanned leather, with a shock of golden hair. Loki took hold of his shoulders and turned him over, his whole appearance still white as a sheet, so that the youth lay on his back.

Bird.

Limp. Eyes closed. Blood trailing down his chin.

"Oh, God, oh, God," Loki keened, his face twisting. Quickly, he pushed his forefinger hard against Bird's breastbone, leaned down and pressed his lips to his forehead and squeezed his eyes shut.

"*Leita...leita...leita...*" he gasped against Bird's brow. "*Finna...finna...finna...*"

Just then, Thor thudded to his knees next to Loki, tears running down his cheeks and lighting his brilliant eyes.

"Is he dead?" he choked, pressing his fingers to Bird's throat. "Loki, I cannot...There's no—"

"*Leita, leita, leita,*" Loki whispered urgently. "*Finna, finna, finna...*"

"Loki—?" Thor begged. "Loki, he is not *breathing...!*"

Loki sat up, his hands shaking, and pressed them to either side of Bird's head.

"*Vanka,*" he commanded. "*Vanka. Vanka...vanka...*"

He squeezed Bird's head, then his neck, then pressed both hands hard down against his heart.

"*Vanka!*" he cried, and shoved *down*—

Bird jerked.

Gasped.

His eyes flew open, and he broke out in violent quivering.

"Ha!" Thor yelped, snatching Bird by the hair—

And Loki jerked Bird into a sitting position, pulled him into his chest and pressed the side of his face to his, tears trickling down. And as Loki fervently held him, his white hair rushed through with gold brighter than the sun. Thor flung his arms around both of them, and the three men sat, wordless, in the grassy field, gasping and weeping.

Marina drew a breath that tore through her—but she could scarcely recover before the scene dissolved, replaced by a vision of Bauldr standing alone on the road in the moonlight, facing Yggdrasil, on the very night Marina had seen him last.

Footsteps sounded on gravel, and Loki—dressed in his frivolous ribbons, his arms crossed, a smirk on his face—strode out to stand beside the slightly-shorter man.

"Thinking of breaking off your engagement?" Loki asked, facing the great tree as well and giving Bird a sideways look. Absently, Bird frowned.

"What are you talking about?"

"Dunno," Loki shrugged. "You're just standing out here in the middle of the night, gazing wistfully at the place where your betrothed is slumbering tonight, just after giving gifts to and kissing a young Midgardian woman on the head."

Bird didn't answer—but a line appeared on his brow, and he glanced down.

"It's a pity you didn't try her mouth," Loki remarked, lifting his chin. "You know, she tastes exactly like sweet cream, with a touch of honey and cinnamon."

"I had hoped your intentions would be more honorable than that," Bird said sharply, his voice low. "That's why I didn't knock you straight to the floor when I saw what you were doing."

"Oh? And how do you know they weren't?" Loki objected, facing him, his eyebrows going up. "How do you know I wasn't trying to see what *you* saw, to get inside and find out what made her so broken and crooked to discover if I could fix it?"

Bird said nothing, folded his own arms, and didn't look at him. The levity vanished from Loki's face, and a hint of urgency entered his eyes.

"You cannot think me so callous as that."

Bird lowered his head slightly, his expression hardening.

"I do not doubt your devotion to me, my brother or my father, Loki," he said. Finally, he turned his head, and met Loki's eyes. "But after what I have seen tonight...Any woman would be a fool to trust your sincerity."

Loki just stared at him. Bird held his gaze for just another moment, then stepped past him.

"Goodnight," he said, and left Loki alone.

Loki stood just as he was, empty space before him. He did not sneer—his eyelashes flickered, and he stood off balance, as if absorbing a sting.

Marina's whole head felt hot, her heartbeat staggering and potent. She wrapped her arms tight around herself and didn't dare glance to her right to see Loki's expression.

The image of Loki in the fire soon dissipated, and a very different sight emerged.

Bird lay on his back on an unkempt bed, bathed in a bright moonbeam that spilled in from a skylight. White sheets had been thrown back and halfway dragged on the floor. One of his legs was bent, one arm lay sprawled, as if he had been hurriedly flung down by someone who had carried him there. Blank eyes stared at the ceiling. Skin white as alabaster, covered in a sheen of sweat. His golden hair spread across the crooked pillow. And the shaft of a black arrow protruded from the center of his chest. Blood as red as the dawn soaked the whole of the front of his white shirt.

He was not breathing.

Marina pressed both hands over her mouth. But she couldn't look away.

Movement in the corner of the dark room where Bird lay. The opening of a door. Someone slipped inside.

And then, Loki stepped into the moonlight.

He wore black. His hair, a deep chestnut. And she saw a shimmer of sapphire in his eyes for a moment as he entered, and caught sight of the graceful body.

His left hand came up in reflex. He lost his balance, and swayed.

"Oh!" he moaned shakily, his brow knotting. Then, he slowly sank toward Bird...

Fell to his knees, and began to sob.

He grabbed fistfuls of the bedsheets, his knuckles turning white. He lifted his face, tears streaming down, and his hands reached out and floundered toward the arrow.

"No, no, no..." he whimpered, pressing down hard against the bloody wound, uselessly grasping the shaft in different places—as if longing to pull it loose, his palms stained scarlet. His breathing came in quick gasps as he searched Bird's face—let go of the arrow and and pressed his fingers to Bird's throat, smearing his white skin with red.

"Not *you*," Loki sobbed in a whisper. His face suddenly twisted with violent anger as tears rolled down his cheeks. He wrapped his hand around behind Bird's neck and shook him, as if fighting to draw that blank gaze to his own. "You little idiot, what were you...What were you *doing?*" Loki gasped, and his features broke with pleading. "What were you doing?" he wept. "Not *you*...Not..." He shook his head, more tears welling up and streaming down as he let go and stroked Bird's hair away from his face.

Then, as if a tidal wave built inside him, Loki curled his fingers desperately through the front of Bird's shirt, bent and let out a wretched howl into Bird's chest. His whole body shuddered, his muscles binding tight as iron. And Bird lay dead, staring sightlessly at the moon, while Loki screamed into his silent heart.

More movement at the back of the room.

Guards, gleaming in armor, burst in.

"So you've come back to lay a curse on his *soul* now, have you?" one of them bellowed—

And grabbed Loki by the hair, flung him around, and struck him in the face with his gloved hand.

Loki's head whiplashed back. He collapsed against the side of the bed. He choked, letting out a stunned, watery cry. He fell to the floor, trying to brace himself up on his elbows...

The guard kicked him in the side.

He yelped and curled up...

And then the other two guards commenced lashing him in the head, shoulders and back with their fists, cursing him and spitting on him. Then, they hauled him to his feet.

Blood ran down his mouth, nose, chin and cheekbone. He sagged against them as they bound his hands behind his back. Then, they grabbed him by the arms and the hair and roughly threw him out of the room.

Bird lay in the ensuing quiet, Loki's bloody fingerprints marring his neck and face, the moonlight gleaming against the feathers of the arrow.

And then he faded away.

The green light vanished. The golden flames died down. The emerald stone rolled out of the embers and onto the rug.

Teardrops burned Marina's skin, and dripped from her chin. Her whole chest heavy as lead, she turned just slightly, terrified of what she would see...

Loki sat on the floor with his back against the heavy armchair, one foot tucked under the opposite knee. His hands lay limp in his lap.

And he looked at her. Hair like midnight, eyes like a winter sky. Eyebrows drawn together.

Tears running freely down his face.

She didn't say anything.

Deathly quiet reigned.

Then, Loki's lips parted, and he pulled in a low, shallow breath.

"It was an accident."

Marina didn't move. Just waited.

He blinked and more tears ran down.

"I had learned from a fairy in the woods that my sister...my sister was planning to kill Thor. That she had made...amorous advances and Thor had rejected her," Loki said softly. He drew another careful breath. "As fairies can be fickle, and sometimes wrong, I went to Hel and warned her that if such a plot had entered her head, she would not only have to contend with Odin himself, but with me." Loki swallowed, and his gaze drifted off. "She denied everything. But she accused me of favoring the Aesir over my own flesh and blood, and told me to leave with her and Fenris, rather than stay in Asgard even one day more. I refused." Loki's fingers closed. "She assured me that, in the end, I would choose to return to my...rightful family."

His attention lingered on the emerald, though his sparkling gaze grew distant.

"I couldn't substantiate the threat, so I said nothing to anyone. Instead, I placed trigger spells around Thor's chambers that would alert me if anyone but an Aesir tried to pass through. One night, one of the spells woke me. Like a fly at the edge of a spiderweb. I got up, and I brought my bow and arrows with me. My arrows have mistletoe hearts—mistletoe breaks all spells. I knew that, if it was my sister, the protective spell she would cast around herself would shatter when the arrow hit it—and so would the arrow. So I...I made my way through the halls and I stopped in one corridor. And there at the far end of it, just outside Thor's doorway, holding a long knife, was a *myrkalfr*. A dark elf."

Marina blinked, listening so hard she couldn't breathe.

Loki bit the inside of his cheek, and said nothing for a long time. Finally, though, he went on, studying his own hands.

"I surmised that my sister had bought an assassin from Svartalfheim. And that an elf would be powerful in both strength and magic. Thor, if he were surprised, might not be able to contend with him. And so, I sighted down my arrow and..."

His throat closed. His eyebrows twitched together, more tears tumbled...

And he wrapped his arms around himself.

"It was him," he gasped, looking up at Marina helplessly. "As soon as my arrow came loose of my string, some kind of spell broke and it *wasn't* an elf. It was him." He shook his head, and teardrops fell from his jaw and tumbled onto his jacket collar. "Hel must have lured Bird out of his rooms and triggered my guarding spell herself, since she's not an Aesir, and then when Bird passed her she put an illusion around him to..." Loki stopped, covered his face with his hand and bent forward, pulling his arms in tight.

Marina's whole heart ached. She couldn't move, and she couldn't look away.

"It was Bird she hated, not Thor," Loki whispered, lowering his hand to cover his mouth, staring at the floor—at nothing. "And she wanted *me* to hit him. To prove her point." He dropped his hand and closed his eyes. "To show how stupid I was to try to make my home in Asgard. To hope...for once...to find some...little bit of happiness."

Marina blinked, feeling more tears slide down well-worn tracks. She couldn't say anything.

Then, Loki twitched, sucked in a panicked breath and looked up to the back of the room—

Thor stood there in the doorway, arms over his chest. Expression filled with dull pain, eyes bright with tears.

"Did you..." Loki rasped. "Did you see—?"

Thor's face twisted, and he nodded hard.

Loki's frame broke. He turned, and crawled toward Thor, his head hanging low, then knelt in the center of the rug—weeping uncontrollably.

Thor took three strides toward him, bent and grabbed him roughly by the upper arms, and hauled him to his feet. Before Loki could catch his balance, Thor had flung his arms around him and folded him into his chest, burying his face in Loki's collar.

Loki immediately encircled Thor's waist with his arms, taking hold of his shirt, incoherent with sobs.

"I'm...I'm sorry, I'm sorry," Loki stammered between harsh gasps. "I'm so

sorry—"

"No, *I* am sorry," Thor protested, backing up and taking Loki's head in his hands. "Forgive me for my lack of faith in you, and for leaving you to such a fate." Thor leveled a fierce, tearful gaze at him. "I beg that you might someday call me a friend again."

Loki reached up and grasped Thor's hair and pulled him close, and the two men stood, foreheads pressed together, tears staining their clothes.

Chapter Twenty Five

PURPLE LIGHT FADED in the western sky. Marina buttoned the top button of her coat and let her breath out slowly—it puffed in vapor around her head. She stood calf-deep in snow once more, in front of her house, facing the darkening woods.

Silence had dominated the sitting room after Thor and Loki's weeping had abated. Then, as if by unspoken contract, they had cleared their throats, dried their tears, stepped back from each other and moved into the cloak room. There, they had noisily retrieved their armor, coats and weapons—as well as Marina's. Loki handed them to her, and, startled, she got up and put them on, trying not to fumble.

Now, Loki stood with Thor on the porch, having just shut the front door with a resounding *thud*.

"*Loka*," Loki ordered quietly, touching two fingertips to the center of the door—and Marina realized he had just put a spell around the house. No one would be able to get in. Then, the two men faced her, hopped down the steps, and began striding toward the forest.

"Come, my lady," Thor urged. "We do not have much time."

"Where are we going?" Marina asked, hurrying to keep pace with them as they moved swiftly across the side yard.

"To Helheim," Loki answered, looping his bow over his shoulders. "Now that we have all the stones, we need to find his body. Otherwise, all of this has just been academic nonsense."

"How do we get in?" Marina wondered.

"The gate," Thor told her.

"The gate!" Marina repeated. "To Asgard?"

"Same gate, different spell," Loki replied.

"What do we do once we're inside?" Marina asked. "I thought there were monsters and spirits..."

"I've been thinking of that," Loki said, glancing over at Thor as they passed the first line of trees and began descending the hill. "I'm going to dress you up, *vinkona*."

Thor looked at him, alarmed.

"What, as *your* bridesmaid, this time?"

Loki smirked.

"Almost." He glanced down at Marina. "You've of course heard of Pesta."

"Yes," Marina answered, confused. "She's the Black Plague personified—an old woman in black who comes through the town and kills everyone..."

"Mhm," Loki nodded, and one eyebrow quirked up. "She was killed recently on Alfheimr—very quietly, by a group of three elvish assassins who have lost the ability to speak, and her body disintegrated. I only know about it because of the fairies that go back and forth between our realms."

"Why do you bring her up?" Thor wondered.

"Well, what if *she* were to accompany me into Helheim, to visit my sister?" Loki looked over at Thor. "It would prove all of our sincerity, and I could easily hand a little Midgardian woman to her as a hostess gift."

"What, *me* as Pesta?" Thor cried.

"Hand me to—what?" Marina interrupted.

"We're not going to be able to fight our way through," Loki said quietly, weaving between the trees as they achieved the bottom of the hill, and darkness gathered around them. "It's better to go along with what she wants until she reveals her hand. We don't know where Bird is—and we won't know unless she shows us." He glanced meaningfully at the others. "I can only speak for myself, but I don't relish the idea of tangling with wraiths, trolls, goblins, wolves *and* my sister all at once."

"Nor I," Thor agreed, facing ahead. "Do what you will, Loki—I will play along. As long as you give me leave to crush her skull when I have the chance."

Loki glanced at him. Thor met his eyes. Loki's expression turned dark.

"With pleasure," he growled. And Thor nodded.

The sun set. Blackness covered them.

"Marina," Loki said quietly—and she heard his steps shorten. Then, his gloved hand grasped hers, and held on. She immediately returned the pressure, her wide eyes searching the darkness all around.

After a few minutes of traipsing through the icy shadows, trusting Loki not to lead her into a tree, she felt a tall, stoic presence rise up in front of them. And then, like a match in the dark, bluish light *snapped* to life...

At the crest of the archway.

The symbol of Mjollnir glowed faintly, as if with inner lightning. By that illumination, Marina could just barely glimpse the two men with her. Loki pulled Marina closer to his side.

"All right, Pesta," Loki said, nodding to Thor. "Are you ready?"

"Mhm," Thor nodded back.

"It's just an illusion, not a transformation," Loki reminded him. "When you draw Mjollnir from your belt, it'll break."

"Understood," Thor said.

Loki took a deep preparatory breath, then another. Then, he lifted his right hand and touched it to Thor's forehead.

Loki closed his eyes, muttering words Marina couldn't make out—but they hissed and slithered through the forest.

Black wisps began swimming around Thor's mountainous form, clinging to his cape, marking his gleaming gold armor, snagging in his wild hair.

Loki backed up, keeping his hand aloft, even as Thor's figure shrank and dimmed and hunched. Ragged black robes frothed over him and draped down to the ground—a deep hood swallowed his head. A splintered broom materialized in his left hand—which had turned bony and gnarled. Then, at last, a very different face peered out from the cowl.

Luminescent green eyes, large as an owl's. A long hooked nose and chin, both covered in warts. Hollow cheeks, skin like leather. Threads of wiry hair framing the cheekbones.

"Well?" Thor gnashed in a high, grating voice, showing five razor-sharp teeth. "How do I look?"

Loki opened his eyes and peered at him. Frowned.

"Horrid," he answered. Then, he stretched out his hand and pushed on that long, hooked nose...

And it moved. Turned crooked, as if it had broken a century ago, and healed badly.

"Ah, yes," Loki said in satisfaction, withdrawing. "Much better."

Thor smacked his lips.

"Not a word of this to anyone," he rasped.

"Any memory of *that* face gives me nightmares, so *no*," Loki assured him, waving it off. "Not a word."

"Shall we go?" Thor asked, thumping his broomstick into the snow.

"I think we ought to," Loki murmured, gripping Marina's hand tighter. He took another deep breath, faced the arch, and spoke. "Helheim, if you please."

Marina's head came up. No magic words?

The next moment, the space beneath the archway rippled, and fog drifted down from the Mjollnir symbol, until a curtain of mist hung from top to bottom.

"You first," Loki said grimly, lifting an eyebrow at Thor. Thor smacked his lips again, gathered the front of his robes in his right hand, hobbled through, and vanished.

"Well," Loki cleared his throat, and started forward.

Marina didn't move. Their hold snagged—she held onto him. He stopped, and looked back at her.

"What?" he wondered, watching her face. "What's wrong?"

"Loki, I'm..." she said, her heart fluttering. "I wanted to tell you I'm sorry."

He blinked. Said nothing. Marina jerked her head away and looked anywhere but at him.

"I'm sorry you thought...that *I* thought you were guilty of willfully doing such a terrible thing." She kept hold of his hand, feeling its long, slender strength within her fingers. "That I've...I've not trusted you sometimes, as we've traveled. And that now...you don't trust *me*."

She paused, then risked lifting her face and looking up into his eyes.

He gazed back down at her, open and quiet. But she couldn't tell the color of his hair or eyes, for the blue light masked them.

And he didn't say anything. Just ran his gaze over her features, studying the depth of her eyes in return.

Then, he drew a breath.

"We ought to go."

Marina's face heated and she nodded quickly, turning away again. Loki adjusted the way he held her hand, and pulled on her...

And together, they stepped through the frosty curtain of mist, and into Helheim.

A gust of warm, dry wind hit Marina's face before she could see anything. When the mist and darkness cleared, her lips parted...

But she couldn't find words.

They stood in absolute barrenness. A white sun burned in a listless sky, covered by a thin shroud of gray clouds. Slate-colored earth crunched beneath her boots. Beaten rocks formed the rolling terrain, which culminated in craggy mountains on the horizon before them. She turned, and cast all around her...

Black stones, and dust, as far as she could see.

She turned to find Thor—still a withered old woman—with his mouth gapped open as he surveyed the land.

"Loki..." he creaked. "When was the last time you came home?"

"A long time," Loki answered, narrowing his eyes at the mountains.

"What?" Marina wondered. "Should it be different?"

Loki let go of her, pulled off his gloves and dropped them on the ground, then knelt and felt the crumbly earth. He picked up sand in his hand and worked it through his fingers. His expression darkened, and he tossed the dirt straight down.

"You probably expected it to look like this, Marina, due to the fact that Christian translators borrowed the word 'hel' to use for that realm that exists in the absence of God," Loki explained, slow and deliberate. "*That* realm is one of the spirit—complete darkness, complete lack of God himself, where dwell those who, in life, have chosen *not* to abide with him, and have died. And as you can see, one does not have to be dead to walk *here.*"

"Then why is Bird here?" Marina wondered.

"Because some people and animals have magic in their blood, and in their bones," Loki answered, straightening up. "And when people die who house magic in their bodies, those bodies are carried to Helheim, and whoever rules Helheim is to dispose of the body properly, filtering the magic in that body back into the nine realms.

It's part of what helps flowers grow, and birds sing, and people fall in love."

Marina's face heated again, but Loki didn't look at her.

"When I lived here as a boy, Helheim was the greenest, most living place in all the realms," Loki answered, rising up and starting to walk forward. "Like Ireland on Midgard, in the spring." He slowed to a stop, gazing at those mountains. "I've hear rumors that it's since filled with all kinds of awful creatures, and that the land has dried up. I didn't really believe it." His tone hardened. "What has my sister been doing?"

Just then, a ripping shriek cut the sky. Thor clamped down on his broom. Their heads jerked up.

Giant wings eclipsed the sun.

For a terrifying instant, Marina thought it was a dragon.

Until she focused, and she realized it looked like an angel.

A dark, awful angel.

Loki grabbed Marina and pushed her behind him, holding on tight to her left wrist.

The great wings folded. The figure plummeted.

THUD.

A giant, enfolded in black feathers, crushed its booted feet into the earth. Then, with a tornadic gust, those mighty wings flared up and back, and a towering woman stood before them. Half of her head had been shaved. The other half bore long, tattered golden hair. She wore bronze armor, with fur around the collar, and a jagged sword at her belt. She had long, black claws instead of fingernails. Her eyes burned like glowing embers, her lids blackened with khol. She stood half again taller than Loki, and her wings stretched three times her length.

"Hello, Valkyrie," Loki greeted her casually. "Fancy seeing you here."

"What business do you have in this realm, Loki?" she demanded, her voice like the snarl of a tiger—and she had fangs.

An awful shudder raced through Marina's whole frame.

"I'm Loki's guest," Thor, in his keening old-woman's voice, spoke up. "I was too weak to make the journey alone."

Valkyrie turned and saw him—and something changed in her expression.

"Mistress Pesta?" she realized. "I thought you died in Alfheimr!"

"Almost, my dear, almost!" Thor cackled. "But not quite. Which is why I wanted to meet Hel—I thought she would wish to rejoice with me!"

Valkyrie gave a pleased grin.

"And she will! Yes, she will!" she agreed. "How did you meet Loki on Midgard?"

"I called for him," Thor replied, leaning on his broomstick with both hands. "Simple enough, but a little loud. Had to get his attention."

"Ah, so that was what all the flash and bother was about," Valkyrie said, her wings fluttering as she looked back to Loki. "And what have you come for, besides escorting an old friend of your sister's?" Valkyrie raised an eyebrow. "And with a little piece of meat along, besides?"

Marina swallowed hard.

"I doubt Hel realizes it," Loki interrupted. "She probably thinks I'm incapable of listening to her nowadays...But I did a great deal of thinking after our last meeting. And I want to talk to her about what I've come to realize."

"What, that the Aesir are nothing but philandering, arrogant weaklings after all?" Valkyrie offered, folding her arms across her chest. Loki's expression grew sad.

"Something like that," he murmured.

Valkyrie smirked.

"All right, I'll show you in," she said. "You ought to take off your coats, though. Far too hot inside."

Loki reached up and pulled off his bow and arrows and set them down, then turned to face Marina to unbutton his coat.

He met her eyes—gave her a pointed look.

She gave him a miniscule nod, knowing what he meant. Earlier, before they had left her house, he had given her the Wishtones in a black velvet pouch, which she had tied firmly to her belt. In turn, she had given him all of Bauldr's tears, and he had disappeared them. As long as she kept hold of her pouch, she needn't worry about any other garment. Quickly, she unbuttoned her own coat and tossed it on the ground, as well as her gloves. Thor stayed as he was, absently smacking his lips.

Loki tossed his coat down, put his bow and quiver back on and faced Valkyrie again.

"All right, lead on," he gestured ahead.

Valkyrie spat on the ground. Then she clapped her hands, and stomped on the place where she had spit.

Lightning flashed—and with a *bang*, a doorway leaped up out of nothing and opened up in the air...

Into a corridor.

"After you, Pesta; my prince," Valkyrie purred, neatly folding her wings, stepping aside and waving toward the door. Thor immediately walked through. Loki grabbed Marina by the upper arm and shoved her out in front of him—rather roughly. Marina bit down, suddenly remembering she was supposed to be the hostage. She felt Loki follow closely as they approached the flickering, snapping doorway...

She gritted her teeth, braced herself, and stepped through...

And her feet hit smooth, beaten earth. Her footfalls echoed. And she felt the temperature rise considerably—she didn't remember being this warm since she'd stepped outside her house into the sunlight in June. She gulped, glad she'd shed her coat when she had.

Loki bumped her from behind, and she quickened her pace, trailing after Thor's limping form, trying not to gape at the vast hallway.

A hundred feet up, the strangely-formed ceiling soared. Thick, twisted pillars flanked their path, marching off into the distance—pillars that looked like massive, petrified roots of incredible trees. Pitch darkness waited beyond those pillars. Eerie, winking lights peered from hollows and cracks in the roots, glowing a dull orange.

BANG.

Marina twisted to see that the door in the air had vanished, leaving behind a solid rock wall. Valkyrie had not followed them.

Loki pushed Marina in the back, and she faced forward again...

To see the corridor open up into a vast chamber.

A craggy ceiling even higher than in the hallway, pulsing with orange and red lights. A wide, circular floor of black, polished marble. At the far end, directly across from them, sat a sprawling throne, over which towered a colossal obsidian statue of a young, fierce woman wearing clinging robes, daggers at her belt—and whose face bore half of a skull. Marina's mouth fell open as her neck craned to see the height of that terrible idol...

Until a cold, seeping sensation invaded her bones, and she pulled her attention down to the one seated on the throne.

It was Hel.

She wore a good deal less than she had the other times Marina had seen her. A black corset with a plunging neckline, a shredded gray skirt, bare feet; her midnight hair halfway unbound and flowing around her as if touched by an unfelt wind. Her full lips had been rouged scarlet, her skin whiter than marble, her eyes reflecting every bit of light.

She rose to her feet, and languidly stepped down the dais—and for the first time, Marina could see what a powerful, full, serpentine, hourglass figure she had—perfection that clearly filled her with pride. The fringe of her hair had even been decoratively pulled back to show off the ghastly skull on one side of her face.

The way she moved, the very manner in which she walked, the black flash of her gaze, made Marina feel thin, small, weak and broken.

She sauntered to the center of the room and stopped, placing a hand on the curve of her hip. She raised her one eyebrow, her mouth quirking into a smile.

"Hello, Loki," she said quietly. "What have you brought me?"

"An old friend of yours," Loki answered brightly, pushing Marina out of the way. She slipped around behind him, her attention fixed on Hel.

"Mistress Pesta!" Hel said in surprise, turning to Thor. "I was told you were killed!"

"Fortunately, you were misinformed, my queen," Thor grated, holding out a wrinkled right hand. Without hesitation, Hel reached out and took it, and "Pesta" managed a crooked curtsey.

"I'm so relieved the rumors were false," Hel said, squeezing those bony fingers. "Why did you not come back straightaway?"

"I wanted to," Thor replied, letting go of her hand and leaning on his broom. "But after what happened on Alfheimr, I was afraid you wouldn't allow me past the gate unless I had...some kind of introduction." Thor nodded toward Loki.

"Nonsense," Hel scoffed, giving Loki a look. "You don't need *him* to pay a visit. You're always welcome."

"Thank you, my queen," Thor grinned, showing all the gaps between his horrid teeth. "It is truly an honor."

Hel's attention returned to Loki, and cooled somewhat.

"So," she said, slowly folding her arms. "How's the arm?"

Loki smirked in return.

"You don't plan to make this easy, do you?"

"Make what easy?" she asked, halfway smiling, watching his face. Loki drew a breath, and sighed.

"You were right," he said, his shoulders sagging. He ran his fingers through his dark curls. "I'll never be accepted back with the Aesir. I don't...belong with them. I never have. No matter how much I wanted to."

Hel studied him a moment, then lifted her chin.

"What made you change your mind?"

"Fenris came to see me," Loki confessed wearily, folding his own arms.

"Ah, Fen," Hel shook her head. "What a good brother."

"Is he here?" Loki wondered, glancing around.

"No, he's out running," Hel waved absently. "What did he tell you?"

"He told me that you and he were just trying to protect me," Loki answered. "That you missed me. Obviously more than the Aesir do. And you want me to come home. That's all."

"Hm," Hel said thoughtfully, her sneer gone. "And why did you bring this thing?" She nodded to Marina. Marina shrank back.

"You said you wanted her," Loki answered. "You never told me why. But I assumed you would accept her as a peace offering."

"Oh, I don't need her anymore," Hel answered. "Not when there's so little time left, and she isn't a threat anymore. I appreciate the thought, though." And she winked at him.

"Time left?" Thor repeated, hobbling closer. "What do you mean, your highness?"

"I'm not sure if you heard, Mistress," Hel turned to Thor. "But in your absence I obtained Bauldr, son of Odin."

"Ah!" Thor's big green eyes widened.

"He managed to keep his soul from going to Valhalla for a while, though—he used Soul Anchors, and tried to hide them all over Midgard," Hel explained, rolling her eyes.

"Ack," Thor spat.

"Mhm," Hel agreed. "But there's just *very* little time before those links break and his body shatters—and when that happens I'll have enough to finish the potion I was telling you about."

"Mhm," Thor muttered, nodding and gumming.

"Sorry, what?" Loki canted his head. "Potion?"

Hel attended to him again.

"I'm going to take Asgard," she answered.

Thor straightened. Loki frowned.

"Take it? How?"

"I turned the forge. Changed the flow," she said, gesturing behind her. "I drained Helheim first—all that magic was just lying around, anyway—and then I was fortunate enough to receive Prince Alfhild of Alfheimr. Terrible accident—fell from a lame horse." Her mouth quirked up, and she winked at Loki again.

Marina thrilled with horror. For just an instant, Loki's hair flushed blue.

But Hel didn't see it. She had turned her grin to "Pesta," who mirrored it instantly.

"With what I get from Bauldr, the draught will be finished, and even Odin's Gungnir will be no different from any ordinary spear," she said. "To me, anyhow. Less, since, even if he threw it at me, it would break apart."

"So you *haven't* been returning magic from the dead into the realms? Any of it?" Loki pressed, his brow furrowed. "You've been siphoning it out to put into a *potion*? For how long?"

Hel shrugged.

"Since Nanna came to Yggdrasil."

Loki straightened, his gaze intensifying with penetrating curiosity.

"That was two-hundred years ago." Loki canted his head—and a bluish tinge returned. "Did *you* lame Bird's horse?"

Hel laughed flippantly and looked off.

"You did," Loki realized.

"I'm amazed you remember that," she remarked.

"I was there," Loki bit out. "I've always known you hated Nanna—but what did *Bird* do to you that you wanted to kill him?" Loki demanded.

"He loved *me*," she snapped, pushing her forefinger into her breastbone. "And then Odin and Frigga chose another woman for him. A feeble, timid, fair-haired, 'suitable' woman. And he *agreed*." For a moment, vivid pain crossed her face. "He *proved* that all Aesir promises are just empty words. And that acting civilized and being beautiful to look at are more valuable qualities in Asgard than heart, strength or character."

"So you killed the one you claimed to love," Loki countered. He snorted. "Well, I'll admit, that certainly isn't *civilized*."

Hel glared at him.

"It took me two hundred years to fall out of love with him and do what needed to be done."

"Then why did you lame his horse such a long time ago?" Loki wondered.

"I wasn't trying to kill him *then*," Hel answered. "I was after Odin."

Loki just stared at her, his jaw tight, his brow knotted. Hel gazed back at him.

"You weren't the only one they deceived, brother," she murmured. "They broke my heart, too."

"And what of Thor?" Loki asked quietly. "He won't let Asgard go without a fight—and Mjollnir will be quite a force to be reckoned with."

"No, it won't," she answered. "Once I have one more specific ingredient, he'll go down easily enough. And when I siphon *Thor*, I'll have enough power to subdue all nine realms. Midgard will be especially easy. All I have to do is release a little magic and bring springtime back, and they'll believe I'm a goddess. And they won't be scared of me—they'll enjoy worshiping me." She shrugged again. "They already love the combination of death, violence and beauty. I'll fit right in."

Loki's hair cooled to black, but his eyes abruptly flashed scarlet. Hel held his gaze, softly sneering.

"What specific ingredient do you need?" Loki asked slowly. "It must be harder to come by than the others."

"Oh, not at all," Hel answered lightly. Then, she took half a step toward him—steel flashed in her hand—

And she plunged a two-inch dagger straight into Loki's gut.

Chapter Twenty Six

MARINA SLAPPED A HAND over her mouth and leaped backward.

Loki jerked—his lips parted, he stared into his sister's face. His hair rippled with blue.

Hel yanked the blade loose and held it aloft. Loki bent his head and pressed his fingers to the new wound, then gazed in bewilderment at his bloody fingertips.

"What did you...do?" he gasped—and his face drained of color. He crashed to his knees.

"No!" Marina howled, and flung herself down next to him. He toppled onto his back, trembling hands twitching up. Marina caught his head and shoulders, her arms breaking into violent shaking. Loki's wide eyes paled to silvery blue, the ends of his hair turned white.

"Thank you for making it so easy for me," Hel said, wiping the blade off on her skirt. "It's a slow-acting poison, but you shouldn't be in much pain. I'll need to take your heart magik right before you die—the fresher it is, the more potent, you know. It'll break Mjollnir in half."

Marina took fistfuls of Loki's shirt as he panted beneath her hands, her eyes clouding with tears. Hel stepped closer, her shadow falling across them.

"I know you better than anyone, Loki," Hel muttered. "Your tricks are obvious by now."

"Perhaps not," came a creaking voice. Hel frowned and turned...

Just as "Pesta" reached beneath her robes—

And withdrew a mighty hammer.

That instant, the ragged black robes melted away—the hag's stature shot up, her chest broadened, her hood fell back—

With a swift shake of his shoulders, a thunderhead cape billowed; golden armor gleamed, a mane of wheat-colored hair caught an unseen wind—the haggard face transformed to one of rugged beauty, a beard appearing, and the eyes changing from emerald to the blue of summer lightning.

"*Thor?*" Hel yelped, and darted three steps backward—

Thor's face snarled. He heaved his hammer high over his head, brought it down and slammed it into the marble floor.

Thunder *cracked*.

The earth *shook*.

The room split.

Immense rocks shattered loose from the ceiling and tumbled.

Marina flung herself on top of Loki's chest and head, shielding him—

Static danced across her skin.

Hel shrieked and leaped backward—a boulder *smashed* into the ground right where she had been. Marina lifted up and twisted around—glimpsed Hel fleeing down a dark side corridor.

"Loki!" Thor cried, thudding onto his knees on the other side of him, letting go of Mjollnir and grabbing tight hold of Loki's right hand. Loki squeezed Thor's fingers in return, finding his gaze.

"Couldn't have been a bit quicker?" Loki rasped.

"Forgive me for that," Thor winced. "What do we do about you?"

"It's some kind of elvish hemlock," Loki said, his voice quivering. "The kind that...turns your muscles to water before you simply can't breathe anymore."

Marina felt her throat spasm as her fingers clenched around his shirt.

"Can you do stop it?" Thor demanded, pressing his hand to the side of Loki's face.

"I...I have a bottle of the queen's hoarhound in here somewhere," Loki said, pulling loose of Thor. "It'll slow it down. And I have...armor that will keep me moving..."

Weakly, Loki rubbed his hands together. Red sparks shot from his palms, and a small bottle full of blue liquid materialized. Then, he almost dropped it.

Thor quickly caught it, popped the cork loose, slid his hand under Loki's head and lifted it, and pressed the bottle to his lips. Loki quickly drank it all, then took a rough breath and nodded. His quivering calmed. He breathed more deeply, then, grimacing, slowly sat up. Thor and Marina both kept hold of him.

"What should we do?" Thor asked, watching him intently.

"You have to go find that potion," Loki said, gripping him by the collar of his breastplate. "I have a feeling it's behind the forge, in what used to be the healing rooms. Probably hanging over the great fire. You have to get it, and take it back to Asgard."

"I cannot leave you here," Thor insisted. Loki shook him.

"If Bird turns to dust and she drinks that potion, it won't matter what any of us do," he barked. "Take it to Asgard, give it to Odin, and if we're not back by then, come back to get us."

Thor nodded firmly.

"It's likely to be guarded by a pack of her wolves," Loki warned. "Don't let any of them bite you."

"What will *you* do?" Thor asked.

"Marina will find Bird," Loki told him. "And I will distract my sister so she doesn't come after either of you."

"Can you kill her?" Thor wanted to know. Loki's mouth tightened.

"No," he murmured. "So you'd better hurry."

Thor looked at him for just another moment, then slapped Loki's chest.

"I will find it, and I will come back for you," he promised. Then, he reached out and laid his palm on Marina's head. "May heaven guard you, my lady." And he grasped his hammer, turned—and with a deadly crackle of thunder, he bolted down another hallway, lightning snapping in his wake.

Loki silently watched him go, his hair and eyes going silver. Then, he turned his head and looked at Marina.

He saw her—and suddenly frowned. His hair blushed blue again, his eyes flushed green as his eyebrows drew together.

"You're crying."

Marina choked on a sob and pressed shaking fingers to her lips—then reached out with both hands and helplessly curled her fingers through his collar. He sat up straighter, leaning toward her, concern flooding his softened face—and his hair became a lustrous auburn, his eyes the tint of a deep spring sky. Hot tears clouded Marina's vision and rolled down her cheeks, even as she struggled to breathe.

"Are you going to die?" she stammered desperately, searching him.

He watched her for a moment, then smiled weakly.

"Most likely."

A strangled cry broke loose from her before she stifled it hard with her hand, every watery breath hurting her whole frame.

"It's all right," Loki murmured, reaching up and tucking her hair behind her ear. "I am quite old, after all. I used up all my good luck a long time ago."

Marina dropped her hand and shook her head.

Loki smiled gently at her, his eyes twinkling.

"It's all right," he whispered again. "Just knowing that at least one person would cry for a fool like me is enough good fortune for a lifetime."

She gasped, and then her jaw locked and she gazed straight back at him, her whole body quivering. Her brow twisted, and she couldn't speak.

His smile faded. He sat up a little further, tipping closer, his eyelashes fluttering.

"Marina?"

"Mm?" she moaned painfully.

"I'm..." He swallowed, his gaze flittering all over her face. "I don't make promises lightly..."

Marina's breathing sped up as stabbing pains lanced into her heart. Loki's eyes turned bright aqua, and his hair the color of summer wheat.

"So..." he whispered. "Forgive me for breaking mine."

Confusion darted through her...

Loki reached up, slipped his warm hands around her neck and cradled her face between his thumbs. His eyes closed. He leaned in.

And he kissed her.

Familiar lips—lips soft as rose petals, warm as evening sunlight. Lips that tasted like peppermint.

A dam broke inside her.

She flung her arms around his neck, opened her mouth and kissed him back.

Instantly, he pulled his hands down from her neck, wound his arms around her waist and crushed her to his chest.

Their mouths moved in wild concert—she sucked in deep breaths of him, drowning in his sharp, sweet scent—savoring spices on her tongue, the feel and push of his lips, the corners and feathery edges...

They kissed each other frantically, over and over—and then Loki began pressing deep, lingering on her mouth, reaching up with one hand to take hold of her neck, pushing his thumb against her pulse.

And then, golden light swelled through her brain. A metallic taste coursed across her tongue and slid down her throat.

The gold faded—Loki pulled back, turned his head and kissed her fiercely.

White light, with silvery hems—a taste like sugar and frost...

He captured her head in both his hands, broke the kiss and then overwhelmed her with another.

The scent of rain, the taste of fire—rolling sapphire clouds...

Loki pushed her back, back—a new kiss burned her lips...

Cinnamon and honey and sweet cream. Flickering scarlet light that seared her vision...

Her back met a wall. Loki pinned her there with his body—his heart thundered against her chest...

His mouth broke from hers. He gasped roughly. She felt his nose brush hers, his breath mingle with hers...

Then, he tilted his head, bent down and pressed his fiery lips to the base of her throat.

Electricity shot through her whole body.

She grabbed his hair with both hands as a green brighter than any jewel nearly blinded her—her mouth and nose and lungs filled with mint and frost and the luster of autumn. It almost tore her in half.

His lips lingered there as the powerful flash faded. Marina blinked her eyes open, shudders and chills racing all across her even as her fingers looped tighter through his hair and she fought to catch her breath.

Loki's lips traced up her neck, along her jawline, and then he withdrew just enough to look down into her eyes again.

Brilliant as the Mediterranean Sea. Filled with tears that slid down his pale face. His eyebrows twitched together, and he swallowed again.

"I do trust you, Marina Feroe," he gasped, his lower lip trembling. "And...now that I see it..." His face twisted, he reached up and shakily wiped her tears away. "I don't want you to cry for me."

Marina shattered with weeping. More of Loki's tears fell—he bent close and swiftly kissed her on the forehead, then on the cheek.

Then, he tore out of her arms—she tried to catch hold of him...

He grimaced, and climbed to his feet, covering his wound with one hand. Marina took fistfuls of the skirt of her dress, her heart nearly stopping.

"Go find Bird," Loki said breathlessly. "Use the Wishstone to hide while you look—it will make you invisible. Then use 'unbind' to get him loose of the bier. The one called 'flee' will take you to Asgard if you ask it to."

"Where are you going?" Marina asked, scrambling up onto her knees.

"I have to distract Hel while I still have the strength," Loki answered. "Keep her from finding Thor or you."

Marina squeezed her eyes shut for a moment, feeling as if something inside her was ripping. When she opened them, she found him gazing softly at her.

"Please don't cry," he said. Then he chuckled sadly. "After all, as a great Midgardian once said... 'If a man has not discovered something he will die for, he isn't fit to live.'"

Marina swiped the tears off her face, fighting to see him clearly, to memorize the sight of him...

He lifted his left hand, and snapped his fingers.

A black cloud *burst* all around him, and swallowed his whole form.

The lamps blazed brighter—the air pulled to him. The pillar of mist around him swirled and spun...

The shadow melted off.

It drained and dripped down from the figure beneath.

Crisp raven hair—strands like the feathers of a crow. A face pale as winter moonlight—stunning, handsome, sharp and hard. Sharp, coal eyebrows, cultured features, a soft and delicate mouth. Eyes that literally blazed red—luminescent as a cat's when a light is shined upon them. Black enfolded his lean figure, hugging his waist, flaring sharply at his shoulders, and draping in jagged skirts around his legs. The lamplight caught the smooth, multi-faceted texture of his armor, flashing light back in sinister winks and sparks.

Scales.

Snakeskin.

It clothed him from throat to wrists to ankles, fitting him as if it were part of his own lean, knife-like body. He turned toward her with silent, deliberate ease, the shadow swimming around his knees.

An elegantly-shredded cape slithered along through the fog behind him, and more tatters dripped from his elbows and forearms. He took a slow breath, reached to his belt, and drew out a short, slender sword that glowed with a wicked green light, its blade dancing with swimming runes.

"Take the same corridor Thor followed," he said. "Turn left at the first chance you get, and follow the stairs all the way down. Keep walking, Marina." His eyebrows drew together. "Keep walking as strong and straight as you can, no matter what you find. Walk all the way through the door ahead of you, and into the chamber that holds the furnace." Then, Loki met Marina's eyes, and sorrow crossed his features. He lifted his chin. *"Til Valhall."*

He waved his hand in front of his face—

Rose into the air on a cloud of vapor, and shot off down the corridor through which Hel had fled.

Shivering, gripping the bag of Wishstones that hung at her belt, Marina hurried down the dark corridor, trying to keep her echoing footsteps and her jagged breathing quiet. Shadows draped all around her like thick cobwebs. Dank, dungeon scent filled her nose and throat. Flickering lamps winked like ancient, malevolent eyes from out of the twists and snarls of petrified roots.

A sigh of cold air—like a death rattle—touched the left side of her face and the edges of her hair.

She froze.

Slowly, she turned her head that direction.

A thrill of dread crawled through her.

It started at her fingertips and traveled up her arms, into her chest, and through her veins. Her throat closed.

Before her yawned a huge doorway. A broad descending staircase waited beyond. Torches upon hooks flickered with a leering yellow light.

And by their illumination, she could just glimpse the texture of the walls.

Hundreds of bodies lying on their backs, each one in its own rectangular cavity set into the walls. Floor to ceiling, on both sides. None of them moved. And Marina could see the haunting outlines of skulls, the curl of white knuckles...

A catacombs.

Another terrible shiver passed through her.

With trembling fingers, she opened her little bag, reached down inside, and fumbled until she found the blue one. She brought it up to her lips, and whispered:

"Hide me."

A watery ripple passed over her vision. Instinctively, she glanced down at her left hand...

Only a ghostly silver outline showed that she even had a hand or arm at all.

She gulped, vaguely horrified, closed her fist around that stone, and started toward the threshold.

She hesitated at the top of the staircase, feeling that deathly breeze against her skin again. Finally, she gritted her teeth, closed her eyes, and forced herself to take the first step.

She landed safely. Nothing happened. She opened her eyes, chills scattering through her body, and made herself take another step. And another. Another.

Her instincts told her to hug one of the walls, but she couldn't bring herself to do it. Those walls stretched up into the blackness, far beyond the reach of her sight. All stacked full of motionless figures shrouded in blankets of dust.

A library of the dead.

Occasionally, grand armor or jewels gleamed through the grime, flickering dully in the flamelight. Jawbones sagged. Empty sockets gazed out at her from beneath crooked helmets. Long finger bones curled around the hilts of rusted swords.

Some of the figures stretched twice as tall as Marina. Others could not have stood as high as her hip. One or two lay in what appeared at first to be a basket of bones—but, upon second glance, had to have been the remains of giant wings.

Down and down she climbed, at a slight curve, until a quiet sound rose up before her. A low trickling, dripping...

Finally, the staircase straightened, and ended in a broad landing. And in front of her waited a wide canal of black, smooth water. A low stone ceiling curved overhead, and a few grim torches lit the chamber. Marina stopped, her heart stuttering as she stared at the fathomless water.

Then...

Breath. Breath. *Breath...*

Behind her.

She went ramrod straight, clutching the stone hard to her chest, her own breathing sharpening...

A touch of hot air on the side of her neck.

"I smell you, little one," a deep, resonant voice purred—it vibrated through her bones. "Clever. But not quite invisible."

"Fenris," Marina gasped, her heartbeat thundering.

Shadow moved in the corner of her eye, and suddenly the looming man swept around from behind her.

Black coat, black hair, white skin and burning eyes. And in a moment of absent realization, Marina finally glimpsed the real family resemblance between the three shape-shifting Jotuns.

She tried to take a step back, tried to turn and race back up the stairs—

Fenris reached out with both hands and grabbed her by the neck.

She jolted, almost screaming—

He didn't strangle her. Just cradled her head firmly, and then directed his gaze at where her eyes would be if he could see them. It turned her blood to frost.

"Where is my brother?" he demanded through his teeth—low and deadly. "How did you come to be here without him?" He squeezed her, and shook her—though not nearly as hard as he could have. "He is in danger—I can feel it. *Where is he?*"

Marina twitched, suddenly confused.

"What? You...You *know* what happened to him," she stammered, feeling strength pulse from his hands and through her skull. "You and Hel planned this—*you* wanted to poison him—"

Bewilderment flashed across Fenris' face.

"Poison?" he repeated, the intensity of his gaze red-hot. "What are you talking about?"

Marina stared at him.

"You...really don't know?"

He shook her again—harder.

"What poison?"

"He said it was an elvish hemlock," Marina answered, trying not to fall down.

Fenris' gaze unfocused, and his breathing unsteadied. His lips parted, but for several minutes he didn't say anything. Then, his jaw tightened.

"Drop that stone."

"I can't," Marina tried. He pinned her with a glare and bared his teeth.

"Do it now, or I will break your neck."

Marina braced herself...

Opened her fingers, and the stone fell to the paving with a musical *clink*.

A ripple crossed her eyes, and she could see herself again.

Fenris instantly fixed on her.

His attention flashed all over her features, and he took deep breaths, leaning closer to her, smelling her...

His breathing slowed. He pulled back, blinked, and looked into her eyes.

And his eyebrows drew together.

"What has my sister done?" he whispered, his tone entirely different.

Marina swallowed hard.

"She tricked Loki into killing Bird," she rasped. "So that the Aesir would blame him and throw him out of Asgard."

Fenris' eyes blazed, but he said nothing. Marina went on.

"Now she's going to use the magic in Bird's body to finish a potion to kill everyone there—and she's going to steal Loki's...Loki's heart magik to help her kill Thor—"

"She can't take Loki's heart magik," Fenris snapped. "Not without—"

"She stabbed him," Marina said, suddenly trembling. "I saw it. She stabbed him with a poisoned blade and he's dying."

Fenris suddenly let go of her. His gaze drifted away—he backed up, his eyelashes flickering. He raked a hand through his curls, then pressed it to his mouth.

"You didn't *know?*" Marina realized, stepping toward him. He looked down at her, resting his hand lightly on his chest.

"I knew she loved Bauldr and that he did not love her in return," he said flatly. "And that she hated him for it and wished to leave Asgard with me, and with Loki." His expression hardened, and he turned away. "But I have not been here, to Helheim, in a hundred years. And..." He swallowed. "I find I do not know it anymore."

Marina's heart beat faster than a rabbit's, but she dared to take a step closer.

"Thor is here with us," she revealed. "He's trying to find the potion before she can use it. Loki sent me to find Bird and get him out of here. He went to find Hel to distract her. Where...Where is Bird's body? Do you know?"

He looked at her again. His eyes burned like mounting embers.

Then, he spoke.

"Through that doorway and down the stairs," he said, pointing across the way. "That is where the forge is, and the biers for the newly-dead."

"How do I get across?" Marina asked frantically, gesturing to the water. He raised an eyebrow.

"You cross," Fenris answered.

She stared at him, then at the black water.

"Swim?"

He snickered and shook his head.

"No, you cannot swim it. It's impossible."

"What? Then what do I do?" she demanded.

He openly sneered at her.

"Typical Midgardian—you make complicated what is simple." He leveled a look at her. "You *simply* decide whether or not you trust the one who sent you down these stairs. And you cross the water."

Marina's mouth opened, but no sound came out. He tipped his head at her.

"Now, if you'll excuse me, I'm off to find my sister."

And with that, he bolted up the catacomb staircase, leaving Marina alone.

Chapter Twenty Seven

MARINA STOOD MOTIONLESS for several minutes, staring at the place where Fenris had vanished. That steady, distant *drip-drip-drip* dominated her hearing. Otherwise, all stood silent.

She turned, her heart suddenly jumping, and bent down to pick up the fallen blue stone.

"Hide me," she whispered, standing back up. She pulled it close to her mouth. "Hide me!"

Nothing happened.

And with a terrible shudder, she remembered that each Wishstone could only be used once.

She set her teeth, fighting back a low cry.

The black water captivated her attention.

A silvery surface, languid as ink, hiding hundreds of fathoms of depth.

And Fenris had said *"just cross."*

What did he mean, just cross? And cross *without* swimming? What was he talking about? Was there a spell on the water? Would it make her fall asleep, or would it suck her under, if she tried to swim?

She hurriedly glanced back and forth, up and down the tunnel, straining to see...

But she could glimpse no bridge, or boat, or stepping stones. Nothing but the wide stretch of canal, far too broad to jump.

And a tall, square door directly across from her.

It might as well have been on another planet.

She dropped the useless stone and took a fistful of her hair.

What had Loki said?

Take the first left, go down the stairs, keep walking. Keep walking strong and straight, go through the door and to the furnace...

She squeezed her hair between her fingers.

He'd said himself that he hadn't been here in two centuries. He probably had no idea this water was here. He probably thought this was just a hallway, a harmless hallway, not some vast ocean between her and the door she so desperately needed to get to...

She frowned.

Wait. If he remembered a *hallway*...

That couldn't be right. Because there would be a chasm crossing her path even if there wasn't water in it. He wouldn't tell her to just walk right into a chasm without a bridge to carry her across...

What if he remembered a bridge being here, and there wasn't one anymore?

She quickly searched again...

But she found no trace of anchorage for any sort of bridge, neither on her side, nor the far side. Just smooth stone.

Now she reached up with both hands and grabbed her head, her pulse ragged, her breath short.

"Keep walking, Marina. Keep walking as strong and straight as you can, no matter what you find. Walk all the way through the door ahead of you, and into the chamber that holds the furnace."

That's what he had said. But it couldn't be right! She couldn't just *walk* to the door. There was no possible way for her to do that. She couldn't use the Wishstone that would take her from one place to another because she needed it to get her and Bird back to Asgard. And the "unbind" stone was useless here. Loki had to be mistaken. She needed to go back up, retrace her steps, find some other, more plausible way...

"You simply decide whether or not you trust the one who sent you down these stairs." Fenris' voice suddenly echoed in her head. *"And you cross the water."*

Marina's breath paused.

Then, she let it out—long, slow and tight.

That was it.

Making complicated what was simple.

She had to trust Loki.

She squeezed her eyes shut as her heartbeat skyrocketed. Memories flashed through her head: driving snow, bright blood against Bird's chest, chains slithering on stone...

Plummeting over the edge of an icy cliff—to land softly at the bottom.

A barked refusal through the frosty night—jaws clamping onto his arm—blood flying...

Swirling, freezing water—a mighty *thud*—being yanked out of the dark depths and into the air and the light...

A beautiful, fresh, living, tingling sensation pulsing through her crippled arm and banishing that old, constant ache...Her fingers stretching out and open as they hadn't in so long...

His mouth searing her lips.

His tears illuminating his brilliant eyes and rolling down his pale cheeks.

She opened her eyes. Lowered her hands.

Stared ahead at the door in front of her.

Straightened to her full height, took a broad stride—

And stepped out onto the surface of the water.

Her foot sank—

Splash!

Her frame jerked.

The bottom of her foot hit a hard, smooth surface. She quickly looked down.

Water covered her shoe up to her ankle.

The canal was only four inches deep.

Fierce, joyful relief surged through her. She smiled, strength rushing through her muscles—and she broke into a run.

Water noisily flew out behind her, soaking her skirt. In moments, she had crossed the wide water—no more than a puddle—and grasped the huge iron latch of the door. She worked it—it creaked. And she pulled the door open.

Heat washed up toward her, gusting through her hair and clothes.

More stairs. Unlit this time. But the staircase was short, and strong light throbbed in the chamber beyond. Gritting her teeth and closing her fingers, Marina started down.

But when she reached the last step...

The skin on her arms tingled, and the hair on her neck stood up.

BOOM.

The whole earth shook. She fell sideways and grabbed the wall to keep from collapsing. Wide-eyed, she slipped forward to see around the corner...

A cape like a thunderhead lashed the air, sending out showers of icy water and white sparks. Two titanic bodies fell and shattered the paving stones, both roaring like tigers. They viciously struck and battered each other—massive wings beat the air, sending the stormy cape billowing upon a great wind. The two thrashed wildly for half a moment, then tore apart, leaping again to their feet and facing each other.

One—the towering, winged form of the dark angel, Valkyrie. Blood running down her lip, her eyes like the sun, her sword laughing in her hand. The other—half her size but mighty and quick as coiled lightning—his lionesque mane feral in the gusts, his hammer gnashing and snapping—

Thor.

To the right of them waited a waist-high railing, and beyond that, the chamber ceiling leaped high, and the floor plunged away into a fathomless pit.

Directly beyond the two combatants opened a dark hallway, down which Marina could see nothing.

And to the left of them, in a vast hearth thirty feet wide, burned a white-hot flame like the mouth of a dragon. Alabaster elves knelt, holding the white mantel up upon their shoulders, their long hair hanging in curtains around their faces. The fire spat and writhed hungrily, breathing dry clouds of heat out into the room.

Before this fire stood two ornate biers decorated in flowery vines of ivory and brass. A body lay upon each one of them, feet toward Marina, head toward the flame. The one to the left wore beautiful silver armor and helmet, his sword slack in his left hand. But he had no flesh anymore—his features were all dry, white bone.

And the body to the right...

Bird.

Marina's heart leaped, and then *banged* so painfully that tears sprang to her eyes.

Draping white clothes, a metal belt, bare feet. Brown blood staining the front of his tunic. Beautiful face placid, the skin of his cheeks, neck and bare arms glowing as if he had just fallen asleep—his golden hair in a curling wreath around his head.

BOOM!

Marina grabbed the wall again as the foundations of the mountain shook, and white lightning blazed through the balcony room.

Thor bared his teeth and roared, and threw himself at Valkyrie. She slashed at him with her brilliant sword—its blade struck Mjollnir.

Marina shocked down onto her knees and covered her head.

The two fighters crashed into each other, smashing and hacking with the fury of a tornado. Static skipped through the air currents, through the seams in the stone.

Marina could never cross while they were fighting.

They clawed at each other, screeching and howling—Valkyrie battered him with her wings, tearing at his cape with her talons; Thor struck her with his free fist and entangled her sword in shafts of lighting. The energy exploding out from them threatened to shatter the balcony.

Then, of a sudden, Thor twisted, raised his hammer and landed a crushing blow to Valkyrie's shoulder.

Bone cracked. She screamed and staggered sideways.

With a terrific bound, Thor leaped high, somersaulted in the air, and hit the ground running, his cape snarling behind him—and made for the dark hallway.

Valkyrie bared sharp fangs and hissed. Her eyes raging, she switched her sword to her other hand and flapped her incredible wings.

With a clap of wind that nearly knocked Marina onto her back, Valkyrie took to the air and sped after Thor into the shadows.

Gasping, Marina clawed her way to her feet, shook her head to clear it, and darted out into the chamber.

Her footsteps echoed deafeningly, her breath rasping in her ears. The fire growled ravenously—the sinister warmth gushed out across her skin.

Then, in a moment, she was beside him.

Her hands slapped down on the marble surface, her gaze falling upon his face.

Angelic and still as stone.

Yet, somehow...

Not dead.

"Bird," she whispered, bending closer and pressing her hand to his silent heart. His body felt cold, his clothes soft.

"Bird, I've come to get you." More tears sprang to her eyes. "I'm so sorry it took so long!" With shivering hands, she reached down to pry open the bag at her belt.

CRACK.

Red light blasted through her skull.

Her whole head spun.

The next instant, she felt herself suspended in the air—

And then her back slammed into stone.

She rolled like a rag doll, then flopped onto her back—pain screamed through all her bones.

She choked, trying to pull in air and clear her eyes...

When she could see enough, she realized she was lying at the foot of the stairs again.

Panic seized her.

She twisted her head—

Hel stood beside Bird's body.

Poison dripped from her shoulders and chaos burned in her fiendish eyes. She showed her fangs, and began striding slowly toward Marina. In her right hand, a long black blade snickered. Midnight rolled behind her like a million snakes.

Marina struggled to sit up, but dizziness grabbed her and spun her balance sideways. She squeezed her bag in a death grip.

Hel's shadow spilled over her. Marina looked high up into her face.

Hel canted her head, her lip curling.

She exhaled a low hiss—smoke breathed from her teeth.

And, without a word, she lifted her sword—

And slashed it down toward Marina's face.

Marina threw up a hand—

CLASH!

A shadow hurled itself over Marina's head and caught the swinging blade. Emerald chewed ebony for half a second, and then two figures roiled away, back onto the stones that Thor and Valkyrie had broken.

They ripped apart. Hel, seething and spitting sparks, hopped back and then set her stance, hefting her lithe blade.

And before her, a figure slowly raised himself to his full height.

Loki. Clad in darkness just as black as hers—but more magnificent and terrible. He held his own weapon easily in his left hand, his skin pale as snow.

And he turned, just slightly, and met Marina's eyes.

His had turned the color of a summer sky. He raised his eyebrows at her.

And, in the depths of her heart, Marina knew what he meant.

Hel chuckled, rivulets of fire trickling down her chin.

Slowly, with resignation in all his features, Loki faced Hel again.

"How are you feeling, *alskling?*" Hel asked.

Loki gave her a minute smirk.

"Ready to die," he replied. "You?"

"Not quite yet." She licked her lips.

He shrugged.

"That's too bad."

And he shot toward her like an arrow.

She spun—slashed with her whip-like sword—

Loki's blade met it, caught it in its teeth—the weapons bandied and snarled with blinding speed.

The two fencers charged back and forth, dodging and dancing, the liquid shadow from their capes swimming and swarming around their feet.

SHINK!

Loki's sword went flying.

Marina's heart stopped.

Loki bared his teeth and clapped his hands.

Hel's sword burst.

Shards of metal flew. She jerked her face back to protect her eyes—

Loki clapped again, and red fire exploded in his palms. With a swift spin, he hurled it at her chest.

It hit her and blasted her backward. She crashed to the ground.

Loki advanced, conjuring another comet in his hands.

Hel leaped to her feet, throwing down the useless hilt of her sword.

She quickly rubbed her palms together, then yanked her hands apart—a bolt of darkness appeared in the space between.

She snatched it up. Loki threw his comet—a pulse of blue-white light—

She sliced through it with her beam of shadow—it splattered apart on either side of her.

She let go of the shadow, lunged forward and thrust her hands out in front of her—

A mighty concussion punched out—

Loki brought his hands together in front of his face and lunged toward it, pointing his palms—

The concussion split. Smoke burst.

Loki leaped up, a knife of blue fire appearing in his right hand. He lanced down toward her head.

She dodged and rolled—Loki landed and swiped the empty air. Hel jumped to her feet and flung her cape out—it became a tangling tendril that caught at Loki's left arm.

He spun, wrapped it around his wrist and grabbed it, then jerked her toward him.

Hel tripped to him, snarling—then jumped and lunged at his throat.

He staggered back, let go of the knife—she snatched at him—they toppled and rolled.

A frenzy of scrabbling and eruptions swallowed them. They careened away, toward the railing.

Marina saw her chance.

She scrambled to her feet and hurried across the floor once more, knocking away her dizziness. An eternity later—the crackling of the battle snapping around her head—she thudded against Bird's bier again. She swept around to his other side, so she could keep Loki and Hel in view...

The brother and sister ruptured apart, both flying backward high in the air—but instantly regained their balance. They spun and faced each other midair, magic seething in their fingers and enflaming their eyes. Sparks shook from the ends of their hair, their capes spread like great wings.

They landed. The floor trembled.

In a furor of fluid, concerted motion, the two began flinging shadow, light, fire and thunder at each other. Their swift, graceful hands moved like birds and snakes and battering rams—catching, cutting, batting away and hurling deadly, furious power that sparkled, cracked and hissed like fireworks. The stones beneath their nimble feet began to fracture. Deflected spells speared the ceiling, the walls, and the railing.

Marina found herself gripping Bird's cold hand in both of hers. She couldn't move, couldn't think—

She couldn't rip her eyes from Loki.

Then, two spells caught each other in the middle. Like dueling giants clasping hands. Both fighters threw out their arms and braced their legs, leaning in, pushing as hard as they could...

With a sound like snapping wood, the spell broke—

—and one shaft blasted straight up, striking the ceiling. Hel knocked back, gasping. Loki fell to one knee.

Marina's breath caught.

The thunder of the concussion rolled through the room.

Loki pressed a hand to his wound. It came away dripping with blood.

Loki—!

Marina's mouth didn't move. Silence smothered them all. But her heart screamed.

Loki turned his head.

Looked right at her.

That same look.

And mouthed one word.

"*Go.*"

CRACK.

Marina jerked her head up.

A giant fissure had appeared in the ceiling. Little rocks began tumbling down like snowflakes—and shattered like hailstones when they hit the ground.

She stuffed her hand in her bag, and pulled out the red Wishstone and pulled it to her mouth, then turned to face Bird. She squeezed his wrist, and fought to keep her voice from shaking.

"Let him go."

Snap!

A blue flash of light all around his body—and his head lolled to the side.

CRACK.

Another fissure opened up, this time in the wall.

Hel cackled with glee. Marina looked up to see flames spew from her mouth and roll down her chin and throat. She whirled her hands and conjured a sword of fire, and held it aloft in both hands.

Loki hauled himself to his feet. Blood ran in a river down his front, down his leg, and pooled on the floor by his boot. His face went ashen—grey around his eyes and lips.

But he spat back at her—and red sparks issued from his lips. Steaming liquid gold spilled from his mouth, and his eyes burned like embers. He spread his arms out to the sides, his hands like claws. His cloak rapidly swirled in vapor all around his legs, building and rising like a boiling cauldron...

Movement.

Marina turned her head to see a massive wolf dart down the stairs and skid to a stop at the base.

He saw her. Their glances caught.

Then, he turned and glimpsed his brother and sister.

Terror shot through Marina's heart.

That instant, another terrible CRACK broke through the room—

And the towering ceiling caved in.

Loki roared.

Hel shrieked.

Fenris charged toward them.

Hel and Loki sprang toward each other, coiling their magic like scorpions.

A flashing green dagger appeared in Loki's hand—

They slammed into each other—bound up in a deadly embrace—

Fenris hurtled into them—

And all three pitched over the railing and plunged into the infinite pit.

Marina ripped the last stone from her pouch and threw herself across Bird's chest.

"*Take us to Asgard!*" she screamed, her heart tearing in half.

A giant stone punctured the floor right next to the bier—

FLASH.

—and everything drowned in devastating white light.

Chapter Twenty Eight

WARMTH.

But not hot, dry, ravenous warmth. It caressed her head, and a soft breeze stroked her hair.

Shivering, she dared to lift up, just an inch.

Bird lay beneath her. She grasped his tunic in an iron grip with both hands. And they both sprawled deep in waving, golden grass.

Gasping, she hurriedly sat up, loosening her death hold on him.

A friendly wind caught her hair and blew it back...

As she gazed out over a beautiful, sunlit hillside bordered around by tall, leafy oaks.

And far out on the horizon, past a knotted emerald wood, stood the highest tree she had ever seen—stretching to heaven itself. And above its reaching branches arched a pure, infinite blue sky, gently joined by shimmering, gold-lined clouds. Swallows twittered and flitted past this banner, diving into the trees or skimming the stalks of the meadow grass. The sweet scent of alfalfa and hay filled her lungs.

Tears trailed down her cheeks.

She climbed to her feet, all her muscles shaking, and blinked through the water in her eyes.

Such warmth. Like spring.

A soft jingling reached her.

She turned to her left to glimpse two horsemen riding on a nearby road toward the great tree. They wore fine, bright scarlet clothes, had reddish-golden hair, and short beards. They cantered easily, laughing together. They each wore a sword, and the tack on their horses glimmered in the afternoon sunlight.

"Hello!" Marina called, her voice breaking. She cleared her throat, and raised her tone. "Hello! Here!" She raised an arm and waved.

The two men turned their heads and looked. Pulled back on their reins and stopped.

"Can we help you, my lady?" one of them shouted.

"Yes," she answered loudly. "I need to get to Yggdrasil to speak to Odin."

They spoke to each other, then urged their mounts off the road and up to her at a quick trot.

"What is your distress?" the other young man asked. "Are you lost?"

"No," Marina answered as they drew near and she could see their faces better. "I'm...I'm Marina Feroe. And I've brought Bauldr back."

The two men drew up beside her, frowning—

And then they saw him.

One of them went pale. Both men froze.

Then, the first handsome man pinned Marina with an astonished blue gaze.

"How did you do this?"

"It's a very long story," Marina answered, more tears running down her cheeks. "And I'd like to tell it to Odin."

"Of course," he rasped. "Erick, get hold of him and lift him onto your horse!"

"Yes—All right," Erick stammered, leaping off and diving into the grass next to Bird. He grabbed his arm, heaved him up, and then laid him across his shoulders and carried him to his startled horse.

"My lady, come with me," the first man held his hand out to her. "I am Erling. This is my brother Erick. We are huntsmen for the king."

"Thank you, Erling," Marina managed, reaching up to grasp his hand. With no effort at all, he pulled her up and set her on the saddle in front of him. Marina looked over to see Bird's body limply sitting in the saddle in front of Erick, who had wrapped an arm around his waist and pulled him against his chest. The brothers glanced at each other, nodded, and then kicked their horses.

The next moment, they were flying through the meadow, caught in the living wind, headed straight toward the world tree, and the home of the king of Asgard.

The tree obscured the sun, the sky, the rest of the world.

Its gnarled trunk—so wide that Marina could not now see around it—its edges and surfaces deep black but burnished with gold. In its center stood a great gate, carved with a hundred pictures from a hundred stories. Guards in vivid, flashing silver armor lined the lane leading up to it, flags flying from their lances.

"Open in the name of the king!" Erling bellowed, and the guards sprang into action, grasping a handle and working a great wheel that groaned deep in the foundations of the earth, slowly heaving the massive doors ajar.

The horses pranced in place for just a moment—Erling's arm tightened around Marina's waist—and then they darted into the new opening, hooves clattering on worn cobbles.

Coolness washed over them as they entered the shade. They galloped through a low, deep tunnel, their passage thundering like cannon fire...

And in a moment, they burst out into the most awesome chamber Marina had ever seen.

Higher than any building on earth, wider than any cathedral. The hollow heart of Yggdrasil, with walls of smoothed pale wood—walls that leaped up far taller than Marina could see. A chamber more vast than she could fathom.

High, high overhead, thick, graceful branches within the tree reached out from all the walls and intertwined with each other, and heart-shaped emerald leaves grew amongst them. Bright flickering lanterns dangled from many of these boughs by jeweled chains, filling the highest reaches with twinkling fairy lights.

Massive knots bulged out from the great walls, and these knots had clearly been carved out—Marina glimpsed chimneys, windows and doors in the faces of these knots, and winding staircases leading up to each entrance. Scents of food and cooking smoke wafted from these open doors and chimneys—and laughter, and voices. Staircases and hanging bridges decorated the walls around these little dwellings, leading round and round, higher and higher, toward the internal branches that held hands so far above.

Their horses sped through the narrow cobblestone streets of this living, wooden city, and then beneath a giant archway sculpted to look like two fierce, bearded men standing guard in full armor.

"Open the doors, open the doors!" Erick shouted, his voice ringing through the great space. Ahead of them stood an immense doorway decorated around with fantastic carven knotwork. The two guards that flanked it leaped toward the handles, grabbed them and heaved the doors open just as their horses plunged through.

They swept down a long, brightly-lit golden corridor. Marina could just glimpse paintings on either side of them: women dressed in white, seeming to be bathing, bandaging, and feeding other people.

The doors at the far end already hung open, and through it Marina could see what had to be sunlight. They raced through, and found themselves in a great round chamber, surrounded by pillars, and pierced down through with a shaft of sunlight from straight overhead.

In the very center stood a white stone bier, completely bathed in this sunlight so it shone.

At the racket their hooves caused, several people emerged from doorways past the pillars. Women, all dressed in white as well, their curly hair bound up.

"Call for the king!" Erling commanded, leaping off his horse. "We have brought his son!"

The women cried out, their hands flying to their mouths, and two of them dashed away.

"My lady," Erling panted, reaching up toward Marina. She swung her leg over and leaned, and slipped down into his grasp. He caught her and set her down easily, then hurried over to help his brother.

Together the two men lifted Bird down very gently, then carried him to the bier. They laid him out, his skin and hair illuminating like alabaster and gold in that bath of sun.

In a moment, several of the women emerged completely and hurried up to the other side of the bier, surrounding him. In hushed, hurried tones, they began asking questions of the huntsmen, and touching Bird all across his head, neck, chest and shoulders. Marina stepped forward to listen...

A strange scent rose up within her and filled her nose.

She stopped. Pressed a hand to her chest.

The scent of metal. Hot metal.

From *inside* her.

And then, something soft and small materialized on her tongue. Something that grew, and hardened, and pressed against the roof of her mouth like a...

Like a stone.

Her eyes went wide.

She opened her mouth, reached in and pulled it out...

A brilliant golden jewel lay there in her palm.

Her throat locked shut. But just as she was about to let out a yelp—

The smell of frost, and cooking sugar overwhelmed her. An object swelled on her tongue and nearly cut her gums...

She pulled it out.

A silvery, laughing jewel that caught every scrap of light in the room.

Marina stepped back, ducking down beside the horse's flank, her heart crashing wildly against her ribs as yet another scent flooded her head.

Windswept summer rain—followed by the scorch of a forest fire.

And she pulled out a deep sapphire stone that swarmed with storms inside.

Before she could process the wondrous shiver that shot through her at the sight of the flashing gems in her hand, yet another smell rose up.

Cinnamon, honey, and sweet cream.

She withdrew a vibrant ruby—one that she remembered down to each facet. Tears began filling her eyes...

Just as the luster of an autumn wind...

And the deliciously-stinging taste of peppermint washed through her mouth.

She closed her eyes as this warm jewel pressed against her tongue, filling her body with pleasant heat and her mind with light. Slowly, she reached up and drew it out between her lips...

Her lips burned at the touch of it—a laugh rang through her head...

She pressed it to her mouth, her eyes still shut, holding her breath, peppermint lingering on her taste...

The gem grew cold. The peppermint faded.

She opened her eyes, lowered the stone, and looked at it.

A deep emerald, faintly winking.

She set it down beside the blue stone, and gazed through tears at the rainbow in her hand.

"What do you have?"

Her head jerked up.

And her heart nearly stopped.

Two new figures stood beside the bier, facing her.

One: a tall, beautiful woman with golden ringlets that hung down to the floor. A circlet of diamonds rested on her head, her eyes—chocolate brown and warm—wide and alight. She wore a light blue dress like the spring sky which trailed on the stones behind her.

The other: a man, even taller, with long, flowing white hair, and a snowy beard braided with beads, wearing majestic silver clothes embroidered with sapphire, and a cape of dark maroon stitched with white. He also wore a patch over one eye—and the other, the color of winter clouds, pinned Marina where she stood.

"Your Majesty," she gasped, trying to incline her head.

"What do you have?" he repeated—but his low voice carried no bite. In fact, it filled her with gentleness, and her hammering heart calmed.

She stepped forward, very carefully, and held out her hand to the shaft of sunlight.

When her palm entered it, and the light struck the stones, they seemed to catch fire. They blazed against her skin, shooting fractured likenesses of themselves across all of the people standing round about.

Marina lifted her head, and looked up into Odin's wizened face. He gazed softly down at the stones, and his lips parted.

"Bauldr's Tears," he murmured. "She has found them."

"How?" the woman—clearly the queen, Frigga—stepped close and gripped her husband's harm, desperately searching Marina's face.

"We will all find out soon," Odin replied, touching her hand. "But now, time runs short for our son."

Frigga pressed a hand to her mouth and fought back tears.

"Eir, what can be done?" Odin asked one of the women who stood across from him. She seemed to be the age of Marina's mother, and had curly, brilliant red hair piled up on her head.

"Let me see the tears," she asked, holding out her hand to Marina.

Marina hesitated, visions of caves, rocks, burnt trees and fireplaces flashing through her mind...

She carefully tipped them out of her palm, and watched them tumble into Eir's. Eir then produced a short, pearl-handled knife, stepped up close and pushed Bird's tunic aside, baring his chest.

His heart wound stood out against his white skin like a stain. Eir set the stones on his belly, then leaned in and slowly pushed the point of the knife straight down into the wound. Frigga gasped and pressed close to her husband. Eir gently worked the knife blade to the side, creating a larger opening. She withdrew the knife, kept her left-hand fingers within the opening, set the knife down and picked up the golden stone.

"Bauldr's tear for his father, Odin All-Father," she declared—and the gem flashed in recognition. She held it up. "May regrets be purified, sins wiped clean, and fellowship restored."

Odin's tear hummed deeply in reply, and its surface swam. Eir took it between her fingers and pushed it hard down inside Bird's wound. Then, she picked up the silvery stone.

"Bauldr's tear for his mother, Frigga, Queen of Asgard," she announced. "May regrets be forgotten, words pardoned, and love renewed."

She drove this stone inside right behind the other, then picked up the sapphire.

"Bauldr's tear for his brother, Thor, Prince of Asgard," she said. "May fear be washed away, wounds healed, and fellowship revived." She pressed this stone in as well, deep and firm, then picked up the ruby.

"Bauldr's tear for his ally, Marina Feroe of Midgard," she said, glancing over to meet Marina's eyes. "May deceptions be clarified, hurts soothed, and joy returned."

Marina swallowed as Eir slid that gem inside Bird's wound. And lastly, she took up the emerald, and gazed into it with furrowed brow, as if reading something in its depths.

"Bauldr's tear for his...friend...Loki of...Asgard," she said—in a slightly-stunned murmur. She drew a deep breath. "May all be forgiven."

Frigga, Odin, the huntsmen and the other women all glanced at each other in profound surprise. Eir looked to Odin, hesitating—but he nodded to her. So, she thrust that jewel into the wound as well, then laid both palms down over the opening and leaned her weight upon his chest. Then, she rested her upper body against his, lowered her head and pressed a kiss to his lips.

She lingered there for just a moment, then lifted just an inch...

"*Lifa*," she whispered into his mouth.

She rose up, keeping her hands right where they were...

He breathed.

His chest lifted—air rushed into his lungs.

Marina slapped a hand over her mouth.

And he opened his eyes.

Frigga let out a stifled cry before she too covered her mouth with her hands.

Bird blinked—his sky blue eyes focused and blinked against the radiant sunlight. He swallowed.

His left hand lifted up, and gently came to rest on top of Eir's. His eyebrows drew together, his head slowly tilted to the side...

He saw Marina.

Looked directly at her. And the quiet, gentle power in his gaze filled the silence.

A smile touched his soft lips, and lit the edges of his eyes. He breathed again.

Impossibly. Beautifully. He breathed.

His lips parted.

"Well done, Marina," he murmured.

Frigga threw her hands in the air and let out a loud, joyous shout, then flung herself onto her son's chest. He sat up and wrapped his sobbing mother in his strong arms, burying his face in the ocean of her curls.

Eir clapped her hands together, then pressed them to her beaming mouth, tears flooding her eyes. The other healing women broke into shouts of desperate delight, and took off through the other corridors, happily shrieking like schoolgirls.

Frigga laughingly relinquished a few inches of her boy, enough so that Odin could come around and envelope him as well, kissing Bird's head, tears glittering in his beard.

"We must tell everyone!" Erling declared, hopping toward the door. "I mean—we should—May we tell everyone?"

"Yes, yes!" Odin laughed, briskly waving him off. "The two of you go—spread the word as fast as you can!"

"Yes, your majesty!" they both grinned, and pelted noisily back up the corridor, their horses trotting confusedly behind. Marina watched them go, tears dripping from her jaw...

"Marina?"

She spun back around—

Bird was looking at her again, his parents on either side of him—who looked at her, too. She swallowed once more.

"Yes?" she asked softly.

"Come here."

She hesitated, then cautiously stepped forward.

"Mother, Father—may I present my dear friend, Marina Feroe," he said, his gaze never leaving hers. "The one who has saved my life."

"Not alone," Marina cut in, twisting her hands together. "Loki—" Unexpectedly, her throat closed. She ducked her head, tried to breathe evenly, then looked up at them again. "Loki helped me so much."

Frigga and Odin's eyes flashed—but Bird's filled with warmth.

"Loki?" Frigga whispered, closing her fingers around Bird's tunic. "How?"

Marina hesitated again, glancing at Bird...

Who just watched her, and smiled. She took a breath.

"Hel came to my house, asking for something that Bauldr had left behind. She chased me out into the snow—but I used one of the Wishstones Bauldr gave me to escape...and it took me to where Loki was being held. He told me that, without him, Hel and Fenris would kill me, so I freed him. And together we..." Her heart started pounding again, but she made herself go on. "Together we gathered up all of Bird's tears from all over Midgard, went into Helheim and got him back, and brought him here to you."

Odin and Frigga glanced at each other.

"But why would Loki help you to do such a thing?" Odin asked.

"Because," Marina replied. "It was an accident."

"An accident?" Frigga repeated.

"Yes," Marina said. "Hel was trying to force him to leave Asgard with her and Fenris—and so she disguised Bird as a dark elf. Loki believed he saw a dark elf trying to enter Thor's room with a knife. And so he shot it with a mistletoe arrow, hoping to break whatever protective spells the elf had put up. He..." Marina squeezed her hands together so hard it hurt, and her gaze fell upon Bird's. "He had no idea it was Bird," she said, more tears tumbling as her lip quivered. "He never...never would have done that to you. Not ever."

"Can this be true?" Frigga gasped, blushing crimson as she turned to Odin. "Did we sentence the wrong man to death?"

"More than the wrong man," Odin muttered darkly. "Our dearest friend."

"It's true," Bird said, glancing up at his parents. "But it's all right in the end, isn't it?" He reached up and fingered his mother's collar, smiling encouragingly at her.

She leaned in and kissed him fervently on the forehead, her tears falling onto his glowing skin.

"Oh, my dearest boy," she said brokenly, rocking him back and forth. "Yes!"

Bird laughed.

"Well, call that rascal in here, then!" he declared. "Marina, go tell him it's safe to come in."

Marina's hands clenched so that her knuckles turned white. She didn't move. Bird's smile faded.

"Wait," he sat up straighter, pulling back from his mother. "Where is he?"

Marina's lip trembled and her jaw clenched. She couldn't speak, couldn't breathe. Only shook her head, once.

Bird's features changed entirely—shocked sorrow flooded his eyes.

"Father! Father!" The roaring voice thundered through the corridors outside.

"Thor!" Odin bellowed back, coming off the bier and standing up to face the door. "Thor, come! We are here!"

The next moment, Thor burst into the room, Mjollnir gripped in one hand, a bottle of glowing potion in the other. Hair torn and wild, armor dented, cape shredded and limp, burning eyes frantic, blood running down the side of his head.

He slowed to a trot, then stumbled to a halt, staring at Bird.

Bird's brow knotted. He said nothing. Just held out his arms.

Thor dropped Mjollnir.

It *clanged* against the stones. He stepped forward, tears spilling down—

And caught Bird up in a mighty embrace.

He took a fistful of Bird's golden curls and swayed back and forth, crushing him close—and Bird hugged him back just as ferociously.

"You look half dead," Bird choked. "Where have you been?"

"To Helheim to find you!" Thor answered raggedly, backing up and pressing his hand to Bird's head. Tears marked tracks through the ash on his rugged face. He beamed through his weeping. "Look at you!"

Bird reached up and took hold of Thor's collar.

"Where is Loki?"

The smile fell from Thor's face, and his brow twisted. He shook his head.

"He was poisoned. By Hel," he said, his voice shaking. "And yet he fought her, even as the chamber collapsed all around us. Marina got you out, and I found the potion Hel was making that would have given her the power to overthrow the realms. But Loki, Hel and Fenris all fell into the chasm beside the furnace, and the mountain fell upon *them*." Thor squeezed Bird's shoulders. "I went back inside many times, calling his name. But everything had been crushed."

Frigga pressed her fingers to her lips. Odin hung his head.

Tears of his own trickled down Bird's cheeks. Thor shook him lightly.

"He died for you," he said through his teeth, and nodded. "Our truest friend indeed."

Bird nodded as well, then pressed his forehead to Thor's heart. Thor wrapped him up again, letting his tears trail into his hair.

"*Alskling?*"

A quiet, bright voice rang like a bell through the room. Everyone turned...

A young woman dressed in rosy pink, with ringlets of soft red curls all undone, paused mid step on the threshold, her vivid green eyes wide.

Bird stood up off the bier. For half a moment, he hung there, on the edge—

And then he ran to her.

She shouted and darted toward him—he caught her up, swung her around and pulled her against his chest—she wrapped her arms around his neck and entwined her fingers through his hair.

She released a giddy, shattered laugh—he set her down, took her face in his hands and kissed her ravenously. She answered with equal fever as he then wound his arms around her body, and the two of them got lost entirely.

Thor chuckled—a rumbling sound that shook Marina, who stood watching with empty hands, her own mouth burning.

Aching with everything in her to taste peppermint again...

And sinking slowly to the floor, her left palm easily stretched out and open on her lap.

Chapter Twenty Nine

MARINA ABSENTLY TOUCHED the petals of one of the soft white flowers wound through her hair, and lifted her eyes to the rafters of Bilskirnir.

Garlands of pale yellow blossoms wound around all the beams and warp and woof of the mead hall. Tiny lights slowly issued from the each flower's center, drifting down toward the feasting floor like snowflakes from the sun.

A hazy afternoon radiance showered down from the skylights at the far end of the wooden room, catching in the crystal bowls of punch, sending dancing reflections across the silver and gold goblets standing on the table—a table which overflowed with red and white roses and oak leaves.

Musicians perched on stools in that far corner, strumming a lively, untamed tune that Marina seemed to remember hearing somewhere before, even as all the royal Aesir, dressed in splendid golds and scarlets, laughed and swirled in the shimmering luster.

At the heart of their company, Bauldr—resplendent in white and silver—held his new bride, Nanna, in his arms. She looked beautiful, fresh as the dawn, and lovely beyond compare, in a cloud-white dress, with a leafy silver circlet in her fiery hair, her cheeks blushed, her eyes dazzling and her lips red from being kissed, and kissed, and tenderly kissed again.

Many Aesir twirled and swayed around them, but these two remained in the center of the light, seeing no one but each other. Many other Aesir sat at the long table, eating more of the honeyed boar, venison, fruits and nuts, and drinking all the mead and wine.

Marina glimpsed some familiar faces there, such as Sif—who, upon closer watching, had proved to be a gentle, sweet and kindly wife to Thor, and an elegant, but understanding, lady.

Marina sat at the farthest corner of the table from the dancing, exactly where she had been placed so long ago. Though now, her seat stood lower, so she no longer felt so conspicuous. And once more, Thor sat in his great chair just to her right, eating and drinking quietly, his gaze wandering distantly through the hall, haunted by a quiet sadness.

Up in the balcony to her left, Odin and Frigga oversaw the dancing, standing arm in arm. And there, upon Odin's weathered face, Marina could see the same grief reflected, and even deepened.

Marina herself wore a loose, sleeveless white dress with a low neckline and a ribbon belt. Bird's silver pendant, which he had given to her ages ago, rested gently against her breastbone. She had never once taken it off.

That morning, she had watched the wedding ceremony while standing in the company of the royal family, saying nothing all the while. At the feast, she had eaten and drank everything that had been served to her, tasting it all, and watching everyone as if from faraway. Now, she simply gazed and listened, the music and conversation fading to the back of her mind.

The afternoon light dwindled to evening, the skylights closed, and the torches lit themselves. Marina sensed Thor wash his hands, dry them, and then slowly sit back in his chair, releasing a long sigh. Marina's attention drifted from the revelers, up the surface of the table, across the way...

And lighted upon the empty wooden chair to Thor's right.

A chair that had been festooned with the branches of a cinnamon tree, wound in with purple hyacinth.

Her gaze hung there, seeing nothing else, as her thoughts wandered back...

A hand touched hers.

Her eyelids flickered, but she didn't turn. She felt a warm, calloused hand gently slip underneath hers, and twine through her fingers.

Thor held her hand there under the table, softly rubbing his thumb back and forth along the back of it. Marina's breathing unsteadied, and she didn't dare look over at him. But she closed her grasp and returned the pressure.

"May heaven bless you for all that you have given my family, Lady Marina," he murmured. "And may the great Ring-giver grant you peace, and freedom from all your sorrows."

She swallowed, knowing she ought to speak, ought to at least look at him...

She could not. So she nodded, and lowered her gaze to her lap.

For a long time, neither of them moved nor spoke. The herald called out an announcement inviting the wedding guests to return to the table for desserts of strawberries and cream, and more wine.

Marina slipped her hand out of Thor's, stood up, and stepped up to his side—though she could still not look at him.

"Thank you, my lord, for coming to help me when I called you," she whispered. And Marina bent down, and pressed a kiss to the side of Thor's head.

With that, she turned, climbed the stairs and left the mead hall, pushing through the double doors and stepping out into the night.

Owls called and night birds twittered in the trees and the shrubs. A cool breeze touched the edges of her loose hair, and the hem of her skirt. She stood in the center of the moonlit road, arms wrapped around herself, gazing into the distance at the colossal silhouette of Yggdrasil, and the myriad lamps that hung like fairy lights in its vast boughs. The full summer moon bathed everything in white and hoary light, turning all shadows to deep blues and violets.

A soft movement to her left. She didn't turn, but her gaze unfocused.

"Hello, Marina," a gentle voice emerged. "How do you suppose that rosebush is doing without you?"

Marina's eyes clouded. Then, she reached up, and wiped away the single tear that trailed down her cheek.

Bauldr quietly stepped up beside her and paused. She could feel him studying her.

"Walk with me?" he asked.

Marina glanced over at him. Flawless and pale, nearly elvish, his earnest eyes luminescent, his curls like the feathers of a swan.

"Won't she miss you?" she asked, with low pointedness.

Bauldr glanced down and smiled crookedly.

"No," he said. "She knows where I am."

Marina said nothing. He turned his back on Yggdrasil, and raised his eyebrows at her.

Slowly, she turned toward him, keeping her arms wrapped around herself. He took a step forward, and she followed suit. And soon, they were walking slowly back up the road Marina had followed in the back of a cart when she had first come to Asgard, all that time ago.

"You are different," Bauldr remarked. "I can see it in you: that strength I only caught glimpses of before. You wear it like a crown, now."

Marina lifted her chin, gazing out ahead of her, listening to the lonely coo of a dove nearby. Bauldr clasped his hands behind his back and walked closer to her. Occasionally, their shoulders brushed.

"I'm sure you have heard, in fairytales," he began carefully. "Of the magical power of 'true love's kiss.' Well, your myth-makers were not entirely wrong. Though it is not so much the 'true love' as it is the *kiss* that carries the power. From the mouth flows life, breath, and the purest forms of magic. Doubtlessly on your travels, you noticed that Loki often breathed into his hands, or whispered spells—and his breath was the catalyst for the change he desired. I'm sure that Eir used some of the same when she revived me. In cases of near death and terrible strain, magicians have been known to bleed magic from their mouths."

Marina glanced over at him again, going cold with recollection. But he looked placidly straight ahead.

"Upon the lips of a powerful practitioner, Kiss Magick can be used to tremendous effect. It can discover the location of broken bones or torn muscle, seek out scars or deformities, convey secrets...and even, in very special circumstances, actual objects."

"That's how you gave me those visions," Marina realized quietly. "Of where to find your tears. You kissed me on the forehead."

Bauldr chuckled softly.

"Yes. And thankfully, it worked. I'm only a novice when it comes to Kiss Magick. Loki, being a natural healer, is the master." He paused, then swallowed. "Was."

Marina pulled her arms tighter around herself.

They walked some distance further, saying nothing—and she sensed that Bauldr was gathering his words. A low gust of wind pushed at their backs, cooling their skin, and the night birds quieted.

"The first day I met you, I saw how much pain you were in," he murmured carefully. "How it swallowed you, crippled you, kept you up at night. I also knew that you would never tell me what it was. And that I could never fix it. But...I knew someone who could."

Marina's heart started beating faster.

"I put a spell on that Wishstone to take you to Loki, wherever he might be," Bauldr went on. "I knew that your resolution and wisdom, paired with Loki's talent and raw nerve, was the best chance that Asgard, and I, had. I was also certain..." he slowed to a stop, and faced her. Marina stopped too—but she could not lift her face to his.

"I was *certain*," he pressed. "That you could reach a depth of Loki's heart that no one has ever seen, not even here, in a thousand years. That you could heal wounds he has carried all his life, that you could give him the courage to confront the ones who have been slowly poisoning him." Bauldr reached out, and gently took her by the elbows. "And I was certain that *he* would persist so stubbornly to know you, to *fix* you, that he would finally get inside of you and mend what was broken—what I could *never* mend." He took a shaking breath. "I had no idea that you...That we would all lose him." He swallowed. "For that, I am...desperately sorry."

Marina's face twisted, still unable to lift her head.

"I would also say that I am sorry that you fell in love with him," Bauldr murmured. "And that he fell in love with you."

Now her head came up. She stared at him, some sort of strange, thrilling panic shooting through her. He gazed back at her, smiling weakly.

"But, for a selfish reason, I cannot be sorry for that," he said, kindly taking up her hands and squeezing them. "Because that is where your myth-makers got it right. Only *love* can give and receive something so potent and mercurial as my tears through Kiss Magick. And so...I am alive." He shrugged, his eyes shining. His brow knotted and his voice unsteadied. "But, for an *un*selfish reason...I cannot be sorry that you loved my friend. He has never been loved by one as true as you." His tears fell, and glistened in the moonlight. "He waited long, his heart often broken. And he died for *you*, as much as he did for me."

Marina's own tears tumbled now, and she couldn't look away from him.

"Carry him with you all your life, Marina Feroe," Bauldr urged. "He gave you a gift you cannot see, but it is beyond the value of anything on earth."

"I will," she promised, gasping.

"And take this gift from me," he added, reaching down to a pouch at his belt, and pulling out a vial. Inside glowed a turquoise blue liquid, the surface of which sparkled with green flame.

"What is it?" Marina asked, blinking away her tears.

"It is some of the magic that Hel stole," Bauldr said, laying it in her palm. "I want you to take it back to Midgard. I want you to stand in the middle of your garden, remove the cork and pour it out. And as you do, I want you to say *lifa, lifa, lifa.*"

"What will that do?" Marina asked, closing her fingers around the vial.

But Bauldr only smiled.

Just then, a low thud rippled through the earth beneath their feet. Confused, Marina turned...

To see a stone archway standing beside the road. Through it, a curtain of fog waited.

Marina stared through that gateway, her heart skipping a beat. Slowly, she frowned, and looked to him again.

"Now?"

Bauldr said nothing. Her gaze wandered across his features.

"Will I ever see you again?" She breathed the question so low, she thought he wouldn't hear it. But his smile returned.

"If you wish," he said. "As long as you wear that pendant."

A flame of pleasure guttered in her chest for a moment.

Just a moment.

Her lip trembled again.

"Thank you."

Bauldr grew solemn.

"No," he shook his head—then knelt on the ground before her, took her left hand, and kissed the back of it. Then, he pressed it fervently to his forehead. "Thank *you*, fairest and kindest and bravest lady of Midgard."

Pain traveled all through her body. She squeezed her eyes shut.

"Goodbye, Bird," she rasped, squeezing his fingers hard—then letting go.

"Goodbye," he whispered—suddenly sounding sad.

She turned, refusing to look at him—but feeling his angelic warmth touch her back. She clutched the vial to her chest, stepped off the road and into the dew-covered grass.

She swished past the little daisies, the gate looming over her.

And, before her will had a chance to break, she lowered her head and charged forward, straight into the mist.

She strode through the fog, head down, following the progress of her feet against the paving stones. She felt the vast, clouded space around her, the walls that formed the railing of the bridge...

She paused, her heart panging, and turned back.

She couldn't see anything but a wall of mist.

Biting the inside of her cheek, she faced forward again, and continued.

On and on she walked, listening to the echoes of her footsteps. Until finally, she caught sight of another archway, and darkness beyond.

Chill air wafted out toward her. She shivered—then ground her teeth and plunged through.

Her sandaled feet sank up to her calves in snow. She instantly snapped her jaw shut as her vision swam...

And there she stood, in the dark, in the middle of the forest by her house.

"Gah!" she rasped in alarm, shivering hard and binding her arms around her chest. Her breath burst out into vapor in front of her face. She dashed forward, kicking through the snow, her feet going numb, frost needling the bare skin of her arms and neck.

She scrambled up the hill, battling to see by the shafts of moonlight that pierced through the laden branches. Finally, she achieved the height, and emerged onto her own side lawn.

She paused, puffing and shuddering, staring down at the three sets of deep footprints that led toward the darkened hulk of her house.

Thor's. Hers. And Loki's.

"Gaaaah..." she gasped again, her whole frame quivering violently, and she hurried out into the moon-soaked yard, where the snow glittered like spilled sugar.

In the dead center, she planted her feet squarely in two of Loki's footprints. She pulled out the vial, popped the cork loose, and held the bottle out in front of her.

The moonlight glimmered secretively through the multi-colored liquid.

She tipped it. The liquid eased toward the opening.

And then...

Drip.

"*Lifa,*" Marina breathed. She tipped the bottle more, letting the potion run out in one continuous stream. "*Lifa...lifa...*"

It struck the snow. Let out a low, contemplative hiss...

WHOOSH.

Hot wind burst outward from her feet—and the snow shot back.

She hopped, almost spilling the potion in shock.

The snow vanished in a rolling, widening circle all around her, fleeing into the woods, disappearing from the branches, leaping off of the flowerbeds, curling away and off the roof.

Hundreds of low branches noisily heaved upward, suddenly relieved of their terrible burdens. Heat swelled against her bare legs, sending goosebumps racing up her skin. Wild crackling issued from the depths of the forest as the trees creaked and sighed and the snow jetted into the air in sparkling clouds of dust and disappeared.

"*Lifa...lifa...*" Marina kept muttering, only halfway realizing she was doing it as she frantically turned her head back and forth to catch what was happening—

The crushed blades of grass righted themselves and filled with strength and moisture. She could feel the lawn soften beneath her feet. All the shrubs and rose bushes lifted from their frostbitten limpness, shook themselves and stretched upward, sprouting out dozens of new leaves in an instant.

A high wind abruptly rushed through the topmost boughs, and the thin winter clouds folded and dissolved. The sky warmed, and seemed to press closer—the stars brightened like living diamonds.

"Lifa...lifa...lifa..."

The hot, teasing wind dove and swirled around her, catching her dress and tossing her hair.

And Marina gasped.

A million winking fireflies rose from the grass. They looped and swung through Marina's yard, swimming through the velvety night, pushed to and fro by the playful breeze. And they lit the fathoms of the forest—countless glimmering yellow lights as far as she could see in all directions.

Then, a cloud of bats dashed by overhead, squeaking with delight, and sweeping down into the branches.

As if on cue, a chorus of fluttering shook the night, and a thousand birds began twittering, shrieking, sputtering and singing. Their raucous noise surrounded Marina, drowned her. Then, in harmony, innumerable grasshoppers and crickets began chirping and clicking.

A few minutes later, dew wetted her feet and soaked the hem of her dress. It beaded on her bare arms, her hair and her brow. The birdsong rose to a joyous cacophony...

And the sky lifted.

The darkness eased back from the eastern horizon.

And, as Marina stood breathless, the empty vial loose in her hand...

The dawn came.

First, it painted the edges with the softest grey, which soon bloomed into a gentle pink that spread across the sky, gradually rolling back the night and hiding the stars.

She gazed, captured by its quiet advance...

Until the sun violently broke the canvas of the heavens—pierced the violets and blues with overpowering gold and blinding white.

The leaves, the grass all illumined with greens of all shades—so many greens! Her lawn bubbled with purple and yellow flowers, the trunks of the trees pulsed with reds, auburns and chestnuts. The rose bushes throbbed, and never-ending roses broke from their buds in a stunning wave, spilling their gaudy blooms across the walkway and up the side of her house.

The voices of the birds rang out a riot through the morning. Swallows wove through the towering blue sky, chasing through a flock of dragonflies.

Slowly, Marina sank to the ground, and sat in the grass—grass which now stood hip high. She set the empty vial down, and wrapped her arms around her knees and tilted her face back, taking a full breath of the sweet, fresh scent that now filled the air.

Warmth coursed through her blood as she listened to the rolling, rising noises of the glorious dawn, a deep quiet in her heart. The sun rose. The sky brightened to a blue as vibrant as Bauldr's eyes.

And, as ruby-red ladybugs crawled up her arms and onto her skirt, Marina reached down with her left hand and pressed it softly against the ground...

Into the place where Loki's footprint used to be.

Chapter Thirty

One Year Later

"Hi, Mr. Larson? This is Marina Feroe. Haha, yes, *again*," Marina smiled into the phone as she kept loose hold of the steering wheel with her right hand. Sunlight flickered past her open truck window as she drove down the two-lane highway. "Listen, I really need some help at my house. The underbrush from the woods around my yard is just taking over, my rose bushes are covering my walkway, and there's a bunch of ivy that's worked its way through my upstairs windows and into my hall. It's too much."

"Well," came the crackling reply. *"Before, I wouldn't have believed you, since me and Peter just came out there three weeks ago to clear all that out! But ever since that freak snowstorm cleared up...!"*

"Yes, I know," Marina chuckled. "It's like living in a jungle."

"It is!" he cried. *"And I've been getting calls from everyone in town saying the same thing as you all spring and summer—I've had to hire more guys to help out. Is it all right if I send a couple of the new ones out to you? You don't know them, but I've been watching them work for the past few days and they do a good job."*

"Yeah, that's fine," she agreed. "Just tell them to hurry before I drown!"

Mr. Larson laughed.

"We'll do our best! Thanks, Marina."

"No, thank *you*," she insisted, grinning, and hung up. She set her phone down on the passenger seat and ran her left hand through her windblown hair, then draped her arm out the window, feeling the sun glow against the side of her face.

She followed the winding road along the rocky coastline, taking deep breaths of the cool, salty air, watching the rows and rows of tall, dark pines flash by.

Eventually, she turned off, came to a parking space, and got out. The slamming of the door rang through the silence, and the wind caught her hair. She gathered up her satchel, swung it over her shoulder, and began her hike.

She wandered down a long lane flanked by thin young pines, hundreds of birds flittering around her, the sunlight dappling the ground before her. She took another deep breath and smiled. She had always loved the scent of pine.

Finally, the woods opened up to a broad beach of rough, reddish sand and rocks. There, she found a lone tree—one that she greeted as an old friend—and sat down underneath its shade, gazing out across the silvery blue sea, and the great, wide sky beyond.

"And when the sun falls and twilight pulls its cloak over the sky, night never truly descends. For a quiet light remains in the west, touching the edge of the silver water on the far side of the great tree. Sometimes, if one stands alone and listens, he can hear the sea birds sing his name, feel the surf call on the wind, and many a man will begin to wish to make sail, and meet that light where it stands..."

Again, Marina smiled. Softly. And she reached in her satchel and pulled out her work.

A stack of paper, all written on, and many pages illuminated. She gazed down at the title page, fully colored and inked.

THE LIVING EDDA by *Marina Feroe*

Carefully, she lifted that page off and set it behind, and scanned over the next bit.

Cast of Illustrious and Infamous Inhabitants of the Nine Realms: *The Sons of Odin*

Only two.

Both of them were born to Odin All-Father and his wife Frigga, the king and queen of Asgard.

Thor: Eldest and wielder of Mjollnir, the thunder-hammer. He dwells in a vast mead hall called Bilskirnir, encircled by ancient oak trees and standing anext the country highway, with his wife, the beautiful and golden-haired Lady Sif. There, he entertains his many friends with glorious, sun-bathed feasts, music and dancing. He is a gracious host, a kind master, and a fearsome friend, fair and just in all his dealings.

Bauldr: Youngest, bringer of light and warmth, friend to all things that grow. His kin have also given him the pet name of "Bird." He is married to the Lady Nanna, Keeper of the Roses, and they live together in the vast palace-tree of Yggdrasil. Bauldr is wise, quiet and gentle, always seeking to benefit his friends, and prevent his enemies from harming his father's kingdom.

THE THREE CHILDREN OF FARBAUTI

LOKI

Loki was the youngest, most talented and unconventional of the three children of the Jotun giant. His most remarkable trait was that his appearance changed with his mood. Red hair and bright green eyes meant amusement, blond hair and deep green eyes signaled tenderness; violet eyes and grey hair showed his irritation, while red eyes and black hair revealed his rage. Sarcasm and disbelief made themselves known with deep blue hair and emerald eyes, whilst sadness came through in black hair and slate-grey eyes. Seriousness took a similar turn, with black hair and brilliant blue eyes, while perceptiveness lightened to chestnut hair and vivid turquoise eyes.

He was very unlike both Thor and Bauldr in manner and character, yet the sons of Odin and Frigga deeply enjoyed his company, and reveled in his storytelling, his jokes and his laughter. He could be forward, flirtatious, and flippant, yet he had no equal in the crafts of magic, illusion and healing. And while he seemed insincere and rakish on the outset, such was the façade of false-bravado he erected to conceal deep fondness, unshakable loyalty, uncompromising bravery, and a sacrificial heart, which earned him the place of dearest friend of the house of Odin, and indeed, all of Asgard.

Loki Farbautison perished with his sister Hel and his brother Fenris by the furnaces of Helheim, locked in a battle against them to save the lives of the only two sons of Odin.

Marina paused, her fingertips ghosting over the heading.

After her return, she had secluded herself inside her house for two months, only erratically eating and sleeping, and sometimes listlessly organizing her possessions that remained in boxes. She ignored calls from her mother, her family friends, and Mr. Larson. She sat on the rug and stared at the blank mantelpiece, arms wrapped around herself. She had let her garden go to seed, and forgot to listen to the birds.

Finally, her tall, short-haired, firm-mouthed mother showed up at her doorstep. And, to Marina's great surprise, she had collapsed in her mother's arms and started sobbing.

Right then, her mother decided she should come home with her back to New York. Marina, too weak and tired to protest, had watched while her mother packed her things and hustled her out the door.

Marina had spent the next six months living in her mother's penthouse in New York City. In the past, when Marina had been a teenager, the bustle and chaos of the city had driven her crazy, and she had longed to escape with her dad to the wide-open, quiet Irish, Swedish or Norwegian wilds. But now, the noise and constant motion stimulated her—shook her out of the depths of the silence that had smothered her in her lonely house, and forced her to interact with it. Thankfully, her mother's penthouse was located on

Park Avenue, a slightly quieter section of Manhattan, and not far away at all from Central Park. When her mother went to work at the publishing house in the morning, she would rather ungently push Marina out the door as well, warning her not to return until three in the afternoon. And so Marina wandered through Central Park, and also discovered many little shops and bookstores she came to adore. She also discovered Fraunce's Tavern, and the cemetery of Trinity Church, and visited both places often. As she rambled through Manhattan, listening to the roar of the city, her thoughts began to flow more freely, with less pain. And the day of the Macy's Thanksgiving Day Parade found her locked in her mother's loft, transforming it into a writing studio.

By Christmastime, she had made great progress, and her mood had brightened. Instead of walking through the streets every morning, she found solace exploring the deepest, frosty sections of Central Park, and hiding in the corners of the public library, taking notes and painting illuminated letters.

By the beginning of May, she had recovered sufficiently that her mother did not protest too loudly when she declared she would like to return to her house. But her mother did not allow her to go until she had made copies of some of Marina's loveliest and most interesting pages, so she could show them to the proper people at her office, and begin the process of having Marina's book published.

Marina had filled these pages with descriptions of Asgard—of the hall at Bilskirnir, the healing rooms at Yggdrasil; the gates and the Asbru bridge; of Traust, of the Aesir guests, the feasts, the wedding, the songs the harvesters sang on the road home from working in the fields, the dance on the lawn, the taste of the mead...

All the details of Festning, especially Bestemor and Skjønnhet, the bath lady; the little library and pokey staircase; the height of the house when one stood outside versus its uncanny height when one stepped inside.

A list of Jotun and Aesir riddles.

She had also vividly described Helheim, and Valkyrie. Helheim's history, and what it had become because of Hel's schemes, its barren landscape, its underground heat, its strange corridors, its throne room with its forbidding idol of its mistress, its catacombs, shallow river, and ravenous furnace.

But most of all, she had detailed everything she could remember about magic. The sparks that flew from Loki's hands to make Festning; his breath and words that caused objects to appear or disappear, grow and shrink; healing and exploring, transporting and renewing of Wishstones; potions and draughts...

And kisses.

Just yesterday, her mother had phoned with congratulations and then faxed her the publishing contract to sign. Marina just had to give the manuscript one last look-over today before she put the whole thing in the mail.

She scanned through each crisp page, as she had done a thousand times already, absently smiling to herself, with that distant, familiar ache settled at the back of her chest.

As midday faded to late afternoon, she reached the last page, read it through, and nodded. She reached in her pack, pulled out the addressed envelope, slid the manuscript inside and sealed it. Then, she got to her feet, and paused for a moment to listen to the lonely cries of the gulls, watching the sunlight glimmer against the water.

She picked up her pack and envelope, and started back up the trail. She would drop this envelope off at the post office first, then head home to make an assessment of the work that needed doing, so that the men Mr. Larson sent tomorrow would know what to do first.

Marina sighed, running her fingers through her hair again as she drove up the dirt road toward her house. It was just about five o'clock. She had plenty of time before it got dark to take stock of everything, and then go inside and start making dinner—

She slammed on the breaks. Her truck skidded to a stop, dust flying out around her tires. She gaped out her window at her house.

She could see it. That was the first thing. When she'd left that morning, she hadn't been able to—the shrubs by the road had been growing so high, and the vines had been hanging down from the tree like a curtain.

Now, everything had been tamed back. And she couldn't see the ivy climbing up her outside wall anymore.

She threw the truck into park right there and leaped out, leaving her empty satchel there.

"What...*What*...?" she stammered, looking all around her and nearly stumbling up the walkway—for her rosebushes no longer sprawled threateningly across the pavement, but stood much smaller, straight and tall and blooming beautifully. Her grass had been shorn and smelled sweet again.

She hurried around to the side, to her vegetable garden...

To find it neatly weeded, and the bricks around it put back in order. She jerked to a stop, then turned around swiftly.

"Hello?" she called. "Is somebody still here?"

No answer.

Someone from Mr. Larson's must have com while she was gone—but *how* could two men have done all this work in just three hours?

She spun and looked at the wall of her house, to confirm that yes, in fact, all the ivy had been pulled down and cut off and disposed of. Her confusion mounting, she dashed around to the other side...

To see that the wild, menacing climbing rosebush that she loved so much had remained untouched. It still sprawled its gangly limbs all over the yard, the side of the porch, and up the chimney. She frowned hard, her mind racing.

"How did he know not to touch that...?" she whispered.

After lapping the house a few more times, taking note of all the spectacular changes, and how beautiful and neat everything looked now, she hurried inside and headed for the kitchen. She had to pause for a second so that her eyes could adjust to the dimmer light, then she charged ahead to find the phone to call Mr. Larson and ask him...

Heat washed past the left side of her face. She stopped.

Soft crackling reached her.

And the sound of smacking gums.

Her heart skipped a beat.

Slowly, she turned, and peered into the sitting room.

The wooden face of an ancient old man protruded from the mantel, contentedly working his gums and smiling to himself. A fire burned in the hearth.

Marina stood there, frozen and staring, for five minutes.

Finally, her fingers closing around the collar of her shirt, she dared to open her mouth.

"Farfar?" she croaked.

The wooden man's mouth suddenly formed a tight "O," and he looked over at her. Then, he broke into a toothless grin.

"Ah, the little *krigare!*" he greeted her, his voice like a rusty hinge. "Brightest of midsummer days to you!"

"Farfar, what...what are you doing here?" Marina cried, stepping further into the room and pressing her hand to her heart.

"I am always here...?" he gummed, his brow wrinkling in bewilderment.

"But you haven't been!" Marina told him. "I sat here waiting for you for two months, and you never once said anything to me!"

"Oh?" his brow wrinkled further and he studied her. "Then who was it that tapped on my forehead just now?"

Marina didn't move. Thoughts crashed together in her head.

Then, she yanked her attention toward the door.

For half a second, she stood bolted to the rug, unable to even breathe.

Then, she dashed out of the room, flung open the door and leaped off the porch.

Her breath snagging in her chest, she hurried out into the center of the walkway, searching the corners of the yard...

No one. No one...no one...

There.

She stopped.

She went cold, and then her face flushed with heat—and her pulse skyrocketed.

A dark figure at the border of her woods. Tall, with dark hair, and a pale face, his hands in his pockets.

He didn't move.

She recognized him instantly.

Marina, fists tightening, dared to maneuver around the rosebushes, and walk slowly across the lawn toward him.

Twenty feet away, she stopped, and folded her arms. For a long while, she did nothing except study him with as severe an eye as she could muster.

Short, combed back dark hair, carven features, high cheekbones and piercing grey eyes, and a set mouth. A slate-colored, long-sleeved shirt, a sleek long coat and black trousers and boots.

Fenris.

He raised his eyebrows at her.

"Good afternoon, Lady Marina."

She didn't answer for a few minutes.

"You ought to be dead," she finally said, quietly.

He lifted his chin and blinked.

"Ah. Meaning...under the circumstances you believed me to be dead, or...you rather wish I were so?"

Marina said nothing. He gave her an almost invisible smirk.

Then, he turned and started walking into the forest.

"Follow me."

Marina's arms tightened.

"Why would I do that?"

"You don't have to," he said lightly, moving easily through the underbrush. "Unless you'd like to thank the one who has taken such pains to beautify your home."

Confusion nearly knocked her over. She hesitated for just an instant—

Then dropped her arms and hurried after him.

She kept her distance, remaining at least ten feet behind him at all times—all the while knowing, of course, that should he wish to close that distance, she couldn't do anything about it.

However, he made no threatening moves. He walked casually ahead of her, his hands in his trousers pockets, glancing around at the birds and the thick forest foliage.

At last, Marina glimpsed a break in the woods, and what looked like a disused logger's road. Fenris hopped up out of the ditch and onto the dirt path, and halfway turned to her. Frowning, Marina hesitated—

Someone else moved.

A young man sitting on a stump on the other side of the road got to his feet.

He was tall. He wore soft tanned leather, without sleeves, and long tassels decorating the back of his tunic. He wore leather bracers on his forearms, and quiet hunter's shoes—a quiver full of arrows also hung from his shoulders, and a bow leaned against the nearby tree.

He had chestnut curls, dark blue eyes, and was lean as a blade, with good-looking, pale, angular features—eloquent dark eyebrows, a perfect nose and an expressive mouth.

"What, did you get lost, Fen?" he asked, giving him a look. "You'd think, after a hundred years of running this territory, you'd learn where the..."

He saw Marina.

She met his eyes.

The chestnut washed through with deep blue, and his eyes turned luminous green.

Of their own accord, Marina's feet carried her three steps out of the woods, and onto the road. And she stood there, motionless as he was, unable to draw breath.

His hair then flushed with a complex mix of gold, red and black, and one eye turned red while the other turned blue, and his panicked glance flashed to Fenris.

"Fenris, did you...?"

Fenris didn't say anything. And Marina couldn't look at him if she tried.

She took two more steps, closer. Her gaze flew all across him, missing nothing, her heart thudding but her lungs locked.

His hair swept through with deep golds—brighter with every step she took. And his eyes changed to the most brilliant emerald. But he didn't back up.

"You..." Marina whispered. "You died."

"No," Loki breathed back, his gaze locked with hers. "No, Fenris saved me."

"Fenris?" she murmured, feeling faint—as if he might disappear at any second.

Loki nodded once, his eyebrows coming together.

"He caught me, and pulled me into a tunnel before the ceiling fell," he said, his voice soft. "And...seeing as he's almost as good a magician as I am..." The corner of his mouth lifted briefly. "He cured the poison. And watched over me all these months as I recovered." At this, he lifted his gaze from Marina and looked at his brother, with an open, quiet expression Marina had never seen. Then, he looked back down at her. She could feel him breathing unsteadily—saw his jaw tighten—and got lost in his eyes.

He couldn't be real.

"Why didn't you come?" Marina asked, barely a whisper, a shiver running through her whole body.

His gaze suddenly flickered over her whole face, and he unwillingly tilted toward her.

"I'm..." He swallowed, searching her eyes. He didn't continue.

She halfway frowned, entranced by every movement of his features.

"But you took care of my trees?" Marina asked instead. "And my roses?"

"Yes," he mouthed, then swallowed again and took a deep, shaking breath. "I...Yes. I...I didn't want to disturb you, but when I saw that your garden was in such disrepair, of course I had to stop to—"

She grabbed his collar, pulled him down and pressed her mouth to his.

He sucked in a shocked breath.

She pressed deeper.

And then at last—at *last!*—

Peppermint on her lips, peppermint on her tongue, peppermint filling her head and her heart...!

He suddenly broke the kiss.

Pulled back, breathing raggedly.

Her eyes flew open—found his—

"You..." he gasped, his brow knotting, his eyes wide. "You're...not angry with me?"

"I love you," Marina cried softly, tears spilling down her cheeks.

Gold flashed through his eyes.

Fire blazed in his hair.

"I love you and I missed you so much," Marina wept, shaking her head hard. "Don't ever leave me again. I can't do without you."

His mouth crashed into hers.

She melted against him, encircling his neck with her arms, as his kiss overpowered her. He wrapped her in his strong arms and lifted her off the ground.

In desperation, joy pounding through them, they kissed each other over and over, both of them tasting salt on their lips and tongues, until Marina buried her face in his neck, took fistfuls of his curls and squeezed her eyes shut, silently letting her tears flow.

Then, for several long minutes, neither of them said anything or did anything but hold each other as tight as they could, listening to each other's heartbeats.

Finally, Loki let her slip back down to the ground, but held her against him and wiped her tears away, all the while laying sweet kisses against her forehead and cheeks.

Then, he pressed his lips to her temple, and she could feel him smile.

"And when I first met you, I thought you didn't want to be friends," he muttered.

Marina chuckled. And then, Fenris spoke up.

"Ask her to marry you, you fool."

Marina's head came up.

Loki's smile faded into sudden, breathless vulnerability. His hair remained gold, but his eyes faded from gold to silver. Marina's fingers closed around the front of his shirt. She felt his hands settle on her hips, as he gazed down into her eyes.

"I don't..." he managed. "I don't know what she'll say."

"That's why you ask," Fenris growled.

Loki swallowed again.

Marina raised her eyebrows, glanced down for a moment, then addressed him as frankly as she could with tears still wet on her face.

"Actually, you're required to marry me," she said. "The prince already arranged it."

Loki blinked.

"What?"

"Mhm," Marina said. "He told me so himself."

"Who?" Loki demanded. "Which prince?"

"Bird."

Loki stopped. His brow knotted again—he looked helplessly at Fenris, then back to her, his eyes filling with tears.

"It worked?" he rasped.

Marina canted her head, and smiled at him.

"Shall we go ask him?"

Loki's tears fell, and trailed down his cheeks. He said nothing.

"Come on," she said gently, slipping out of his arms but taking hold of his hands.

She finally turned to see Fenris—who just stood there smirking with his arms folded, leaning against a tree.

Marina faced Loki. Stepped back from him. And gently tugged on his hands.

He gave way. Took a step forward, then another, fear filling his face...

But she turned around, and pulled him onward, through the woods, back toward her house. She gripped his hand firmly, entwining their fingers, constantly glancing back at him to catch his eye, to memorize him, to make sure he was really, truly *there*...

Finally, they arrived at the stone archway, completely covered up with vines now.

Loki pulled back on her hand. They stopped, and she faced him.

More tears welled up in his fearful eyes, and he shook his head.

She brought his hand up, and kissed his knuckles.

"Trust me," she murmured against his fingers.

He squeezed. Then slowly nodded.

She smiled.

Pulled on him. And they slipped through the archway.

Fog swallowed them. Silently, breathlessly, they hurried along the stone bridge. Marina's heart thundered, thrills shot up and down her arms. They broke into a trot, gripping each other's hands so tightly...

Light brightened ahead of them, changing from a dull grey to sunshine...

A gust of wind rushed through their hair and clothes. They broke through the fog, and out into full afternoon sun...

Marina slowed down, blinking the dazzle out of her vision.

They stepped out onto an earthen road. To their left, looming, white-barked beeches stretched their leafy branches to the dome of the airy, cloud-dotted sky, lining the road like soldiers at march. Off to the right rolled green fields touched at the edges with the gold of the sunset, and interrupted by wandering stone walls. In the distance stood a carved wooden barn with a prowling dragon decorating its peak. The wind whipped happily through the shorn grain.

"*Oh,*" Loki gasped, and Marina looked up to see tears running freely down his face, sunlight sparkling against his cheeks.

"Come on," she urged, pulling on him, and together they hurried up the road, their footsteps loud on the gravel. The birds dipped and swung overhead, chirping and twittering. But then, two loud squawks joined their singing, and both Marina and Loki looked up...

To see two broad ravens swoop past, watching them brightly, and commenting all the while. Then, they pivoted midair, and flew back the way they had come.

"They're his," Loki realized. And not long after the ravens had disappeared from sight, Marina felt a rumbling beneath her feet.

A shout went up. Loki stopped, his attention catching on movement on the horizon.

And then Marina saw them too.

Three riders. One with hair like a lion's mane. Another with golden locks like the dawn. The other with braided bands of snow. And they bore the banner of the king. They rode on great bay stallions that ate up the ground before them, tails flying wildly.

Loki squeezed Marina's hand so tight her bones came together.

In a matter of minutes, in a cloud of dust, the three regal riders had reached them. They slowed their snorting horses, and for an instant, sat poised above the two on foot.

Thor, in blue and gold, with no sleeves—a knotted tattoo showed on his muscular left arm. Bird, in white—shining like a star, his eyes sky-bright. Odin, in black and gold, his ancient brow furrowed.

Then, Thor swung off his horse. His smile beamed brighter than the day, and at the sight of it, a watery chuckle broke loose from Loki's chest. He let go of Marina just in time for Thor to wrap him up in a fierce bear hug—one that he returned with equal force. Only Marina could see that Thor was crying. For he swiped at his face as he withdrew, and grinned brilliantly, taking hold of Loki's head and shaking him. Loki laughed again, eyes still sparkling, and turned to see Odin dismount and approach him. Loki's expression faltered, and he gulped...

But then Odin held out his hand to him.

Loki gazed at it a moment, then grasped it tightly. And Odin brought Loki's hand to his lips, and kissed it. Loki's lip trembled, and more tears fall.

Bird had not moved.

Slowly, Thor and Odin turned, and regarded the prince still atop the horse. Loki's breathing picked up, and he lost some of the color in his face. His hair paled, as did his eyes.

Bauldr and Loki's gazes locked.

Deliberately, Bauldr dismounted his horse, and landed easily on the dirt. He stepped up to Loki, and stood for a long moment, not stirring.

Loki reached up, and took the quiver of arrows off his shoulders. Gripping it, he held it out to Bird.

Bird looked at it. Took it from Loki. The arrows rattled quietly.

He held it there, running one hand down across the delicate feathers.

Then, he dropped it.

It struck the ground with a loud clatter—

And he wrapped his arms around Loki, and closed his eyes.

Loki let out a sob, and crushed Bird to him. Marina giggled like a kid and wiped her own tears away. Thor stepped close to them, leaned his head in and pressed his forehead to theirs. Odin also laid his hands on Bird and Loki's hair, beaming.

Bird finally released Loki, only to take his head in his hands and give him an earnest, solemn look...

One that slowly, enchantingly, broke into a delighted smile, as soft and affectionate as the dawn.

And Loki's hair turned the color of wheat as he returned the smile.

The next moment, Thor caught sight of Marina—and he bounded around the group to embrace her. He nearly smashed her, but she didn't care. Laughing, he hauled her over to the rest of them. Odin graciously took her hand, Bird cried her name and happily bent in and kissed her on the cheek, leaving a scent of cinnamon hovering all around her.

And then, she felt an arm wind around her waist, and pull her into a warm, soft, familiar chest. Loki bent, and pressed his cheek against her neck, bound his arms around her...

And let out a great, powerful sigh that washed through her whole frame. She closed her eyes, curled her arms against her chest, and let him hold her.

At long last, he lifted his head. The sunlight caught his blond locks, the winds of Asgard played through his clothes, and his eyes had turned a purer gold than she had ever seen. He reached up, and barely touched her chin with his fingertips.

"I love you," he said. "Will you be my wife?"

"Yes," she whispered.

He gazed at her lips, then closed the distance and kissed her—and the scent of sweet summer grass mingled deliciously with peppermint again.

"Loki!" Bird called. Their mouths parted, and they turned to see the other three standing by their horses. Bird, grinning, waved to him.

"Come home with us!"

Loki's brow twisted again as he gazed at his friend—and he nodded firmly.

"I'm coming," he choked, then smiled beautifully. He looked down at Marina. "Coming too?"

She just smiled, biting her lip, and tugged on his hand again.

He watched her and laughed, then caught up her hand and pulled her into a run. Together, they caught up to the men of the house of Odin, and all of them followed the evening road back toward the mead hall of Bilskirnir, singing all the way.

THE END

Don't miss out!

Visit the website below and you can sign up to receive emails whenever Alydia Rackham publishes a new book. There's no charge and no obligation.

https://books2read.com/r/B-A-MQLEB-OUCZC

BOOKS 2 READ

Connecting independent readers to independent writers.

Did you love *Bauldr's Tears: Retelling Loki's Fate*? Then you should read *Glass: Retelling the Snow Queen*[1] by Alydia Rackham!

What if your very first assignment is impossible, because the one you were sent to help has a heart of stone?Rose has lived in a mountain fortress with curse-breakers almost all her life, never venturing out into the wilds. But now, her masters have sent her on a mission to free a lost kingdom that crafts unbreakable glass. But this task may prove impossible, for the prince has an unyielding, selfish heart, and he and the kingdom are frozen under the hand of the Snow Queen.*A suspenseful and unexpected reimagining of the timeless romance of "The Snow Queen" continues Alydia Rackham's epic fairy tale series. If you enjoy magic, mystery, and*

1. https://books2read.com/u/bx9RRv

2. https://books2read.com/u/bx9RRv

the power of true love, you will relish this tale.Live anew this classic story when you read "Glass: Retelling the Snow Queen" today.

Read more at https://alydiarackham642036291.wordpress.com/.

About the Author

Alydia Rackham is a daughter of Jesus Christ. She has written more than thirty original novels of many genres, including fantasy, time-travel, steampunk, modern romance, historical fiction, science fiction, and allegory. She is also a singer, actress, avid traveler, artist, and animal lover.

Read more at https://alydiarackham642036291.wordpress.com/.

Milton Keynes UK
Ingram Content Group UK Ltd.
UKHW010020030424
440481UK00001B/78